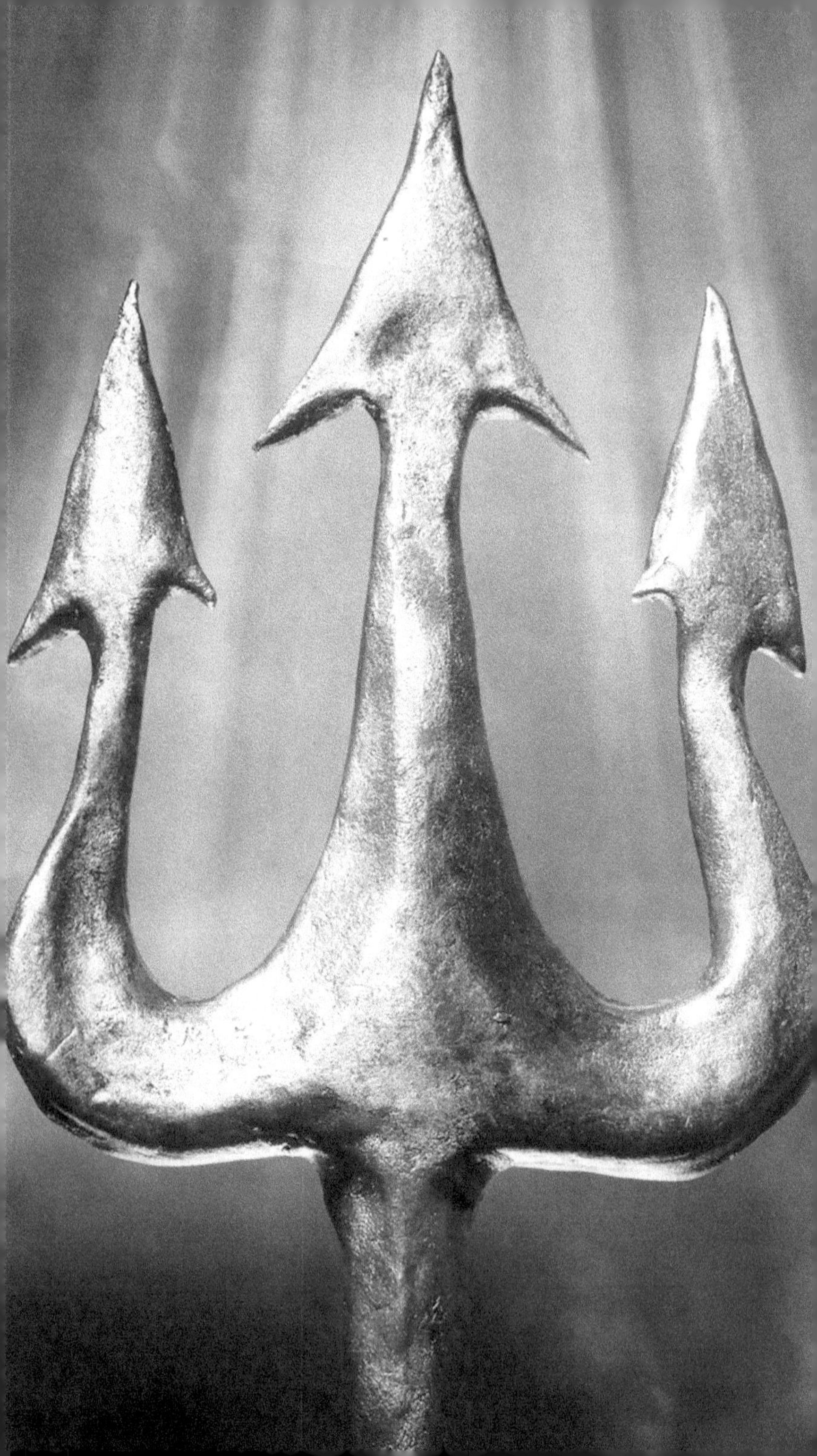

TICKLE
His Fancy

Trident Security Book 8

SAMANTHA COLE

To my grandmother who introduced me to my first romance novels as a teenager.

Valentine's Day will never be the same without you.
RIP Grandma
Dec. 30, 1909—Feb. 14, 1998

ACKNOWLEDGMENTS

As always, I want to thank my Beta Readers—Jessica, Julie, Brandie, Charla, Jen, Debbie, and Abby. You all are the best!

I also want to thank my editor, Eve Arroyo, for putting up with my quirks and loving my characters as much as I do!

For Milynn for letting me pick her brain and helping me with some of the technical stuff. You were awesome!

Thanks to my Facebook group—The Sexy Six-Pack Sirens—for all your support, shout outs, input, and putting a smile on my face every day.

AUTHOR'S NOTE

The story within these pages is completely fictional but the concepts of BDSM are real. If you do choose to participate in the BDSM lifestyle, please research it carefully and take all precautions to protect yourself. Fiction is based on real life but real life is *not* based on fiction. Remember—Safe, Sane and Consensual!

Any information regarding persons or places has been used with creative literary license so there may be discrepancies between fiction and reality. The Navy SEALs missions and personal qualities within have been created to enhance the story and, again, may be exaggerated and not coincide with reality.

The author has full respect for the members of the United States military and the varied members of law enforcement and thanks them for their continuing service to making this country as safe and free as possible.

Healing Heroes, and its founder Tori, are real and used in this book, lovingly, with permission, for fictional purposes only. (This in no way implies that she is involved in the lifestyles depicted in this book).

WHO'S WHO AND
THE HISTORY OF
TRIDENT SECURITY
& THE COVENANT

***While not every character is in every book, these are the ones with the most mentions throughout the series. This guide will help keep readers straight about who's who.

Trident Security (TS) is a private investigative and military agency, co-owned by Ian and Devon Sawyer. With governmental and civilian contracts, the company got its start when the brothers and a few of their teammates from SEAL Team Four retired to the private sector. The original six-man team is referred to as the Sexy Six-Pack, as they were dubbed by Kristen Sawyer, née Anders, or the Alpha Team. Trident had since expanded and former members of the military and law enforcement have been added to the staff. The company is located on a guarded compound, which was a former import/export company cover for a drug trafficking operation in Tampa, Florida. Three warehouses on the property were converted into large apartments, the TS offices, gym, and bunk rooms. There is also an obstacle course, a Main Street shooting gallery, a helicopter pad, and more features necessary for training and missions.

In addition to the security business, there is a fourth warehouse that now houses an elite BDSM club, co-owned by Devon, Ian, and their cousin, Mitch Sawyer, who is the manager. A lot of time and money has gone into making The Covenant the most sought after membership in the Tampa/St. Petersburg area and beyond. Members are thoroughly vetted before being granted access to the elegant club.

There are currently over fifty Doms who have been appointed Dungeon Masters (DMs), and they rotate two or three shifts each throughout the month. At least four DMs are on duty at all times at various posts in the pit, playrooms, and the new garden, with an additional one roaming around. Their job is to ensure the safety of all the submissives in the club. They step in if a sub uses their safeword and the Dom in the scene doesn't hear or heed it, and make sure the equipment used in scenes isn't harming the subs.

The Covenant's security team takes care of everything else that isn't scene-related, and provides safety for all members and are essentially the bouncers. The current total membership is just over 350. The fire marshal had approved them for 500 when the warehouse-turned-kink club first opened, but the cousins had intentionally kept that number down to maintain an elite status.

Between Trident Security and The Covenant there's plenty of romance, suspense, and steamy encounters. Come meet the Sexy Six-Pack, their friends, family, and teammates.

The Sexy Six-Pack (Alpha Team) and Their Significant Others

- Ian "Boss-man" Sawyer: Devon and Nick's brother; retired Navy SEAL; co-owner of Trident Security and The Covenant; fiancé/Dom of Angelina (Angel).
- Devon "Devil Dog" Sawyer: Ian and Nick's brother; retired Navy SEAL; co-owner of Trident Security and The Covenant; husband/Dom of Kristen; father of John Devon "JD."
- Ben "Boomer" Michaelson: retired Navy SEAL; explosives and ordnance specialist; husband/Dom of Katerina; son of Rick and Eileen.
- Jake "Reverend" Donovan: retired Navy SEAL; temporarily assigned to run the West Coast team; sniper; fiancé/Dom of Nick; brother of Mike; Whip Master at The Covenant.

- Brody "Egghead" Evans: retired Navy SEAL; computer specialist.
- Marco "Polo" DeAngelis: retired Navy SEAL; communications specialist and back up helicopter pilot; husband/Dom of Harper; father to Mara.
- Nick "Junior" Sawyer: Ian and Devon's brother; current Navy SEAL; fiancé/submissive of Jake.
- Kristen "Ninja-girl" Sawyer: author of romance/suspense novels; wife/submissive of Devon; mother of "JD."
- Angelina "Angie/Angel" Sawyer: graphic artist; wife/submissive of Ian.
- Katerina "Kat" Michaelson: dog trainer for law enforcement and private agencies; wife/submissive of Boomer.
- Millicent "Harper" DeAngelis: lawyer; wife/submissive of Marco; mother of Mara.

Extended Family, Friends, and Associates of the Sexy Six-Pack

- Mitch Sawyer: Cousin of Ian, Devon, and Nick; co-owner/manager of The Covenant, Dom.
- T. Carter: US spy and assassin; works for covert agency Deimos; Dom.

- Parker Christiansen: owner of New Horizons Construction; husband/Dom of Shelby.
- Shelby Christiansen: stay-at-home mom; two-time cancer survivor; wife/submissive of Parker.
- Curt Bannerman: retired Navy SEAL; owner of Halo Customs, a motorcycle repair and detail shop; husband of Dana; stepfather of Ryan, Taylor, Justin, and Amanda. Lives in Iowa.
- Dana Prichard-Bannerman: teacher; widow of retired SEAL Eric Prichard; wife of Curt; mother of Ryan, Taylor, Justin, and Amanda. Lives in Iowa.
- Jenn "Baby-girl" Mullins: college student; goddaughter of Ian; "niece" of Devon, Brody, Jake, Boomer, and Marco; father was a Navy SEAL; parents murdered.
- Mike Donovan: owner of the Irish pub, Donovan's; brother of Jake.
- Charlotte "Mistress China" Roth: Parole officer; Domme and Whip Master at The Covenant.
- Travis "Tiny" Daultry: former professional football player; head of security at The Covenant and Trident compound; occasional bodyguard for TS.

- Doug "Bullseye" Henderson: retired Marine; contract bodyguard.
- Rick and Eileen Michaelson: Boomer's parents; guardians of Alyssa. Rick is a retired Navy SEAL.
- Charles "Chuck" and Marie Sawyer: Ian, Devon, and Nick's parents. Charles is a self-made real estate billionaire. Marie is a plastic surgeon involved with Operation Smile.
- Will Anders: Assistant Curator of the Tampa Museum of Art Kristen Anders's cousin.
- Dr. Roxanne London: pediatrician; Domme/wife (Mistress Roxy) of Kayla; Whip Master at Covenant.
- Kayla London: social worker; submissive/wife of Roxanne.
- Chase Dixon: retired Marine Raider; owner of Blackhawk Security; associate of TS.
- Reggie Helm: lawyer for TS and The Covenant; Dom/boyfriend of Colleen.
- Alyssa Wagner: teenager saved by Jake from an abusive father; lives with Rick and Eileen Michaelson.
- Dr. Trudy Dunbar: Psychologist.
- Carl Talbot: college professor; Dom and Whip Master at The Covenant.

The Omega Team and
Their Significant Others

- Cain "Shades" Foster: retired Secret Service agent.
- Tristan "Duracell" McCabe: retired Army Special Forces
- Valentino "Romeo" Mancini: retired Army Special Forces; former FBI Hostage Rescue Team (HRT) member.
- Darius "Batman" Knight: retired Navy SEAL.
- Kip "Skipper" Morrison: retired Army; former LAPD SWAT sniper.
- Lindsey "Costello" Abbott: retired Marine; sniper.

Trident Support Staff

- Colleen McKinley-Helm: office manager of TS; girlfriend/submissive of Reggie.
- Tempest "Babs" Van Buren: retired Air Force helicopter pilot; TS mechanic.

Members of Law Enforcement

- Larry Keon: Assistant Director of the FBI.
- Frank Stonewall: Special Agent in Charge of the Tampa FBI.

- Calvin Watts: Leader of the FBI HRT in Tampa.

The K9s of Trident

- Beau: An orphaned Lab/Pit mix, rescued by Ian. Now a trained K9 who has more than earned his spot on the Alpha Team.
- Spanky: A rescued Bullmastiff with a heart of gold, owned by Parker and Shelby.

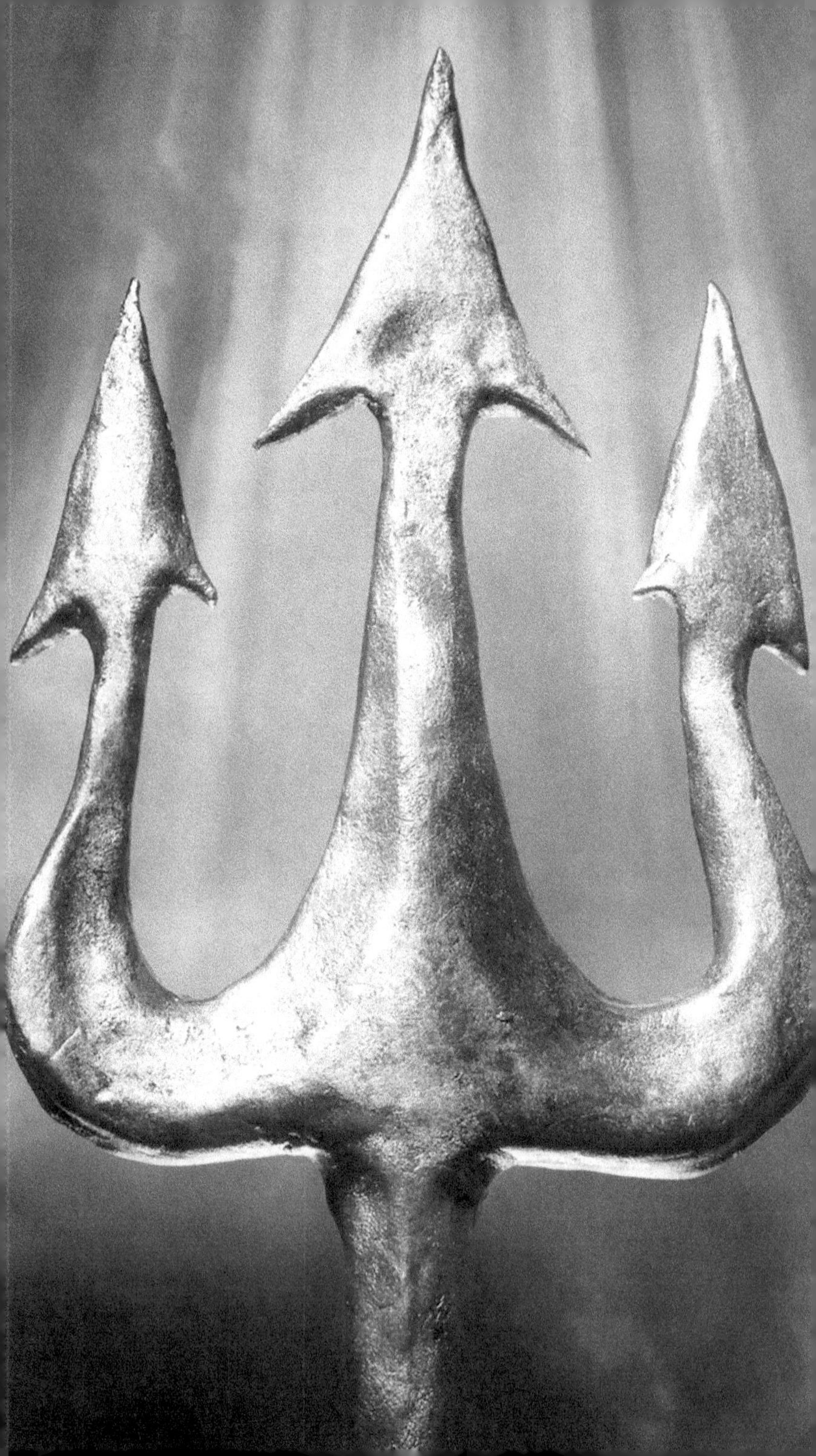

PROLOGUE

"Oh, my darlin',
      Oh, my darlin',
Oh, my darlin', Clementine.
You are lost and gone forever,
Dreadful sorry, Clementine."

The song being sung repeatedly helped Christie emerge from a deep sleep. As the fog slowly cleared from her mind, it occurred to her she had no idea where she was or who was singing. Realizing it wasn't a dream, she opened her eyes but couldn't see a thing. A blindfold only allowed a small sliver of light to show through. She struggled to sit up, but her limbs wouldn't move—they were restrained to the point where she was spread eagle on a mattress. Her first thought was she must be in a private room at the club, Heat, and coming out of subspace. But the stench of urine and lack of thumping club music told a different story.

Panic was starting to set in, and she thrashed against the restraints. A ball gag in her mouth prevented her from screaming at the top of her lungs.

"Oh, goodie. You're awake, my darling Clementine. Now the fun can begin."

Christie turned her head toward the deep voice she didn't recognize. Whoever he was, he knew the nickname she went by in the BDSM club she frequented. That's where she'd been last... wasn't it? No... wait... the last thing she remembered was leaving her friends at a bar they'd gone to and going home. Her visit to Heat had been the night before. Or had more time passed since then? She had no clue.

Her naked body trembled as footsteps scraped across the floor, approaching her. The blindfold was yanked from her face, and she blinked against the harsh overhead lightbulb. When her vision focused, she stared at the man standing over her with an evil grin and a bullwhip in his hands. They were in a damp room with concrete walls covered in dirt and... oh God! Was that blood?

Fear, unlike anything she'd ever known, attacked every cell in her body. She finally recognized him. He was a Dom, but she'd never played with him before. He was into the stuff she had on her hard limit list, so she'd avoided him the few times he'd shown up at the club. So what was she doing with him now? She couldn't remember when she'd seen him last—it had to have been, at least, a few weeks ago.

Struggling to pull her arms and legs free, she tried to ask him what was going on as tears rolled down her temples. *"Mmm-umm-mmmm?"*

"What's that?" He dramatically cupped his ear. "I couldn't quite hear you. Oh, that's right, you can't exactly talk with the ball gag, can you? Sorry, Clementine, but that stays in place for now. Don't worry, though. When I return in a little while, I'll remove it. After all, I want to hear you scream before you die."

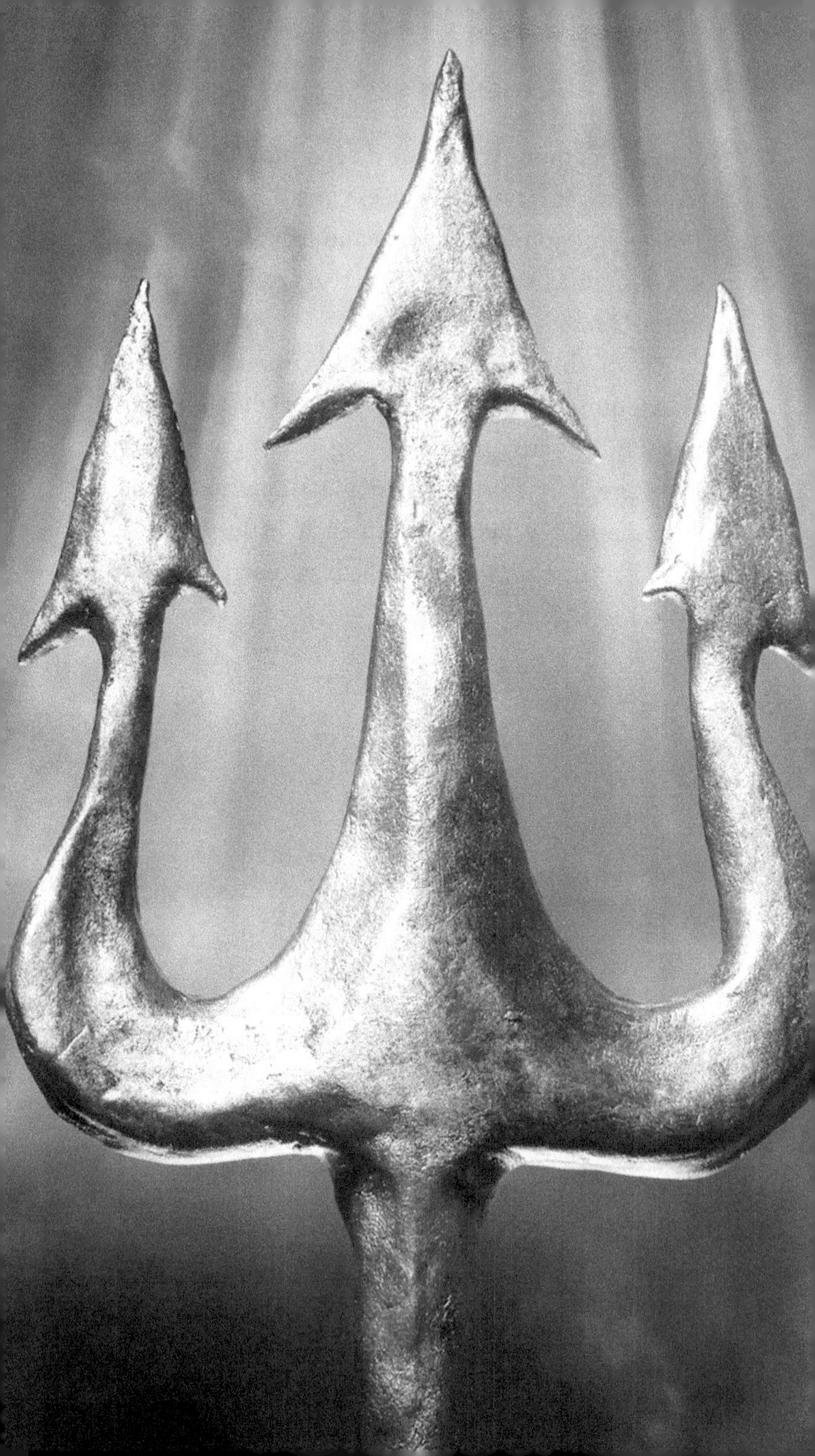

CHAPTER ONE

Turning off the engine of his Ford F150, Brody Evans sighed. How the fuck he had been roped into this, he didn't know, but his boss definitely owed him. Ian Sawyer, co-owner of Trident Security, had been called away on urgent business at the Pentagon. Meanwhile, the rest of their six-man team of former Navy SEALs-turned-private security operatives were all scattered on either professional or personal business. That left him to escort Ian's fiancée, Angie Beckett, to a local bakery to taste-test wedding cakes. The big event was six weeks away, and the couple suddenly found themselves without a baker after the one they'd hired closed up shop without notice. At least Brody would satisfy his sweet tooth with some, hopefully, yummy pastries.

Across the bench seat, Angie opened her door at the same time he did. Meeting her in front of the truck, he scanned the area. Being aware of his surroundings was second nature, especially when Angie was with him. The two had become friends after he'd bought the house next to hers over a year ago and then ended up on her protection detail when her life had been in danger. He loved all his teammates' significant others, but he'd developed an extra special bond with his boss's woman—strictly platonic, of course. Not that he didn't think she wasn't downright smokin' hot, but he valued his job, his friendship with Ian, and his life too much to do something stupid like hit on her. And even though they all participated in the BDSM life-style, Ian didn't share as some of them did.

Holding open the door to Fancy Creations for Angie, he followed her inside and inhaled deeply. *Holy crap, it's a diabetic's nightmare in here.* Thank God he wasn't a diabetic. His mouth watered at all the delicious smells. He would have to take some of the sweet confections home with him.

A college-age woman putting a tray of goodies in a display case smiled and greeted them. "Hi, what can I get you today? We have some fresh cinnamon rolls that just came out of the oven."

Angie stepped over to the counter between the display cases, which had several covered trays filled with cookies and cupcakes. "Hi. We have an appointment with Fancy about a wedding cake."

"Oh, sure. She'll be out in a minute." The cute blonde pointed at a few tables on the opposite side of the shop, several of which were taken by people chatting and eating pastries. "You can have a seat over there. Can I bring you some coffee?"

"That would be great, thanks."

Stepping over to the coffee machine, she glanced at Brody and got her first unobstructed view of him, her eyes growing wide as she took in his six-foot-two, two-hundred-fifteen-pounds-of-solid-muscle body. His mouth moved upward into the dimpled grin which made many a woman drop to her knees in front of him and let his Texas drawl rumble out a little stronger than usual. "Thanks, darlin'. Milk and sugar in both. Can ya'll box up a dozen of those cinnamon rolls for me, too? I'll bring 'em back to work for everyone."

When he winked at her, a blush appeared on her cheeks before she nodded and almost knocked over a tower of unused coffee cups. Following Angie over to the table, Brody sat beside her as she rolled her eyes. Leaning closer to him so she couldn't be overheard, she teased, "You're such a man-whore, Egghead."

"It's a God-given talent to make women of all ages blush, and I'm damn glad he blessed me with it." Part of him was being cocky, but his friends all knew it was true. He was a natural flirt, and nothing turned him on more than when a woman blushed as he imagined what other parts of her body would turn the same shade of pink.

She laughed at him, then her eyes shifted toward the door to the shop's kitchen. He followed her gaze, and his mouth watered again at what he saw. The woman walking toward them was about five-foot-five with curves that could knock a man's eyes out of their sockets. The fact that she was wearing an unflattering white chef's outfit did nothing to stop his appreciation of her luscious body. Her auburn hair was pulled up into a neat bun at the crown of her head, and her brilliant, green eyes reminded him of the soft moss found in the forest surrounding Trident's safe house in North Carolina. In his mind, her movements slowed, and some cheesy porn music began to play. Her smile lit up the room and caused a stirring in his groin.

She was only a few steps away when he realized he was staring. Giving himself a mental shake, he stood as she reached them.

"Hi, I'm Fancy Maguire." Her gaze was focused on Angie, who had remained seated. "You must be Angie and Ian. It's so nice to meet you."

Brody snorted. "Not." At her startled expression, he scrambled to clarify. "Sorry. This is Angie, but I'm not Ian."

Glancing at a clipboard and papers she'd brought with her, along with a photo album, she frowned. "I'm sorry. Did I get that wrong when I spoke to you on the phone?"

Smacking Brody's hip, Angie rolled her eyes again. "No, you didn't. This is our friend, Brody. My fiancé, Ian, was called out of town on business, so I dragged him along."

The baker was clearly relieved with that information if her sigh was any indication. "Oh, good. Thought I'd made an error from the get-go, which isn't a way to make a good impression in this business."

When Fancy extended her hand toward Brody, he took it in both of his and brought it to his lips. After kissing her knuckles, he winked at her. "There is absolutely no way you could make a bad impression, darlin'. My name is Brody Evans, and it's a pleasure to meet you."

Narrowing her eyes a little at his boldness, Fancy tugged on her hand, attempting to remove it from his grasp while trying not to be rude. He knew if they weren't in a business setting and he wasn't a customer, she would have no problem blurting out the words, which had to be on the tip of her tongue. *Awesome.* He loved when he had to work a little before cozying up to a woman. The chase drew him in and made the end result that much better. And since the lovely lady didn't have a ring on her finger, she was fair game for his charm.

The second her mouth began to turn into a frown, he knew it was time to let go. Releasing her, he gave her another wink and then waited for her to take the seat across the table from them before he sat down again. "Not that I wouldn't mind the beautiful Ms. Angelina Beckett being my fiancée, but I have no desire to be Ian. He doesn't have enough fun in his life unless Angie is with him. Me? I'm all for fun and games."

"I'm sure you are," Fancy murmured to his delight before turning her attention to Angie. "Now, I remember you saying your baker closed up shop, and the event is in six weeks."

The bride-to-be nodded as the young woman manning the counter brought over their coffees and placed them on the table. Brody grinned at her, causing the blonde to turn pink again, while Angie thanked her before responding to the baker. "Yes. Without warning, his place closed. I know many people are trying to get their deposits back. Our wedding date is October 15th."

"Do you have a picture of the cake you chose? We can start there."

Pulling out printouts she'd made this morning, Angie handed them over. "This was what we had decided on, but honestly, looking at them now, I'm not sure if it's what I want anymore. There just seems to be something missing, but I don't know what it is."

Fancy studied the two pictures—a close-up and a wide-angle version—then opened the photo album and flipped through several pages. "It's a good start, but I think we can jazz it up a little more. Where is the wedding being held?"

"The Vinoy in St. Petersburg."

"Great. Love that place—it's so elegant—and we've done several weddings there recently." She found the pictures she sought and turned the album around for Angie to see. "This we did just a few weeks ago. Instead of the white plastic separators between the tiers, the venue supplied the wine glasses, which we inverted. Then the bride arranged for the small floral pieces that we put under each glass to match the table centerpieces."

"Oh, I love that! It's different, and that's exactly what I'm looking for. Brody, what do you think?"

He'd barely been paying attention to their conversation. Instead, he'd been studying Fancy's face. It was rounded and full, with just a hint of dimples when she smiled. A smattering of freckles rose up and over her nose from one cheek to the other. While he had no doubt she was a headstrong, competent businesswoman, he'd bet a year's membership to The Covenant she was a sexual submissive. Being in the lifestyle for over ten years, he could spot one a mile away. The problem was sometimes women didn't know it, or if they did, they were too afraid to explore that part of their sexuality. "Hmm? What?"

Angie pointed to the album as his gaze went back and forth between the two women. "The cake. What do you think of this cake?"

Glancing at the photo, all he saw was a huge white cake with lots of flowers. "It's nice, but don't go by my opinion. All men care about is what it tastes like. Sweet and yummy is all I need to satisfy me."

This time, Fancy rolled her eyes while Angie groaned beside him. It was clear they both knew he was talking about something other than a cake. "Why did I bother to bring you with me?"

It was a rhetorical question, which he didn't bother to answer as he continued to observe the woman sitting across from him. Fancy turned her head to address her employee, who returned to her post behind the counter. "Jamie, can you ask Sal to bring out the samples for Ms. Beckett to try?"

"Sure."

A grin spread across Brody's face. It didn't escape his notice that he was intentionally omitted from her question. *Well, we'll just see about that.* He was looking forward to tasting anything the beautiful baker was offering.

Sal, a short, older man dressed in white with an apron wrapped around his waist, brought out a tray laden with several small plates, topped with slices of assorted cakes—each more delicious-looking than the last. The man had also supplied two forks so Brody didn't have to search for one or use his fingers. Either way, he was definitely sampling the delicacies. He listened as Fancy explained each one, from the type of cake and filling to the icing, and then stole a bite after Angie had taken hers. They were so scrumptious that he had no shame in taking a second taste of each. If the rest of Fancy's pastries were this good, he would stop in often. The bonus to that was he'd be seeing a lot more of her, and a plan of seduction began to take root in his mind.

Ultimately, he and Angie agreed the best was the champagne cake with a strawberry buttercream filling and fondant icing. The women then discussed the decorations for the cake, and Fancy explained what Angie needed to order from her florist. As the baker finished writing up the order and took the deposit check, Brody sipped the last of his coffee. When she gave Angie the receipt and a business card, he held out his hand. "Mind if I get one of those business cards, too?"

If he hadn't been observing her so intently, he might have missed the fraction of a second's hesitation before she gave him a forced smile. "Sure. Are you planning on getting married soon, too?"

He smirked as he accepted the small card. "You never know, darlin'. I'm just waiting for the right woman to come along, and one never knows when their soul mate will cross their path."

The sadness that briefly clouded her eyes wasn't lost on him, and he wondered what had brought it on —the word "soul mate," maybe? Whatever it was from, it didn't scare him off. In fact, it made him want to take her into his arms and comfort her, among other things. For now, though, he would leave things be and look forward to the next time he visited Miss Fancy Maguire's bakery—which he planned on doing tomorrow.

After they'd climbed into his truck with the bag

full of cinnamon rolls, Brody noticed Angie grinning at him in amusement. "What? What's that look for?"

Shrugging her shoulder, she snickered. "It looks like the pretty baker teased more than your taste buds."

Laughing, he started the engine. "That she did, you little brat. And I plan on having her tease me some more real soon."

"Well, you still haven't told me who you're bringing to the wedding. Maybe you can bring her. I like her."

He pursed his lips and tilted his head to the side. All of his buddies had settled down, and the funny thing was everyone had thought Brody would be the first to fall. "Maybe... and I like her, too."

There was a moment of silence between them as he pulled out of the parking lot into the afternoon traffic. "Brody? Do you mind stopping at Donovan's for another cup of coffee? There's something I want to talk to you about."

At her wistful tone, his eyes narrowed as he glanced at her. "Everything all right, sweetheart?"

"Yes! Oh, sorry. I didn't mean to worry you. I just... well, I'll explain when we get there."

Relieved there wasn't anything seriously wrong, he nodded, then prepared to change lanes. "Okay. Sure."

Since Donovan's was only two blocks away, it wasn't long before they walked into the pub, which belonged to Mike Donovan, brother of Brody's coworker Jake. The owner waved from behind the bar where he chatted with two old-timers who were constant fixtures during the weekday afternoons. Instead of taking his usual seat at the far end of the bar, Brody followed Angie to one of the booths along the left side wall. Knowing all of the Trident men hated having their backs to the front door of any place they were in, Angie sat in the booth facing the rear of the restaurant.

Brody glanced around before sitting across from her, noting that Jenn Mullins wasn't working today. The twenty-one-year-old was considered a niece to the men of Trident Security, as they'd been her father's teammates on SEAL Team Four and watched her grow from an infant to the beautiful young lady she'd become. In the aftermath of her parents' murders two years ago, she'd come to live with Ian, who was her godfather. Now, she had her own apartment in the secure Trident compound while attending classes at the University of Tampa.

After asking the older, dark-haired waitress for coffee for both of them, Brody rested his elbows on the table and stared at Angie curiously. "Spill it. What's on your mind?"

Taking a deep breath, Angie let it out slowly. "I was talking to Ian the other day about an idea I had, and he agreed I should ask you. Since we're one bridesmaid short, and you're supposed to walk down the aisle with Marco and Harper, I was wondering if you would… well, if you would walk me down the aisle, instead, and give me away?"

Stunned, his mouth fell open, but he didn't answer her as she rushed to continue. "I mean, I always thought my dad or brother would be here for me, and after they both passed away, I thought Jimmy would. But…" She swallowed hard and fingered the BDSM collar her Dom/fiancé had given her. "Since that's no longer an option, I would really love it if you would do it. Ian and I might have never met if it hadn't been for you."

She had lost her older brother when she was a child and then both her parents when she was in college. Her best friend, Jimmy Athos, had been there for her since high school and had become her family as both of them were alone in the world after he'd lost his sister and mother. Athos had worked for the DEA, and it was the result of one of his undercover ops that Ian and the rest of Trident had been tasked with keeping his best friend safe. It was during that time that Ian and Angie had fallen in love. When dirty DEA agents kidnapped Jenn and Angie as a way to get to Athos, the man was shot and killed during the otherwise successful rescue.

All choked up, Brody cleared his throat as he reached across the table for her hand. "I'd be honored to give you away, Angie. Absolutely honored."

CHAPTER TWO

After Fancy had completed the deposit slip for the past two day's receipts, she slipped it into the canvas bank bag along with a stack of cash and checks. Miguel, an assistant pastry chef, was out in the kitchen, decorating the popular oversized cupcakes they sold, which had been baked earlier. He would start cleaning the counters and appliances in a little while before clocking out at 5:00 p.m. Sal had left two hours ago at the end of his nine-hour shift, which had begun at 4:00 a.m. Having arrived at the shop an hour after him, Fancy felt the effects of the long day and couldn't wait to get home to a nice hot bath.

Grabbing the deposit bag and her purse, she glanced around her office to ensure she hadn't forgotten anything. She locked the door behind her, then said goodbye to Miguel before heading to the front of the shop. Her afternoon staff, Carol and

Bernice, had been working for Fancy since she'd first opened the bakery a year ago, and she trusted them to close for her in the late afternoons.

Waving goodbye to them as they helped customers, Fancy headed for the door, digging into her purse for her keys. When the bell on the front door jingled, she glanced up to see Corey enter, and she smiled at her brother-in-law. "Hi. What are you doing here?"

"I came to take you to the bank, and then I thought we could grab dinner if you're hungry."

Corey had been a godsend these past few years since his brother, who'd been Fancy's husband, had died in a car accident, which had left her in a coma for several weeks. He'd taken care of the funeral and everything else until she'd recovered physically and mentally and then supported her decision to open the bakery. It had been Patrick's and her dream before his death, and one she knew he would want her to have with or without him.

She sighed because as much as she loved Corey's company, she was too tired tonight to go out. "I'm actually not hungry and really just want to go home, take a hot bath, read for a bit, and go to bed early. And you don't have to take me to the bank."

His brown eyes narrowed as he held the door open for her. It never stopped to amaze her how much the dark-haired brothers had looked alike despite being born two years apart. Corey had been the younger sibling, which made him her age of twenty-nine, but many people thought the men had been twins, especially once they'd hit their teens and puberty. Not Fancy, of course. She'd never had trouble telling them apart, but she could see why other people did. "After the vandalism yesterday, I want to make sure you have no problems carrying all that money."

Heading to her car in the attached parking lot, she glanced up at the outside brick wall of her shop. Her landlord had arranged for it to be power-washed yesterday after the police took a report and pictures, but she could still see faint traces of the spray paint that had been used to write vile things. "I'm sure it was just a bunch of kids being jackasses. I wouldn't be surprised if it were those teens I kicked out of the shop last week for being loud and rude to the customers."

She used her remote to unlock her Altima, and Corey opened the door for her. "It could be, but I'd still rather go with you to the bank."

Smiling up at him as she climbed in, she tossed her purse and the deposit bag on the passenger seat. "Who am I to turn down a six-foot-one firefighter who wants to double as my bodyguard?"

"Smart ass," he retorted with a grin. "I'll follow you over."

It was only four blocks to the bank she used, and when they arrived, Corey got out of his pickup truck and escorted her to the outside money drop-box. "Are you sure you don't want to go grab dinner? Or we could bring something in."

They strolled back to where they'd parked after she'd deposited the canvas bag into the secured box. "I'm sure. Sorry, but it's just one of those days, and I'm exhausted."

Gently grabbing her elbow, he stopped her in her tracks. "Don't apologize, Fancy. You've come a long way this past year and should be proud of yourself. But I don't want you pushing yourself to the point of exhaustion. And if you're tired, you're tired. No big deal. Go home and get to sleep early, and maybe we'll go out tomorrow night. After that, I'm on duty four nights straight."

She went up on her tippy-toes and kissed his cheek. "Dinner tomorrow sounds great. You can pick me up at the shop, and we'll go to that new Mexican place."

His grin widened. "Now you're talking. I'll see you tomorrow, but text me when you get home so I know you got there safe."

It wasn't an odd request from him. When Fancy started driving again after recovering from the acci-dent, she was so tense she was surprised she didn't get into another one. At first, Corey had followed her home, but then she gained more confidence, so he didn't need to. However, he still insisted she call or text him when she had gotten to her destination without incident.

After saying goodbye, she started the engine and drove home to her little apartment. It was much smaller than the house Patrick and she had bought a year after they married. While the three-bedroom ranch had been more than they needed for the two of them at the time, they'd hoped to fill it with children as soon as possible. Sadly, they never had the chance.

Locking the door behind her, she dropped her purse on the couch on her way to her bedroom, undressing as she went. No matter how clean they kept the kitchen in the shop, she always felt sticky and covered in flour when she got home, and the first thing she wanted was a shower or bath. Today, she was going with the latter.

Passing several pictures on the hallway wall, she stopped and adjusted the one of Patrick and her the day he proposed to her on a picnic. They'd gone to the Tampa Riverwalk, and after they'd eaten lunch, he'd pulled a small ring box out of his pocket. He'd told her he'd been trying to think of a memorable way to ask her to marry him, but everything he'd thought of was too cliché. In the end, he just did it on the spur of the moment after carrying the ring around with him for two weeks, waiting for the right time. People enjoying the beautiful, sunny day had stopped to watch him get on one knee and waited for her to say yes before applauding. Another couple offered to take several pictures with Patrick's iPhone, and the one in front of her had been perfect for blowing up and printing.

They were smiling while gazing into each other's eyes, the world at their feet and happy times ahead. Who knew it would all end far too soon?

Stepping away before the tears she'd fought for the past two and a half years started again, she entered the bathroom and turned on the tub's faucet. After checking the temperature of the water, she left it to fill while she shed the rest of her clothes and grabbed her robe from the back of the bedroom door.

Her phone rang, and she checked the caller ID. It was her cousin, Kerry. Sighing, she sent it to voice mail because she wasn't in the mood for another lecture on why she needed to get on with her life. She *was* getting on with it. In fact, the only thing she hadn't done yet was date... and she still wasn't ready for that. But her mind flitted to the handsome man who'd come in with her new client today.

Brody Evans was drool-worthy, as Jamie had pointed out after he'd left with Ms. Beckett. However, the man knew it. He was an obvious flirt and the complete opposite of Patrick or any other man she'd ever been attracted to. So why couldn't she forget how her skin had tingled when his lips had brushed the back of her hand? Her body's response to him had startled her, and she'd tried to yank her hand away, but he'd held on tight for a few moments longer before finally releasing her. Well, whatever it was about the man that had triggered her reaction wasn't something she would act on. She wanted stability in her life, not some charmer who probably had a new girlfriend every week.

Before she tossed her cell phone on her bed, she quickly texted Corey to let him know she'd arrived home safely and would talk to him tomorrow. Grabbing her new book, *Velvet Vixen* by Kristen Anders, she decided to open a bottle of red wine and have a glass. Between the fruity alcohol, a good fictional story, and a hot bath, she would sleep well tonight. That was all she needed for now.

Leaving the locker room, Brody took the stairs back up to the bar area of The Covenant, dressed in his usual Dom-wear of snug, faded jeans, a black T-shirt, and his favorite cowboy boots. He'd seen several people at the bar who he wanted to say hello to first before going into the pit, as the play area of the BDSM club had been dubbed. That was on the lower level, with the bar and sitting areas in a balcony above it.

At the far end of the pit were two hallways leading to private playrooms. A club member, Parker Christiansen, who owned a construction company, had started on a new addition last week. More private rooms, a few with themes, were being added, but the plans for the second floor were amazing. The area would have a retractable roof for play under the moonlight, weather permitting. And to ensure privacy when the roof was open, there would be specially made netting in its place. It would let the air in, and the people could see out, but anyone trying to take pictures via a helicopter or satellite camera would only get a fuzzy, dark gray photo. The Sawyers—brothers Ian and Devon and their cousin Mitch—take their club's security seriously, and no expenses are spared when it comes to safeguarding their members. It helped that Ian and Dev's father was a self-made real estate billionaire, and the brothers have enormous trust funds. But you would never know it unless you were close to them, as Brody and the rest of the Trident team were. The men didn't flaunt their wealth and had successfully established their own businesses and reputations while only using the trust funds for start-up expenses.

Glancing around, Brody noted it was a little quiet in the bar area for a Thursday night, but based on the volume of noise from the pit, the level of activity down there was high. A few people were enjoying a pre- or post-play drink, and he headed toward a small group he knew well. The rules for pre-play drinking were strict—only two alcoholic beverages allowed—and with the computer system Brody had set up for the business, the bartender and waitstaff kept track of who was served what. Then, the security guards had hand-held computers that scanned the club members' access cards before allowing them entry to the pit. No one was permitted in the play areas if they had exceeded the limit, but they were welcome to relax at one of the pub tables or sitting areas along the balcony and watch the scenes from there.

As he approached the four women and two men he wanted to chat with, he noticed the serious and worried looks on their faces. His teammates, Ben "Boomer" Michaelson and Marco "Polo" DeAngelis, were there with their fiancées/submissives—Kat Maier and Harper Williams, respectively. The other two women were a married couple, Dr. Roxanne London and her submissive/wife Kayla, and it was the latter who seemed the most upset.

He signaled the bartender, Dennis, for a bottle of his regular beer, then joined the discussion. "What's everyone frowning about?"

Kayla London gave him a small smile, but it didn't reach her eyes, reminding him of the cute baker from that afternoon. But the sweet sub greeted him politely as always. "Good evening, Master Brody. We were just talking about a friend of mine from Heat, Christie Lawrence. She's been missing since last Friday night, but we just heard about it today."

Heat was the second most popular private BDSM club in the Tampa area behind The Covenant. Roxy and Kayla had been members there before they'd been granted memberships here.

Brody's eyes narrowed. He hadn't heard about any missing persons cases recently, but then again, he'd been busy with upgrades to the Trident computer system for the past two weeks. "Where'd she go missing from?"

His best friend, Marco, handed him the beer the bartender had placed on the counter since he stood between the bar and Brody. "From what we've heard, there's no sign of foul play. Her car was parked and locked in front of her condo as usual. Her phone was in the car, but her purse was gone. No sign of a struggle. She left her friends at some bar downtown, drove home, and disappeared from the face of the earth. There's no indication she made it into her condo either."

"That doesn't sound good." He took a swig of his beer.

"What doesn't sound good?"

They all turned to greet the newcomer, Master Carl Talbot. The middle-aged man with slicked-back, salt-and-pepper hair was distinguished-looking, but he could pass for a vampire in a movie when he dressed in his black pants and dress shirt. At least the older movies. Nowadays, the Hollywood men with fangs were young and handsome, catering to teenagers who think it would be romantic to have a vampire shower them with attention. It also didn't help Master Carl's image when the subs found out the man was a sadist and a Whip Master at the club—not that he minded, of course. But there was also a gentle side to him, which he showed during the aftercare for a sub following a scene—after he inflicted whatever pain they were into.

As another couple, Master Reggie Helm and his submissive/fiancée, Colleen McKinley, joined the group, Kayla and Marco went over the details again. Reggie was a lawyer whose firm handled the legal business for Trident Security and The Covenant, while Colleen had been Trident's secretary for over a year. It had taken her a while to break the habit of calling the team members "Master" during business hours, but she was damn efficient and had just received a handsome raise for all she did for them.

Sipping his beer, Brody scanned the bar and sitting areas. Sometimes, he and his former ménage partner, Marco, tag-teamed Harper, but only when his friend approached him about it. Brody would never ask to join them since it would make him sound like a desperate third-wheel, which he was definitely not. There were plenty of available submissives in the club he'd played with before, and he honestly had no preference over a duo or trio scene.

When the subject changed among the group again, he turned back toward Kayla. Between her and another sub, Parker's wife, Shelby Christiansen, they kept up-to-date on the status of the submissives— who was currently collared or in a contract. They were kind of the mother-hens of the club, along with Mistress China, a Domme and one of the Whip

Masters. "Hey, Kayla. Have you been down to the sub area yet tonight?"

"Yes, Sir, about fifteen minutes ago while my Mistress was busy."

"Who's available this evening?" he asked.

"Sasha is working in the store, Sir, and Georgia was negotiating with Master Cain earlier. Oh, and Cassandra signed a temporary contract with Master Stefan last night."

His eyes narrowed, but Mistress Roxanne beat him to it. Her voice was deep in reprimand. "My little subbie, I don't think that helps Master Brody. Instead of telling him who's *unavailable*, skip the gossip and tell him who *is*. Then we will have another discussion about your chattiness when you're asked a direct question."

"Yes, Ma'am." Remorse was evident in her eyes, but Brody wasn't concerned about Roxy disciplining her sub. Kayla was a bit of a brat and masochist at times. "I apologize, Master Brody. Several new submissives passed their final training class last night, so they're available. A few of them are downstairs already." She paused. "Is there anything else I can help you with, Sir?"

He shook his head, not needing any further help from her since he'd overseen several training classes and done the initial background checks on them before their memberships had been approved. He analyzed every aspect of a potential member's life before forwarding all the information to Ian, Devon, and Mitch for final approval. "No, thanks. I'll wander down there and do my own negotiations."

Excusing himself from the group and leaving his half-empty beer on the bar, he ambled over to the stairs, nodding hello to several people on the way. When he reached the security guard dressed in black dress pants, a red, button-down shirt with a black bowtie, he handed the man his membership card. The only people in the entire club who didn't have to have their cards swiped before entering the pit were the three owners since they had written the rules.

After getting his card back, he descended the stairs to find out what fun there was to be had for the evening. He was sure no matter what he found, it was bound to be entertaining.

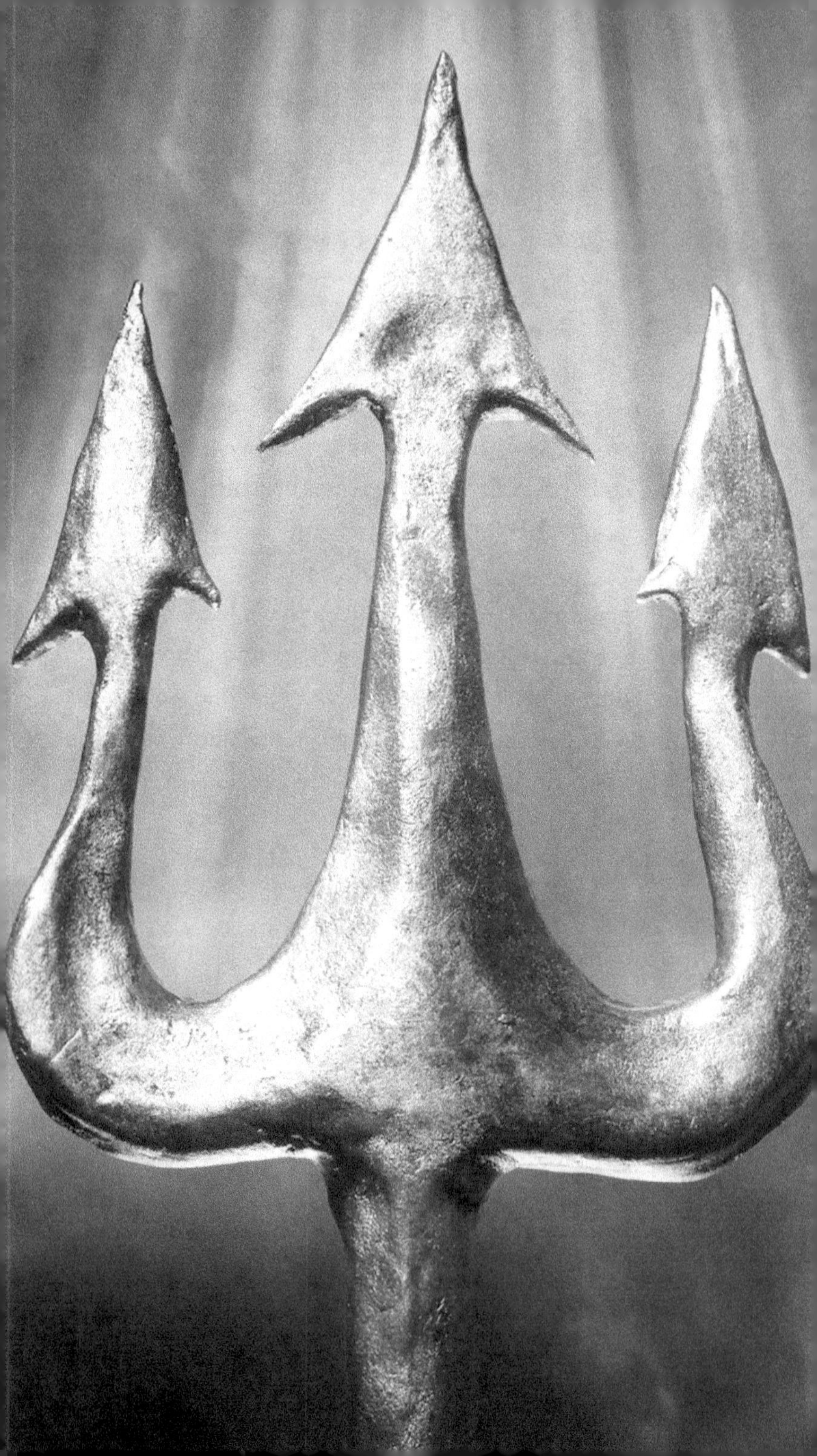

CHAPTER THREE

Whistling loudly, Brody drove toward his destination, anticipating seeing *her* again strumming through his veins. *Her* being Fancy. She would have arrived at the shop ten minutes ago at 5:00 a.m. on the dot. Through her talkative employee Jamie—the cute blonde—he'd learned a few things about the bakery owner, but not enough to satisfy his curiosity. While he could easily find out anything he wanted via the internet, he'd held off doing a background check on her past for some reason. He wanted to hear it from her instead.

He wasn't sure what it was about the sexy baker, but she hadn't been far from his thoughts since he'd met her two weeks ago. Although seeing her practically every morning when he stopped in to get pastries for the office probably had something to do with it. Add in the fact his usual flair for seducing a woman was falling flat at her feet, and he craved Ms. Fancy Maguire like mad. But she seemed immune to his flirting and charm, so he was trying to think of a new way to get past her barriers.

It wasn't that she didn't appear to be interested in him, it just seemed she was a little more standoffish than the women he was generally attracted to, and for some reason that made her more appealing. Sometimes, things were better the more one had to work for them, and he felt Fancy was worth the effort —at least, he hoped so. Each time he saw her, she seemed a little more at ease with him, but when it came to his subtle, probing questions, she would clam up or suddenly need to do something in the kitchen.

Usually, his seduction of a woman lasted only a day or two, if that, before she fell into bed with him or, as in the past, with him *and* Marco, who had been his best friend since boot camp. His buddy had introduced him to the pleasures of sharing a woman when they'd visited an underground BDSM club in Paris while on a joint training mission there between the U.S. and French militaries. From then on, they'd participated in many ménages together. The only thing that had taken some getting used to was the occasional unintentional contact between them while pleasuring a woman since they were both straight as arrows. Now, he didn't even notice it most of the time.

Since Marco and Harper had permanently hooked up, Brody had been an occasional third with them, once every four to six weeks or so. The only other ménages he'd been involved with in the past seven months had been with Carter when the U.S. government spy had been in town and once with Mitch and Cassandra for the cute waitress's birthday.

While he enjoyed ménages—a great way to please a woman—he didn't necessarily need them as some people did. He could take them or leave them. All was good as long as the woman he was with was completely sated by the end of the night, along with himself.

Making a left into the bakery's parking lot, he was surprised to see a police car and the Tampa PD Bomb Unit's truck. The sun wasn't up yet, but it was light enough to see one uniformed officer standing on the sidewalk with Fancy and Sal, staring at the store's shattered front display window. *Fuck! What the hell had happened?*

He didn't see the bomb guys, but since the cop, Fancy, and her employee were standing so close to the shop, he assumed there wasn't any chance of an explosion. Throwing his truck into Park, he jumped out and hurried toward the trio. Unable to keep his concern from showing, he headed straight for Fancy and gently took her elbow until her troubled gaze met his. There was no mistaking the tears that threatened to fall, but she managed to keep them at bay—barely. "What happened?"

Shaking her head, she was about to answer when the cop interrupted. "Who are you?"

Annoyed but knowing not to step on any local law enforcement toes unless it was necessary, he turned toward the uniformed man. "Brody Evans. I'm with Trident Security." The recognition of the company name flashed in the officer's eyes, so Brody knew no further explanation was needed. "What's going on, and why's the bomb squad here?"

"Hey, Egghead. What are you doing here?"

He sighed in relief when Sgt. Barry Templeton and Officer Freddie Mendoza appeared in the shop's doorway, sans their bomb gear. Mendoza was on his cell phone and stepped aside as his supervisor approached the group. "I was going to ask you the same thing, Sarge. I was stopping in for my morning sugar rush to bring to work with me. We've got some early training today since it's supposed to be over 100 degrees later. Can someone please tell me what the hell is going on?"

Templeton offered his hand, which Brody shook. "No explosives. Just a shattered window from a brick thrown through it." He tilted his head in Sal's direction. "Sal is Freddie's cousin. He was in the kitchen when it happened about twenty minutes ago."

Brody switched his attention to the shorter man, who held up his hands in frustration. "But I didn't see anyone. I wish the fuck I did. I would've kicked the bastard's ass." He grimaced when he realized his employer still stood next to him. "Excuse the language, Fancy."

Giving him a reassuring pat on the shoulder, Fancy remained silent, biting her lip. Brody wanted to rescue the abused flesh and nibble on it himself, along with a few other places on her body. Damn, he had it bad for this woman.

"Anyway," Templeton said, interrupting Brody's wayward and inappropriate thoughts. "We were only a few blocks away when the call was dispatched and recognized the address. Unfortunately, whoever it was, he did a good job of making himself unrecognizable. We just took a look at the security camera feed. Black sweats, black hoodie, dark shoes or sneakers—hard to tell because the recording is so grainy. Hell, I can't even figure out if the guy is white, black, or green with purple polka dots."

Letting out a deep breath, Brody chuckled. One thing he loved about men and women in the military and law enforcement was their wry sense of humor. Addressing Fancy, he asked, "Were you here?"

She shook her head and spoke for the first time since he arrived. "No. It happened right before I got here. In fact, I pulled up at the same time the officer, Freddie, and the sergeant did. Freaked me out until they said there wasn't a bomb."

"Yeah, well, they tend to do that, but I can't complain since they've helped my team out a few times."

"And vice versa," the sergeant added.

As Sal headed inside to start sweeping up the mess and the uniformed cop finished taking notes for his report, a navy blue truck flew into the parking lot. Brody stepped in front of Fancy to protect her from any threat as a frowning dark-haired man jumped out and ran toward them, leaving the driver's door wide open. "Fancy, what happened?"

The worry on the man's face and in his voice was evident. When he reached the group, Fancy stepped around Brody and threw her arms around the man's neck as he embraced her. Disappointment filled Brody's gut. It was evident Fancy was close to this man, and he wondered if his shot at getting to know her better was as shattered as the store window. He took a step backward as she told the newcomer what had happened.

Someone bumped his shoulder, and Brody turned to see Freddie had closed the distance between them. Keeping his voice low so only Brody could hear, the cop said, "Don't worry. That's her brother-in-law—he's with Tampa F.D. But be forewarned, Fancy's like family to my cousin. If you're looking for a little something on the side, then look somewhere else. She's had enough heartache in the past."

His jaw tensed. It was a friendly warning, and he knew it meant Fancy had people who cared about her, whether or not they were close to her. But it didn't mean he had to like it. "Understood."

He wanted to ask what "heartache" the cop was talking about, but this wasn't the time or place. Clearing his throat, he was about to say her name to get her attention, but he overheard her brother-in-law say something about this not being the first incident. He stepped forward. "What else happened?"

The fireman's eyes narrowed as he glared at Brody. "Who are you?"

Stepping to the side, Fancy gestured back and forth between the two men. "Corey, this is one of my new regular customers, Brody Evans. Brody, this is my brother-in-law."

Not letting it show, Brody was surprised she used his full name. He had never heard it sound so lyrical before and wanted to hear it again. Instead, he temporarily pushed aside the warm fuzzy feelings it brought as neither man did anything more than nod while sizing each other up. As if she noticed the tension between them, Fancy turned back toward him to intercede. "Corey was referring to some vandalism I had last week. A bunch of nasty comments were spray-painted on the wall facing the parking lot. I filed a report, and my landlord cleaned it with a power washer. It was really no big deal."

Seriously? "Well, one incident might not be a big deal to you, but this just upped the ante. How good are your cameras and security system?"

When she looked a little confused, his gaze shot to Freddie. "Tell me."

The cop shrugged. "Not the best. Certainly not on the level I know you're referring to."

"Well, that'll change."

The uniformed officer handed Fancy his card with the report number on it so she could contact her insurance company and gave her the standard "what to do next." It was to call a glass company, which wouldn't be available until at least 9:00 a.m., so Brody pulled out his cell and scrolled through his contacts to find the number he wanted. Hitting send, he brought the phone to his ear and waited for the call to connect.

"—ello. Oose this?"

"Parker, wake your ass up."

The owner of New Horizons Construction had obviously been sound asleep. "Brody? What the fuck, man? It's... shit, it's not even six o'clock. What the fuck is wrong?"

"I need a favor."

Within five minutes, arrangements were made for two of Parker's workers to head over with sheets of plywood to close up the window until Fancy's insurance company ordered the glass to be replaced. When he disconnected the call, Templeton and Mendoza said their goodbyes, but it was the stunned expression on Fancy's face that caught his attention. "What?"

"You just called someone to cover my window at six o'clock in the morning?"

"Yup. A friend of mine has a construction company. His workers will be here in about twenty minutes. In the meantime, let me look at your security setup."

"Why?" This time, it was Corey who spoke—truthfully, it was more like a growl—and he clearly wasn't happy that not only was Brody still there but was taking over. *Well, too fucking bad.*

He shrugged. "Because it's what I do best."

Shaking her head, Fancy gaped at him. "That's awfully sweet of you, Brody, but I can't afford a new security system right now."

Ignoring the brother-in-law's glare, Brody smiled at her. "That's not a problem. Just pay me in pastries."

Her eyes widened. "You're crazy."

"Nope. I have an enormous sweet tooth that loves your baking." And now he had the perfect excuse to be around her some more. It was a win-win for both of them. She just didn't know it yet.

Striding into the Trident Security building with the company dog, Beau, on his heels, Brody went straight to Ian's office and rapped on the open door. His friend glanced up before returning to his computer screen. "Egghead, what carbs did you bring today to make my teams fat?"

He snorted while taking a seat in front of the boss's desk. Ian had been enjoying Fancy's delicacies just as much as everyone else had. "Some sticky pecan things. You'll love them." He paused until Ian shifted his eyes back to him. "I need today off, Boomer's help, and a new system, which I'll pay for."

Ian's eyes narrowed as he frowned. "You fucking serious? For what, or should I say, for whom?"

"Fancy's having some problems at the bakery. Vandalism. And she's got a shit system. I told her she could pay me by satisfying my sweet tooth."

Rolling his eyes, Ian leaned back in his leather chair. He knew exactly who Fancy was between Angie raving about their new wedding cake baker and Brody bringing in the pastries every day. "Just your sweet tooth? I have a feeling you want her satisfying more than that."

Not bothering to deny the truth, Brody shrugged. "So, can I have Boomer and the training day off?"

"Yeah, okay. Marco can play drill sergeant today. Just don't fucking forget you're on Princess duty later. She's got that shindig tonight, and you're on with Omega. Be here in your monkey suit by 1600 for the briefing. Amar will be here to run through everything."

Shit, he'd almost forgotten all about the detail. Timasur's Princess Tahira was in town and had a charity function on her schedule, which meant more security than usual. Mousaf Amar was the head of the royal bodyguards, and Trident worked well with him when members of the royal family visited one of their vacation homes in Clearwater Beach. The man had been trained with special ops teams from several countries and Brody was impressed with his eye for detail in security. He rarely missed anything when it came to protecting the royal family.

Brody stood and headed for the door. "I'll be here, no worries. And thanks, Boss-man. I owe you."

"Just keep sharing the baked goods."

A half-hour later, he was pulling back into the parking lot next to Fancy's bakery with several boxes in the bed of his truck and Boomer sitting in the passenger seat. Brody wasn't surprised to see Fancy's brother-in-law leaning against his own vehicle with his arms crossed, trying to look intimidating. While the fireman was physically fit and stood over six feet, the former SEAL could take him with one hand tied behind his back.

As they climbed out of the truck, Corey approached Brody with a scowl on his face. "If you think this is going to get you into her pants, think again."

Rounding the back of the truck, Boomer raised his eyebrows, giving his teammate a silent, "*What the fuck?*" But he didn't interfere. Brody crossed his arms over his massive chest and scowled back at the man glaring daggers at him. "Seriously? You think that's why I'm doing this? I would think you'd be glad she'll be better protected."

Corey mirrored his stance. "Fine. But I'm paying for the system. You can show me how it works when you're done. I don't want Fancy worrying about a thing. After that, leave her the hell alone."

"Huh?" The guy was getting on his nerves, so Brody changed tactics. "So you're married to her sister?"

"What? Who the fuck told you that? Fancy doesn't have any sisters. She was married to my brother." At that moment, Brody realized he didn't know the man's last name. "He was killed in a car accident a few years ago, and she ended up in a coma for weeks. So excuse me if I'm a little over-protective of her. I'm the only family she's got around here."

Brody noticed the slight shake of his teammate's head, and he knew he had to put this pissing match to rest. "Look, man. I like her. She's really nice. I met her through a friend who hired her for a wedding. But I'm not some asshole who would expect sex in return for helping her stay safe. I understand where you're coming from, and the last thing I would ever do is hurt her. That's not the kind of guy I am. Let me just do this for her so we'll all know she's safe, all right?"

After a long pause, Corey nodded and held out his hand. "Truce?"

"Truce."

For the first time since they got there, the fireman acknowledged Boomer. "Hey, sorry about that. Corey Maguire." He extended a hand.

"Ben Michaelson, but everyone calls me Boomer. And no worries. I'd do the same."

As the two shook hands, Brody dropped the tail-gate of his truck bed and started sorting through the multiple boxes they'd brought. With Maguire's help, they had everything inside within a few minutes. With the plywood covering the window, the table area on the right side of the store was darker than the rest of the shop, so Fancy had turned the light dimmer on high for them. After ensuring his sister-in-law didn't need anything, Maguire left, promising to return later to see how the new system worked since he had the spare keys to the place.

By noon, Boomer and Brody had the camera system up and running, as well as new security locks and alarms on both the front and back doors. All they needed to do was wire the new window currently being put in place. Fancy's insurance company had sent an adjustor out immediately since the only damage was the broken window. As soon as the man had taken his pictures, Brody had gotten Parker's glass company on the phone. As a favor to Brody, Parker had asked the owner to put them at the top of the repair list.

The teammates were packing up their tools and things they were done with when Fancy walked over with two large water bottles. "Here, you two look like you could use these."

While the air conditioning had been blasting earlier due to the 103-degree temperatures soaring outside, it had done no good with the hot air coming through the empty window frame, which had just been filled. Brody grinned at her. "Thank you, ma'am."

Rolling her eyes, she fought a smile and lost. "Does that fake accent actually work on women?"

When Boomer barked a laugh, Brody smacked him hard in the gut, causing him to cough and gasp for air instead. He winked at Fancy. "It's not fake, darlin'. I was born and bred right outside Dallas. I just learned to hide it in the Navy. But it tends to come out a little stronger when I'm relaxed."

She cocked her head to the side, and her eyes narrowed in confusion. "Why would you have to hide it?"

"I was a Navy SEAL, and we had to go into places where having a southern accent stuck out like a sore thumb. The only thing worse was my buddy Marco's New York accent."

Swallowing some water, Boomer nodded his head. "Yup. It's the Yankee meets the hick when those two get going. And if you think hiding his accent was bad, you should see him with his hair dyed. Most of the countries we went into didn't have people with blond hair."

"So you were both SEALs?"

Widening his stance, Brody got comfortable and tried to hide his satisfaction at her sudden curiosity. *Three questions in under two minutes?* Wow, that was a record for her with him over the past two weeks. Usually, it was him asking questions, trying to get to know her better, and Jamie jumping in to answer when Fancy wouldn't.

As Boomer explained the little he could about their careers on SEAL Team Four, Brody thought back to what Maguire had said earlier. Actually, it had been on his mind ever since he'd learned she was a widow. He guessed she was about thirty, which would have made her twenty-seven or so when she lost her husband—way too young to have to go through such a horror. *How long had they been married?* His gaze roamed her face and then her body. She had no noticeable scars or disabilities from the accident and subsequent coma. *How long had it taken her to recover?*

Sometime in the past few hours, his feelings toward her had changed. They had gotten stronger, and she was no longer just some woman who was a potential conquest. She was bringing out the inner Dom in him. He could switch it off now and then. He had dated plenty of "vanilla" women, some who enjoyed a few D/s things he introduced them to, and others who he knew it was a line they wouldn't cross. *What category did Fancy fall into?* While he didn't mind dabbling in the vanilla world occasion-ally, he did know any long-term relationship would need a D/s dynamic for him—at least in the bedroom.

The bell over the front door jingled, and he glanced over his shoulder to see the glass guy stride in with a clipboard. He had Fancy sign off on the work order so he could submit it to the insurance company and then gave her a copy of the receipt.

Brody was about to start grabbing what they needed to alarm the window when a hand on his forearm stopped him. His eyes traveled up the feminine arm to the shoulder, neck, face, and then the eyes of the woman who had been invading all his dreams lately. The contact sent a tingling through him, and he fought the urge to shiver. Damn, he couldn't remember a single time a woman's non-sexual touch had made him want to pin her to a wall and do wild, nasty things to her.

Fancy's brown eyes stared back at him, and when her eyebrows shot up, he realized she was waiting for an answer. And God help him, he had no idea what the question was. He gave his head a slight shake. "I'm sorry. Zoned out there for a second. What did you say?"

The corners of her mouth turned up in a smile, and for a brief moment, he knew he was seeing the real woman behind the multiple masks she had used to keep him at a distance. "I asked what I could get you both to eat for lunch. I'm sending Jamie across the street to the Italian deli, and the least I can do is feed you for all you've done for me. I know I said the upgrades weren't in my budget right now, but I can make monthly payments. I can't let you do this for free."

Placing his hand over hers, still resting on his forearm, he purposely lowered his voice to Dom mode. "I offered to do this, Fancy. And I meant what I said. Pay me in sugar and whatever else you put into all those yummy things behind the counter. That and seeing a smile like the one you just gave me every day will be payment enough."

She blushed as she giggled. "Sugar and a smile *every* day? Hmmm. I'll think about it. Today, though, you definitely earned them."

They stood there staring at each other as the seconds ticked by, and the rest of the shop faded away. Brody was about to lean forward and kiss her, but thankfully, the bell on the door sounded again as new customers entered, pushing the thought from his mind. As much as he wanted to kiss her, here and now was neither the time nor the place. He had to take this slowly. This woman was turning him inside out without even trying, and for the first time in his life, he thought he might have found "the one." He only hoped she would give him a chance.

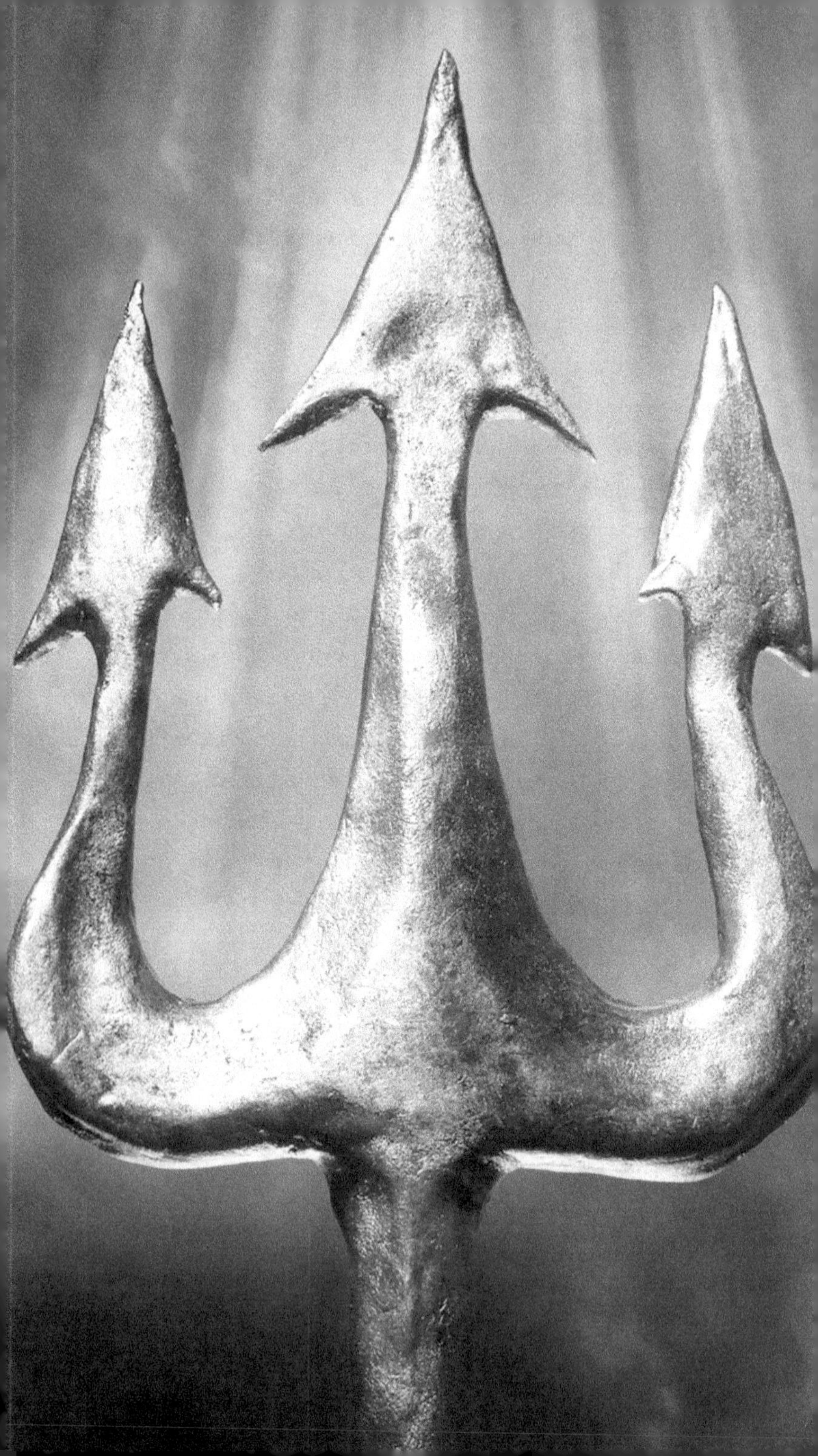

CHAPTER FOUR

With his black tie hanging undone around his neck, Brody climbed from his truck and grabbed the tuxedo jacket he'd put on the hook behind the driver's seat. *Who the fuck had thought of holding a black-tie event on a Friday night in the middle of September in Tampa?* It was a quarter to four in the afternoon and the outside temperature was still over the one hundred-degree mark. Damn, he was ready to fucking melt. At least the air conditioning would be on full blast in the offices and later at the Hilton, where the gala was being held.

Entering the warehouse that'd been turned into the Trident offices, he hung the jacket up on the coat rack in the reception area before heading to the conference room. As he passed the secretary's desk, Colleen was packing her things to leave for the day, but she paused long enough to give him a wolf whistle. "Looking good, Brody."

He laughed and winked at her. "You know it. Have a good time in Miami."

She and Reggie were headed there for a relative's wedding this weekend. "Thanks. See you Monday."

Waving over his shoulder, he walked into the conference room, which had doubled in size with the renovations they'd made two months ago. Parker's company had originally transformed the warehouse into office space downstairs, bunk rooms and living quarters upstairs, and a vehicle garage in the back half of the building. Some unused space had been walled off until Trident needed it, which happened when they hired more personnel—the Omega team. Returning, Parker had added more offices and expanded the conference room and Brody's war-room. While he loved having more space for his computers and electronic toys, he wasn't exactly thrilled Ian and Devon had hired another computer geek. Their reasoning was they would be screwed if anything happened to him, which, although he didn't like it, he understood. At least when the new guy, Nathan Cook, arrived next week, he'd be in charge of the Omega team's intel gathering, so Brody's workload wasn't doubled to accommodate both teams. He and Parker had designed the updated war-room so both geeks would have their own space yet have full access to whatever computer setup was needed.

Most of the Omega team was already in the conference room, which he'd expected since all but two of them were still using the bunk rooms upstairs until they could find permanent housing. But there was no rush for that. He noted who was present and accounted for since he was leading tonight's detail. Valentino "Romeo" Mancini, Cain Foster, and Tristan McCabe were studying the floor plans of the ballroom and surrounding areas of the Hilton. While across the room, Darius "Batman" Knight and Kip "Skipper" Morrison conversed with Ian and Mousaf Amar. The only person not dressed in various states of formal wear was Ian, wearing black dress pants and a gray golf shirt. He'd go with them to introduce the new team to the princess, but then he had the rest of the night off. It must be nice to be the boss and make the rules.

Two team members were missing, but they still had a few minutes before the briefing was about to start. Stepping over to their client, Brody greeted the man with a handshake. "It's been a while, Amar. How are you doing?"

The dark-haired, olive-skinned security agent was of Malian descent, although his family immigrated to the small, neighboring North African country of Timasur when he was ten. "Good, my friend. It is a delight to be back in Florida for a bit. I like the change in scenery."

"How's Her Royal Majesty doing? Better, I hope."

Queen Azhar had fallen ill with unexplained renal failure earlier in the year, forcing Princess Tahira to cancel a visit to the States with two of her cousins. "Her Highness is doing much better and responding to treatments. According to the press release issued last week, the doctors expect a full recovery. And thank you for asking. I will tell her you were inquiring about her well-being."

He was about to respond when a chorus of wolf whistles filled the air as a brunette bombshell walked in wearing a female-cut tuxedo, and Amar's eyes widened. "Who is that beautiful creature, and why haven't I met her before?" he asked in a low but interested voice.

Chuckling, Brody leaned closer. "She can kick your ass and snipe you from a mile out."

"That just makes her even more attractive," the man murmured.

Rolling her eyes, Lindsey "Costello" Abbott groaned at the heckling she was getting from the team. Over the past few months, the former Marine sniper had more than proven she deserved to be on the Trident team as much as the men did. While she had been hired to fill the sniper position in place of Jake Donovan, who was putting together a West Coast team, she'd been on assignments and training with both teams over the past seven months. She held her own in combat and physical training and had already protected their sixes on a few missions. But clean off her camo grease paint, and the woman was a walking hard-on. To fit in with the extravagant venue this evening, her hair was in some fancy updo that kept it out of her way while still stylish. Add the subtle makeup she wore and her toned yet curvy body, and the woman would turn heads all evening without even trying. Nevertheless, any guy who tried to interrupt her security assignment tonight would be either taken down and talking soprano or peeing his pants when her 9mm was shoved into his face. Underneath the custom-fit black attire was certainly a variety of weapons.

When she approached, Brody introduced her to their client. "Lindsey, this is the head of the royal security detail, Mousaf Amar. Amar, this is our newest sniper, Lindsey Abbott. She'll stay the closest to Princess Tahira in case she needs to go to the restroom or anywhere else the men shouldn't be."

Smiling, Amar bowed his head slightly in her direction. "It's a pleasure, Ms. Abbott."

Lindsey responded with her own polite yet professional smile. "Thank you, Mr. Amar. And it's my pleasure to meet you as well."

The last man they were waiting for walked in. Logan "Cowboy" Reese was introduced to Amar, and then Ian called the room to order. "All right. Let's go over tonight's detail. Rule number one: I don't care how much Princess Tahira comes on to you—Abbott, this doesn't apply to you—keep it in your fucking pants. She's off-limits. Not only will you be fired, but I will kick your ass from here to Timasur, where King Rajeemh will castrate you. Got it? Good."

An hour later, a caravan of black SUVs drove through the gate of the royal family's vacation home—well, with its twenty-nine rooms, "mansion" was a more appropriate word. The team poured out of the vehicles and hurried into the air conditioning to keep from getting drenched in sweat. The temperature had only dropped two degrees to ninety-nine, but the forecast had called for it to fall even further to the high eighties after the sun went down. Still, not weather you wanted to be formally dressed in, though.

Amar quickly made the introductions to his own team members, some of whom had been on duty all day and would be off for the next few hours. It was one of the reasons the palace had hired Trident to supplement their security personnel here in Florida.

The sound of high heels on granite tile had everyone looking at the top of a curved staircase leading to the foyer. Princess Tahira made her grand entrance, dressed in a stunning emerald evening gown. The fabric shimmered with her every movement, and her diamond necklace, bracelet, and earrings also caught the light. Her long, black hair was swept up off her neck, with a few curls framing her exotic features. Brody noticed several new team members' eyes widen as the woman floated down the stairs with a regal, half-nurtured and half-natural posture. They had seen several photos of the princess earlier at the briefing, but those paled compared to the real thing.

As Tahira reached the last step, Ian moved forward, taking her proffered hand. She smiled warmly at him. "Hello, Ian Sawyer." She habitually used a person's first and last name together. "It's wonderful to see you again. How is Ms. Angelina doing?"

The princess met Angie last year when she and Ian accepted King Rajeemh's invitation to visit the small, North African country. The two women had hit it off, much to Ian's surprise. Before that, Ian had been on Tahira's flirt list, which didn't extend to men in committed relationships. Every other male, however, was fair game, and Brody was sure she would be flirting with him and the rest of the team very shortly. "Very well, Your Highness. She's been busy with the wedding plans and was thrilled to hear you and Prince Raj will be attending."

"My brother and I wouldn't miss it for the world. My parents send their regrets, however. Father doesn't like to travel so far from home with Mother still recovering." She turned her attention to Brody, and he bowed his head slightly in respect of her title. "Well, hello, Brody Evans. It's always a pleasure to have you on my security detail. You look…"

Pausing, she tilted her head and stared intently at him. Unsure of what she was scrutinizing, Brody glanced down to see if there was something on his tuxedo. Not noticing anything, his gaze returned to hers. "Is there a problem, Princess Tahira?"

Instead of answering him, she directed her response to Ian. "It appears I've lost another of my favorite American bodyguards to his soul mate."

Ian's eyebrows shot up, and Brody was just as startled, if not more. "Um. I'm sorry, Your Highness, but I'm not sure what you're talking about. I'm not dating anyone."

A knowing grin spread across her face. "Maybe not yet, but you have met her. I can see it in your eyes and body language, Brody Evans. But you have doubts. Don't. She will come around soon enough, and I'm happy for you. Sad for me, but very happy for you. Truthfully, I had expected you to be the first of my Trident men to fall in love. But better late than never, as you Americans say."

His eyes narrowed in shock and thought as Ian introduced Tahira to the members of the Omega team. Brody knew the woman firmly believed in soul mates and things being "written in the stars." When she met Angie, she knew immediately that Ian and his fiancée were meant to be together and had told Ian so. But how she knew Brody had met his soul mate was completely lost on him. Yeah, he'd been thinking that maybe Fancy was the one since he'd never been so attracted to a woman to the point of jealousy at seeing her embrace another man—even if it had been her brother-in-law. However, he didn't think he looked or acted any differently. At least enough that the princess would notice within thirty seconds of observing him.

One of Amar's men announced the arrival of the limousine, which the princess would be taking to the gala, just as a dark-haired man dressed in formal wear came hurrying down the stairs. It was Tahira's cousin, Farid, who was her escort for the evening. Brody didn't bother greeting the younger man since Farid had made it quite clear on numerous occasions that he thought anyone who wasn't royalty was beneath him. The smug bastard would answer to Amar because he had to, but he just sneered or glared at all the other bodyguards if they spoke to him.

Once they confirmed everyone was ready and the head of security over at the gala had given the all-clear, the group of royals and guards exited the mansion. Ian bid the princess a pleasant evening before leaving in one of the vehicles they'd arrived in. Brody climbed into the back of the limo with Tahira and Farid while McCabe rode shotgun with Amar's guard, who was driving. The others would lead and follow the limo in the SUVs.

Settling into the soft leather seat, the former SEAL sighed. *It's going to be a long, fucking night in this damned monkey suit.*

Pulling the cupcake pans out of the industrial-sized oven, Fancy lined them up on the long butcher block table to cool. It was just after midnight, and once again, she couldn't sleep, so instead of tossing and turning, she'd come to the bakery to at least be productive during her insomnia. This was the last batch because she needed to try and get *some* sleep before she had to be back at six-thirty in the morning. Maybe she'd leave Sal a note saying she would be an hour late. They didn't open until seven on Saturday mornings.

Removing her protective mitts, she turned off the oven. She'd cleaned up for Sal, so she just had to cover the cupcakes, and he could decorate them when he came in. The tarts were already taken care of and would go out in the display case in the morning. Reaching for the foil and plastic wrap, she froze when someone knocked loudly on the locked front door. While it was bright in the kitchen, the only lights on in the main shop were the red security lamps.

Unsure who the hell would be at the door so late,

she grabbed a large knife and her cell phone. Dialing 9-1-1, she held her thumb over the "Send" button, ready to hit it if needed. Pushing the swinging door open just enough for her to see out, she was shocked to see Brody Evans standing outside the front entrance, looking in. He knocked louder this time, and Fancy sighed. Leaving the knife on the counter, she hurried through the shop to find out what he wanted. She didn't realize until she'd entered the new security code, then unlocked and opened the door that he was dressed in a tuxedo, sans bowtie, with the top shirt button undone. "Hi. What are you doing here?"

His gaze scanned her body as if assuring himself she was okay. "I was going to ask you the same thing. I was driving home and saw the kitchen light on with your car in the lot. Is everything all right? And what smells so damn good?"

She chuckled. The man hadn't been kidding when he mentioned his sweet tooth, but you would never know it by looking at his hard and sculpted physique. "Cupcakes and raspberry tarts. And, yes, everything is fine. Sometimes, when I can't sleep, I come here to bake."

The relief on his face was evident, but his eyes narrowed slightly. "By yourself? And why can't you sleep?"

Shrugging, she made light of it. There was no way she was going to tell him the real reason. "Just occasional insomnia. Can't shut my mind off some nights. And I keep everything locked, so I'm fine here alone." He opened his mouth to say something else, but his stomach picked that moment to growl—loudly. His blush made her laugh, and she opened the door wider. "Come on in, and I'll give you something to go."

After locking the door again behind him, she walked back toward the kitchen with him following. Glancing over her shoulder, she asked, "Where are you coming from, all dressed up? You look good in a tux, by the way." Now, what had made her tack that on?

"You like my Sinatra impersonation, huh? We had a security detail at some fancy gala tonight at the Hilton. A bunch of people showing off how rich they are and making sure everyone knew how much they're donating to AIDS research.

"Oh, my God, it smells even better in here. Woman, where the hell did you learn to bake, and who should I thank for teaching you?"

She chuckled. "My Aunt Denise. She still owns a bakery in Ohio, where I'm originally from. I'll tell her you said thanks. Do you want a tart or an un-iced cupcake? They won't be iced until the morning."

"I can't have a cupcake without icing. That's like having a steak without potatoes, so I'll take a tart, please. Do you mind if I eat it here? Otherwise, I'll be drooling the whole ride home unless I put it in the truck bed."

Her chuckle morphed into a belly laugh. "Sure, I

don't mind. One tart coming up." Pulling a wooden stool over to the counter, she gestured for him to sit. She slid one of the treats in front of him and handed him a clean fork. "Sorry, I don't have the coffee machine on, but I can offer you a glass of milk."

"Perfect, thanks." He took a bite, and his eyes nearly rolled back into his head. "Holy cow. This is delicious."

Fancy smiled and placed a full glass of milk next to his plate. "Glad you like it."

While she started covering the trays of cupcakes, Brody ate his tart. The silence between them was comfortable, but her body's awareness of his presence was a little unnerving.

Glancing over, she saw his plate was empty except for a few crumbs. "Want another one?"

"Does the sun rise in the east? Of course, I want another one. What I'd like even more, though, is if you'd join me. Nothing goes better with a sweet treat than an even sweeter woman."

She laughed as she slid another tart on his plate. "Is that all you know how to do with the opposite sex? Flirt, I mean?"

"Nope. I also know how to treat a woman as if she's the only one in the world. Just the way my dad taught all his sons."

After pouring another glass of milk and pulling over another stool, she sat beside him. When he held up his fork in question, she shook her head. "I'll join you, but I'll pass on the tart. You tend to lose your taste for sweets when you're always around them."

His eyes grew wide. "Perish the thought."

"So, you're from a big family?"

He nodded as he swallowed. "Yup. I'm the fourth of six kids. Two older sisters, one younger, and two brothers—one older, one younger. What about you? Any siblings?"

"I have one older brother who lives in Hawaii and two half-sisters from my father, but I've never met them."

His eyebrows arched. "Never? How old are they?"

A heavy sigh escaped her. She wished she had the close family most of her friends had, but it wasn't meant to be. "Fourteen and sixteen. They live in California with my father. He and my mom were never married, but they did try to make a go of it. It obviously didn't work out. I haven't seen him in about fifteen years, but every once in a while, I'll get a card in the mail, or he'll finally get around to answering one of my emails. I wanted to go to California to meet his wife and my sisters years ago, but he kept putting it off. I get the impression his wife has no desire to meet me, and he abides by it."

"Sorry to hear that. What about your mom?"

She took a sip of her milk. "She's still up in Ohio. I wasn't very close to her growing up because she always worked two jobs. Once I was old enough to take care of myself, she sort of had a midlife crisis.

She's on husband number three right now. I guess she's trying to make up for being single most of her life." She gave her head a slight shake. It had always bothered her that her family wasn't the perfect little family with married parents, a house with a picket fence, and a dog. At least when she met her husband, she'd gotten used to his brother and parents being around a lot. And when she and Patrick moved to Florida, Corey followed. Her in-laws had remained in Ohio and planned to retire to nearby Sarasota, but when they lost their oldest son, their grief had them staying where they had the most memories of him. "Anyway. I have a few aunts, uncles, and cousins up north, but my Aunt Denise and I have always been the closest. She never married or had kids, so she tried to fill in where my mom was lacking. Oh, don't get me wrong. My mother worked her ass off for my brother and me, but because of that, we rarely had her to ourselves." Her eyes widened. "And I can't believe I just told you all that. You probably want to leave after I dumped that on you."

Blushing, Fancy stood, but before she could move away, Brody's hand on her elbow stopped her. "Hey. I didn't mind at all. Haven't you realized that I'm interested in getting to know you better? And no, that's not why I offered the security system. Okay, scratch that. A little part of me knew it was an excuse to see more of you, but your safety trumps every-thing." He gave her a sad, puppy-dog look. "And I really do love your baking, so please don't send me away."

That last part made her chuckle and roll her eyes as he had probably intended. "Fine. You can stay. At least until I'm done here."

"Good. Then I'll follow you home." He took another bite of the tart, ignoring her startled look.

"Um, you don't have to do that."

He licked the fork, and her eyes followed his tongue involuntarily. "Um. Yes, I do. And before you ask why, I'll tell you. Because I'm a gentleman in the security business, who would hate to see anything happen to you before I had a chance to take you on a date. And because my momma would slap me upside the head if I didn't." He placed a hand over his heart. "Please don't make my momma do that."

Her laughter spilled forth. What was it about this man that made her feel lighter than she had in years? His brown eyes danced with amusement as his grin made his dimples appear. Oh, Lord, that smile was devastatingly handsome—actually, the whole man was devastatingly handsome. And for the first time since her husband died, she wanted a man to kiss her.

Pushing the thought from her head, she finished covering the cupcakes and put away the foil and wrap. "Okay. God forbid I get you in trouble with your *momma*. You can follow me home." She pointed a finger at him. "But don't expect me to invite you in. It's late, I need sleep, and I don't invite men into my home until at least the third or fourth date." Well, at least she wouldn't if she ever went out on a date.

His eyes shot up. "So, does this mean you're willing to go on a date with me?"

She shrugged coyly. "Maybe. You're starting to grow on me. One of these days, I might say yes."

"Then I look forward to that day, sweetness."

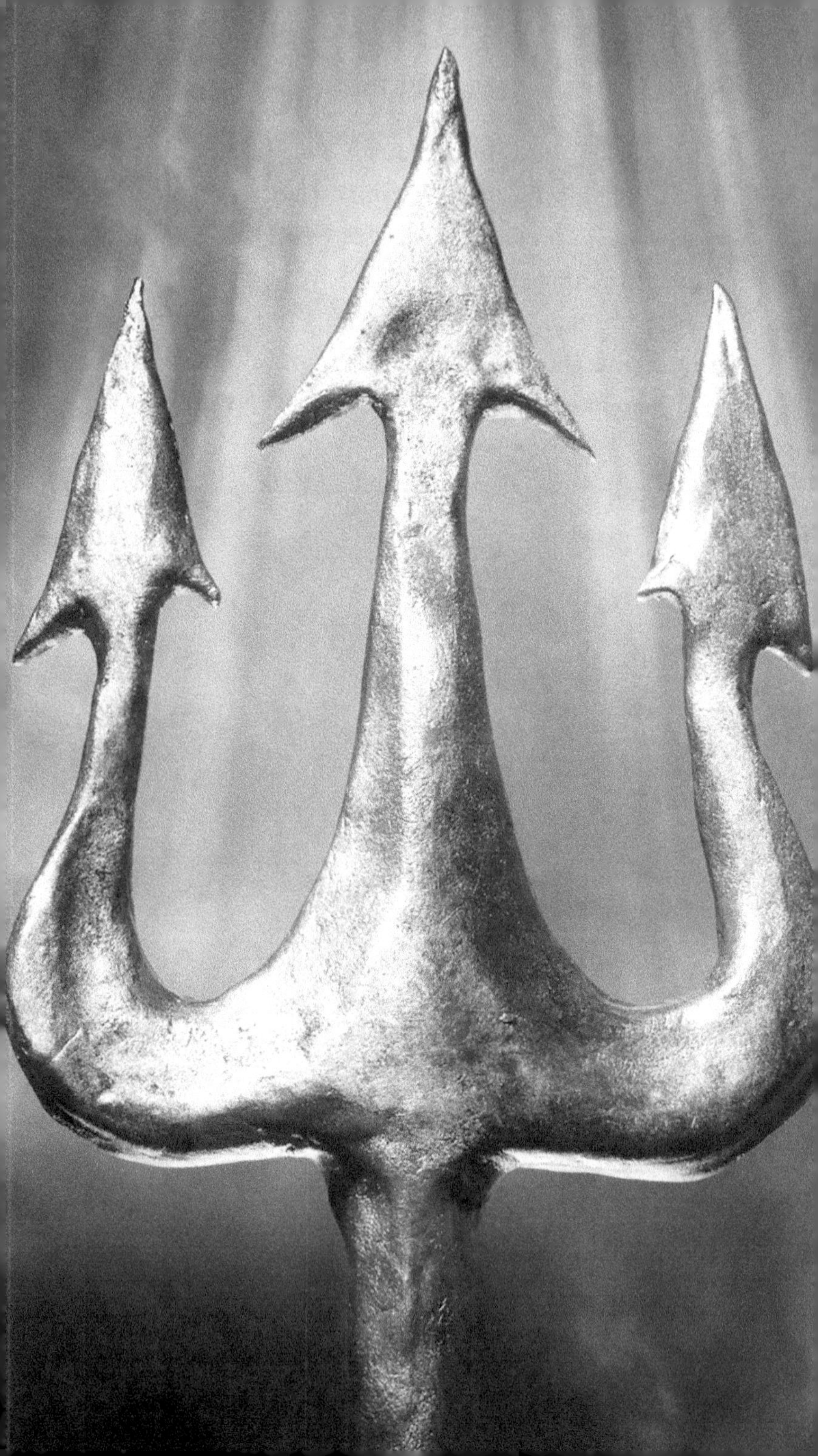

CHAPTER FIVE

The Dom sat in his car, staring at the entrance to the club. The submissive bitch should be coming out any time now. Her dominant boyfriend was working at the hospital, and instead of being a good sub and staying home on a Monday night where she belonged, she'd sneaked out and come to the BDSM club, the Devil's Dungeon. It wasn't one of the high-scale, private ones because she had been banned from The Covenant and was only allowed in Heat with her Dom. Well, tonight, she was going to get what she deserved for being such a naughty slut.

He thought back to all the gossip he'd been hearing the past week and a half. Word of the missing Christie Lawrence, aka Clementine, had spread among the members of several BDSM clubs, including The Covenant, and the few people who'd met her before were worried about what had happened to her. He was the only one on this earth who knew what *had* happened to her. She'd screamed, cried, begged to be let go, and, in the end, she'd begged to die. And he had been all too happy to oblige her.

Clementine had stayed alive longer than the first sub he'd brought to his lair. That bitch had been new to the lifestyle, and while he had seen a blurb in the newspaper about her disappearance, it seemed as if no one had connected her to the munch she'd gone to. That's where the Dom had met her. There were munches at least once a month in various places in and around Tampa. They were events where newbies interested in BDSM could meet and talk to those experienced in the lifestyle without play. Initially, introducing her to his world had been fun, but she hadn't lasted long. It was then he'd decided to seek out more experienced subs.

If he were honest with himself, he desperately wanted to tell everyone what had happened to Clementine and the other bitch, and where their destroyed bodies were located—in the middle of the Gulf of Mexico. But that would be the end of his fun and games. This time, however, he planned on leaving Heather Davis where she would be eventually found. If he couldn't let people know who was putting these whores in their place, at least he could let them admire his work.

The unmarked door to the Devil's Dungeon opened, and out walked his intended target, wearing her slutty clubwear. Her hair was messier than when she went in, and her face was flushed. It was clear she'd played—and not with her Dom.

Well, you bitch, you're going to be playing a lot more over the next few days.

Starting his vehicle, he waited for her to climb into her little sports car and then followed her home.

Holding on tight to the "oh-shit" strap behind his head, Brody grinned at Marco, who was laughing, as another green-looking Omega team member puked his breakfast into a barf bag. This time, it was Morrison, who was retired Army and a former LAPD SWAT sniper. The chopper they were all in was spinning and tilting as if it were caught in a tornado. Brody had known damn well what the pilot, Tempest Van Buren—call sign Babs for "bad-ass bitch"—was going to do once they were in the air, so he'd held off eating his morning treat from Fancy's bakery. But it was waiting for him in his office.

It had been four days since he'd found Fancy working late that night, and this morning, she had finally caved when he'd asked her to tonight's Tampa Rays vs. Cleveland Indians baseball game. She'd been a lot more talkative over the past few days, and once he'd heard she was an Indians fan, he knew he'd have to call in a few favors to get good seats. She didn't know it yet, but they would sit right behind home plate. One of the best things about working for Trident was the perks and contacts.

Abbott was the next to puke on a fast incline, followed by a nasty drop in the stealth helicopter, and Marco glanced at his watch and then nodded. Brody spoke into his headset. "Babs, take it down. Time to take these pansies on their run."

Several groans came over the air as Van Buren acknowledged him and cranked her disco music on high. The beat of the Bee Gees singing "Stayin' Alive" thumped through the bird as it tilted back toward the Trident helipad, and everyone leaned to the side from the Earth's gravity. From overhead, the compound appeared to be what it had been before the Sawyer brothers bought it—a bunch of warehouses formerly owned by drug dealers. Trident had added the heliport and a track with an obstacle course to the north. To the south was a shooting gallery designed to look like a small town's main street and a five-story training building where many walls could be moved to vary the setup. A security fence surrounded the entire compound, and several hundred acres of woods were on the other side of that.

The first warehouse was where The Covenant was located. No signs were advertising the private BDSM club, and it was hard to gain membership. An interior fence line separated the club from the other buildings that housed the Trident offices, bunk rooms, maintenance garage, gym, storage, and a panic room. The last warehouse had been converted into four large apartments, one for each of the Sawyer brothers—Ian, Devon, and Nick—and their significant others, and Ian's goddaughter, Jenn.

Babs set the helicopter down with practiced ease, and the Omega team scrambled to get the hell off, just in case she decided to take flight again. They didn't need to worry because the female pilot was already shutting down the engine. Heads low, everyone cleared the rotors before standing upright again. They all looked nauseous, but Brody and Marco were not going easy on them today. As he shouldered his fifty-pound pack, which matched theirs, Brody barked, "Let's go, you pansies! Packs on and fall in. We're going on a nice, long run—sixteen klicks— and then you'll get the break you'll be begging for."

"What the fuck's a 'klick'?"

Brody forgot Foster had always been in law enforcement, without a military background, and wouldn't know what a klick was. "Klick is military for kilometers. Sixteen klicks are just under ten miles."

A few dirty looks and groans were sent his way, but no one argued. The six-man Omega team lined up with Abbott on the far end. Brody wasn't worried about her lagging behind. In fact, she would probably be pushing the other guys forward. "Move out!"

They headed for the west fence line, and Marco

jogged ahead to place his hand on the security scanner, which would open the gate leading to a trail in the woods. Brody shut it again after everyone was through. With their current business and past missions as SEALs, the original Trident team took the compound's security seriously. There were plenty of hi-tech measures, armed guards at the front gate, and Ian's rescued dog, Beau, who had been trained by a company that supplied dogs to the military and private security companies.

The only things he heard for the first few miles were soft footfalls and the sounds of nature, and then the heavy breathing started. It was only 0900 hours, and they wanted to get this run in before the temperatures rose into the nineties. At least the hundred-degree marks had eased off over the past few days. He eyed the team. McCabe, Abbott, Reese, and Knight were no longer green, but Foster, Mancini, and Morrison still had an ugly tint to their faces. Foster stepped to the side to puke again, but as soon as he was done, he quickly rejoined the ranks. Brody knew Ian and Devon were trying to decide who would head the Omega team, Foster or McCabe, and it would be a tough decision. Both men had strong leadership abilities. Where one was lacking, the other made up for it, and vice versa. They came from two different backgrounds—Foster from the Secret Service and McCabe from the Army Special Forces—with similar and vastly different advanced training.

By the time they circled back, everyone was drenched in sweat. A bottled water cooler waited for the overheated runners in *Ian's Oasis*, the "backyard" Angie had designed for Boss-man as a birthday present. It ran the length of the warehouses and was located between the buildings housing the apartments and the gym. The asphalt had been removed, and sod had replaced it, then an outdoor kitchen, multiple sitting areas, cooling sprays, a fire pit, and a koi pond with a waterfall had also been added. There were many nights when everyone had gotten together there just to chill.

Each team member dropped their packs, grabbed at least two bottles, and crashed into a seat. Marco flipped the switch to activate the cooling spray tucked under the eaves of both buildings. Several people removed their soaking-wet T-shirts, including Abbott, who wore a black sports bra underneath. Brody glanced at her. She was in top physical condition and had an impressive body, but he preferred Fancy's softer one. He'd spent many a morning jacking off to what he imagined the delicious baker looked like under her chef's whites. The only time he had seen her in regular clothes was the other night. She'd been wearing a comfortable pair of jeans, which had only enhanced her curves, and a blue V-neck tee that had given him a teasing hint of her cleavage. The memory had his dick twitching, and he forced the image from his mind. Now was not an appropriate time to be getting a hard-on about the woman he couldn't wait to have in his bed.

Cracking open a second water bottle, he guzzled half of it as Marco's and his cell phones alerted them to simultaneous messages. Instead of checking his own, Brody raised an eyebrow at his buddy reading the text. Standing, Marco tilted his chin in the direction of the offices. "Ian wants you and me in there. Something's up."

Brody stood and addressed the team before following Marco. "Hit the showers. You've got an hour before you're due on Main Street for some target practice."

Striding into the reception area on his teammate's heels, Brody shivered as the air conditioning hit his sweat-covered skin and shirt. Goosebumps appeared on his arms. After finding out what was happening, he'd hit the showers over in the gym since the Omega team would be using all of the ones in the bunkrooms upstairs. Colleen stopped them from heading to Ian's office, telling them everyone was in the conference room. On the way, Brody veered off into his war-room and grabbed his cinnamon rolls, taking a huge bite of one as he walked down the hall and entered the room where everyone else had gathered.

He was surprised to see Detective Isaac Webb from Tampa P.D. with Cal Watts from the local FBI's SWAT team sitting at the long table with Devon, Ian, Marco, and Boomer. Webb was a tall, slender black man in his forties, while thirty-seven-year-old Watts was about four inches shorter at five foot ten, stockier, and had red hair. The former wore one of the Tampa PD golf shirts the department let their detectives wear in warmer temperatures instead of a suit and tie. But Watts was off duty, unless the bureau had changed its dress code to include cargo shorts, Metallica T-shirts, and sneakers.

Brody wiped his sticky hand on his wet shirt, then realized that was just as bad, so instead, he gave them a short wave. "Sorry, guys. What's going on?" He sat between Boomer and Marco and pulled one of the laptops in front of him. Whatever was up, he was probably going to need some intel.

Before anyone answered, Ian stood, shut the door, and sat back down. There was no mistaking the grim expression on his face. "This stays in this room for now, but I'm sure it'll get out soon enough. It seems as though we have a big problem. Cal is here off the record."

At the others' curious looks, Cal stated, "Isaac took Jake's spot on our Tuesday night basketball games at the 'Y,' so we know each other from there. He'll explain what's going on."

They all knew Jake Donovan had gone to the local YMCA for bi-weekly games before he headed out to San Diego to get the West Coast team of Trident up and running. It had been a win-win decision for everyone to send Jake because he was in a Dom/sub-committed relationship with Ian and Devon's younger brother, Nick, who was on SEAL Team Three stationed out there.

Webb cleared his throat. "Dispatch got a call this morning about a missing person. A woman who I believe you all know. Heather Davis."

Boomer and Devon groaned while Brody rolled his eyes. *This was the "big" problem? Seriously?* Heather was the biggest bitch in the world. When Devon's wife, Kristen had first come to the club as a guest, she had gotten into a knock-down, hair-pulling fight with Heather and another sub in the women's locker room. The two bitches had been bullying none other than Trident's secretary, Colleen, when Kristen had interrupted. Colleen had been very timid at the time and shied away from controversy. She also hadn't been working for the team back then. Heather and the other sub had already been on probation for bullying, and their memberships had been revoked that night. Kristen ended up being dubbed "Ninja-girl", and a few months later, Colleen had been hired by Ian, which her Dom/fiancé, Reggie Helm, was grateful for. Even he had seen the positive changes in his woman. Since they first met, the two women had become good friends, and Colleen had flourished under the training and watchful eyes of the Trident employees. Now, she knew how to defend herself and even had a concealed weapon license to carry a gun.

"Knock it off, assholes, and listen to the man."

Ian's tone had them all pausing, then sitting up straighter. If they had been in the club, everyone would have said it was his Dom voice, but in this setting, it was his "I'm your Lieutenant, and you just fucked up" one. It was obvious he was already privy to whatever was going on.

Webb took over again. "Well, whatever issues you had with Ms. Davis, I can assure you she's missing, and she's not the first." Brody's eyes flashed to Marco and saw his friend also made the connection to Kayla London's missing friend from Heat. "Her live-in boyfriend, Dr. Scott Harrison, got home from a shift at the hospital, which, due to a multi-vehicle crash, had him in the ER until 2:00 a.m. When he arrived home twenty minutes later, he found Ms. Davis's car parked in the driveway as he expected it to be. However, she wasn't at home. He went back outside and saw her car was locked with her cell phone in the center console—her purse was missing. He called 9-1-1 when she didn't return by eight this morning. Typically, this wouldn't have raised any alarms, and everyone would assume she ran off or something, but as I said, this isn't the first one with the exact same circumstances. I'll get to the others in a moment. What did differ this time was one of Ms. Davis's high-heeled shoes was found under the car by the driver's door when the patrol units first responded. According to Dr. Harrison, he had no idea where she'd gone last night and thought she was staying in.

The last time he spoke to her was just after 6:00 p.m. by phone."

He slid an 8 x 10 photo of the missing blonde onto the table, followed by another of a different woman—this one was a brunette. "Christie Lawrence, age twenty-eight, has been missing for three weeks. Last seen at a bar down on the Riverwalk by some friends a little after midnight. She drove home and disappeared. Her car was locked with her cell phone inside. Her purse was missing too." Christie was the one some of them had already heard about. Brody studied the photo—she was cute. Webb tossed a third picture on the table for the team to see—this woman had black hair. "Melody Barnes, age twenty-five, missing for six weeks. Last seen leaving her job as a waitress at eleven p.m. And like the others, her car was parked at her condo and locked—cell phone inside. No purse."

Devon crossed his arms and leaned back in his chair. "Okay. So we have three missing women, and since you haven't said you found any bodies, they are still *just* considered missing. I understand your concern because the similarities and circumstances don't bode well, but what's it got to do with us?"

Sitting forward, Ian rested his elbows on the table. "You already know Heather is a submissive in the life-style." He pointed at the photos. "The brunette is a submissive and a member of Heat. And the other one attended her first munch a few days before she went missing. One of her friends went with her, but they weren't always together, so she doesn't know who Melody spoke to, but she was there as a potential submissive to the lifestyle."

"Oh, fuck." Boomer slid the photos closer to inspect them. "Are you telling me we have some nutcase kidnapping submissives?"

Webb nodded. "That's what we're starting to believe. It's too much of a coincidence to ignore. For several reasons, my captain doesn't want to bring the feds in yet. One, he doesn't play well with others. Two, he hates Special Agent in Charge Stonewall." Brody snorted. Everyone in the room hated the SAC of the Tampa FBI office—the guy was a real asshole. "And three, we have no bodies. Just three missing person cases. Cal called me about something unrelated this morning, and I asked, off the record, if he knew any connections to the lifestyle. He brought me to see Ian. I had no idea there was a club on the premises here."

"That's the way we like it," Ian responded.

"I hear you. Anyway, I know there are other clubs in the area. I want your help getting the word out to women who attend them to be careful until we have more to go on." The detective stood, and Cal and Ian followed suit. "And it goes without saying, but if you hear of anything that might give us an idea of what the fuck is going on, give me a ring."

Ian shook the man's hand. "Of course. I'll call my cousin Mitch, our manager and co-owner, along with the owners of the other clubs, and have a meeting. I'll make sure they have your contact info in case some-thing comes up."

"Thanks."

After Cal also shook hands with Ian, the fed and detective left the room. The boss raised his voice. "Colleen?"

Within seconds, Trident's secretary was standing in the doorway. "Yes?"

"Pull up the list of kink clubs. I want a meeting with every owner and/or manager of the clubs within a fifty-mile radius. Tell them it's imperative, and I'd appreciate it if it could be this evening at The Covenant." He glanced at the wall clock. "Let's make it for seven. Let me know if someone can't be there, and I'll contact them later."

When Colleen hurried off to make the calls, Ian turned back to his team. He placed his hands on the table and leaned his weight on them. "Since we're closed tonight, I'll send out a mass text and email to the members. As of now, no female submissive leaves the club without an escort home and is secured behind locked doors. Right now, it doesn't look like male subs are being targeted, but if they want an escort, they'll get one to be on the safe side. Those without Doms will be followed home by a volunteer or security. No fucking exceptions. I'll be damned if this fucking asshole takes a member of my club."

The men all agreed. They were extremely protective of the submissives who belonged to The Covenant, no matter who they were.

Ian eyed Marco and then Brody. "How's the training going?"

After popping the last bit of cinnamon roll in his mouth, Brody swallowed and grinned. "Everyone but Batman puked for Babs, but he's already been on several of her roller coaster rides. They're doing well on the rescue simulations and starting to think like a team. When are you planning on dropping them in the middle of nowhere?"

The last training exercise would consist of letting the Omega team fast rope into the midst of the wilderness of the Rocky Mountains with a two or three-day hike out. They would have less than the bare necessities to survive and need everyone's input to make it to the prearranged extraction point in one piece. "We've got a few cases and missions on the front burner, and this missing submissives thing just added to it. At this point, it'll probably be after my wedding."

Devon's cell rang, and he answered the call. "What's up, Pet?"

Obviously, it was his wife. Kristen was ready to give birth any day now, and it couldn't happen fast enough for her. She was already nine days overdue. Baby JD—John Devon—was taking his sweet-ass time. Brody knew Kristen had been extremely uncomfortable these past few weeks with the sweltering weather following months of morning sickness, which had worried her husband to no end. Devon froze. "You're sure?" Standing quickly, he sent his chair flying and raced for the door, shouting over his shoulder, "She's in labor!"

Sitting next to Brody, Boomer groaned. "Fuck! I had Thursday in the baby pool. Who has today?"

Egghead hit a few buttons on his laptop and brought up the document with everyone's bet. With twenty people putting up fifty dollars each, the winner would get a cool thousand bucks. "Nick's got today. And Reggie has tomorrow if it's a long labor."

"Figures."

Crumpling up the now empty bakery bag, Brody stood. "Well, I'm hitting the shower, then we'll have the team down on Main Street if you need us. But please don't because I've got plans tonight with one very fancy lady."

CHAPTER SIX

Behind her locked office door, Fancy changed from her chef's whites into a denim skort and red tank top. Over that, she pulled on a cotton, button-down Cleveland Indians shirt she had stolen from Patrick years ago. It was one of the few items of her late husband's clothing she'd held onto. Leaving the buttons undone, she pulled her hair from its bun, brushed it out, and then put it back up in a ponytail. She turned to a small mirror on the wall and applied a subtle eyeliner, blush, and lip gloss. Her stomach quivered for at least the hundredth time that day. Her last first date had been with Patrick, but that had been nine years ago when she was twenty.

A knock on the door had her startling. Taking a deep breath, she tried to get her nerves under control. "Who is it?"

"Carol. Brody's here." Her employee singsonged

the second two words. Jamie, Bernice, and Carol had been urging her to go out with Brody for the past two weeks and almost threw a party when they'd heard she had finally relented.

"Tell him I'll be out in a minute."

"'Kay."

Sliding her feet into the sandals she'd brought, she shoved her work clothes and shoes into a duffel bag and left it on her chair. She'd bring it home after work tomorrow. Grabbing her purse and the canvas bank bag with the day's receipts, she took another look in the mirror. The butterflies in her stomach took flight again, and she inhaled, then exhaled slowly. "Here goes nothing."

Locking the office door behind her, she walked into the kitchen and said goodbye to Miguel, who was decorating large cookies in the shapes of several *Sesame Street* characters—they were a hit with the kids. Entering the main shop, she found Brody paying Bernice for a box of something, which had already been tied off with string, along with two large bottles of water and a quart of milk. He was wearing tan cargo shorts, a Tampa Bay Rays T-shirt, and sneakers, and he looked absolutely yummy. The shirt was just snug enough to show off his incredible physique, and her hands itched to brush against the hard contours of his torso.

Stepping around the counter, she approached him

with her eyebrows raised. "You know they have food at the stadium, right?"

He grinned at her as he tucked his wallet into his pants pocket. His gaze went quickly from her face to her feet and back up again. "You look fantastic." She blushed as he continued. "And yes, I know they have food there. This isn't for us. Ready?"

Nodding, she held up the bank bag. "Mmm-hmm, but can we drop this off at the night deposit at my bank? It's just a few blocks away."

"Sure thing." He turned back to the counter and said goodbye to her employees as he gathered up the box and the bag Bernice had placed the bottles in.

Fancy waved to the women, who paused in their prep for closing, giving her a covert thumbs up before she followed Brody to the door. She couldn't believe how much she looked forward to this evening and hoped she wasn't reading too much into his attention. He stopped at his truck and opened the passenger door for her to climb in. "I'll be right back."

Confused and curious, she watched as he hurried toward the back of the parking lot. There was a homeless man she had never seen before, sitting on a crate in the shade of a few trees. Brody squatted down beside him and spoke as he opened the bakery box and bag so the man could see what was inside. His clothes were worn and dirty, and his hair was long and disheveled, but it was clear none of that bothered her date. As

Brody stood again and said something else, he pulled out his wallet and handed over a small white card. The man nodded, took the card, and then shook his hand.

Jogging back to the truck, Brody climbed into the driver's seat, shut the door, and started the engine. Fancy stared at him. "You know him?"

"Nope." He backed the vehicle from the parking spot and steered toward the exit.

"No? You just bought a homeless stranger food and water? How did you know he wasn't a violent, crazy person or a criminal or something?" She knew she sounded shocked, but the man continued to surprise her in many ways. And each time, it made her like him even more.

He shrugged and pulled out into traffic. "It's no big deal. And, yeah, he could have been either of those things, but he's a Navy veteran, and that was good enough for me."

Her eyes narrowed. "How did you know that?"

Rubbing his right forearm with the opposite hand, he glanced in her direction. "The tattoo on his arm is a Navy insignia. He was walking past me as I pulled in, and I saw it. His name's Russell Adams, by the way, if you see him again, and he's harmless as far as I can tell."

"We don't get many homeless hanging out in this area, but I'll tell Sal and Miguel if they see him, it's okay to give him some food and stuff."

"I'm sure he'll appreciate it." Throwing on his left

turn signal, he slowed and waited for a break in the traffic. He held out his hand after parking in front of the night-deposit drawer. "Give me the bag. I'll drop it in."

He was back in a flash, and with the evening traffic, it took them almost an hour to get to Tropicana Field in St. Petersburg, and he held her hand almost the entire time. They chatted about everyday, ordinary things, and Fancy relaxed as the butterflies stopped bouncing around her stomach. Brody was so easy to talk to, and he made her laugh often. There were so many layers and sides to the man, each one more attractive than the last, and she wondered why no other woman had snatched him up by now.

It was a beautiful evening, and the stadium dome was open to let in the night air. They stopped at a kiosk and grabbed two beers, then again he surprised her by heading toward the section behind home plate. Her eyes bugged out when she realized they were sitting at the field level, three rows behind the batters. "Oh my God. I've never sat behind home plate at a Major League game before. Little League, yes. Major League, no. Are these your regular seats?"

He gestured for her to proceed him into the row. "No. With my work, it doesn't make sense for me to buy season tickets since I never know if I'll make it to a lot of games. I just had a few favors owed to me, so I cashed them in, hoping to make a good impression on you." He paused, then grinned at her. "Is it working?"

Chuckling, she sat and took the plastic cup filled with Bud Light, which he handed her. "Maybe. I'll let you know by the end of the game."

It was still a few minutes before the first pitch, and she glanced around. While most people were wearing Tampa Bay shirts and hats, a fair share still supported the Indians. That was one of the reasons why she loved Florida so much—many people had moved there from other states and countries, so there was always a diverse mix.

A waitress, who catered to the elite section, came over to take their food order—another first for Fancy at a baseball game—and Brody ordered a sausage and pepper hero while she decided on a gyro.

After they had stood for the national anthem, the game started, and they talked throughout the slugfest, mostly about baseball. She could tell he was surprised and pleased she knew quite a bit about the game. The lead changed hands several times, which had them booing and cheering with the crowd, depending on who took the lead.

Sitting in the seats in front of them was a couple with a baby about eighteen months old. The little boy wore a shirt that said "New Rays Fan." He was adorable, and Fancy felt a moment of sadness as she always did in the presence of young children. To her amazement, every time the boy looked over his father's shoulder, Brody waved at him and made funny faces that elicited a smile or giggle.

"You're great with kids," Fancy told him. "You must have a lot of nieces and nephews."

"Oh, yeah. At last count, thirteen, ranging from twenty-one to six months old between my family and close friends. The oldest is Ian's goddaughter, Jenn, who calls all of us 'uncle.' Her dad served with us on Team Four. And number fourteen is due any moment now. Devon and Kristen are having their first, a boy—" He was interrupted by the crowd's roar for a long fly ball heading into the home run territory but went foul. His attention returned to her. "Anyway, little JD sent his mother into false labor this morning, so after a round trip to the hospital, she's back at home, and Dev is pulling his hair out in frustration. I think the guy is going to crack if that kid doesn't make an appearance soon. There's a huge baby pool at work, but my guess at the due date has come and gone."

Fancy loved how Brody's face lit up when he talked about his two families—his blood family in Texas and his family of friends here in Florida. He was one of those people who appreciated the little things in life. She had been that way before Patrick's death and realized she missed finding joy in the simple things. It was time to start living that way again, and maybe this man could be the one to help her do that.

With a final out, it was the end of the fifth inning. The Kiss Cam appeared on the scoreboard, and after two couples, a third popped up. It took Fancy a moment to realize it was Brody and her as they stood while stretching their legs. As people around them cheered for them to kiss, she blushed and looked up at him. At six-foot-two, he towered over her. Grinning, he cupped her cheeks in his hands and slowly leaned down for a kiss, his eyes on hers the entire time. Her breath hitched a second before their lips touched, and she swore everyone and everything else disappeared except for the two of them and the fireworks that filled the sky—at least in her mind. The kiss was tender and sweet and ended all too soon. The cheering around them quieted as the Kiss Cam switched off and the at-bat player was announced.

Getting her hormones under control, the edges of her mouth ticked upward as her eyes narrowed at him. "You planned that, didn't you?"

Brody let out a barked laugh. "I'll never tell."

"Uh-huh." The man was incorrigible.

"I do have one question, though."

She eyed him warily. "What's that?"

Leaning down again, he whispered in her ear, "Can we do that again later without an audience?"

Oh, heaven help her!

Scanning the bar area of The Covenant, Ian took a head count. Fifteen owners and/or managers from the public and private BDSM clubs in the area had been able to make it. Only two had been unable to attend, and he had spoken to their representatives earlier to fill them in. Travis "Tiny" Daultry, a former professional football player turned bodyguard and the head of security at The Covenant, had agreed to come and be the bartender for the meeting as a courtesy to the others. Mitch had plans with a few college buddies who were in town, and Ian had filled his cousin in earlier, saying he would handle the meeting.

Double-checking they weren't waiting for anyone else, Ian stepped over to where the people at the bar and the others in a nearby sitting area could all see and hear him. "All right, everyone. Can I have your attention?"

Several conversations were cut short as they turned to face him.

"I want to thank everybody for coming despite the short notice."

"Your secretary said it was urgent, Sawyer," said Seth Markowitz, the owner of The Devil's Dungeon, from where he was leaning against the brass railing overlooking the pit. "What's up?"

Ian crossed his arms and widened his stance. "Had a visit from Tampa P.D. this afternoon." Groans and eye rolls filled the room. He held up a hand to get their attention again. "I know, I know. But this was necessary. Hey, listen up!" A few people who had started whispering among themselves shut their traps. "I know the detective who came to me, and it wasn't to harass anyone. We have three missing female submissives from the community."

"Missing? What do you mean missing?"

"Exactly what I said, Seth. About six weeks ago, a new sub attended a munch and disappeared from her driveway a few nights later. Three weeks ago, a sub and a member of Heat went missing—again, from her driveway, without a trace. I spoke to Heat's owner, Chad Thomas, earlier since he couldn't make it tonight. The detectives have already interviewed him and his staff but couldn't come up with any leads. The woman's name is Christie Lawrence, but she goes by the club name 'Clementine' and wasn't collared by any Dom at the time of her disappearance. The third missing sub is a former, and now banned, member of The Covenant—Heather Davis."

A few "fucks" were spat out. Heather may not be on everyone's list of friends, but she was known throughout the local BDSM community, as well as her Dom/boyfriend, Scott. "Her Dom reported her missing at eight this morning, but she wasn't home when he got there after 2:00 a.m. Like the others, her car was in the driveway, but there's no sign any of them made it into their homes. In Heather's case, a high-heeled shoe was found under her car."

Markowitz raised his hand to get Ian's attention. "Heather was at my place last night. I'm not sure what time she left, but she was there at eight when I arrived. I can check the video feeds at the front door, narrow down what time she left, and see if she was with anyone."

"Great. That would help a lot. See me before you leave, and I'll give you Detective Webb's number at TPD. See if you can get a close-up of the shoes she had on too." The man nodded, and Ian continued. "Now, at this time, we have no idea what happened to these women, but the coincidences are too high to ignore. I've already initiated a standing order here that no female sub goes home unescorted. Those uncollared will be escorted by either a volunteer Dom or someone from security."

"Fuck, Sawyer." This time, it was the owner of one of the public clubs, which tended to be a little lax in the security and house rules departments. "We don't have the staff for that."

"I know, Tim. But you can spread the word and get a buddy system going. I'm asking that you make your members aware that submissives are missing under unusual circumstances. Encourage them to look out for each other. Ask the Doms to do what they can to help. Do whatever you can to make sure your subs are safe because, in addition to not boding well for those who are missing, the word will spread whether you like it or not. And when it does, you may see a drop in club attendance. Ensuring your subs are safe protects them and you. Any questions?"

Twenty minutes later, Ian sat at the bar, drinking with Tiny. Everyone else had filtered out after a bunch of questions, some of which he didn't have answers to. A few people took down Isaac Webb's contact info in case they needed it, and Markowitz would call the cop first thing after he reviewed the security tapes for his club.

Tiny took a swig of his beer. "You did the best you could, Boss-man. You can't police every club. We just have to hope we find out what's going on before anyone else goes missing."

Ian sighed heavily and ran a hand down his face. His gut was churning. "I know. But I get the feeling things will get a lot worse before they get better."

Brody glanced at the dashboard clock and winced. It was almost twelve-thirty, and they were returning to the shop for Fancy's car. The game had gone into extra innings, and she had been having such a good time she hadn't wanted to leave before the end, despite the fact she needed to be at work at 6:00 a.m. She had assured him that she would call one of the afternoon girls to come in early so she only had to work a half day. But that still meant she had to get up in about four and a half hours. Truth be told, he was happy they had stayed for the whole game because it meant more time to just be with her. And seeing the smile on her face and the glee in her eyes when the Indians won had been worth every minute of it.

Pulling into the parking lot, he immediately noticed something was wrong. Fancy's silver Altima was tilting toward the driver's side. Cursing under his breath, he parked next to her car, and she gasped when she saw both tires were flat. Opening his door, he grabbed the heavy Mag-lite flashlight from under his seat and ordered, "Stay here while I check it out."

When she nodded, he climbed out and circled the front of his truck, his eyes taking in and assessing every corner of the lot for danger. No one was in sight, and nothing else appeared out of place. He squatted down and cursed when he saw the visible knife-induced puncture. Someone had deliberately stabbed her tires. He stood and walked around to inspect the passenger side, but those tires were still intact and full —probably because that side faced the roadway. Glancing up at the building at the other end of the lot, he berated himself for not putting up enough security cameras to monitor the entire lot. They covered the first row of parking spaces parallel to the building. Well, he'd remedy that in the morning.

Stepping over to the truck's passenger side, he opened her door. "Hand me my phone in the center console there, please."

She retrieved it for him. "Someone slashed my tires, didn't they?" From where she sat, she couldn't see the knife marks he'd seen, but what were the chances of both tires going flat without involving criminal mischief?

"Yeah. Who has it in for you, Fancy? The graffiti and brick were one thing, but it's obvious now that someone is targeting you and not just your store."

Her eyes widened as he found the number he was looking for in his contacts. "It has to be the teenagers I kicked out a few weeks ago. At least one of them must be holding a grudge."

After hitting the send button, he brought the phone to his ear and waited for someone from the towing company Trident used to pick up the phone. When a male voice answered, he gave him the vehicle's location and told him to tow it back to the Trident compound. Brody would change the tires and then ask Babs to do the alignment while he gave the entire vehicle a thorough inspection to ensure nothing else had been done to it.

Taking Fancy's keys, he removed the electronic key for the Altima and put it behind the front flat as the tow guy had requested, then got back in his truck. "I'll drive you home and come get you in the morning to take you to work. I'll have the tires changed and the car back to you by noon so you can still leave early."

When she didn't respond, he glanced over and saw wet droplets rolling down her cheeks as she stared out the windshield at nothing in particular. Reaching over, he brushed her tears away. "Hey, it's going to be okay.

We'll find out who's doing this and file charges with the police."

Her bottom lip quivered as she looked at him and nodded. "Sorry. I just don't know why someone would be so mean. I only asked them to leave because they were making so much noise and being rude to the customers. Then one of them started cursing at me, so Sal came out with a baseball bat and told them if they didn't leave, we were going to call the police. They threw their garbage on the floor and made a mess, but they left. I swear, if my friends and I ever acted that way when I was in high school, I would have gotten my ass kicked by both my mom and my aunt."

Her tears ebbed as she spoke, and anger replaced them, which he preferred to see. "I was raised the same way. Trust me, my parents just had to give us a look that said they were not only pissed but disappointed, and we straightened right out. Nobody does guilt better than a Texas mom or dad."

She laughed. "I'll have to remember that."

Leaning over, he gave her a quick, gentle kiss. As much as he wanted more, it was really late, and she needed sleep. "Let's get you home."

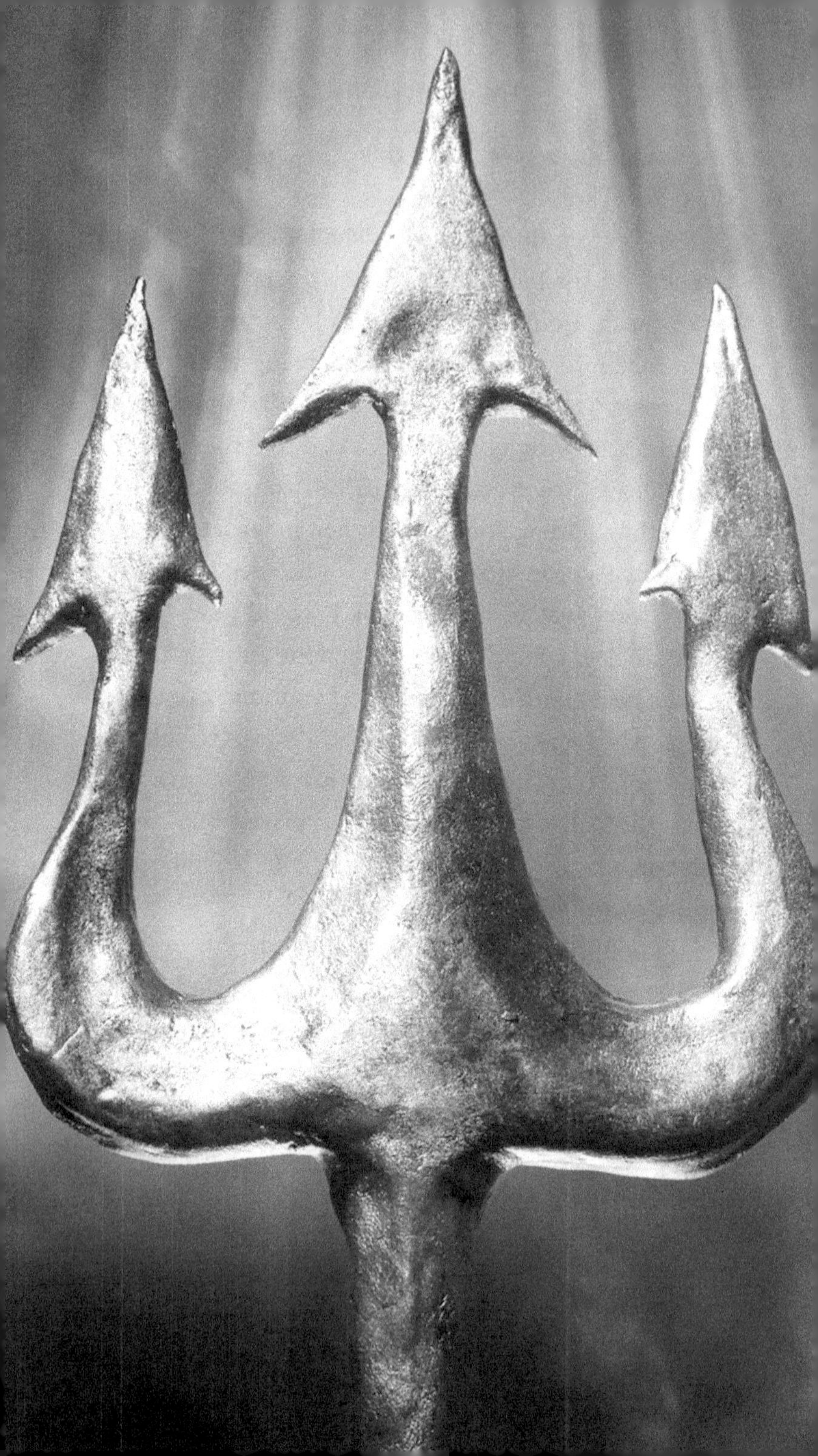

CHAPTER SEVEN

The sound of a car door opening and then closing nearby made Heather Davis's muscles tense. She had no idea where she was, how she got there, or how long she'd been there. She'd awakened with a severe headache a short while ago to silence and the fact that she was naked, tied spread eagle to an uncomfortable bed, with a blindfold over her eyes and a ball gag in her mouth. Her bladder was painfully full, and if she didn't get free soon, she was going to pee herself—again. The stench of urine and the wetness she felt under her thighs and ass told her she must have relieved herself at some point while she'd been unconscious.

Once again, she tried unsuccessfully to pull her arms and legs free, but the restraints on her wrists and ankles held fast. Even if her muscles hadn't been achy and weak, she doubted she could get out of them. The last thing she remembered before waking up here was leaving The Devil's Dungeon. Scott, her Dom, had been working at the hospital, and she'd been in the mood to go out and have fun. Knowing she wouldn't get in trouble unless she didn't get home before the end of his scheduled shift at midnight, she'd snuck out. Scott never went to the public BDSM club, preferring the private ones, Heat and The Covenant. And since she'd been banned from The Covenant, thanks to that bitch who'd married Devon Sawyer, Scott and she now only played at Heat.

They had been in a D/s and live-in boyfriend/girlfriend relationship for about three years now, despite the rumors she often heard that he was too good for her. Maybe it was true, and maybe she wasn't the most perfect submissive girlfriend, but in her own way, she did love him—as much as she could.

An interior door opened, and she heard footsteps on concrete or rock. Panic bubbled in her chest. She tried to speak, but the gag muffled her words. "*Ooo ehhh?*"

"Ah, good. You're awake. Perfect timing."

The male voice sounded familiar, but she couldn't place it. She began struggling against the restraints with what little strength she had. Whatever was going on, she knew without a doubt it couldn't be good. She flinched when hands touched her face, but all the man did was remove the ball gag. She coughed and tried to swallow, but her mouth was too dry. Her voice rasped.

"W-who are you? What the—*cough*—hell—*cough*—is going on? L-let me go!"

"Now, why would I want to do a thing like that when we're about to have so much fun?"

"You bastard! Let me go!"

The blindfold was ripped off, and she blinked against the harsh light. When she could finally see, her mouth gaped at the man standing over her. He was a Dom she knew from The Covenant and Heat, but she'd never played with him before. "You? What's going on? Let me go! Why are you doing this?"

His smirk was pure evil. "Why? Two reasons actually. One—because you're a bitch and a whore who deserves it. Two..." He shrugged. "Because I can."

Heather wished she could spit in his face, but her mouth was too dry. She yanked hard on her restraints again. "Let me fucking go, you asshole!"

"Tsk, tsk. Such foul language coming from you. What does your Dom say about your dirty mouth? Clearly, he doesn't know how to put you in your place... but I do."

When he released the hook keeping her right leg immobile, she kicked out at him, but her reflexes were slow and muscles stiff after being restrained for so long. He easily grabbed her ankle before her foot made contact with his body. Without warning, he stepped forward and slammed his fist down on her stomach, forcing an "*oompf*" from her mouth as she lost her breath. Bile shot up her throat as she gasped for air while he released her other leg. The pain in her abdomen was almost unbearable. She lost control of her bladder, soaking the mattress once again, but it didn't seem to bother the fucking bastard. And now was not the time to be embarrassed about it. She had much worse to worry about.

Before she could recover enough to struggle, he freed her arms. He grabbed her by the hair and hauled her off the bed. Her scalp screeched in agony when her legs gave out, and the only thing keeping her from hitting the floor was his hand. Her fists struck out as her feet tried to gain purchase, but he was so much stronger than her that the attempts to do damage were useless. He dragged her flailing, naked body across the cement floor to a St. Andrew's cross like he was bringing a bag of trash to the garbage. Terror coursed through her veins as he quickly restrained her to the contraption so she was facing the wall. One last attempt to kick him resulted in a painful punch to her side in the fleshy part above her hip.

Sweat and tears poured down her face. When he stepped away, she turned her head to see what the Dom was doing. Her blood ran cold as he picked up a bullwhip from a wooden table and sneered at her. "It's time to scream for me."

Brody stared at the picture accompanying the nearly three-year-old newspaper article on his computer screen. He'd finally broken down and done a Google search on Francine "Fancy" Maguire. Curiosity had gotten the best of him, and he had some questions he didn't know how to approach her with.

The top twenty URLs had to do with the car accident she and her husband had been in, while a few more were about her business. From what he saw in the photos shot from different angles, he had no idea how Fancy had survived the crash in the first place. Some bystanders had also taken a video with their cell phones, showing the off-duty police officer and two other men who'd stopped to help, rescuing Fancy from the passenger seat moments before the Jeep Wrangler burst into flames. According to the coroner's report, which had been posted a few days after the accident, Patrick Maguire had been killed on impact after he ran a red light and was T-boned on the driver's side by a box truck.

Brody had watched as the rescuers carefully but quickly pulled the limp woman from the wreckage, and his heart squeezed. He'd come this close to losing her three years before he'd ever met her. And long before she started creeping into his heart.

The only thing he couldn't access was the official police department accident report. He could easily hack into the Tampa P.D.'s computer system—that was a piece of cake for him. But Ian had promised the local Chief of Police his computer geek wouldn't do that again, after the last time unless absolutely necessary—for example, something which concerned national security. This didn't qualify, so he'd go the accepted route.

He was about to look up the number he needed when Boomer walked into the room. "Almost ready to go? After I drop you back here, I have to do a security inspection for a new client."

Brody glanced at the time. He had a few more minutes before they had to get Fancy's car back to her. "Yeah, but first, do you have Freddie Mendoza's cell number? I need to ask him something."

Trident's explosives and ordinance expert often did cross training with the local and federal bomb teams. They kept Boomer up-to-date on the new nightmares some chemists dreamed up, and he showed them stuff he'd learned while diffusing IEDs and suicide vests while in the devil's sandbox, otherwise known as Afghanistan and Iraq. "Yeah. Here it is."

As he rattled off the number, Boomer's phone rang. Answering it, he stepped back out of the warroom. "Hi, Kitten."

While his teammate chatted with his fiancée, Kat Maier, Brody dialed the TPD officer's number. The man picked up on the third ring. "Hello?"

"Hey, Freddie. It's Brody Evans."

"Egghead, what's up?"

He relaxed back in his comfy leather office chair with its ergonomic design. "Got a question for you."

"Shoot."

"What do you know about Fancy's car accident? The one that killed her husband."

There was a pause as Mendoza acknowledged someone else in the room. "I didn't know her back then, so I never looked at the report. Sal's wife is a nurse's aide and met Fancy during her rehab after she came out of her coma. You want to tell me why you're asking me and not her?"

Brody sighed. "I'm just curious—and I'm really interested in her, but haven't quite brought up the subject of Patrick and the accident. We went on a date last night, and when I took her back to get her car at the bakery, her tires had been slashed."

"Fuck. Anything on the cameras?"

"No. She'd parked out of range. I'll add two more to pick up the entire lot later today. Fancy thinks it's some kids she kicked out a few weeks ago."

"Yeah, she mentioned that. What's that got to do with her accident?"

He shrugged despite the fact the man couldn't see him. "Probably nothing. But I can't find any news reports of the results of the investigation."

Over the line, a door slammed somewhere in the vicinity of the cop, and voices in the background got louder. "I'm at a training gig that's about to start right now, but I'll look it up later and call you back."

"Thanks, I appreciate it."

"No prob. Later."

After the call had disconnected, Brody closed his computer browser and headed out to find Boomer. He drove Fancy's car back to the bakery, with his teammate following, and parked right under the camera closest to the front door, not wanting her to walk further than she had to. Holding two fingers up to Boomer sitting in his truck, he indicated he'd be back in a few minutes.

As he reached the shop door, he was surprised when it opened and Russell Adams came shuffling out with a carton of milk and a bakery bag in his hands. Brody grabbed the door and held it open for him before letting it shut again. "Hey, Russell. How're you doing?"

The retired Navy Petty Officer appeared to have taken advantage of the showers at the nearby shelter Brody had told him about, which catered mostly to homeless veterans. While his clothes were still disheveled, they were cleaner, along with his brown hair and fair skin. He was much thinner than he should be, and his clothes hung on his tall frame. Brody wished he could do more for the guy, but Russell had refused anything other than some free food, information on the shelter, and a few kind, understanding words. The former SEAL was all too aware that many veterans couldn't go back to being the people they'd been before going into combat, seeing and doing things most civilians could never imagine.

"I'm good, Senior Chief," he answered, using Brody's former rank, which he'd inquired about yesterday. "Ms. Fancy was kind enough to invite me in for some food. She told me to sit down at one of the tables, but..." He shrugged, his gaze flitting in all directions. "Having a homeless bum with PTSD sitting around can't be good for her business, so I told her I'd take it to my tree out back. She's really nice."

Brody smiled. "Yes, she is. And she wouldn't have invited you to sit if she didn't mean it."

The man shrugged again. "Yeah, but I don't do too well around people anymore, and I wouldn't want to have an episode in there."

Knowing he was probably referring to horrific flashbacks and/or temporary loss of reality, Brody nodded in understanding. Very few vets came back from combat without some form of PTSD, but some were luckier than others in that they were able to function day-to-day without breaking down or worse. "Well, if you need anything, you've got my card, right?"

"Yes, Senior Chief. Thanks."

"You're welcome." He watched as Russell shuffled around the side of the building, headed for the shade of the trees where he'd been sitting yesterday. Shaking his head, Brody thanked his lucky stars he'd come home from all his missions in one piece for the most part—mentally and physically.

Opening the door, Brody strolled into the shop and was assaulted by all the delicious aromas he'd come to expect. Yup, he was definitely going to have to bring something back to the office with him. A few customers were at the counter, and he had to wait until Fancy was done helping someone. She smiled when she spotted him and waved for him to follow her into the kitchen. She picked up two white boxes tied with string from the butcher block work table and handed them to him. He traded her car keys for them. "What's this?"

"One is pineapple crumb cake, and the other is a bunch of white chocolate raspberry tarts."

He groaned as his eyes almost rolled back into his head. His mouth watered. "God, woman, you're killing me here. How do you expect me to get these back to the office without digging in on the way there?"

Fancy giggled. "I'm sure you'll survive. Thanks for taking care of my car. What do I owe you for the tires?"

She narrowed her eyes at him when he stayed silent and shook his head. Her fists went to her hips in annoyed defiance. "Oh, no, Brody. No way. You wouldn't let me pay for the security system, but you're not getting away with that for my tires." She held out a hand, palm up. "I want to see the bill for them so I can reimburse you."

He gave her a sheepish grin. "I lost it."

Crossing her arms and cocking her hip, she frowned. "You lost it? You expect me to believe that?"

"I was kind of hoping you would." Before she could respond, he quickly continued. "Tell you what, you can pay me in food. They cost about as much as a home-cooked steak dinner with baked potatoes, asparagus, and something for dessert." He gave her the boyish "aw-shucks" expression, which usually had women falling at his feet.

"They did, huh?" Yeah, she didn't believe that for a minute, but it was still worth a shot.

"Yup. What do you say? You can cook at my place since we've only had one date, so I'm not allowed in your place yet. And I'll even be your sous chef and help cook."

She hesitated, thinking it over, but when the corners of her mouth began to turn upward into a smile, he knew it was a done deal. Leaning over, he placed a chaste kiss on her forehead. "That'll have to do for now, but later, I'm going to kiss your lips for as long as you'll let me."

Turning on his heel, he left her gaping at him as he sauntered out the door. Over his shoulder, he added, "See you at six, Fancy-girl."

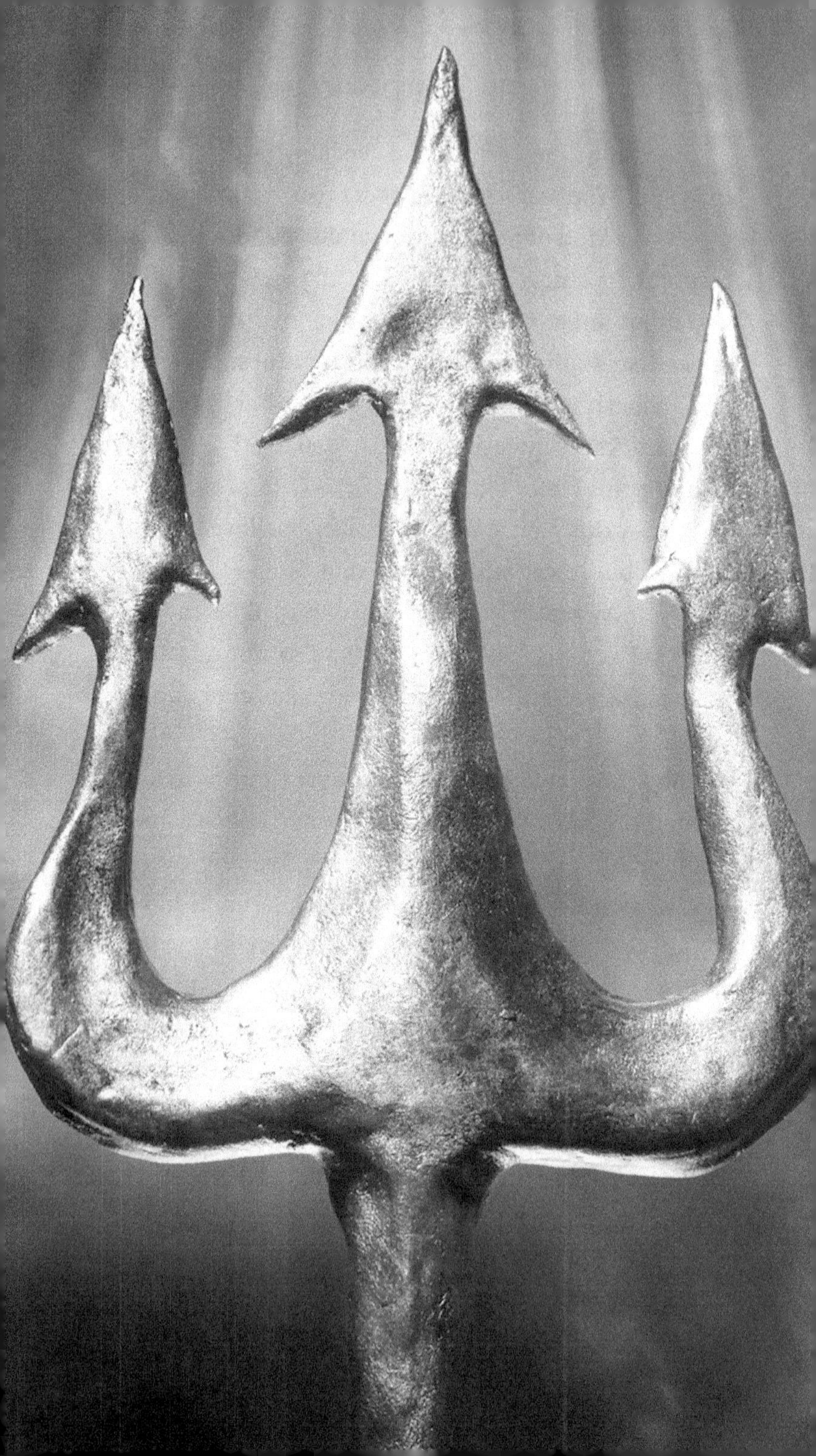

CHAPTER EIGHT

Biting her bottom lip, Fancy trailed behind Brody as he led the way to the front door of his house. She was so nervous about tonight but also excited. The more she got to know the man, the brighter her world was becoming, and, damn it, it was about time. Existing under a shroud of grief over the loss of her husband was expected, but after three years, she was ready to return to the land of the living. Patrick wouldn't want her to be alone, mourning him for the rest of her life, and now that she'd met someone who made her laugh and smile so often, she didn't want to be alone anymore, either.

After Brody had left earlier, she'd begun to look forward to this evening in earnest. She'd checked to be sure her staff had everything under control, then made a beeline to the gourmet grocery store up the street. While a little more expensive than her usual supermarket, she found the quality of meat and other fresh food was worth the extra cost. She'd picked out two juicy T-bone steaks, baking potatoes, fresh asparagus, and a beef seasoning rub the butcher had recommended, along with the fixings for a salad. Then she'd returned to the bakery and made a strawberry shortcake. Now, Brody was carrying the bags from the store while she had the box with their dessert in it. When he'd spotted the large, white cardboard box, he begged for a peek, but she told him he'd have to wait until after dinner for the surprise.

She'd followed him in her car to his house, which was located in a nice, quiet neighborhood. The land-scaping was well-maintained, reminding her of the house she and Patrick had owned. Shaking her head, she brought her mind back to the present. As Brody unlocked the front door, she said, "Your house is beau-tiful. Have you lived here long?"

He pushed the door open and indicated with a tilt of his head that she should go in before him. "About a year and a half now. Angie owns the white house next door. She lived there when I first moved in, and that's how she and Ian met."

"Sounds like it was meant to be."

Chuckling, he headed toward the large eat-in kitchen. "A little divine intervention, huh? Well, despite a few bumps in the road in the beginning, Boss-man has definitely met his match. When Ang moved in with him, she rented the house to a young couple with four-year-old twin girls. They're too cute —they call me *Mista Brophy*." She laughed as he set the bags on a granite-covered island. "Now, what can I do to help?"

"Um... well, first, do you have an outdoor grill, or am I using the broiler?"

His eyebrows shot up. "I'm a guy. What do you think? I'll go light the grill." He pointed to a drawer next to the stove. "Aluminum foil is in there for the potatoes, and pots and pans are below that for however you're preparing the asparagus. I'll be right back."

As he passed through the large family room, she watched him through the half-wall cut-out separating it from the kitchen. He grabbed the TV remote and turned on one of the music channels. Tim McGraw's voice filled the air. When he opened the sliding door to the patio, Fancy glanced around and began opening drawers and cabinets, looking for bowls, plates, utensils, and anything else she needed to prepare their dinner. Brody returned moments later, and after washing the cucumbers and tomatoes she'd brought, he pulled out a cutting board, then grabbed a knife and started slicing them.

They worked in comfortable silence for a bit, then he suddenly smacked his forehead. "I'm sorry. Here you are slaving over dinner, and I didn't even offer you something to drink. Forgive me?"

She smiled at him. "Nothing to forgive. I'm all right."

"I've got beer, wine, soda, sweet iced tea, and water. What can I get you, Fancy-girl?"

Needing something to calm the butterflies that suddenly took flight in her stomach at his endearment, she answered, "Wine would be great. A red if you have it."

"Is Merlot okay?"

Nodding, she rubbed the spices into the steaks. "Perfect. Thanks."

He selected a bottle from a nearby wine rack and opened it with a corkscrew before pouring two glasses. Fancy was surprised, expecting him to have a beer or something else. At her curious expression, he chuckled. "Yes, I like the occasional glass of wine. I do have a few refined moments now and then." He placed her wine in front of her. "So, tell me about Patrick. How did you two meet? I think you said something about him working at your aunt's bakery."

Stunned, she gaped at him. "You-you want to know about my husband? Why?"

Reaching over, he grabbed her hand, ignoring that her fingers were covered in the rub, and pulled it closer. His thumb brushed the skin of her wrist a few times. "Darlin', I want to know everything about you. Patrick was a huge part of your life, and your relationship and his death helped mold you into the woman you are today. The woman I am very attracted to. If you don't want to talk about him right now, I'll understand, but don't *not* talk about him because you think it would bother me because it won't."

With that little speech, he just wormed his way further into her heart. There were very few people to whom she could talk about Patrick and her loss. Her friends from back then didn't know what to say to her after she'd emerged from her coma, only to be plunged into a state of grief that resulted in her being hospitalized again. She'd lost touch with most of them since then. And his parents wouldn't talk to anyone about the loss of their son. Her family didn't bring him up either, and several of them, including her cousin Kerry, had been pushing her to move on since a few months after the accident. Corey, Aunt Denise, and Fancy's best friend Suzanne, who lived in Ohio, were the only three people who still talked about Patrick. Everyone else had let him fade away into oblivion as if he'd never existed.

She gently tugged her hand from his grasp, took a sip of her wine, and swallowed the sweet and pleasant liquid. He had exquisite taste in wine, she thought. "Okay... um... well, yes, we met at my aunt's bakery. He was going to the community college for business administration, and I was there for my liberal arts degree, but we never ran into each other before we started working together. He and Corey were the only two children their parents had, and they were devastated when they lost him."

"Understandable. Where did you go on your first date?"

She raised an eyebrow at him, but his expression told her he was really interested in hearing all about Patrick. "A movie. The *Rocky Horror Picture Show* to be exact."

"'Time Warp' fans. Awesome. I love practically everything Tim Curry was ever in, but *Rocky Horror* was his best."

"I agree." A grin spread across her face. "It was a midnight showing, and we brought all the props with us. You know, newspapers, water pistols, rice, toilet paper, the works."

He laughed. "Oh, yeah. I remember all that. In high school, my friends and I must have seen that movie a dozen times our senior year. We brought everything too."

Grabbing the potatoes she'd wrapped in foil and pierced with a fork, he said, "Hold that thought. Let me throw these on the grill since they'll take a while."

While waiting for him to return, she washed the rub from her hands and realized everything else was set for when the steaks went on. The asparagus she'd cleaned was ready to be seared in a splash of olive oil and garlic in a pan on the stove. The salad was all prepared, too, so she picked up both glasses of wine and strolled out to the family room just as Brody entered through the sliding door. "Everything else was ready, so I thought we could sit while the potatoes were cooking."

"That's fine. It's too muggy outside to be comfortable tonight, so we can eat in the dining room instead. It doesn't get much use with just me in the house."

Handing him his glass, she sat at one end of the brown leather couch and got comfortable as he sat in the middle, turning his body to face her. Martina McBride's sultry voice came over the speakers. "So tell me about Texas. I hear it's hot and flat."

"Definitely hot and flat, but aside from the occasional tornadoes, it was a great place to grow up."

"Do your brothers and sisters still live there, or have they scattered around?" She couldn't imagine growing up with five siblings under one roof.

Brody sipped his wine and then placed the glass on the coffee table. "They're all still in the same vicinity, within forty minutes of each other. My oldest brother Brett was the only other one of us to leave at all. He served in the Marines for four years and is now a cop in Dallas but lives in the suburbs near our folks. Everyone else went to college nearby and stuck close to home."

"You never thought about moving back there?"

He shrugged. "Yeah, I've thought about it. But I love my job and my family at Trident too. I visit Texas several times a year, so it's kind of like having the best of both worlds. What about you? Ever think about moving back to Ohio?"

"Not really." Fancy shook her head. "Many of my friends from back then have moved on, and there's not much for me up there besides my aunt. I would have considered it after Patrick died if Corey wasn't down here. But I love my shop, the people who work for me, and being close to the Gulf and the beach. I kind of feel like I was always supposed to be a Floridian who just happened to grow up in Ohio."

"Yeah, that's something a lot of people down here say if they grew up somewhere else. My buddy Marco is like that, having grown up on Staten Island." He paused and seemed to weigh his next words. "What, uh—what happened that day? When you—?"

"The day Patrick was killed?"

His eyes filled with compassion as he nodded. Suddenly, Fancy felt a strength she hadn't felt in a long time with someone. She couldn't deny her attraction to him any longer, and if they were going to date, then he had the right to know about what she'd gone through. "We—" She cleared her throat. "I wasn't even supposed to be with him. We had been talking about starting a bakery but hadn't done it yet, figuring it would be a few more years before we could afford to try it. Patrick worked in the sponsorship department of WRBQ radio station, and I had a job in the cafeteria at St. Joseph's Children's Hospital."

"Making desserts?"

She grinned. "Yes. My cartoon character cookies were a big hit there."

"I'm sure. By the way, Marco's daughter, Mara, loves the PAW Patrol cartoon. Can you make any of those characters for her?"

"Absolutely—I'll do some next time I make them —I'll even send some for your little fan club next door." He chuckled, and she took another sip of wine. "Anyway. Like I started to say, I wasn't even supposed to be in the car with Patrick that morning, but my car wouldn't start—I'd left the interior light on all night by accident, and the battery was dead the next morning. Patrick was running late, and dropping me off near the hospital was faster than trying to jump the battery. The last thing I remember is we were getting off the exit to the hospital. Then everything was blank until I woke up in the ICU six weeks later. I never had the courage to look at the pictures or video of the accident Corey told me were online, but from what I know, the brakes failed, and we went through a red light. A truck T-boned us on the driver's side and... and Patrick was..."

She hadn't realized she'd started crying until a sob escaped her and Brody cupped her cheeks in his big hands, brushing away her tears with his thumbs. "It's okay, sweetness. Come here."

He pulled her into his strong embrace and held her as she cried. There was more she needed to tell him, but she couldn't right now—it was too much. This was the first time she'd ever told the story to someone she hadn't known back when it happened. Her head rested on his shoulder as his hands rubbed her back. He was murmuring words of reassurance and understanding. When her sobs eased, he pulled back so he could see her face, and her cheeks reddened in embarrassment. "I-I'm sorry. I didn't mean—"

"Shhh. It's fine. I think you needed that."

She nodded. She had needed that. It had been a long time since she'd relived what she knew had happened the morning her world had shattered. "Still. This wasn't what you expected when you asked me out."

Grinning, he wiped the last of the tears from her face. "You'll find I'm an easygoing guy, Fancy. I go with the flow. I don't freak out when a woman cries. I just hold her until she's done and then do what I can to make her smile again."

And a little bit more of Fancy's heart opened to him.

Agony wrenched Heather awake. Tied face down on the mattress, her body was on fire from head to toe, but all she had the strength to do was moan. It didn't matter, though, because the ball gag was back in her mouth, preventing her from screaming in pain. But she'd screamed earlier—*for him*, the bastard.

He'd tied her to a St. Andrew's cross on the other

side of the windowless concrete room and then taken a bullwhip to her body. She'd never experienced it before—it was on her hard limits—but she'd seen Whip Masters and Doms at the clubs wield them with expertise, which made the whips sing. They never broke a submissive's skin. She'd even seen *him* whip a sub, but never like this. She couldn't see her back, torso, or legs, but her arms bore the same slash marks she knew covered the rest of her. Dark blood still oozed from the deep lashes. She didn't think there was an inch of her body that hadn't been licked by the leather implement from Hell.

She'd tried not to scream, not to give him the satisfaction, but it had been impossible as he'd cracked the whip over and over again. She'd screeched her throat raw, and when she could no longer make a sound, she passed out. Now, she was alone and didn't know which was worse—being alone or wondering what would happen if and when he returned. Never in her life had she wished for death, but as she plunged back into the painful abyss, her last thought was praying she would never wake up again.

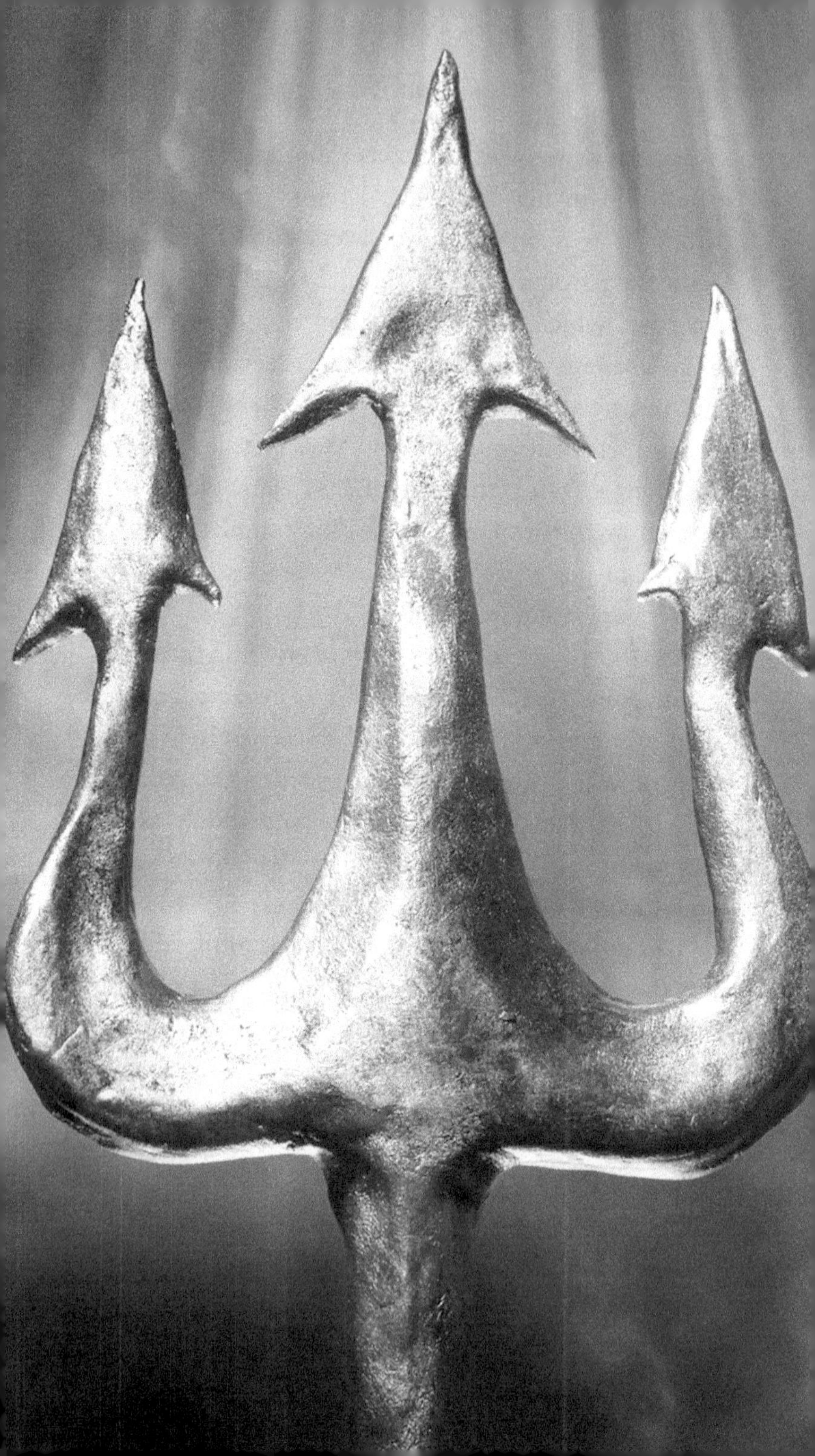

CHAPTER NINE

After drying the sauté pan Fancy had made the asparagus in, Brody placed it back in the lower cabinet. Giving the rest of the kitchen a quick glance, he ensured everything else was clean and in its place. After she'd pulled herself together earlier, Brody had intentionally switched the conversation back to safer, less upsetting topics. He felt there was more to the story about the accident than she'd told him, but he thought saving it for another time was best. There was something about this woman that sent all his Dom and alpha male instincts rising, to not only protect her but to make her his. Eventually, he would know everything he possibly could about his Fancy-girl, but that also meant he would have to open up and reveal a few things about himself he'd kept hidden up until now—namely, that he was a Dom.

He'd been a dominant in the BDSM lifestyle for so

"

long now he wasn't sure he could do without it being a part of his life. While he had no problem dabbling in the vanilla world now and then, any long-term relationship would have to include a D/s factor. How Fancy would respond to that, he wasn't sure. But tonight wasn't the night to divulge that information. He wanted her to be invested in their relationship before he came clean so that, hopefully, she wouldn't run into the night. He prayed she would at least be open-minded enough to try it. She was a natural submissive despite her outer strength, and the combination had him craving her more and more each day.

"Brody?"

He hadn't realized he'd been standing there doing nothing until she called his name. Shaking his head, he cleared his mind and focused on her beautiful face. "I'm sorry. What did you say?"

"I asked if you wanted dessert now or to wait a bit."

A grin spread across his face. If the woman only knew what he wanted for dessert—it wasn't in the box, but he'd settle for that now. "We can have it now. Do you like flavored or plain coffee? I have both for the Keurig. And decaf if you want."

"Mmm. French vanilla or hazelnut if you have it. And caffeine doesn't usually bother me at night, so regular is fine."

He stepped over to the counter, where he had a rack of coffee pods for the machine. Selecting a vanilla/hazelnut mix, he popped the pod in the slot and waited for the light on the brew button to turn green. "Maybe that's why you're having bouts of insomnia." He glanced over his shoulder at her and then did a double take as his mouth watered. "Oh my God, woman! Is that strawberry shortcake?"

"Uh-huh." She reached for a knife from the butcher block set and smacked his hand when he tried to dip his finger in the frosting. She wasn't fast enough, though, and he shoved a dollop of the fluffy white confection into his mouth. His eyes rolled back in his head, and she laughed at him. "Well, I guess you're proof of the old saying that a way to a man's heart is through his stomach."

"Amen to that." He placed a mug on the tray of the Keurig and hit the brew button. "You should have seen my brothers and sisters and I fighting over who got to lick the bowl when my mom was baking."

"I guess that's one good thing about growing up with only one sibling—no fighting over the bowl of cake or cookie mix. It also helped that my brother wasn't big on sweets."

"Is he not human or something?"

Fancy giggled. Damn, he loved that sound. Switching mugs, he brewed a second pod for himself. After all was set, he carried both coffees to the family room. Fancy followed with two plates of strawberry shortcake slices—one much bigger than the other. Yup, he would have to start adding more sit-ups to his workout routine if she kept feeding him all these goodies.

"So tell me more about Trident. Do you just do security systems and bodyguard work?"

He tilted his head to the side and swallowed a piece of the delicious cake. "Not really. We have a few government contracts, which I can't talk about. It's similar stuff to what we were doing in the SEALs. We also do security consulting and even some private eye stuff—you know, 'follow my cheating husband or wife and get me proof so the prenup is invalid.'"

"Seriously? People really do that?"

A small snort escaped him. "More than you'd ever think. We don't take many of those cases anymore, but when we first started out, they paid the bills. Now we've grown so much, we're training a new team here in Tampa, and my buddy Jake is out in San Diego putting together a West Coast team. He's in a relation-ship with Ian and Dev's brother Nick, who's out there on SEAL Team Three for another eighteen months or so. Then they'll decide whether to stay in California or come back and work for Trident here." He paused, then put his empty plate and fork on the coffee table beside hers. Leaning toward her slowly, he watched her eyes for any sign she was nervous or scared. "You have a little bit of icing on your lip."

Fancy's eyes widened as he closed the distance between them and used his lips and tongue to clean the frosting from the corner of her mouth. Her breath hitched at the contact, but she didn't move away. Instead, her eyes fluttered shut as she silently begged for more. Who was he to deny her?

Skimming his hand up her arm until he reached her shoulder, he plunged it into her silky hair, reveling in the feel of it as he placed soft kisses on her lips. The instant she took a deep breath and relaxed into the moment, he took possession of her mouth, using his tongue to request entry. Her lips parted, and her tongue danced with his. She tasted like coffee, vanilla, hazelnut, and strawberries—an intoxicating mix combined with her own individual, feminine flavor.

His cock grew hard as his hands went to her hips to tug her toward him. Then he eased her shoulders down until she was flat on the couch with him leaning most of his weight on his forearms and knees. He didn't want to freak her out, giving her a little space if she wanted him to stop, but her arms wrapped around his neck and pulled him down on top of her. He elicited little mewls and gasps from her as he switched from kissing her mouth to the sensitive skin below her ear and back again. Her one hand delved into his hair as the other explored his shoulders and upper back. When she clutched his T-shirt and pulled it out of his khakis, he pushed up from the couch, reached back, and yanked the shirt over his head. Seconds later, he was back to where he'd just been—lying on top of her, kissing the dickens out of her.

Her hands scorched his skin as she caressed the

muscles of his back. Her legs shifted until they straddled his hips, and he ground his erection into her mound, causing them both to moan. Trying to control himself, he leaned on his hands and stared down at her. Her lips were red, swollen, and moist. Her eyes filled with the same desire he knew was showing in his own. "Tell me, sweetness. Tell me now if you want me to stop. Otherwise, I'm going to take you into my bedroom and ravish you until neither one of us can walk. I need to know we're on the same page here because I want you so badly, but you come first. If you're not ready yet, I'll put my shirt back on and follow you home. No worries. No thinking this is all or nothing tonight. If you need to wait, I can be patient."

Tenderness flashed in her eyes, mixing with the passion. She reached up and cupped her hand over his cheek. He turned his head and kissed her palm. "I want you, sweetness. More than any other woman I've ever met. I want to see where this goes between us. Let me show you how good it can be between us."

"Yes."

That one word had barely been audible and would not do. "Uh-uh, Fancy-girl. I need more than a whispered word. Tell me what you want."

She licked her lips, then bit the bottom one. He leaned down and brushed his lips against hers. "Tell me."

"Yes. I want you, Brody. I-I want to see where this

goes. I want to spend the night in your bed, pleasing each other."

He noticed she avoided using the words "making love" but that was okay. She'd been married and in love with Patrick long before meeting Brody, so those words would be hard to say to another man. But as he'd told her, he was a patient man. If passionate sex was all it was tonight, then that was what he would give her. However, someday soon, he would admit to her what he finally realized was happening. He was falling in love with her—his soul mate.

Taking a deep breath, Fancy reached for Brody's extended hand. As soon as she'd told him she wanted to spend the night in his bed, he'd stood from the couch. They were moving this party-for-two into his bedroom, and the thought scared and excited her simultaneously. The nervousness wasn't about him— not at all. Since their first kiss at the ballgame, she knew he would be a gentle and patient lover. No, those butterflies in her stomach had retaken flight because Patrick had been her first and only lover. He'd been so understanding, and they had both taken pleasure in the things he'd taught her and others they'd learned together. But this was nine years later, with a slightly older man who probably had experienced more than his fair share of women over the years. What if she paled in comparison to those women? What if he found her lacking in how to please him? Well, she wouldn't know if she didn't give it a try.

Holding her hand, he led her down the hall to the master bedroom, flipping the light switch in the family room off as they passed it. The music from the TV channel still filled the air but was muted further as they stepped into his bedroom. A shiver coursed through her as she stared at the king-sized bed.

"Hey." His voice caught her attention, and she tilted her head to look him in the eye. All she saw there were desire and understanding. He cupped her cheek. "Sweetness, is this the first time since your husband?"

Her gaze dropped to his chest as she nodded. Her heart sank when he let out a heavy sigh, but then he surprised her by stepping over to the bed and lying on his back. He tucked his hands behind his head and gazed at her from under desire-heavy eyelids. "Come here. I won't bite—at least, not until you ask me to. I'll keep my hands to myself for now and let you explore a little. I promise. When you're ready to move on, then just kiss me on the mouth."

Jeez, he just melted her panties. And holy hell, the man looked like a feast laid out before her. The butterflies in her stomach were still in flight, but the throbbing of her pussy was overriding them. She swallowed hard as she toed off her Keds. Brody said nothing as she pulled the V-neck shirt she'd changed into at the shop over her head. Instead, his eyes stayed on hers. The black of his pupils almost entirely covered the soft brown of his irises. Suddenly unsure again, she decided to take one step at a time. She left her white cotton bra and capri pants on and circled the bed to the far side. His gaze followed her. Climbing up on the mattress, she crawled over to his side, knelt beside him, and lifted a trembling hand toward his naked torso. Her mouth watered. The man had to work out daily to keep a sculpted body like this and still eat all the treats she gave him. She paused inches from his chest.

"Touch me, sweetness." His voice was a little more than a hoarse whisper. "Explore all you want. If this is as far as we go tonight, that's fine. But you will sleep with me tonight, even if it's fully dressed. Understood?"

She nodded, then placed her hand on his ribs just below his left nipple. His breath hitched at the contact, but he didn't move or say anything. His skin warmed her palm, and she relaxed her fingers, enjoying the feel of power beneath them. Slowly, she began to explore every mesa and valley of his upper torso. She noticed him swallow hard and felt his muscles twitch beneath her touch every once in a while. His eyes alternated between watching her face and following the path of her hand. The tenting of his pants was hard to miss, but he kept his promise—his hands stayed behind his head. With every moment that passed, Fancy grew bolder. She added her other hand to the first, testing and learning every inch of him.

Oh God, his flesh was hardened steel covered in soft velvet. She ran her finger down his sternum to the line of dark blond hair leading to his groin but stopped at the edge of his pants and reversed direction. As she reached the base of his neck, his Adam's apple moved as he gulped. That was all the encouragement she needed. Bending over, she kissed the little notch just below that and was rewarded with a groan. She peppered his neck with little kisses and licks as she worked her way around to his ear. Now, she wanted to see if she could make him beg. His hands hadn't moved, but she could see he was opening and closing his fists, trying to keep from reaching for her. She knew he was waiting for her to kiss his mouth.

"You're killing me here, Fancy-girl. If you don't kiss my mouth soon, I'll have to reach down and give myself a little adjustment."

A wicked smile spread across her face. She didn't know where the courage came from but whispered in his ear, "Why don't I do that for you?"

"Oh, shit, yes! Please, hurry."

Walking her fingers slowly back down his bare torso, she reached his pants again, but this time, she flattened her hand against his abdomen and slid it under the waistband and his boxer briefs. As she wrapped her hand around his hard cock, she leaned over and kissed him on the mouth. He reacted as if he'd been struck by lightning. His hips bucked upward as his hands whipped out from under his head and plunged into her hair. He held her head in place while devouring her mouth. Holy hell, she was in heaven. Damn, did the man know how to kiss, or what?

His hands slid down her body and pulled her hips until she was lying completely on top of him. She straddled his waist and felt his erection against her core. She wanted him in the worst way—no, she *needed* him. Their tongues went from inside her mouth to his and back again. He clutched a handful of hair and tugged her away from him, then gasped as he stared at her as she tried to catch her breath. "Take your bra off, baby. Let me see what I've been dreaming of for weeks now."

Fancy sat up, which increased the connection and friction between her legs and his cock. As his hands settled on her hips, he watched as she reached back, undid the clasp, and pulled the bra down her arms. His eyes widened in appreciation at the sight of her bare breasts. "Jesus, you're more beautiful than I pictured. And trust me, I had plenty of pictures of you naked in my head since I met you. Hell, I was picturing you in my own personal porn flick the moment I first saw you. No lie. But none of that did you justice, sweetness." His gaze met hers. "Will you play with your nipples for me? Show me how you like to be touched."

Her cheeks blushed as she raised her hands to her breasts. She was suddenly shy again as her fingers circled the stiff peaks and then tugged on them. "Like this?"

"Whichever way you like to do it is fine with me."

As she played with them, his hands slid up and down her sides, getting closer to her breasts and mound with each pass. Sitting up, he cupped her left breast and nudged her hand away with his nose. His mouth closed around her nipple, and the heat blossomed and spread to her core. She closed her eyes, and her head fell back on her shoulders as he worshiped her flesh with his mouth and tongue. She couldn't control her hips as they began to rock against his cock on their own accord. "More. Please."

Flipping her onto her back, Brody settled between her legs and switched to her other breast, giving it the same attention. He shifted further down on the bed, trailing wet kisses over her abdomen. His tongue circled her belly button, and she giggled because it tickled. He paused at the top of her capris and looked up at her. "Yes?"

She knew he was asking for permission, and her heart melted a little more—if he kept this up, he would be taking up a permanent residency there. Nodding, her hands went to the snap and zipper. "Yes."

Tugging on the pants, Brody kissed each inch of exposed flesh as it appeared. Her hips. Her thighs. Her knees. And all the way down to her toes. Reaching back up, he hooked his fingers under the waistband of her panties and pulled them down as well. His eyes feasted on her naked body, and she fought the urge to use her hands to cover herself—she had always been a little self-conscious of the extra thirty pounds she'd gained over the years. But the heat in Brody's gaze warmed her to the point that her blood was boiling and pulsating through her veins—it was evident her generous curves didn't bother him. In fact, she could swear they turned him on even more as his gaze roamed every one.

Standing, he removed his pants. Her eyes widened at the sight of him. Oh God, he was huge! Well, not exactly huge... but, yeah, huge pretty much said it.

Rounding to the foot of the bed, Brody crawled up and settled between her legs. "Hands behind your head, sweetness. Time for my treat."

When she did as she was told, he spread her thighs wider. His thumbs brushed the fine hair between her legs, and she wished she hadn't stopped waxing. Patrick had loved her bare, but after the accident, there had been no reason for her to keep it up—at least she still kept herself trimmed down there.

Brody leaned forward and licked her pussy in one long and hard stroke. The contact and sensations that shot through her sent her hips flying off the bed. "Oh God!"

"Easy, honey. I'm just getting started. Put your hands behind your head again."

She hadn't realized they were no longer there. Instead, they were in his hair. "Sorry."

"Nothing to be sorry about. I just want all your concentration on what my tongue is doing and nothing else."

Yeah, no worries there. She doubted she'd be able to think about anything else other than him and what he was doing to her.

His head ducked back down, and this time, when he licked her, even though her hips bucked again, she kept her hands behind her head. Alternating between her slit and the tiny bud of nerves above it, Brody licked, nibbled, and sucked, sending her higher and higher. It had been so long since she'd had an orgasm that the powerful wave caught her off guard. She cried out as intense pleasure coursed through her body. Behind her closed eyelids, bright lights flashed in a multitude of colors. "Oh my God! *Ahhhh.*"

Her body shook with the impact as he plunged two fingers into her pussy, drawing out her response before letting her float back to Earth. With a few more swipes of his tongue, Brody ended his assault and lifted his head. He grinned from ear to ear at her in satisfaction, the cocky bastard. Not that she was complaining—no way would she complain after that orgasm.

He wiped his wet mouth and chin with his hand. "When was the last time you had an orgasm, babe?"

"Since..." she panted, "... since the last time... I had a man in my bed."

His eyes widened in surprise. "Seriously? You never masturbate?"

Blushing, she shook her head. It had been so long since she had been intimate with a man, and his bluntness was a little shocking. "No... I mean, I used to, but after Patrick... I thought that part of my life was over, and it didn't feel right without him with me."

The understanding in his eyes was almost her undoing. Reaching for him, she urged him to cover her body with his. She didn't want to think or talk anymore, just feel again. Needing to leave the past where it belonged, she pulled his face to hers and initiated another toe-curling kiss. Tasting herself on his lips and tongue sent her desire soaring again. This man did things to her she'd never expected to feel again, and for the first time in years, she felt like she was home. "More... please..."

Kissing along her jaw, Brody opened the nightstand's top drawer and searched for a moment before retrieving a small square package. He quickly donned the condom. "I'll go slowly, sweetness. Tell me if anything hurts or is uncomfortable."

His hand slid down her torso to her core, and his

fingers tested her wetness. He needn't have worried because she was more than ready for him. Supporting himself on his forearms, he lowered his hips to hers. With slow, short thrusts, he eased into her heat, groaning as she enveloped him. God, it was heaven. Her body yielded to him, but suddenly it wasn't enough. Her nails dug into his back. "More!"

With one final thrust, he was inside her as far as nature would allow. "Are you okay?"

"Yes! But I'd be more than okay if you sped things up a little."

He chuckled, then nipped her bottom lip. "Demanding little thing, aren't you? I don't like taking orders in bed, sweetness. I prefer to issue them, but I'll let you get away with it this time because I'm hanging on by a thread here."

Easing out, he thrust forward again, his eyes remained focused on her face. Her moans urged him on. Faster. Harder. Her body yielded to him over and over as her breathing and heart rate increased. Sensations she'd forgotten existed assailed her. His pelvis hit her clit on each inward stroke. As he slammed into her, she began climbing again, and even though she was prepared for it, her orgasm was even stronger this time, which she hadn't thought possible. "Brody! *Ohhhhhh... yyyyessss!*"

"Fuck, baby! Shit!" With one final plunge, he stiffened as he came, and his forehead dropped to the pillow next to her head as his body shuddered. His release triggered another one in her, and her head spun as her entire body quivered. His weight fell onto her, but she didn't care as they both gasped for air. A contentment she never thought she would experience again came over her. He nuzzled her neck. "That was incredible, sweetness. And I can't wait to do it again."

Neither could she.

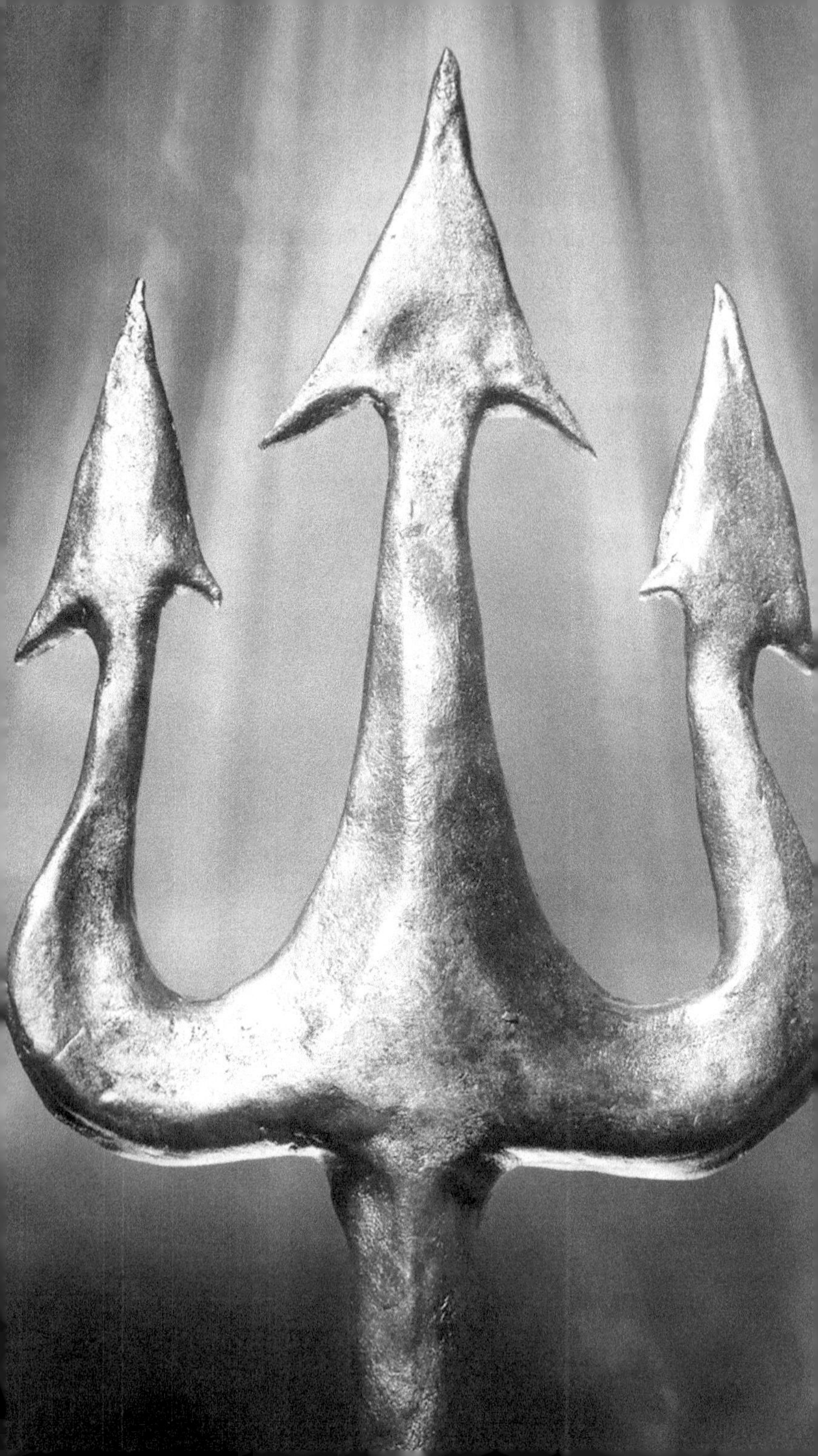

CHAPTER TEN

Rolling over, Brody reached for Fancy but only found an empty bed. His eyes blinked open, and he checked the digital clock on the nightstand. Just after 3:00 a.m. *What the fuck? Where the hell is she?*

Noise from the bathroom caught his attention. The shower was running. Frowning, he threw the covers off his nude body and climbed out of bed. Pushing the door open, he was surprised at the darkness. His heart clenched at what he saw when he switched the light on. Naked, Fancy was sitting on the floor of his walk-in shower. Her knees were drawn up to her chest, and her arms were wrapped around them. Her shoulders were shaking. *Fuck.* She was crying as the water pelted her from above. Her teeth were chattering as she stared at the blank tiled wall.

Stepping over, he realized the water was cold— almost freezing. How long had she been in there? He flipped two switches on the wall next to the shower. When he'd had Parker renovate the master bath, he'd gone all out. There was a reserve heater, so there would never be a lack of hot water, and when you stepped out of the shower, the overhead red heat lamps kept you warm as you dried off. Sticking his hand under the cold water, he waited until it ran hot again, then sat on the tile floor next to Fancy. Without saying a word, he pulled her shivering body onto his lap, then stroked her hair and skin as the water raining down on them began to warm her again.

She tucked her face into his neck. "I-I'm s-sorry."

"Shhh. It's okay, sweetness. I've got you. Let it out."

Her sobs almost broke his heart. He had no idea what had brought it all on, but there was no way he was running away when she needed him the most. Kissing her forehead, he murmured words of comfort and reassurance as her shivering subsided. Being warmed up again also seemed to ease her crying. He smiled when he felt her shift and kiss his neck. "If you're warm enough, let's get you dried off and back under the covers. We can talk there, okay?"

She nodded, and he reached up and shut the water off. Helping her stand, he followed, then brought her out under the heat lamp. Grabbing one of the fluffy towels from the rack, he rubbed it over her skin from head to toe, drying her off. He towel-dried her hair as best he could, then wrapped her in the terry cloth robe he kept behind the door. Once she was cared for, he ran another towel over his body. Leading her back to bed, he let her climb in, then pulled the covers back over her. "I'll be right back."

Comfortable in his own skin, he didn't bother to put anything on his naked body as he shuffled out to the kitchen. He retrieved two glasses of water and brought them back to the room after shutting the music off in the living room. It had been faint enough not to disturb them as they'd slept, and he'd forgotten it was on.

Handing her one of the glasses, he brought the other to his lips and drank half while making sure she rehydrated herself. He climbed back under the covers and noticed she'd shed his robe, laying it at the foot of the bed. Turning on his side, he placed his hand on hers over her abdomen. "Talk to me."

"I'm sorry—"

"Don't apologize, Fancy. Talk to me."

She took a shuddering breath and stared at the ceiling as she spoke. "I don't know what brought it on, but I woke up crying and didn't want to wake you. I-I didn't tell you everything earlier when I told you about the accident." He rubbed his thumb over her wrist, silently encouraging her to continue. "I-I was pregnant... we found out a few weeks before the accident and w-were over the moon about it. We hadn't actually been trying, but we weren't taking any precautions either."

His heart and gut twisted. He was certain he knew where this was going, but it was obvious she needed to get this all off her chest. "What happened?"

"When I woke up from the coma, they told me I'd miscarried. I learned my husband and my baby were both dead six weeks after it happened. Patrick's family had taken care of the funeral and everything—which I understood—but it was like going to sleep and waking up to find everything you knew and loved was gone. I-I flipped out—which is an understatement. I became manic-depressive—crying one minute and screaming with rage in the next. It got to the point that when I was physically well enough to be released from the main hospital, I was sent to the psychiatric ward for two months. Corey and my aunt became my rocks." She swallowed hard, and he patiently waited for her to continue. "If it weren't for them visiting me every day, I don't think I would have ever recovered—mentally or emotionally. Aunt Denise wanted to take me back to Ohio, but I couldn't. This was where Patrick and I were going to follow our dreams, and I knew he'd want me to stay here. It took me a year or so to finally shake off my grief enough to rejoin the living. Patrick had taken out a large insurance policy at work that I hadn't known about. That's what I used to start the business. It's what he would've wanted me to do."

Jesus, this poor woman had been through hell and back several times. That she'd pulled through and turned her life around again proved how courageous and strong she was. He brought her hand to his mouth and kissed the back of it. "Where were your brother and parents through all this?"

She shrugged and swiped at the tears falling down her cheeks again. "My father couldn't be bothered with coming to see me. My brother had been here for the first week but had to go back home to work. He flew back in for a few days after I woke up. My mother... well, let's just say she didn't know how to deal with a grieving widow and leave it at that."

Taking a few strands of her drying hair, he rubbed them between his fingers and thumb. "I don't know how you did it, sweetness, but I'm in awe that you recovered from not only the accident but the loss of Patrick and the baby. And I'm sorry you had to go through it all. I've never wanted to turn back time as much as I do right now. If I had to give up ever knowing you, for you to have not gone through that, I would, and that's saying a lot because you've become very special to me. I can't even remember my life before you came into it, and I don't want to."

That was as close to a declaration of love as he was willing to make right then. She was far from ready to hear that from him. Finally, turning to face him, she stroked his cheek. "It doesn't bother you that I was institutionalized?"

He held her palm to his cheek as he stared into her eyes, wanting her to know his words were true. "Not at all. Everyone deals with grief in their own way. If that's what it took for you to recover, then, no, it doesn't bother me."

Smiling for the first time since he'd found her, she leaned over and placed a soft, quick kiss on his lips. "Thank you."

A yawn escaped her, and he glanced at the clock. She'd told him earlier that she needed to leave by five fifteen at the very latest to run home for a change of clothes and be at the shop by six. "We have about an hour before we have to get up. Roll over, close your eyes, and try to sleep for a little bit." He nudged her to her side, facing away from him, then pulled her tightly against his chest. She was asleep in minutes while he watched over her.

After kissing Fancy goodbye and telling her he'd call her later, Brody walked out of the bakery with his coffee in one hand and a box of pastries in the other. He let her sleep for a few more minutes while he'd gotten dressed for the day and then followed her to her condo, waiting while she ran inside and did the same. She seemed different after their middle-of-the-night talk—lighter, happier. And he hoped that meant they had a future together. He wondered what she would say if he asked her to go back to Texas with him in six weeks—his family had a huge hoedown every year. Brothers, sisters, aunts, uncles, cousins—everyone came. The only ones he'd ever missed had been when his SEAL tours or missions had prevented it. Ian and Dev had it penciled in every year not to send him on any assignments unless it was an emergency during the fourth weekend in October.

Walking across the parking lot, he scanned the area, searching for Russell and anyone who shouldn't be there, but no one was around. As he reached his truck, his cell phone chimed with an urgent text from the Trident line—at just after six in the morning, it couldn't be good.

Opening the driver's door, he placed the box on the passenger seat and the coffee in the center console, then checked the message. It was from Ian.

BOSS-MAN

Body found. Possibly Heather. 575 Winfield Street. Meet me there.

"Fuck!"

Rush hour had not started yet, and it took him about ten minutes to get to the crime scene. It was hard to miss, with the number of strobe lights flashing from multiple police cars, an ambulance, a coroner's vehicle, and CSI units. The closest he could park was half a block away, and after locking his truck, he hoofed it the rest of the way. Bystanders and the media were being kept a fair distance from the scene, and Brody flashed his Trident ID to a uniformed officer, earning him passage to the inner circle. They had worked with Tampa PD on numerous cases in the past and had a good reputation among the officers and detectives.

Ian, Devon, and Marco were already present, and he was confident Boomer was on his way. The three men stood along the "Police—Do Not Cross" tape, which ran from the front of a laundromat across the parking lot to a patrol car. Uniformed and plainclothes officers milled about on the far side. They couldn't see anything from there—the body had to be behind the building.

Brody stopped next to Ian. "What's going on?"

Boss-man ran a frustrated hand down his face. "Just got here ourselves. Webb called and said to get over here. He's still behind the building, so we're waiting to find out what's up. What I do know is it's a female homicide victim who fits Heather's description, and a few cops and two EMTs have come back around and tossed their cookies."

Shit, that's not good. When people who were experienced in seeing the worst that could possibly be done to the human race were puking, the scene had to be horrendous and beyond anything they had seen before.

Long moments passed before an ashen-faced Webb rounded the rear corner of the building just as Boomer arrived. The detective spotted them and strode over, stopping for a brief exchange with another detective on the way. When he reached them, he shook Ian's hand and nodded at the rest of them. "Thanks for coming. I'm going to need your help on this... fuck, I can barely comprehend what *this* is... what the fuck I saw..."

They waited in silence while the rattled man gathered his composure. "It's definitely a dump scene only. Wherever he did... *that*... had to be somewhere they couldn't be heard because I guarantee she screamed the whole time. I can't imagine what she went through."

Before he could explain further, two men from the coroner's office came from behind the building, rolling a gurney between them with a body bag on it. Both men were as pale as everyone else from back there. Webb flagged them to stop, then turned to Ian and the others. "You don't all have to look, but I would appreciate an ID and any insight you might have. This goes beyond anything I've witnessed or even heard of before."

They all stepped forward, not imagining it could be worse than the atrocities they'd seen committed by radical al Qaeda and ISIS terrorists. They were about to be proven wrong.

Webb indicated to one of the coroner's assistants to show them the body. Before he did, the man glanced around, then turned the gurney slightly so no unauthorized eyes could catch a glimpse. Brody took a deep breath as the bag was unzipped and a white protective sheet was lifted.

"Fuck!"

The expletive was spat out by more than one of them. The coffee in Brody's stomach churned and threatened to come back up. He swallowed hard, forcing it down as he stared at the horrifying remains of Heather Davis. While her face was mostly recognizable, the rest of her was not—at least what they could see. The sheet still covered her lower body. There wasn't an inch of skin, from her neck down, left untouched by what had to have been a bullwhip or similar implement. The oozing, pink and red, shredded flesh of her torso and arms conjured up images of beef being freshly ground by a butcher. And that's what the sick bastard who had done this to her was—a psychotic butcher.

Having seen more than enough, Ian nodded at the ME's assistants, and they quickly covered the body and zipped up the bag again. As the gurney was rolled toward the transport vehicle, Ian coughed, then turned to Webb. Everyone else was too stunned to talk. "The entire body like that?"

The detective nodded grimly. "From her neck to her toes, front and back. As you saw, there are only a few strikes to the face, but he left that mostly intact for whatever sick reason. Maybe so we could identify her... I've got no fucking clue. Any ideas?"

"Looks like the bastard used a bullwhip, but you'll

need the coroner to confirm that. I've been in the life-style for years and never heard of anything like this. Whip Masters are usually highly trained and never break the skin. There's no way to tell if the killer is inexperienced or knew exactly what he was doing. Is he... or she, I guess... in the lifestyle? Again, hard to tell. And if your next question is do I think her Dom did this, no, I don't... ninety-five percent certain. I'm sorry. I know this doesn't help, but that's all I've got right now."

Webb blew out a harsh breath. "No, it doesn't help, but hopefully, at some point it will. We're not sure when she was dumped yet, but the estimated time of death is ten hours ago. The ME will narrow that down further during the autopsy. This building has no cameras, but we'll check with the surrounding busi-nesses to see if anyone has one and caught something."

Crossing his arms over his chest, his fists clenched in anger, Ian asked, "Has Scott Harrison been notified?"

"Not yet. That's my next stop." The detective glanced at his watch, which caused Brody and a few others to look at their own—it was just after 7:00 a.m. "The good doctor is about to get a very depressing wake-up call."

"If you want, I'll go with you. I've known Scott a few years and already reached out to him after we heard she was missing."

Again, Webb nodded. "Thanks. I appreciate it. Give me a few minutes to finish here, and we'll go."

"Take your time." As the detective walked away, leaving them on the other side of the crime scene tape, Ian turned to his team. "I... fuck!" He kicked a discarded soda can in disgust.

Yeah, that's pretty much what they all felt right then.

CHAPTER ELEVEN

Striding into the Trident offices, Brody left the box of pastries on Colleen's desk; he'd completely lost his appetite. Entering his war-room, he stopped short when he saw a pair of legs sticking out from under the newly installed secondary work area. "Hey!"

The person startled, and a smack resounded in the room. "Fuck!"

Sliding out from under the desk, holding his hand to the swelling knot on his forehead, the new computer whiz, Nathan Cook, glared at him. Brody gave it right back. He'd forgotten the kid was starting today. "What the fuck are you doing under there?"

"Making a few adjustments—"

"I already hooked up everything you fucking need."

The twenty-seven-year-old, über-skinny geek stood, then flopped into his desk chair. A former

National Security Agency computer tech, Nathan had high government clearance—Ian and Dev wouldn't have hired him otherwise. The NSA had signed off on Nathan coming to work for Trident, and due to the classified missions the team did for multiple U.S. government agencies, they'd allowed Nathan to keep his security clearance.

The guy was about five eleven, with unruly, curly brown hair and matching brown eyes, and wore a vintage Pac-Man T-shirt, jeans, and high-top Converse sneakers. He pushed his wire-rimmed eyeglasses back up the bridge of his nose—yup, they didn't make 'em any geekier than that. The only things missing were a button-down shirt and a damn pocket protector. "Maybe everything you need, but I brought a few toys of my own."

Brody was not happy, which was putting it mildly. He wasn't used to anyone messing around in his warroom and wanted to know what other "toys" were being connected to his setup. "Like what?"

Nathan smirked. "Isn't the saying around here, if I tell you, I'd have to shoot you?"

Taking a threatening step closer, he snarled. "No, it's the other way around—tell *me* or I fucking shoot *you*."

"Chill, Evans. It's just an interface for the mainframe at NSA. Remember? That was in the contract the Sawyer brothers signed with the agency when everyone agreed I could come work here." When Brody just glared at him, the guy held up his hands in surrender and added, "Jeez, who pissed in your Wheaties this morning?"

Letting out a deep sigh, he finally relented. "Not you." He ran a hand through his hair. "Sorry. It's just been a really shitty morning so far. Do what you have to do. Just make a list so there are no surprises for me later."

Taking the seat in front of his own computer setup, he pulled out the keyboard shelf and booted up the hard drive. When it was up and running, he logged into the FBI's secure NCIC—National Crime Information Center. He had access to it through special permission from the FBI. Almost every police department in the United States used it and entered major crimes into it—the exceptions tending to be small departments with few employees and minimal budgets. As each year passed, though, fewer were on that shortlist. The system was also used for statistics, but he wanted to run a search for homicides similar to what they'd witnessed this morning. He was sure Webb and the rest of Tampa PD would be doing the same, but he still entered keywords to be searched for in the vast database. *Homicide. Female. Submissive. BDSM. Bullwhip. Whip. Torture.* If any results came close, he could add more parameters and narrow it down further.

As he hit send, Boomer strolled in and spotted the newcomer. "Hey! Nathan, right? Nice to finally meet you. I'm Ben Michaelson, but everyone calls me Boomer. Welcome aboard."

"Thanks. Nice to meet you too."

The two men shook hands, then Brody's teammate sat on a rolling stool beside him. He nodded at the computer monitor with a scrolling "Searching" message. "You running a check on the homicide?"

"Yeah," he answered. If their new coworker was interested in the conversation, he didn't show it as he continued to move things around to his liking on his side of the room. Most geeks were very particular about their setups, so Brody had expected it. "I've never heard of anything like it, have you?"

Boomer shook his head. "Nope, and I hope I never do again."

When Nathan took a sip from his coffee cup, he must have found it empty. He grumbled to himself as he walked out, heading for the break room and the Keurig machine that was always well-stocked. Day one, and the guy already knew where to get his caffeine fix. He'd be gone for a few minutes, at least, so Brody took advantage of their privacy. "Boom... got a question for you. How did you tell Kat you're a Dom? I know Ian, Dev, and Marco never had a chance—it came out before they could say anything—but you told Kat before she found out. How?"

This was the first time he was nervous about telling a woman he was a Dom since the initial few months of being in the lifestyle over a decade ago. No matter how he worded it, it didn't sound right. The last thing he wanted to do was scare Fancy or run her off in disgust if she didn't understand it.

Boomer grinned at him. "So, what Ian said about Tahira calling Fancy your soulmate is true, huh?" He didn't wait for an answer, and Brody didn't offer one because it wasn't necessary. "Awesome. Um, let's see. I just kind of blurted out that I was a Dominant and asked her if she knew what that meant. But I knew she had to have some idea because she was reading one of Kristen's books before that. She just had no idea the lifestyle actually existed outside of fiction, and I thank God every day that she trusted me enough to explore it. Is Fancy a natural submissive?"

"Yeah. But she's so much more than that. I don't want to get into it here, but she's one of the strongest women I've ever met. Hell, she ranks right up there with Kat, Kristen, Angie, Harper, and even Shelby. She's been through so much, and I'm not sure how she'll take it when I tell her."

Colleen appeared in the doorway and rapped her knuckles on the jamb. "Boomer, your nine o'clock appointment is here."

"Thanks." Boomer tilted his head toward the reception area when she left them alone again. "Talk about kick-ass women. Colleen's come a long way, too. Must be something in the water around here." Standing, Boomer slapped him on the shoulder. "Anyway, you'll never know until you talk to her, bro.

If she's 'the one,' then I'm sure things will work out just fine. Catch you later."

"Yup. Thanks."

As Boomer walked out, Nathan came back in with a freshly brewed cup of coffee, and the aroma curled Brody's stomach once again, bringing back the gruesome images of Heather's brutalized corpse. The NCIC search would take a bit, so he grabbed his cell phone and left the building, needing some fresh air. Beau came running over to him with his favorite hard rubber ball for a game of fetch. Brody took the offering and flung it far across the lot, then strolled over to *Ian's Oasis*. He sat by the unlit fire pit and hit a speed dial number on his phone as the dog returned and laid down at his feet, gnawing on his toy.

The call connected. "Hello?"

"Hi, Mom."

"Brody! Oh, it's so good to hear your voice, honey. I was just thinking about you."

Elise Evans's Texas twang soothed him, and suddenly, he was a teenager again, sitting on the back porch with her, sharing a glass of sweet tea. "Yeah, why's that?"

"Are you coming for the hoedown?"

He smiled. "That's the plan. Ian's got it penciled in, as usual."

"Well, just let everyone know the invitation is always open to all of them."

A few times in the past, one or more of his teammates had made the annual trip with him, but each year, it tended to be a toss-up for who was on an assignment or had something else on the calendar. "They know that, but things have been busy lately. Listen, I was wondering if you'd mind if I brought someone else."

His mom paused. "It wouldn't happen to be a woman, would it?"

Rolling his eyes, his grin got wider. He and his younger brother were the only two not married or engaged, and his mother was dying to make sure all her little ducks were in a row and happily wed. "Yes. Her name is Francine, but everyone calls her Fancy. I haven't asked her yet—not sure if she can take the time away from her business—but wanted to check in with you first."

"Brody, you know this house is open to anyone you want to bring. It always has been and always will be. I hope Fancy can come so I can meet the woman who suddenly put my son in knots."

His brow furrowed. "What are you talking about?"

"Please. The last time you asked permission to bring a date to a hoedown was Jo Ellen Tremont, back in high school."

Had it seriously been that long? "Jeez, Mom. Either your memory is freakish, or you're keeping a record of everyone's dates somewhere."

She chuckled. "It's a little bit of both. Now, tell me all about Fancy. How did you meet her?"

With Boomer and Tiny on his heels, carrying a bouquet of blue and white flowers and helium balloons, Brody entered the hospital room with a bakery box from Fancy's. He grinned at the new parents cooing over their firstborn son. Little JD Sawyer had decided to wake up his mother-to-be at 1:00 a.m. with active labor pains and burst into the world a little more than five hours later. Apparently, Kristen had been in labor since earlier in the day, but the pains had felt like the ones she'd had during the false alarms, and she figured that it was happening again. The team had all gotten the birth announcements via text from Devon after JD had been taken to the nursery so Kristen could rest.

Ian, Angie, and Jenn had come to the hospital after getting the text, and not wanting to overwhelm Kristen, Brody and Boomer had waited until after lunch. Kat was working and would swing by in the early evening with Marco and Harper. And without a doubt, there would be visits from Shelby, Parker, Kayla, Roxy, Mitch, Colleen, Reggie, and Kristen's cousin, Will, at some point during the day.

It had been a great way to start the day after yesterday's horrific wake-up call. There were still no suspects in Heather's death. Brody's search in the

NCIC database had been a bust. The only case that had popped up had been solved, and the suspect had been killed during the rescue of his last victim. In addition to that, the suspect's preferred victims had been of Asian descent, and none of them had been in the BDSM lifestyle. There had been a few other differences, and no other case had come close. Whipping a person to death, while popular back in early Rome and a few other ancient and more modern cultures, apparently was very rare in this day and age across North America. He'd extended the search into Canada and Mexico with no further hits. That morning, he accessed the Interpol crime database and a few others worldwide that he'd hacked into. He wanted to make sure the killer hadn't worked his way into the United States from somewhere else.

Shaking his head, Brody pushed aside the thoughts of the missing submissives and the murdered Heather. Today, they were celebrating a new life. While Tiny let go of the balloons so they settled on the ceiling, Brody set the box on the window shelf, which already had several bouquets perched on it. "Fancy sent over a bunch of blue and white cupcakes."

Kristen was sitting in bed, glowing with motherhood and cradling JD in her arms. With almost a full head of soft, black hair, the little guy weighed in at eight pounds two ounces. From the chair he'd pulled next to the bed, Devon looked more exhausted than his wife did. After shaking hands with the proud father, Brody leaned over and gave Kristen a peck on the cheek. "You did good, Ninja-mama."

She giggled at the new variation of the nickname Devon had given her on their first date. He'd dubbed her Ninja-girl when she'd kicked Heather and another sub's ass in the club's locker room after finding them bullying Colleen. "Thanks. And thank Fancy for sending the cupcakes."

"I will. Can I hold him?"

Out of all of Kristen's Sexy Six-Pack, as she called the original Trident team, Brody had the most experience with infants and toddlers, being an uncle to eleven of them in Texas and Marco's daughter, Mara. Kristen lifted JD and gently placed him in Brody's arms. The little chubster was like a big football with limbs. Brody grinned when the baby opened his blue eyes, which matched his father's, and stared at him. "Hey, JD. I'm your Uncle Brody. I'll teach you everything you need to know about computers and women. This big guy here is your Uncle Tiny." The six-foot-eight, two-hundred-seventy-five-pound man was the only person who had ever made Brody feel small since he'd hit his adult height of six foot two. "He's going to teach you how to play football. And over there is your Uncle Boomer, whose job is to show you how to blow things up without getting hurt."

The men all laughed, but Kristen rolled her eyes. "Oh jeez, Brody. He's not even a day old. Please don't make me think of him blowing things up someday."

"Don't worry, Ninja-mama. I have it on good authority that JD will grow up to be a great man someday. In the meantime, just make sure he eats all his vegetables."

"Yes, sir." There was no mistaking her sarcasm.

"Brat." When the baby kicked his little legs in the swaddling blanket, Brody added, "Not you, JD—you're not a brat. Your mama is. But that's your daddy's problem."

He handed off the little tyke to Tiny. It was funny seeing the huge guy cooing over such a small baby. "Hey there, JD. How's my thousand-dollar jackpot doing?"

Kristen grinned. "So you won the baby pool. I'd forgotten all about it."

"Yup. Drinks are on me tonight. Are Chuck and Marie on their way down from Charlotte?"

Devon shook his head. "No. As much as they can't wait to see JD, Dad and Mom decided to wait two weeks to give us time to settle into a routine. Kristen's mom and stepdad will be flying down on Saturday morning for a few days, and her dad and stepmom told us to let them know what days are good for them to come."

They chatted for a few more minutes, but when Kristen yawned, the men said their goodbyes. The new mother needed all the sleep she could get before being sent home. Life as Devon and Kristen had known it was over, and while waiting for the hospital elevator,

Brody's gut clenched a little as he thought about Fancy. He hadn't asked her if she could still have children after the miscarriage, and he wouldn't. She would tell him when the time was right for her. If their future children needed to be adopted or born through a surrogate, then that was fine with him. But he knew in his heart that she was the woman for him. Now, he just had to convince her of that fact.

The next evening, pulling open the door to the steakhouse, Brody let Fancy precede him. Marco and Harper had already arrived and waved to him from the bar. A glance around told him they had beaten the third couple there. Earlier in the day, his teammate had suggested a double date since Harper's mother had baby Mara for the night. When Brody mentioned it to Fancy, she'd told him Corey and his new girlfriend had also invited them to dinner. Everyone had agreed to all three couples getting together.

When he'd picked Fancy up at her condo, Brody had almost texted everyone to start dinner without them. She had donned a cute red sundress, heeled sandals, and a short-sleeved, white sweater that was light enough for the warm weather but would also keep her from being chilled in the restaurant's air-conditioned dining room. The cut of the dress had accentuated her generous curves, and the urge to drape her over the back of her couch, lift her skirt, and fuck her from behind had been powerful. He'd been sporting a semi-hard-on ever since, and her subtle perfume hadn't helped one bit. He had to remember to ask her the name later so he could purchase a barrel of the stuff—no matter how much it cost.

With a hand on Fancy's lower back, he led her to the bar and introduced her to his friends. Marco shook her hand and smiled. "So you're the baker supplying us with all the goodies. It's nice to meet you finally."

"Same here. I hope Brody's been sharing everything."

Marco good-naturedly slung an arm around his buddy's neck. "If he didn't, I think everyone would mug him."

Harper chimed in, "And thank you for the cookies for Mara. She loved them, although most ended up as crumbs on the floor. That's what happens when you have a nearly one-year-old. Speaking of which, Angie is bringing me to your shop on Saturday, so I can order a cake for the baby's birthday. She said you have the most adorable cake ideas for kids."

"Wonderful. I look forward to showing you some options, and I'm glad she liked the cookies."

Only because Brody was aware of her loss did he see the quick flash of sadness in her eyes at the discussion of babies. However, she hid it well, and the others didn't seem to notice—not even her brother-in-law. One of Brody's sisters had miscarried her first child two weeks after announcing the pregnancy to everyone. That had been over eight years and three healthy children ago, and he knew Doreen still felt the loss as strongly as she had back then.

The bartender stopped in front of them, and after checking with Fancy, Brody ordered a Merlot for her and a beer for himself. The conversation flowed, and it wasn't long before the front door opened, and a petite brunette walked in with Corey behind her. Everyone was surprised when Harper and Corey's date, Nora Parsons, let out squeals of recognition and hugged each other. When they separated, introductions were made all around.

Corey glanced back and forth between Harper and Nora. "How do you two know each other? From school?" Fancy had mentioned to Brody that Nora was an elementary school teacher.

Harper started, "My—"

At the same time, Nora also tried to explain. "Her—"

They both laughed, and Harper gestured for the other woman to continue. "My cousin, Monica, is Harper's paralegal. We've hung out a few times. And Marco, it's nice to meet you finally. I've heard so much about you from Monica and Harper, so I feel like I already know you."

Placing her arm around her fiancé's waist, Harper

hugged him close and gave Brody a subtle glance. "Well, I haven't told you everything about him—a woman has to have some secrets about her man."

Brody grinned. *Thank you, Harper. Message received.* He doubted Corey was in the lifestyle, but Harper just confirmed for him that Nora was definitely not a member of the BDSM community and also not aware the others were. That was a big thing in their world—privacy. Many people had misconstrued conceptions about the lifestyle. When community members ran into each other in the real world, they either pretended to know each other from somewhere else or not at all.

He planned to tell Fancy later when they were alone again. She'd been so open and honest with him and deserved the same in return. Communication was what the BDSM lifestyle was based on, and even though they weren't a D/s couple at the moment, he wanted that to be their next step. They could work out any wrinkles in the relationship together if it were meant to be between them. He just hoped she would keep an open mind until he could explain and show her what the lifestyle was all about. The power exchange between a Dominant and submissive wasn't how most people not in the lifestyle perceived it to be. Some people thought Doms were a bunch of perverted deviants who got off on beating their subs before they raped them, and that was so far from the truth it was beyond ridiculous.

A BDSM relationship is a mutual agreement, either

temporary or long-term, between two adults that is considered to be safe, sane, and consensual. It is the Dom's job to push a sub's limits while giving her—or him—what she needs and desires. But it's also the Dom's job to recognize when a scene needs to stop, whether the sub wants it to or not, and to honor the use of a safeword. Just like there were Doms in the life for all the wrong reasons, there were subs who shouldn't be there either.

An experienced Dom cared for the sub's physical, emotional, and mental health during a scene. A sub's trust must be earned, or the results can devastate both.

The hostess approached the group and told them their table was ready. Everyone grabbed their drinks and followed her to a table for six in a secluded back corner. Brody and Marco quickly and silently evaluated the setup, then chose the seats that gave them the best view of the rest of the restaurant and a vantage point to protect their women, if needed. It was no longer a conscious thought for them. It was instinctual after their years in the military and the private security business. It was highly unlikely someone would start shooting up the place, but in this day and age, they couldn't be one hundred percent certain.

At the round table for six, Brody and Marco sat with Fancy and Harper between them. Nora took the other seat next to Marco, with Corey on her left, next to Brody. After a busboy placed two baskets of warm, fresh bread on the table with a dish of butter rosettes, the conversation picked up again.

Corey directed a question at Marco. "So you work with Brody. Did you serve in the Navy too? Fancy mentioned... um... what's his name?" He glanced at the man seated beside him. "Boomer, was it?" When Brody confirmed Corey was correct, he continued. "Yeah, Fancy mentioned they served together as SEALs."

Swallowing a mouthful of beer, Marco nodded. "Yup. I've known Egghead since basic, and then a few years later, we ended up on the same team together."

"Egghead?"

Marco chuckled. "His nickname. He's a geek of the highest degree, but you'd never know by looking at him."

While Brody gave his buddy a subtle middle finger along the side of the nose, Corey laughed. "Then I guess he's a bit of an anomaly—brawn *and* brains."

Even the women found that amusing, and Brody held up his hands. "Sure, laugh at my expense. Just don't come running to me when your laptops or phones go haywire and you can't figure out why."

Harper chimed in. "You'll probably be the cause of it." He grinned, knowing exactly what she would say while filling the others in on his antics. "Last time he got mad at their boss, he changed all the settings on Ian's cell phone and locked him out. The ringtone was set to the 'Chicken Dance,' and Siri was calling Ian 'Princess Twat-Waffle.'"

The group roared, including Brody. "Yeah. I made him sign a document that Ms. Legal Eagle over there," he pointed at Harper, "drew up for me, saying he wouldn't retaliate before I let him have his settings back."

The waitress interrupted to tell them the specials and ask if they needed new drinks. When she stepped away again, Corey looked back and forth between the two other men. "I don't know how you guys do it. I give a lot of credit to people who sign up for the military, but you guys went even further in special ops. Glad you got out of there alive."

"So are we," Brody replied. And it was true. They'd lost good men and women—good friends—over in the desert hellholes of Iraq and Afghanistan, as well as other places they'd been sent to they couldn't tell anyone about. "But you're in a profession that deserves a lot of credit too. You run into fires while everyone else is trying to get out. Were you a fireman up in Ohio too?"

Corey shook his head. "No. I didn't know what I wanted to do with my life back then. When Patrick and Fancy moved down here, I figured why the heck not and followed. I was sick of the cold winters. One of my new neighbors was on the job and convinced me to take the test." He grinned. "Actually, he said it was a great way to meet women."

Everyone laughed, and Nora beamed at him. "Well, that *is* how we met."

"Very true." He put his arm around her shoulder. "My neighbor was right, *but...* he should've said it's a great way to meet a great woman."

The brunette blushed. Obviously, she was as smitten with Corey as he was with her. Brody glanced at Fancy to find her smiling at her brother-in-law's happiness, and he gave her a wink. Despite a probable serial killer who'd set upon the submissives of Tampa and the issues with Fancy's shop, it was turning into a pleasant evening for all of them.

The Dom smirked as he listened to the chatter around him. The hot topic at the club tonight was the horrific death of Heather Davis. While many people had experienced problems with her in the past, apparently, what he had done to her wasn't something they would wish for anyone. Most of the details were being kept quiet by the police, but a few had gotten out. On top of that, there was plenty of speculation—some of which he found quite hysterical. There had been several times he'd wanted to open up his mouth and correct the ignoramuses—particularly when they'd referred to the killer as a psychotic deviant. He wasn't a psychotic deviant at all, just a man willing to do his part in ridding the world of worthless whores.

Years ago, when he'd discovered the lifestyle, he felt as if he'd found his home—his calling. He trained and studied under some of the best Dom's in the area, but something was always missing—the last piece of a puzzle that would make him feel complete. And now he'd found it. The satisfaction he'd had after whipping those three women had made him feel ten feet tall and bulletproof. Watching the cops tossing their cookies the other morning after discovering his masterpiece had been even more entertaining—making him yearn to find his next victim and start on a new work of art. But rushing things would be a mistake. He had to continue being methodical. Otherwise, he might get caught. Florida had the death penalty, and he'd be damned if someone ended his life before his destiny was fulfilled.

In the meantime, he could enjoy himself tonight. While he was scening with a sub, he would be reliving every scream Heather had let out for him. *Now, who was the lucky lady tonight?*

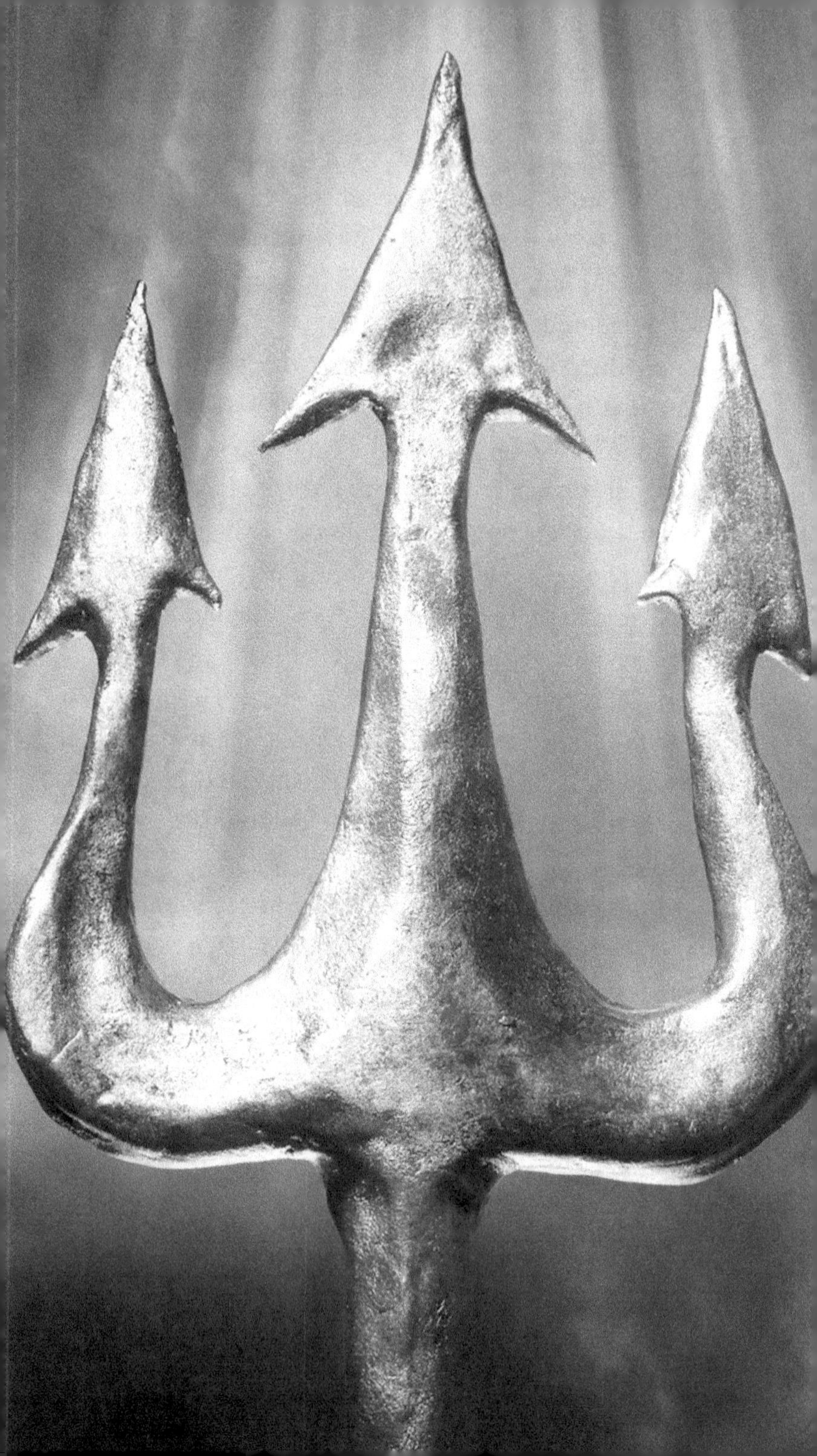

CHAPTER THIRTEEN

Fancy's head spun. While recognizing Brody's alpha tendencies, she'd been shocked by his revelation. Once recovered, though, it all fell into place for her. Was this why she felt so safe with him? Why she felt cherished by everything he did for her, big or small?

The connection they seemed to have was stronger in some ways than what she and Patrick had experienced between them. And part of her was scared by that. She and her husband had been together five years before they discovered the BDSM community, and they started from scratch together. But Brody had been in the lifestyle for years. Could she be a proper submissive for him? What if she screwed up? It had been so long since she'd played that she'd forgotten many of the protocols. And what if their limit lists didn't match up? There were many types of play she'd never experienced, much less learned about. And she was sure more play activities had become available since she'd been in the lifestyle. Kink was an ever-evolving world, pushing limits to satisfy both a Dom's and a sub's needs and desires. Before now, she hadn't realized how much she missed the lifestyle she'd been in so briefly.

"Hey, sweetness, are you okay?"

She hadn't realized her eyes had closed, and she opened them to see his face filled with concern. Smiling to reassure him everything was fine, she said, "Yes... Master Brody."

His relief was evident, and then her use of his title seemed to register as a grin spread across his face. "While I love all three of those words falling from your pretty lips together, I want you to clarify what you're saying 'yes' to."

Taking a deep breath—and a leap of faith—she looked him right in the eye. "Yes, Master Brody, I would like to explore a D/s relationship with you. I want to negotiate a contract and would be honored to wear your collar to The Covenant."

It didn't surprise her that he was a member of the private, elite club, which was so selective in its application process. While she had no clue where the club was, she'd heard it mentioned among the subs at Spice when she'd been there. It was supposedly the best, high-end club in Florida. But none of that mattered to her; the only thing that *did* matter was she would be there as Master Brody Evans's submissive.

"You don't know how much it pleases me for you to say that, Fancy."

With a hand splayed across the back of her head, he pulled her in for a kiss, and not just any kiss, but the mother of all kisses. *Holy cow!* She realized that before now, he'd been holding back with all the other kisses they'd shared. Their tongues dueled, but there was no doubt who was in charge. Her blood boiled, and her pussy was wet... with want... with need. The hand at her head held her in place as he took as much as he gave her. His other hand closed around her breast, squeezing and massaging the supple flesh.

Fancy whimpered when the kiss ended but was thrilled that Brody had been just as affected by it as she had. He gulped for air as a storm brewed in his eyes—a storm she desperately wanted to get caught up in.

"Sweetness, we can keep this vanilla for now since we haven't negotiated or gone through a limit list yet, but it's your choice. Vanilla, or will you let me spice it up? We can keep it simple, and of course, you'll have your safeword."

While this was one of the things she would rather let him take control of, without the negotiations and contract, she had to be the one to make the decision. Once everything was in place, if he thought she needed or wanted to be topped, for whatever reason, he would take the lead and trust her to use her safe-word if anything felt wrong. She knew in her heart he would honor her safeword and stop all play if she uttered it. And right there, she had her answer.

"Spicy, Sir."

His charming grin returned, but this time, she saw the Dom behind it, and a shiver went down her spine. "Then spicy it is. Thank you for trusting me. The Covenant uses the same color system Spice does. Do you want 'red' as your safeword, or would you like to choose something else?"

"Red is fine, Sir."

"Good girl. You can also use 'yellow' to slow things down or let me know if you have questions." He patted her hip. "To start, I want you to go into your bedroom, remove all your clothes, and present next to the bed. I'll follow in a few minutes."

Brody helped her stand and watched her walk to the hallway leading to her bedroom on trembling knees. She glanced over her shoulder at him, and another shiver went down her spine at his expression. It was intense yet playful, and she wondered which would be more prevalent during their scene.

As soon as she reached her bedroom, she quickly removed her dress, bra, and panties. Sinking to her knees next to the bed, she was in position when Brody—Master Brody entered the room. While there were many protocols she'd forgotten, she remembered to keep her eyes cast downward until directed otherwise. All she could see were his feet. He'd removed his socks and shoes but still wore his jeans. She hoped the golf shirt he'd worn was also gone because she loved letting her eyes and hands roam his muscular torso.

"Damn, you're beautiful."

She blushed at his words as he dropped a small, black duffel bag on the floor in front of her. It wasn't hers so he had to have run out to his truck to retrieve it. She knew many Doms had a spare toy bag or two so they were always prepared, and she was nervous to find out what was in his.

She didn't have to wait long. "Open the bag, Fancy-girl."

Pulling it closer, she did as ordered and waited for the next command.

"I'm going to tell you to take out a few things. If any of those things scare you or are on your hard limit list, leave them in the bag. If you're okay with an item, then hand it to me. Understood?"

She hadn't expected that but was grateful he was giving her a choice about what they would use during the scene. But then again, that was the sign of a good Dom, which she already figured out he was. "Yes, Sir."

"Excellent. Hand me the leather cuffs."

She spotted them on top, next to a black, six-tail flogger. *What would it be like to be flogged by Brody?* Her ass tingled at the thought. Grabbing the cuffs, she placed them in his waiting hand.

"There's a bullet vibe in there, still in its package. Let me have it."

It was nice to know what he'd be using on her had never touched another woman—it was considerate of him and didn't surprise her. Yes, an item could be sterilized, but still... *eww*. She found the sealed package and handed it to him.

"Hmmm. Decisions, decisions," he teased her. "The six-tail."

Oh, fuck, yes! Her hand closed around the leather handle of the flogger, and she lifted it out of the bag. When Brody took it from her, he placed the tip under her chin and raised her head until she looked into his face. The heat in his eyes warmed her and made the desire and need in her core flare even higher. His bare chest had her yearning to lick every inch of it.

"Thank you, sweetness." He bent down, picked the bag up by its handles, and moved it out of the way. "Up on the bed, on your knees, hands behind your back."

She complied with his instructions, her heart rate and breathing accelerating with anticipation. Oh, how she'd missed this—handing the reins over to her lover—all she had to do was follow his commands and feel. Her mind could go blank as he sent her into subspace, and there was no doubt Brody would send her there. Hell, if she was honest, she was halfway there already.

Brody stepped behind her beside the bed and

attached the cuffs to each of her wrists. "Spread your legs a little. What's your safeword, Fancy-girl?"

"Red, Sir."

After linking the cuffs together so her arms were restrained, he ran a single finger up the length of her spine, sending a shiver through her as goosebumps pebbled her skin. One hand closed around the nape of her neck while the other supported one of her shoulders. "Put your head down on the bed."

With his help, she bent at the waist, then turned her head to the side so her cheek rested on the comforter. Her ass remained high, and she felt herself grow wetter at the erotic pose. Brody ran his hand across her backside, occasionally squeezing the flesh to bring her blood to the surface. "Damn, you have the nicest ass I've ever seen."

"Thank you, Sir." She was sure he was exaggerating, but she couldn't help wiggle said ass in response.

His hand lifted, then smacked back down, causing her to yelp. The laughter in his voice was unmistakable as he said, "Little brat."

While the single spank stung a little, it only just increased her need for more. His hand dipped between her legs and found evidence of her arousal. Fingers delved into her folds.

"Mmmm. I love that you waxed down there for me, sweetness."

She'd gone to the salon the day after they'd first slept together. While it had been a little more painful than she'd remember, she loved how much more sensitive she was once the initial soreness was gone. And she couldn't wait to feel Brody's mouth and tongue on her bare flesh.

His hand disappeared and she heard him open the vibe package, and it wasn't long before the adult toy was humming. It took every ounce of strength not to clench her legs together because she knew she would jump the second the vibe touched her where she expected he was about to put it. She hadn't been wrong.

Cupping the small vibe in his palm, Brody put it between her legs and held it to her exposed pussy as she nearly flew off the bed. The only things that had kept her in place were the position she was in, her hands being restrained, and his other hand on her hip. "Easy, baby. It's been a long time for you, so I won't demand that you stay still, but do your best."

"Y-yes, Sir."

Damn, he'd never get tired of hearing that from her mouth. Shifting his hand, he gripped the humming vibe and put the tip in her vagina. He grinned when she let out a loud moan.

"There's more where that came from," he said, pushing the toy into her channel. "Don't lose it."

He squeezed her ass cheeks a few more times, ensuring there was enough blood flow near the surface to keep her from bruising. This was going to be a pleasure flogging, so his strikes would be hard enough for a bite of pain but light enough that she wouldn't feel any lasting effects in the morning. Picking up the flogger, he stepped away from the bed to give himself some room. Her ass looked delectable, and he couldn't wait until he prepped her with a progressive set of anal plugs so she could eventually take him there.

"Ready, sweetness?"

"Yes, Sir."

Brody flicked his wrist and let the six leather tails land softly on her right ass cheek, followed by another flick to her left. Slowly, he let the strikes increase in velocity and intensity. A pink blush appeared on the skin of her buttocks and upper thighs. He paused. "Color, sweetness?"

"Green, Sir. I'm good."

"Yes, you are."

Peppering her flesh, he slowed his pace once more, but now he really let her feel the sting as the knots at the end of the leather strands landed harder. Again, it was just enough for the pain to morph into pleasure. Her breathing increased as she moaned louder.

One last strike on her sit spot, and he dropped the flogger to the floor. His hands went to his waist, and he quickly shed his jeans. Grabbing a condom, he anticipated the day he could take her bareback—something he'd never done in his life, but if he had his way, it would be that way forever with his Fancy. After rolling on the latex, he held her steady with one hand, and using the fingers of the other, he removed the vibe, tapping it a few times on her clit.

"Oh! *Ohhhhhhhhh!*"

Clutching her hips, he pulled her to the edge of the bed and lined his rigid cock up with her slit. She was soaked, and he wasted no time entering her. The torturous drag of her tight walls had him seeing stars.

"Please, Sir! Faster!"

He slammed into her, his pelvis slapping against her ass. "We'll have to talk about topping from the bottom, Fancy-girl, but it will have to wait until later. Right now, I agree with you."

Pumping his hips, he fucked her fast and hard. Her gasps and pleadings urged him on. When the pressure in his scrotum was about to peak, he reached around and found her clit with his fingers, stroking it with fervor. Fancy screamed as an intense orgasm took hold. Her walls pulsated around him, sending him over the edge a few thrusts of his pelvis later. Shouting his release, he did his best to draw hers out as long as possible while his legs threatened to buckle and drop him on his ass.

His hands fell to the mattress on either side of her torso, supporting his weight, while his lungs heaved for oxygen. As soon as he was able, he unhooked the clasp keeping her bound wrists together and massaged her arms and shoulders. The only sound in the room was their combined heavy breathing. When his legs continued to protest his position, he reluctantly pulled from her body and quickly discarded the filled condom.

Rolling onto her back, Fancy watched him through heavy eyelids. As much as he wanted to lay down beside her, he had some aftercare to do first. Entering the master bath, he retrieved a wet washcloth and a dry towel to clean her with. He returned to find she had turned her body so her head was resting on the pillows on her side of the bed. *Huh*. He liked the sound of that. She owned that side of his bed, just like she owned his heart.

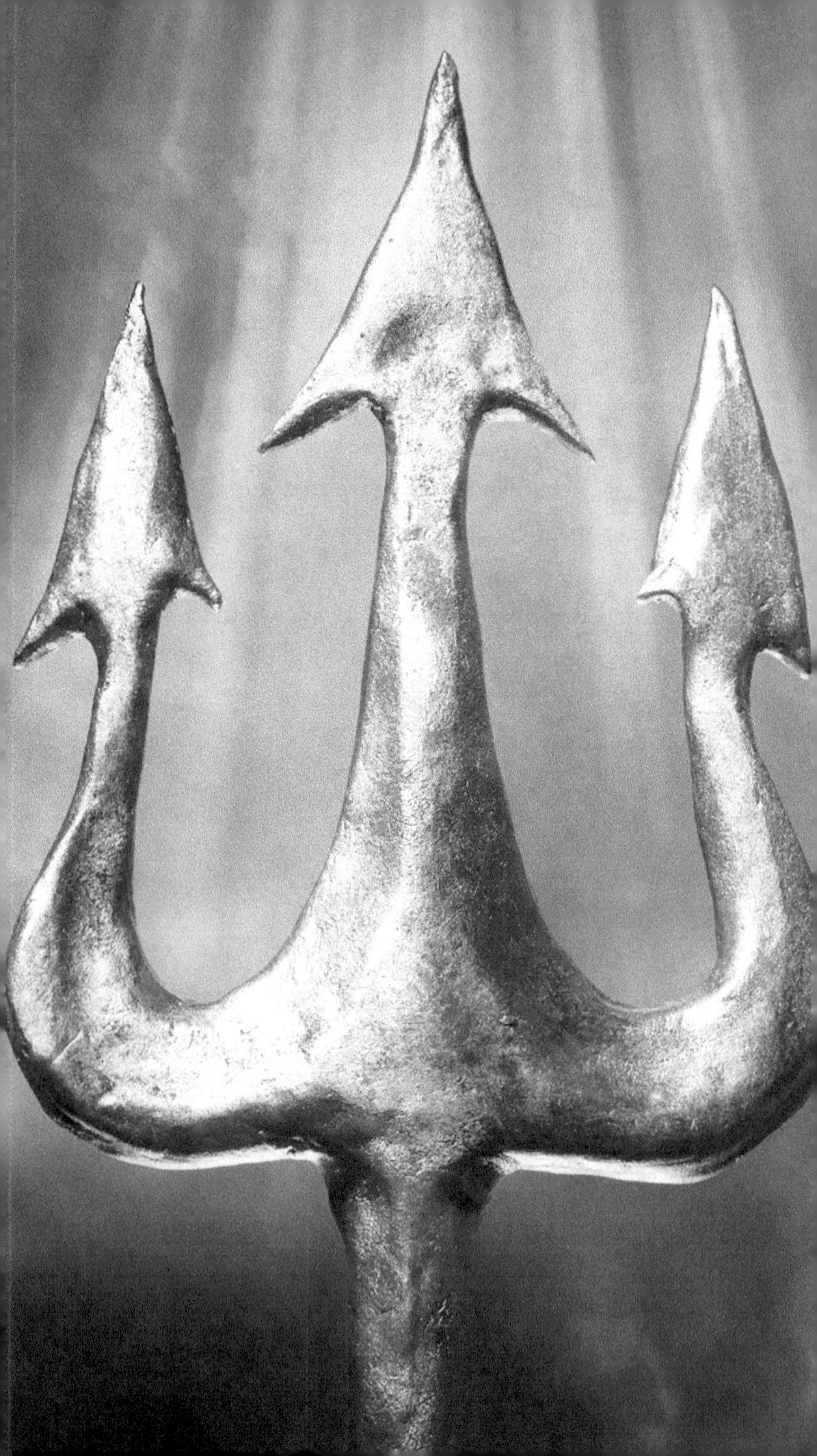

CHAPTER FOURTEEN

With long, freestyle strokes, Brody did lap after lap in his in-ground pool under the late Monday morning sun. He'd had it installed this past winter, using the company Parker had used for his own pool. His friend's was designed to look like a small lake, with its dark floor and walls surrounded by lush landscaping, giving it an overall feel of a natural hot spring, complete with a diving rock. While Brody loved its garden feel, he had wanted a pool long enough to get a decent workout in—being a former SEAL, he could swim for miles. The results had been better than he'd hoped for. He'd had several pool parties since it was completed, along with a Jacuzzi on the patio. The spa was in a little alcove, so he could use it naked if he wanted to and not worry about any neighbors seeing him, especially the four-year-old twins next door. Taylor and McKenna loved chatting with him through the fence, and he hadn't had the heart to change the black chain link to something they couldn't see through. He'd invited the girls over with their parents for a few barbecues, and their adorableness had quickly won over his friends. They loved it when baby Mara visited and couldn't wait to meet little JD.

The entire pool/patio/spa setup was now enclosed in a screen house to keep the bugs and other critters out. It locked from the inside, so he didn't have to worry about the twins coming over for a swim without their parents.

Reaching the end closest to where Fancy was lying on a chaise lounge reading an e-book, he stopped and ran a hand down his face, wiping away the salt water the pool was filled with. He observed her in silence for a moment. At his urging, she'd done something she apparently hadn't done in quite a while—she'd taken the day off—the entire day, to spend it with him. Her curvy body was yummy looking in the bathing suit she'd run out to buy on her way over this morning. Another thing she hadn't done in a long time was sitting by a pool or the gulf in a bathing suit just to relax and enjoy the day. The navy blue tankini, as she'd called it, was a two-piece suit—the top was a body-hugging tank with a racer back, while the bottom was a cute little skirt over an attached, traditional bikini. And she looked tempting as hell in it.

Glancing up, she gave him a smile, which grew as

he put his hands on the hard patio floor and pushed himself up and out of the pool. The water sluiced off his body and dripped from the hem of his swimming trunks. Her heated gaze roamed his body, taking in every contour of his muscular physique as he stalked over to her and grabbed his towel from the chaise next to her. "Keep looking at me like that, darlin', and we'll spend the rest of the day in my bed."

Bending down, he gave her a swift kiss on the lips. As much as he would love to follow through with his threat, he wanted her to remember what it was like to loll around while playing hooky from work. Her employees were more than competent at running the place for the day, and if he had any say in it, she would be taking many more days off. No one could keep up the pace of working every day of the week without burning out. Besides, they would be playing later tonight after a visit to The Covenant.

While they couldn't play at the club until Fancy was fully vetted and had a complete physical and blood work with her doctor, it would allow him to observe her as she watched some scenes. The screening process was mandatory, with no exceptions, and even Kristen and Angie had gone through it despite dating the owners. Not wanting any members to think he skipped over anything on Fancy's behalf, Brody had asked Marco to do the paperwork for her clearance. His buddy had done the club's background checks numerous times when

Brody was busy with other stuff, so it was nothing new.

"Sorry, but I can't help but stare," she replied. "Your body is amazing, and you know it."

He snorted and then stole another kiss. "Not as amazing as yours, sweetness. You're rockin' that bathing suit." He was thrilled when she blushed. There was nothing prettier than a woman blushing when her man complimented her.

Dropping onto the other chaise, he grabbed a bottle of water from the cooler beside it and guzzled half. "What are you reading, anyway?"

"Believe it or not, it's Kristen's *Velvet Vixen*."

"Really?"

"Um-hmm. I started reading it a few weeks ago, but there are days I'm too tired to read, or I start falling asleep after a page or two. And don't tell Kristen that —I don't want her to think it's because of her book since it's not. I loved all her vanilla books, but she writes awesome BDSM books."

Gritting his teeth, he fought the urge to reprimand her about running herself ragged and not getting enough sleep. They hadn't signed a contract yet or gone over her hard and soft limits. But once everything was in order, her well-being would be under his direct supervision—one of the main reasons he enjoyed the lifestyle. It was instinctive for him to want to care for a woman in every possible fashion—he was just wired that way.

There would be no more dark circles under her eyes, and they would find a way to combat her insomnia, although she looked well-rested today. In fact, she'd told him she'd slept fantastically last night, the first time in a long time. He wished he'd been the cause of her good night's sleep, but he had been on a security detail until very late and hadn't wanted to disturb her, so he'd gone home alone.

He finished the rest of his water. "I agree."

"You do? You've read them?"

Rolling his eyes, he said, "Yeah, but don't tell the guys that. As far as any of them will admit, they've only read the sex scenes and skipped over all the sappy romance."

"I can't wait to meet her. But I hope I don't say anything stupid because I'm totally going to be fangirling."

He took her hand in his. "You'll be fine. Trust me, Kristen is as down-home as they come. I've seen her with her fans. She loves them all, treating them like longtime friends. You'll meet her on Sunday afternoon."

Her eyes narrowed in confusion. "What's Sunday afternoon?"

"Just a little get-together at their place for a barbecue. Angie designed this awesome 'backyard,'" he made air quotes with his fingers, "on the Trident compound and called it *Ian's Oasis*. The only thing it doesn't have is a pool, but it's got everything else. Will you come with me and meet the rest of my crazy extended family? Kristen's mom and stepdad will be there, and so will Boomer's folks. Oh, and Jake and Nick are flying in too. Nick took a four-day leave because he's over the moon that he's an uncle. And I promise, no one will bite. Besides, by then, you'll have met most of them anyway."

Before she could respond, a child's shriek, filled with terror, came from next door. "Mista Brophy! Mista Brophy!"

He flew from the lounge and ran out the door of the screen house to the fence. The tears and expression on little McKenna Long's face had the hair on the back of his neck standing up. "McKenna, honey, what's wrong?"

As Fancy joined them, the little girl answered through her sobs, "M-Mommy... she on... the floor... s-sleeping and... and won't wake up!"

Shit! He placed his hands on the top of the fence and said, "Fancy, call 9-1-1. She's a diabetic."

Not waiting for a response, he vaulted over the fence and ran barefoot and shirtless through his neighbor's open back door. The sight greeting him almost broke his heart. Amy Long was lying on the living room floor with little Taylor crying and shaking her mother's shoulders, trying to wake her. Kneeling, he checked Amy's breathing and pulse. No problems there, but her pale and sweaty skin, in addition to her unconsciousness, were positive signs of being in diabetic shock.

Brody hurried to the kitchen and yanked open the refrigerator door. *Orange juice—perfect.* He searched through the cabinets, found a glass, and poured the juice into it. Then, he spotted a sugar bowl on the counter by the coffee machine. *Even better.*

Taking both the bowl and juice, he rushed back to Amy. Fancy stood nearby, talking on her cell phone with the 9-1-1 operator, telling them what was happening, while McKenna and Taylor each clutched one of her legs in fear. Brody gave them a quick, reassuring smile. "It's going to be okay, girls. Just stay there with Ms. Fancy."

Using his fingers, he took some granulated sugar and placed it under Amy's tongue and along her gums. The orange juice wasn't a good option until she came around a little bit and could drink it without choking.

Come on, Amy. Wake up.

A relieved sigh escaped him when her head started moving slowly as the sugar was absorbed into her bloodstream. Putting a hand behind her neck and shoulders, he sat her up a little and held the glass to her lips. "Here we go, Amy. Take a sip, sweetheart."

As her glucose levels gradually increased, she finally understood what he was saying and drank some of the juice, spilling a bit on her shirt, but it was better than the alternative. By the time the police and paramedics pulled up, Amy was more alert and holding the glass on her own. Brody stood and let the professionals take over.

He stepped over to where Fancy did her best to soothe the little girls. Kneeling before them, he held open his arms, and they jumped into them, hugging him tightly. "Mommy's going to be okay, girls. Everything will be all right."

"You a 'ero, Mista Brophy," Taylor said, pulling back a little to look at him before giving him a peck on the cheek.

McKenna put her little hand on his other cheek. "Uh-huh, a 'ero! Mommy's 'ero!"

No matter who you are, when little four-year-old twins kiss your cheeks and call you a hero, you have to grin from ear to ear. "Well, thank you, but you're Mommy's heroes, too. Actually, you're heroines because you did what you were supposed to do and got her help."

"We tried to call 9-1-1, like Mommy showed'd us," Taylor informed him. "B-but we couldn't find her phone, and the one in the kitten is broked."

It took him a second to translate that last part as the phone in the *kitchen* was *broken*. "Well, while the paramedics take care of Mommy, why don't we look for her cell phone so we can call your daddy and let him know what happened."

"Brody..." He glanced at Amy, now sitting on the couch, to see the missing phone was in her hand. "It was in my pocket. Sorry."

Relieved she was okay—embarrassed, but okay—he took it from her. "No worries. Do you want me to call Kevin and let him know what's going on?"

Reluctantly, she nodded as a medic checked her vital signs. "Please. My doctor is going to have to adjust my insulin. The dosage I'm on isn't cutting it anymore. This was my third sugar dump this week, although the other two weren't as bad, and Kevin was home."

After getting ahold of Amy's husband and assuring him she was okay, Brody told him to meet his wife at the emergency room and not to worry about the girls. Fancy was helping them get their bathing suits and arm flotation thingies, while the medics were preparing Amy for transport. Brody hadn't missed how the wet-behind-the-ears cop, who'd responded to the emergency, had eyed Fancy in her tankini as the children led her to their room.

Brody loudly cleared his throat, and when the uniformed man saw his glaring, possessive expression, the bastard had the audacity to shrug. "I'd be dead if I didn't appreciate a fine-looking woman like that."

"You'll be dead if you do it again," he growled.

The younger man grinned and held up his hands in mock surrender. "I'll let it slide that you just threatened a cop, but damn, you're a lucky guy."

And Brody knew it. Since she'd purged her soul to him about the accident and her loss, she'd seemed lighter, more open, and free. She was smiling all the time now as if the last of the grief holding her back from enjoying life had finally lifted. The results made her even more attractive, and men who may not have given the curvy woman a second glance over the past few years were now noticing what they'd been missing. It was almost as if she was going through a second blossoming into womanhood. And there was no way he was letting her slip through his fingers—not when jackasses like this were waiting in the wings for a chance at her.

CHAPTER FIFTEEN

"Tank you, Miff Fancy."

"You're welcome, Taylor," Fancy responded as she pushed a plate with a cut-up hotdog in front of the little brown-haired girl. McKenna had just received her own cut-up meal from Brody. It hadn't taken Fancy long to tell the twins apart. In addition to being fraternal, not identical, twins, the girls' personalities were like night and day. Taylor was quieter than her sister and seemed to analyze and think things through before taking any action. McKenna, on the other hand, was boisterous and plunged headfirst into any situation. In the pool earlier, McKenna had been delighted when Brody had repeatedly lifted her out of the water, high in the air, before letting her plummet back in again. Taylor wasn't the daredevil her sister was and preferred to wade in the shallow end with Fancy.

It'd been the first time since her accident and miscarriage she'd spent more than a few minutes in the company of a child, much less two children. It wasn't that she didn't love little kids—they were just a reminder of what she'd lost. But Taylor and McKenna had quickly won her over, and they'd all had a great time in the pool.

When the waterlogged crew had gotten out and toweled off, Brody had retrieved a package of hotdogs from the Long's refrigerator and thrown them on the grill with the chicken breasts he'd prepared for Fancy and him. While the girls hadn't been fans of the romaine lettuce in the accompanying salad, they'd scarfed down most of the cherry tomatoes and cucumber slices with gusto.

When the girls' parents arrived home from the hospital, it was almost 3:00 p.m. Amy hugged Fancy and profusely apologized for ruining her day off. But Fancy wouldn't hear any of it. "I'm just glad we were here and you're all right. The girls are adorable, and we had so much fun. I think they'll need a nap after all the swimming."

As if on cue, both Taylor and McKenna yawned. Their mother chuckled as she gathered them to leave. "I think I'm going to take one, too. Thank you again, Brody. And Fancy, it was so nice to meet you, but next time, we'll do it without the police and paramedics."

The family of four headed to their own house with several more waves and thanks sent in Brody and

Fancy's direction. When they were alone again, Fancy let her eyes trail over Brody's delicious torso, regretting that he was now wearing a T-shirt to cover up all that sexy, hard flesh. His muscles rippled as he cleaned up the last of their lunch. Grabbing the salad bowl and dressing, she followed him into the house. They worked silently for a few moments, putting things into the fridge and dishwasher.

When everything was finished, Fancy stepped over to Brody and put her arms around his waist. Smiling, he bent down and gave her a kiss that she immediately took advantage of. Heat coursed through her as she kissed him back with all the desire she felt. This man sent her hormones into overdrive, and right now, they were revving high. His hands delved into her hair as he held her head in place. He pivoted until their positions were reversed, and she was pinned against the counter. Clutching her hips, he picked her up and plopped her onto the granite. It was cool against the bare backs of her legs, but she didn't care. Spreading her knees wide, Brody stepped between them and pulled her to the counter's edge. His swim trunks were now tented with his growing erection, and he rubbed it against her core.

Ripping his mouth from hers, he brought her hands to the bottom hem of his shirt. "Take it off me, sweetness. Nice and slow."

Placing her hands underneath the material, she slid them upward over the contours of his torso, reveling in the feel of him. When the shirt was bunched up under his armpits, she took hold of it and pulled it over his head. With the height of the counter, she was staring directly at the notch in his throat. Leaning forward for a lick, she whimpered when he stopped her before she got to her prize. "Uh-uh, baby. We're in D/s mode here, even though it's only a verbal agreement right now. That will change Wednesday night."

She'd asked to observe some scenes at the club before completing her limit list. She and Patrick had only begun exploring the lifestyle when they found out she was pregnant, and then two weeks later, he was gone. So, she was still very inexperienced in the different types of BDSM play. "But right now, any self-indulgence will earn you a punishment, which I guarantee you won't like—at least, not at first. Understood?"

She couldn't help it when her mouth turned into a sexy pout. "Yes, Sir."

Chuckling, Brody grabbed the hem of her tankini top. "Don't worry, sweetness. I'll give you time to play around in a little bit. Right now, it's my turn."

He dragged the spandex material of her suit top up to and over her head. Her large breasts bounced when they were released, and she moaned at their sensitivity.

"Lean back a little. It's time for my dessert. And this time, you're my sweet treat."

When she followed his order, resting her head against the cabinet behind her, he bent over and took one of her nipples in his mouth. Wet heat almost scorched her and spread throughout her body, coming to a stop deep in her core. While his lips and tongue tortured the one peak, his thumb stroked over the other one. Brody's appreciation and attention to every bit of her flesh could only be described as sensual worship. Maybe he was the type of man who didn't mind a little extra weight on his woman.

Holy shit. Where did those words come from? Is that who I am now? Brody's woman? Am I woman enough for him? Or am I too much woman?

Uncertainties she hadn't known since Patrick had started flirting with her all those years ago bubbled to the surface.

Pain shot through her when Brody's open hand slapped her inner thigh, and her eyes flew open to find him scowling at her. She'd been so far into her old teenage insecurities and hadn't even noticed his mouth was no longer on her breast. "Where'd you go, Fancy-girl? Because it wasn't here with me."

"I-I'm sorry... I just..." She bit her bottom lip, not quite sure what to say. How do you ask your lover if he likes your body or not?

Does he wish I weighed less?

His brow furrowed even more as he cupped her chin. "Listen, sweetness. I know you didn't have a lot of time to explore the lifestyle back then, but let me make one thing perfectly clear. I want a complete and honest answer when I ask you a question, especially during playtime. Whether you think I'll be upset or get mad doesn't matter. Communication is vital in a D/s relationship. I can't take care of you properly if I don't know what the problem is. Now, I'll ask you again, and I expect a truthful answer. Where was your sexy little mind a few minutes ago?"

He thought her mind was sexy? No one had ever come close to saying that to her before, not even her husband, and she loved how warm and fuzzy it made her feel. Her body and brain went to mush, and that was the only reason when, without thinking, she blurted out, "I don't think I deserve you."

Her jaw dropped when she realized she'd said that out loud. Brody's expression hardened; the best way to describe it was thunderous. Anger flared in his eyes as his jaw tightened. Holy crap, she'd never seen him mad before, not like this. While she knew in her heart he wouldn't hurt her, the fear she felt at that moment had her shuddering.

He stepped back and pulled her off the counter, setting her feet on the floor. Without a word, he took her by the hand and led her to his bedroom. His silence was deafening, and she wished she'd kept her big mouth shut.

"Brody, I'm sorry. I didn't mean that. Can you just forget I said it?"

Letting go of her hand, he grasped the waist of her

bathing skirt and shoved it down her legs until it pooled at her ankles. She gasped as the cold air conditioning hit her bare mound and ass. He left her standing there, completely naked and vulnerable, then sat down on the bed with his arms crossed over his massive chest. "Rule number one, Fancy—I never want to hear you say anything bad about yourself or that you're not good enough for me. You're beautiful to me, inside and out. I thought that the first moment I met you, and nothing will ever change my opinion. And no, I will not *just forget* you said it. Rule number two—anytime I hear you say anything covered by rule number one, you will be punished, as in a spanking, and not an erotic one like you had the other night. Rule number three—once said punishment is over, the past is erased. We let it go and move on. Understand?"

His voice was hard and rumbling as he was obviously in full-Dom mode. *Shit,* she was in so much trouble. "Yes, Sir."

"Good girl." Thankfully, she remembered to call him "Sir" since he might have added more to her punishment. She shifted her weight from one foot to the other as he continued. "What's your safeword, sweetness?"

"Red, Sir."

"Since we haven't signed a contract yet, I will ask you this—do you want to use your safeword now, or are you willing to take your punishment and wipe the slate clean between us?"

The spanking he'd given her the other night had turned her on. And while she was sure she wouldn't enjoy this one, she had a feeling that in the aftermath, Brody would take care of her other needs, too. Her past and future would fade into oblivion for a while and let her live only in the moment. She wanted to push away the insecurities holding her back from falling for this wonderful man. All she had to do was hand over her body and mind to him and feel how good it was between them—how he made her body sing.

Did she want this? As much as she loved handing over the reins to him in bed, this was entirely different. Something she and Patrick had never had a chance to explore— control over things outside of the bedroom. Her late husband had been more mellow than Brody. If she worried out loud about her weight or anything else, he had just kissed her silly, tickled her, and told her he loved everything about her. Any flaws she thought she had didn't matter to him.

But Brody would not allow her to even *think* about her perceived flaws. He wouldn't allow her to feel anything less than beautiful. If those negative thoughts were spanked out of her, would she finally come to love her body as much as he obviously did?

Brody stared at her, patiently waiting for her answer. This was relatively new to her, and she needed time to think things through. But there was no way he would allow his woman ever to believe she was undeserving of his attention and love. And yes, he was totally head-over-in-heels in love with Fancy.

No other woman had ever raised his Dom instincts as high as she did. She'd spent a total of two nights in his bed, and he didn't think he'd get a good night's sleep without her there ever again. He just had to think of her, and his dick got hard. He could make love to her until he was one hundred and never tire of or stop wanting her. Fancy Maguire was the other part of his heart and soul he'd been searching for all his life, of that he was positive. He just had to be patient until she reached the same conclusion.

She shifted her hips again, then finally said, "I'll take my punishment, Sir."

The knot he hadn't realized was in his gut released. Silently thanking the universe that she was taking this important step in their relationship, he held out his hand. "Good girl. Then we'll talk about those negative feelings you have. I won't tolerate them. Now come over here and lay across my lap."

Stepping out of the bathing suit bottoms still around her ankles, she slowly walked toward him, clearly feeling a mixture of dread and anticipation. While she wasn't going to enjoy her punishment, he was certain she'd be wet and begging for him to fuck her when he was done doling it out. And he'd be happy to oblige her, but first things first.

When she took his hand, he helped her lay across his lap. While the other night, he'd used the bed to support her, this time, she was face down toward the floor with her ass in his lap. Her feet didn't reach the ground, so she was off balance, exactly how he wanted her. She gripped his leg with one hand and reached up with the other to hold onto the bed's poster.

Rubbing her upper thighs and ass cheeks, he said, "Count out loud, sweetness. You'll be getting twenty-five of them."

He ignored her gasp and lifted his hand, letting it smack back down on her bare ass with a resounding *crack*. Her count followed a yelp. "One, Sir."

Crack.

"Two, Sir."

Crack.

"Thr-three, Sir."

By the time he reached number five, the skin on her buttocks and upper thighs was turning an angry shade of red. He hated disciplining her like this but knew she needed it. She was definitely a submissive, with a lack of confidence issue, which wasn't surprising after what she'd been through, but the self-doubt she had about her body would be banished if he had his way. If this was what it took for her to realize she was beautiful to him, and it was he who should be wondering if he deserved her in his life, then that's what he would do.

"Nine, S-Sir," came out on a sob, and he stopped for a moment and caressed her tender flesh, giving her time to take a few deep breaths.

"Are you still green, sweetness?"

"Y-Yes, Sir."

He dipped his finger between her legs to her folds and found them drenched with desire. He knew her body craved his dominance, and this was his proof. When he tapped her clit, she moaned, but that was all the pleasure he'd give her—brief as it were—until her punishment was complete.

Removing his hand, he set about spanking her again, landing a few strikes right on her sit spots. He wanted to ensure she felt this for the next few days, to remind her why she'd been punished. Her body was now his—to care for, love, and cherish—and he wouldn't tolerate any negative thinking about her image or self-worth.

Crack.

"Tw-Twenty-four, Sir."

Crack.

"Twenty-five, S-Sir."

Fancy let out a huge sigh of relief between her sobs and tears before Brody helped her stand for a moment and then laid her down on the bed. After removing his swim trunks, he spooned her, his chest to her back, tucking her sore ass against his groin. There was no hiding his erection, and he smiled when she gently wiggled her hips despite her crying. Any doubts he may have had about her reaction to a discipline spanking were completely gone. She'd handled it well, and he hoped he'd purged those negative thoughts from her mind. While Fancy was a confident, strong businesswoman, when she wasn't working, she needed to be under the care of a Dom—him, to be specific. He wanted her to be just as strong and confident in her private, personal life and would do anything to help her achieve that.

Brushing her hair to the side, he kissed the shell of her ear. "Are you okay, sweetness?"

"Mmm-hmm. I just feel a little perverted since all I want now is for you to make love to me."

While he barked out a laugh, his heart soared at her choice of words. She wanted him to *make love* to her. It was the first time she'd used those two words, and he'd be damned if it was the last.

CHAPTER SIXTEEN

Brody's cell phone chirped, and he rolled over to grab it from the night table, silencing it before the noise woke Fancy up. Looking at the screen, he inwardly cursed. It was the alarm monitoring company Trident Security used. The only properties Brody received alerts for were his place, the Trident compound, his teammates' homes, and Fancy's shop.

Anytime one of the systems they'd installed throughout the city and surrounding area went off, signaling a breach, an alert went to the monitoring company. A tech there would contact the police to respond, and then the person or persons on the property's notification list—usually the owner, manager, or another key holder. But in Fancy's case, he'd made her the backup contact, and she would only receive an alert if he or Corey didn't respond first—at least until the vandal was caught. He wanted to know what damage was done before she found out and then be the one to break the news to her—gently.

After seeing it was the alarm at the bakery, he glanced at the time. *Two-in-the-fucking-blessed-morning.* He hated to rouse her, but she'd worry if she awakened to find him gone. He also didn't want to tell her where he was going, and he wouldn't. Not until he figured out if it was a false alarm or not.

Slipping out from under the covers, he quickly threw his clothes back on and then squatted beside the bed. Placing his hand on her hip, he gave it a little shake. "Fancy, baby, I need you to wake up for a second."

"Mmmm." Her eyes blinked open, her voice filled with sleep. "Br-Brody? What's wrong? What time is it?"

"Just after two. I have to run out... work-related." It wasn't exactly a lie—he just didn't clarify whose work it was related to. "I didn't want you to wake up and find me missing. It shouldn't take long, and I'll be back in a little bit." He gave her a sexy little grin. "Keep my side of the bed warm for me."

"'Kay." She snuggled down under the sheets as her eyes fluttered closed once more.

Brody was confident she'd be asleep again before he reached his truck. With his 9mm in a holster at the small of his back, he grabbed his cell phone and keys. He then ensured the alarm was reset, and the front door's deadbolt was re-engaged before leaving Fancy alone in his house.

When he pulled into the bakery's parking lot, a patrol car and Corey Maguire's truck were at the far end. Two uniformed officers talked with the fireman under one of the overhead lights. They turned their attention to him as he parked and exited his vehicle.

He didn't recognize either of the cops. "Hey, Corey. What happened? The monitoring company's text said the back door alarm went off."

"Yeah." He extended a hand, which Brody shook as the man introduced him to the officers. "Brody Evans from Trident Security, this is Matt Caulfield and Juan Rojas. I run into them a lot on the overnight shifts."

He exchanged handshakes with the men. Caulfield appeared to be in his early twenties, while Rojas had to be about fifteen or twenty years older. However, both seemed fit and alert and probably wouldn't have any trouble taking down a suspect. As a group, the four began to walk behind the building as Rojas spoke. "It doesn't look like they gained entry, but it rattles if you pull on the door handle hard enough. Might have been enough to set it off. The real damage is the graffiti."

"Shit, again?" Brody's anger began to spike. When he got ahold of the little punk responsible, he'd shove the spray paint bottle up his ass. The big, utility-green metal door had been a little loose on its hinges when he and Boomer had inspected it before wiring it for the alarm. While it had rattled, it had taken quite a bit of force to make it happen and would be highly unlikely to have been an accident if it had set off the alarm.

The two officers shined their flashlights on the back brick wall so he could assess the damage. Vile words had been spray painted in bright yellow, and rage overtook his preceding anger. Someone was calling Fancy—his Fancy—a *bitch, whore, and cunt.* Brody's hands clenched into fists. "Fucking bastard. You better make sure you find this asshole first because I'm going to tear him limb from limb." He didn't wait for a reply. "I take it you didn't go inside and check the camera feed."

Corey shook his head, pulling his shop keys from his jeans pocket. "No. It's your system. I haven't had a chance to play with it yet, so we were waiting for you. I didn't want to erase anything accidentally."

"Let's go through the front in case the perp left fingerprints on this door."

Within minutes, they were in Fancy's office, and Brody was rewinding the camera feed on the program he'd added to her computer, looking for the asshole who dared to harass his woman. "There he is. Let me rewind it to when he first shows up."

The suspect's actions ran backward at a rate of eight times the normal speed until he disappeared into the wooded area behind the shop. Brody hit play, and the four men watched as a person, presumably a male, but they couldn't be certain, walked into the frame. He used an umbrella to shield his face and upper body from the security camera he'd apparently known was there. After spray painting the graffiti, the bastard had pulled on the door handle a few times, probably hoping to gain entry and do more damage. Unable to get in, the punk left the same way he'd come.

Corey let out an exasperated sigh. "Well, that was no fucking help. The bastard even wore gloves, so there won't be any prints. I'm going to kill this fucker."

Shutting down the computer, Brody stood. "You and me both."

The two officers followed him out the back as Corey went out the front so he could relock that door. Caulfield and Rojas pulled out their flashlights again, and the latter said, "We'll take a walk through the trees here and see if there's any evidence that might have been left behind."

Pulling one of his business cards from his wallet, Brody handed it to the older officer. "Let me know if you come across anything. My cell number is on the bottom. And thanks for coming out."

"No problem. I'll add the bakery to the patrol watch list, so it'll get a few drive-by inspections during each shift."

"I appreciate it." Brody shook their hands and then left them to their work. He met Corey by their side-by-side trucks. "I'm really not looking forward to telling Fancy about this."

"Want me to tell her?"

"Nah, she's at my house, I'll tell her. In the meantime, do you know anyone who can get that garbage off the wall in the morning? I don't want her landlord pissed at her for something she's not responsible for."

The other man nodded. "We have a power washer at my stationhouse that I can borrow. I don't have to be at work until sixteen-hundred hours. I'll grab it now so she doesn't have to see it in the morning."

"Thanks." Brody pulled his driver's door open and climbed in. "Call me if you have any problems cleaning it up."

Corey shrugged. "I don't expect any, but let me get your number just in case."

He rattled off the digits, and a few seconds later, his cell rang with Corey's number appearing on the screen. "Got it. Thanks."

"No problem. Night."

Driving home, Brody dreaded telling Fancy what had happened. He'd let her get a few more hours of sleep and tell her over coffee. Damn, he wanted to kill the mother fucker who was doing this.

In the locker room of The Covenant, Fancy was nervous as she changed into the fetish club wear she'd bought yesterday. She'd wanted to surprise Brody, so he hadn't seen the outfit yet, but he'd sent her to one of the nicest fetish wear shops she'd ever seen—not that she'd seen many. He had also insisted on paying for whatever she purchased. When she'd arrived at the shop, she'd learned he'd called ahead and requested she not be allowed to see the prices of anything she was interested in. Apparently, the two women who worked there often received requests like that from Doms, and as they'd promised him, she had no idea what anything had cost.

"Fancy, I'm so glad you're here!"

She spun around to see Angie and another woman already dressed in their club wear and suddenly wondered if she was overdressed. "Hi, Angie. Thank goodness you're here. It's nice to see a familiar face because I'm nervous as hell."

The striking blonde grinned. "Actually, Brody sent us in here to calm your nerves. He figured you could use some girlfriends to lean on. This is Kat Maier, Boomer's fiancée and sub."

Dressed in a very, very short, plaid schoolgirl skirt and an adorable matching bra, the brunette extended her hand. "Hi, Fancy. It's nice to meet you finally. Bennie's been raving about all the treats Brody's gets from your shop. And Angie won't tell us what the new cake design looks like—she wants it to be a surprise, but said it looks awesome."

Shaking the other woman's hand, Fancy smiled. "I'm glad you like it, Angie. It's one of my favorite cakes to do."

Angie was dressed in a sheer, black teddy with a

matching thong. The sub was obviously very comfortable in her skin and, with a body like that, she should be. Kat was a little shorter than her friend—she was the same height as Fancy at five foot five, but she was thinner.

Stop thinking like that! Brody said he loves your curves, and you should, too! Do you want another punishment when a pleasure spanking is so much more enjoyable?

The door at the top of the stairs opened, and they heard several women chatting while heading down to the locker room. When they entered, Fancy was relieved to see a variety of shapes and sizes among the four women. One of them was wearing a bright purple wig and a huge smile. "Oh-em-gee! Is this Fancy?"

Startled that a stranger knew who she was, she looked to Angie for help, and the woman introduced her. "Yes, this is Fancy, and she's nervous, so everyone, rally around. Fancy Maguire, this is Shelby Christiansen." She pointed to the purple-haired woman and then to the next woman in line. "Colleen McKinley, who's the office manager at Trident. And this is Mistress Roxanne and Kayla London."

Angie hadn't needed to tell Fancy that the tall redhead was a Domme. She'd known it as soon as their gazes met. Her eyes were kind, but Fancy recognized the take-charge look and how she carried herself as someone who was so not a submissive. Mistress Roxanne smiled warmly and shook Fancy's hand. "It's nice to meet you. The Trident subs have been chatty about the woman who finally caught Master Brody's heart. I always knew he had good taste."

A blush stole over Fancy's cheeks. The Domme's wife was as curvy as Fancy was, if not more, and Mistress Roxy apparently approved of voluptuous women. Feeling better about her outfit and body, she finished getting ready as the others did. A few more women entered the locker room, and Fancy started to lose track of everyone's names. There was Georgia, Cassandra, Sasha, and another Domme, Mistress China.

Harper Williams walked in with two other women and hugged Fancy after spotting her. "I had a feeling you were a submissive the other night, but it wasn't my place to ask. I'm so happy to see you here. We have to go out again with just the girls."

"That sounds like fun. Count me in."

The chatter in the room began to relax her. In addition to the nervousness she was experiencing about being here, she was still upset about the vandalism at her shop. Corey and Brody had taken care of the latest graffiti the other night, and it had been gone when she'd arrived to open the shop. While it was her business, she was grateful they had handled it this time. Hopefully, the teens, or whoever it was, would be caught soon or eventually get tired and stop harassing her.

Several of the women around her laughed at some joke she'd missed. Fancy realized that aside from a few get-togethers with her female employees, she hadn't had an actual girls-night-out in a very long time. Well, that was one more thing to add to her list of how to leave the past where it belonged. She missed having girlfriends to go out with, even if it was just shopping or having lunch. Looking forward to this next phase of her life more than ever, she shut her locker door and took a deep breath before walking out to the club floor where Brody was waiting for her.

Standing outside the women's lounge, Brody acknowledged several people who greeted him as they walked past his temporary, self-assigned post. The sensual jazz music that was usually played over the club's sound system on Wednesday nights coursed through him and conjured up his personal porn flick of Fancy in his mind. He was dying to see what she'd picked out at the fetish wear shop and was positive that whatever it was, she would rock it—which, in turn, would make him rock hard. Hell, he was already halfway there just thinking about her in any fet wear. Thankfully, he wore his usual comfortable, faded jeans, which he preferred over the leather pants many of the Doms wore. Instead of a snug T-shirt, tonight he'd opted for an open leather vest—a brown one that matched his cowboy boots.

The door to the locker room opened, and Brody almost swallowed his tongue. Fancy wore a tight blue corset with some stitched, black floral design—paisley, he thought they called it. The top pushed her breasts in and up, making her tantalizing bosom even more attractive. The short skirt of the outfit was soft, black leather with a tulle underlining that flared it out a bit. He knew underneath she was bare, as he'd instructed her not to wear any panties, and the knowledge had him cursing the fact they couldn't play tonight.

He held his hand out for her to take as she stepped toward him. "You look stunning, sweetness. I have one thing to add, though, to make sure the horny vultures stay away from you."

He pulled out the collar he'd purchased in the club shop yesterday from his jeans pocket and held it up for her to see. The necklace had an intricate design with a thin, black leather cord threaded through the silver links. From the center hung a black, onyx heart. When she was ready, he'd have a one-of-a-kind collar designed for her at the jewelry shop many of the local Doms went to. For now, he hoped she liked the one he'd picked out.

Fancy gasped. "Brody... I mean, Sir, it's beautiful."

"Something fancy for my Fancy-girl. I'm glad you like it." He moved behind her, and when she lifted her hair out of the way, he clasped the collar at the nape of her neck.

She spun around so he could see the delight in her eyes as she fingered the stone heart. "I love it. Thank you, Sir."

Pulling her close, he bent down and kissed her softly on the lips. As much as he wanted to kiss her silly, he had to keep himself in check. *Damn the rules—* he couldn't wait until she was cleared to play. At least there would be plenty of things they could do when they returned to his place later. "You're very welcome, sweetness. Now, let's see what we can check off on your limit list."

He escorted his sub around the club and introduced her to some members. Earlier, he'd told her not to go crazy trying to remember names. There were over 350 people who belonged to The Covenant, so he would use his friends' names often in conversation until she learned them. Most of the stations in the pit were active, and he studied Fancy's reactions to the different types of play.

Mistress China was on Whip Master duty tonight, and they stopped to watch her finish restraining the first sub who'd signed up for a session. Ian, Devon, and Mitch took the art of bullwhipping seriously here. It was a talent to whip a sub properly so the skin was never broken, and only a few people had been approved to use the bullwhips in the club. Many Doms who weren't skilled in the task would sign up their subs for a session with the on-duty Whip Master for the night. Unattached submissives could also request to scene. Mistress China, Mistress Roxanne, Master Carl, and two other Doms rotated the schedule, so one of them was on each night. Jake Donovan was also one of the original club Whip Masters, with China and Carl, but with him out in San Diego forming the West Coast Trident team, the Sawyers had needed to apprentice several more.

While Fancy watched in fascination as the Domme lit up the male sub's bare back with licks of the whip, Brody's mind flashed back to Heather's mutilated corpse. There had been no reports on any more missing submissives, nor had the bodies of the other two missing women been found. The police and forensic techs had yet to develop a viable suspect, which had many community members on edge. The Doms did their best to protect the subs, but they couldn't be watched 24/7.

Brody's attention was brought back to the present as Fancy leaned her body toward his. "It's amazing to watch, but being whipped isn't for me. I'm so not a pain slut."

He grinned. "And *I'm* so glad you're not. Spanking and a little pain for pleasure is one thing, but this isn't my cup of tea, either. Shall we move on?"

When she nodded and replied with a "yes, Sir," he glanced around to see what other scenes were being played out. Master Dennis was playing with one of the new female submissives at a spanking bench station, and Master Stefan was nearby with two subs. The

Coast Guard Lieutenant had recently signed a contract with Cassandra Myers, one of the club's waitresses, who had the night off. Evidently, they had decided to add another female sub to their play tonight. Brody had played with Cassandra before and knew she was fond of rope play, which was being used in their current scene. Shibari is an art in itself, with hundreds of different variations in how the rope can be wrapped around the sub's body, and Stefan Lundquist was one of the local masters of the craft. He taught classes on different techniques at The Covenant, Heat, and Spice and always drew a crowd to watch him create a new design.

At the moment, Cassandra was blindfolded and lying on a leather table that allowed her Dom to wrap the rope around her upper body and under the table-top, securing her to it. Her legs were spread wide using the table's extension attachments. As Lundquist created an intricate webbing on the woman's torso, the other sub, Kenya Phelps, was on her knees between Cassandra's legs, licking her bare pussy. Under instructions from Master Stefan, she kept the pace slow and steady and would continue until he issued a new command. If the restrained sub's increased breathing and moaning were any indication, Kenya's tongue was sweet torture but not enough to send her into an orgasmic state.

Brody studied Fancy's face. Her gaze wasn't on the Dom, but instead was on the one woman pleasuring the other. *Hmm.* He leaned down to speak into Fancy's ear. "Have you ever played with another woman before?"

She turned to face him. Her cheeks were stained pink, which had him wondering where else she was blushing. "No... Sir... but it was on my soft limit list with Patrick. We just never had the chance to try it."

His cock hardened as an image of Fancy and Harper playing together popped into his brain. Marco's fiancée enjoyed an occasional third in their scenes, and the person's gender didn't make a difference to her. Sometimes, Brody joined them, and Cassandra or Kenya had been the third on a few occasions. "Well, then. Will it be going on your new soft limit list?"

"Would that please you, Sir?" Her face lit up in a saucy, seductive expression. Yeah, she knew how to get his heart racing, sending plenty of oxygenated blood to his growing erection.

"Very much so, sweetness." He stroked her cheek with his knuckles. "We'll have to explore that sometime after you've had a chance to get to know the other subs. Then you can tell me who you'd feel comfortable with."

They turned back toward the scene and watched as Master Stefan continued to twist the rope in geometric patterns along the soft lines of Cassandra's body. The more he worked, encasing her in his design, the further she went into subspace. Her body was releasing endorphins, creating a sense of euphoria—basically, the sub was "rope drunk."

After Master Stefan tied the last knot, he ordered Kenya to increase the pace and pressure of her tongue until Cassandra screamed with an orgasm. It was so strong that it brought tears to the sub's eyes. Her legs trembled while the rest of her body barely quivered under the snug ropes her Dom had expertly wrapped around her.

Next to Brody, Fancy shivered, and he knew if he dipped his hand between her legs, he would find her soaked. Yeah, tonight was going to be fucking awesome once they were home and in bed, and he couldn't wait.

CHAPTER SEVENTEEN

"Thanks for following me home, Master Thomas," Naomi Nguyen said as the Dom climbed out of his pickup truck, which he'd parked behind her Ford Focus. It was 1:00 a.m., and he'd given her an escort home from Spice because of the three missing submissives, one of whom had been found dead. The club's owner had asked the Doms to ensure the subs they played with made it home safely, and the two had scened together earlier.

"No problem, Naomi." He glanced around the front yard as if reassuring himself there was no threat. One of her neighbors, who never seemed to sleep, strolled down the street with his little brown pug. Her escort nodded at the man and then turned back to Naomi. "I'll walk you to the door."

She wished she dared to invite him in for a drink—and maybe some more play. Her crush was growing stronger each time they played together, but aside from scening with her almost every week, Thomas Manfred didn't seem to want a steady submissive in his life. The civil engineer was extremely attractive and super nice, and many of the subs at Spice were wagging their tongues after him. She knew it had been three years since his submissive/fiancée had been killed in a car accident, and he'd only returned to the BDSM community a little over six months ago. She wondered how long he was going to grieve before he opened up his heart again. One of these days, she would conjure up the courage to let him know she was interested in signing a contract with him—just not tonight.

Sighing to herself, she climbed the four concrete steps to her front door and slid her house key into the deadbolt lock. Opening the door, she flipped the switch for her interior light and spotted her Calico cat, Tonto, trotting down the hall to greet her. He was an indoor cat, but every once in a while, he tried to make a run for the outdoors. The few times he'd managed to escape, though, he hadn't gone far. He knew who fed him and was content to be waited on.

She spied a toy mouse on the floor at her feet and kicked it down the hall, sending Tonto chasing after it.

Turning to Thomas, Naomi was surprised to see he stood close to her. Her gaze met his, and her heart rate picked up at the heat she saw there. This was how she'd hoped he would look at her one day. Her mouth went dry as she stuttered, "Th-thanks, again... Sir."

The Dom reached up and cupped her chin. "I enjoyed tonight very much, pet." He took a deep breath and let it out slowly. "I've been thinking that I'm ready to start dating again—finally. If you'll let me, I'd like to take you out for dinner and dancing some night. Someplace other than the club where we can talk and get to know each other outside the lifestyle. Do you think we can do that?"

Her breath hitched. *Holy crap—I must be dreaming. My fantasy man just asked me out on a date. Someone pinch me!* "I-I'd like that very much, Sir."

"Thomas. We aren't at the club and playing, so you can call me by my name, Naomi." Leaning down, he brushed his lips against hers in a sweet, brief kiss. "I'll call you tomorrow evening, and we'll make plans, okay?"

Nodding, she replied, "Yes, Sir... I mean, yes, Thomas. That would be great."

"Good. Now, lock the door so I know you're safe."

Elated at the turn of events, she did as she was told and then waved at him through the window. It wasn't until he drove away that she gave Tonto her full attention. Picking up the cat, she spun around and squealed. "Momma's got a date with the cutest guy in the world! Celebration time. Whoops! I forgot your cat food in the car."

Putting him back on the floor, she grabbed her car

keys from her purse on the hall table. "I'll be right back."

Closing the front door behind her so the cat couldn't escape, Naomi hurried down the steps to the driveway. Using the remote, she popped the trunk of her car and started to pull out the shopping bags of nonperishables she'd gotten from Walmart that afternoon after finishing her nursing shift at the hospital. Not wanting to make two trips, she hooked three bags on her left arm and leaned down to grab the last two.

A strong arm grabbed her around the waist while a hand covered her mouth and nose with a sickeningly-sweet-smelling cloth. She struggled against the hold, dropping her grocery bags to the ground. Trying to pull the hand from her face, twist away, or scream was futile as her mind fogged over and an oppressive darkness overtook her. Her last conscious thought was of Thomas's charming smile and kind eyes.

Ian stood in the observation room, watching the activity on the other side of the one-way mirror. He could see Isaac Webb and another detective speaking with Thomas Manfred, but the men in the interrogation room could not see the observer in return—although the policemen knew Sawyer was there. Earlier in the day, when it was discovered Naomi

Nguyen was missing under similar circumstances as the other submissives, the police had hauled in the last person known to have been with her. Webb had then asked Ian to observe the interview to get the perspective of someone in the BDSM lifestyle. Ian did not believe Manfred had anything to do with the missing women, and he was sure Webb would eventually come to the same conclusion. But, in the meantime, Ian had Brody working on tracking Manfred's pickup truck after it left Spice and followed Naomi home. Webb hadn't minded the geek doing some of the investigative legwork—he wasn't too proud to admit they needed all the help they could get to stop this psychopath. But he was also seasoned enough to make sure any outside intel was verified by someone in the department instead of taking it at face value.

The interview had started off as they usually do, with basic, easy-to-answer questions: How did Manfred know the victim? What happened during the hours leading up to Naomi's disappearance? Did he see anything out of the ordinary? What did Manfred do after he'd left her home?

Ian had known the Dom from The Covenant several years ago, but after Manfred's fiancée had been killed in a car crash, they hadn't run into each other until about six months ago. Manfred had explained he'd put an application in at Spice because, if he hoped to move on with his life, he would never be able to set foot in the club where he'd collared his fiancée ever again. The head Dom of The Covenant had understood and wished the other man the best.

Ian watched as Webb placed photos of the two other missing women and Heather on the table in front of Manfred. The detective's voice came through the speakers. "Do you recognize any of these women?"

The Dom nodded. They could all see the pain and worry in his eyes—haunted was the best way to describe it. Ian felt bad for the guy—first, his fiancée was killed in an accident caused by a drunk driver, and now another woman he obviously cared for was missing at the hand of a probable serial killer. Like most people in the area, Manfred had heard all about the missing submissives and that Heather had been found murdered, but not how she'd been tortured and killed. The police were keeping as many details as possible out of circulation. However, being a smart man, Manfred immediately connected Naomi's disappearance with the others. She'd been discovered missing after failing to show up at work for her scheduled shift.

Manfred pointed to the photos of the first two victims. "I only know these two because I saw their pictures on the news but never met them. I knew Heather from a club we both used to go to, but I haven't seen her in two or three years."

"What club is that?" When Manfred hesitated, apparently not willing to out a private kink club, the detective added, "One of the BDSM clubs in the area?

We know there are several and are working with the owners to keep their members safe."

"Okay, yeah. We were both members of The Covenant..."

He paused, and Webb said, "I'm aware of the club and know the owners, the Sawyers." Of course, the detective failed to mention that one of the owners was currently watching the interview.

Manfred's shoulders relaxed a little. "Okay, good. Um... anyway, like I said, we were both members a while back. But we never played together, if that's your next question. My fiancée and I had been together for at least two years before we met Heather and her Dom, Scott, at the club. After Kim, my fiancée, died almost three years ago, I stopped going to The Covenant and haven't been there since. I only got back into the lifestyle about six months ago, and Spice is the only club I've gone to during that time."

"So, you've never been in The Devil's Dungeon or Heat?"

"No, I haven't—wait, I've never been in The Devil's Dungeon. When Kim was alive, we attended a few parties at Heat, but as guests of other members. I haven't been there in years, though."

Webb moved on to questions about Manfred's whereabouts when the other women disappeared. The Dom couldn't recall off the top of his head about the nights when Christie and Melody went missing. However, the night Heather had been abducted, he'd been in Miami for several days, taking a class with other civil engineers on new state requirements for the profession. He told Webb he was more than welcome to check his flight, hotel, and credit card history and contact the state inspectors who could confirm he was there.

The door to the observation room opened, and Brody and a uniformed officer walked in. The Trident operative carried some photos. "We think he's clear. I was able to track his vehicle through the traffic cams from Spice to Naomi's house and then to his. He drives a pickup, and no one appears to be in the passenger seat or bed. Also, Simmons here spoke to Naomi's neighbor, who was walking his dog when they arrived at her house. He saw Thomas escort her to the door, then drive away after making sure she was inside with the door locked. The neighbor went into his own house minutes later."

Ian hadn't expected anything different and knocked twice on the one-way mirror to get Webb's attention. Both detectives excused themselves, leaving Manfred alone in the room. As soon as the door shut behind them, the man dropped his head in his hands, and his shoulders shook under the weight of his grief. Ian hoped like hell they would find the missing submissive alive; he didn't think Manfred would survive another loss of life.

After piling several bakery boxes filled with goodies into Brody's waiting arms, Fancy grabbed the last two and her purse. Waving goodbye to her staff, she held the front door of the shop open for him. She hadn't been able to decide what to bring to the barbecue at the Trident compound, so she made a little bit of everything, including the PAW Patrol cookies little Mara enjoyed.

Russell Adams ran across the parking lot toward them as they approached Brody's truck. "Let me help you with that, Senior Chief. Hi, Fancy."

Brody jutted his chin toward the back of his truck. "Thanks. Just drop the bed."

"Hi, Russell." Fancy smiled at the Navy veteran.

Adams lowered the pickup bed and dragged over the cooler Brody asked for so they could load the boxes into it to keep them fresh from the eighty-nine-degree heat. At least it wasn't supposed to get much hotter during the day—the temperature was bearable in her skort and tank top.

After Russell had taken the two boxes from her, Fancy glanced around and gasped when she spotted two teenagers stopped on their bicycles on the side-walk in front of the shop. Beside her, Brody froze, trying to figure out what she was looking at. "What is it?"

She pointed at the two teens. "Those boys... they're the ones who caused the trouble in my shop." Without thinking, she shouted, "Hey!"

The teens spun in her direction as Brody spat out, "Shit!"

Fancy realized too late she'd warned the two she'd recognized them as Brody ran after them, ordering Russell to stay with her. The teens took off on their bikes, and it wasn't long before Brody returned, having been unable to catch them.

"The bad news is they got away," he said. "But I should have clear pictures of them on the security camera feeds. I doubt they'll be back today, so I'll check the system later." Opening the passenger door to the truck, he reached into the glove compartment and pulled out a cell phone. Turning it on, he entered a number and then handed Russell the phone with a charger. "Petty Officer Adams, you're officially on my payroll. If you spot those little shits again, call me. It's number one on the speed dial. You can charge the phone at the shelter or in Fancy's shop."

Taking the items, the homeless man stood tall and proud, giving Fancy an image of the seaman he'd been before whatever had caused his PTSD. "Aye, aye, Senior Chief."

"Meet me back here at eighteen hundred hours."

"Yes, sir."

Fancy pointed to the front of the shop. "Go inside and grab something to eat and drink, Russell, and charge the phone if it needs it. I made those sticky pecan rolls you like."

The man's face lit up with delight. "Thank you, Miss Fancy."

"You're welcome. And thank you for watching my shop for us."

"No problem, ma'am. I've got nothing to do, so it'll keep me busy. Don't you worry about a thing." He gave her a friendly wink and Brody a quick salute before heading to the shop.

Climbing into the passenger seat, Fancy put on her seat belt as Brody shut her door, rounded the front of the vehicle, and got in beside her. As he started the engine, she eyed him with curiosity. "What's at eighteen hundred hours? That's six p.m., right?"

"Yeah. I know he wouldn't accept an invitation to the barbecue, even though Devon and Kristen wouldn't have minded at all, but I'll bring him back a load of food for dinner."

"He'll love it. I've been leaving some turkey, cheese, and fresh fruit in the kitchen for when he stops in. As much as he loves my pastries, all that sugar can't be good for him, so I make sure I have some healthy stuff ready for him too."

Before putting the car in reverse, Brody leaned over, gave her a quick kiss on the mouth, then stared into her eyes. He started to say something but stopped and nervously stroked her hair behind her ear. Grabbing her hand, he brought it to his lips and kissed the back of it. Then he took a deep breath before letting it out slowly as his gaze flicked to hers again, and she was stunned to see a deep emotion there. "I've been putting off saying this for a while because I wasn't sure if you were ready to hear it, but I can't hold back anymore. I love you, Fancy-girl. I'm totally, helplessly, head-over-ass in love with you."

CHAPTER EIGHTEEN

"Angie, can I help you with anything?" Fancy asked, approaching the other woman standing by the outdoor kitchen in *Ian's Oasis*, putting the finishing touches on a cheese platter. Brody had been right about the beautiful "backyard" Ian's fiancée had created for his birthday last year. It ran the length of the two warehouses it sat between and was nicer than most yards she'd ever seen. In addition to the fully functioning kitchen and huge grill, there was an oblong fire pit, a koi pond with a waterfall at the far end, and plenty of conversation seating areas with shade from patio umbrellas. An all-weather, flat-screen TV with stereo surround sound, a bar, and a cooling spray system for the sweltering Florida summers gave it all the comforts of an indoor living room. The asphalt had been torn up and replaced with sod, along with bushes and flower beds, which resulted in a tropical garden atmosphere.

Angie shook her head. "No, thanks, I think everything is set. Kristen's mom, Jenn, and Kat have worked hard for the past two hours, and now everyone can relax. When Ian fires up the grill, you can help me put all the salads and stuff out."

Quite a few people had come to celebrate the newest arrival, and little JD was handling his local fame just fine. He was such a happy little baby and didn't mind being passed from one admirer to the next. Currently suckling his mother's breast, he appeared to be dozing off in the middle of his meal as Kristen talked with her mom and stepdad, Elizabeth and Ed Finch. The couple were leaving Tuesday to visit friends in Naples before returning to New Jersey.

Fancy glanced around and tried to put the correct names to the faces of the rest of Brody's friends and second family. She'd been introduced to the seven new members of the Omega team, the company's new computer tech, Nathan, and their helicopter pilot, Tempest, who went by her nickname, "Babs." Ian's and Devon's brother Nick and his Dom/boyfriend, Jake, who she remembered was one of the original six-man Trident team, had flown in from San Diego for a few days to meet Nick's new nephew. Ian's goddaughter, Jenn Mullins, sat by the pond, chatting with Kristen's cousin, Will Anders, and playing patty-cake with Marco and Harper's daughter, Mara, who had recently turned one.

Kat and Boomer had arrived a few minutes ago with Boomer's parents, Rick and Eileen, and the older couple's charge, Alyssa Wagner. When the pretty teenager spotted Jake and Nick, she squealed and threw herself into their arms. Brody had told Fancy how the two men had saved the girl's life not too long ago.

Also in attendance were several people Fancy had met at the club the other night, including Colleen and Reggie, Roxy and Kayla, Mistress China, whose real name was Charlotte, Mitch Sawyer, Shelby and Parker, Tiny, and Master Carl. The latter looked so different from how he'd appeared when she'd first met him. In his fifties, the man was six feet tall and slender, with dark hair, a mustache, and a goatee. He'd been dressed in all black on Wednesday evening, and her immediate response had been that he would have made a perfect Count Dracula in an old black-and-white movie. Add in the fact he was a sadist and Whip Master, and the image was an ideal fit. Today, though, he looked more like the college math professor he was in the real world, wearing khaki shorts and a yellow golf shirt.

Her eyes searched for Brody and spotted him talking to Boomer and Rick. She still reeled from his announcement that he loved her—but in a good way. She had suspected he would say those words to her sometime soon and feared how it would make her feel.

But to her surprise, the words had warmed her and caused her heart rate to increase. It was then she knew she was in love with him too. How had she gotten so lucky to have fallen in love with two of the most incredible and caring men to have walked the earth? Despite a few similarities in their personalities, they were totally different—as men and as Doms. And she thanked God she hadn't known them at the same time because choosing between them would have been the hardest thing she would ever have had to do.

After his declaration of love, he said he didn't want her to say it back until she was one hundred percent certain. She'd giggled and responded, "Well, since I'm only ninety-nine percent certain I'm in love with you, you'll have to wait a little while longer."

He'd laughed, called her a brat, and promised to spank her later for teasing him. Of course, that had made her horny as hell, and she decided to let him suffer for a few more hours before professing her own absolute love when it wasn't in response to his words.

Now, grinning that he caught her staring, Brody crooked his finger at her. She stepped over to the trio, and her lover tucked her under his arm, where she loved to be. When Harper and Marco joined them, Mara leaned out of her father's arms, her hands reaching for Fancy. Laughing, she took the baby and cuddled her as she cooed, "Such a big girl."

Brody leaned down and whispered in her ear. "You look beautiful with her in your arms."

Studying him, she responded in a quiet voice so the others wouldn't hear, "You never asked if I could have children after the miscarriage. Why not?"

As the baby played with Fancy's red hair, Brody cupped her chin. "Two reasons. One—I figured you would tell me when the time was right for you. And two—because it doesn't make me love you any less. Our own baby, or one we adopt or have through a surrogate, will be loved by me no matter what. Whether our children grow inside you or not doesn't make a difference. They'll still grow in our hearts."

She gaped at him as Mara wiggled in her arms, reaching out to her mother. Fancy passed the baby to Harper, then grabbed Brody's hand and dragged him around the corner of the building for some privacy.

His brow furrowed as she pushed him against the wall, her hands on his chest. "Sweetness, what's wrong? What did I say?"

Clutching his shirt, she pulled him down for a passionate kiss, her mouth and tongue taking possession of his. He closed the last few inches between their bodies, and she felt his erection grow against her abdomen. When she finally released him, she looked him in the eye. "What did you say? Everything right, *that's* what. I love you, Brody Evans. I'm madly, passionately in love with you."

Brody stormed into the police station's detective bureau and was met by Webb and Freddie Mendoza. He'd given them the photos he printed from the bakery's security system of the two teens yesterday after escorting Fancy to the shop and having breakfast with her. The punks had ridden their mountain bikes close enough to the store's front door for him to get clear pictures of them. After Webb had shown the photos to a few of the day shift cops in turnout that morning, the two had been identified as some local troublemakers. They'd been picked up an hour ago and brought in for questioning.

"Where are the little shits?" he asked, glancing around. "Which interrogation room?"

Webb held up his hands. "Easy. You're not going in there."

"Why the fuck not?"

Freddie pointed behind him and said, "That's why not."

Spinning on his heels, Brody spotted the teens sneering at him as they stood with two men in suits—fucking lawyers, although one of them was probably the father of the similar-looking boys. They had to be brothers.

Brody stepped forward, but a hand grabbed his arm from behind and stopped him from getting too close. "You little shits. If I find out you're behind the vandalism of that shop, I'll make your lives fucking miserable."

"Was that a threat?" asked the man Brody suspected was related to the boys. "I want that man arrested for threatening my sons."

"Yeah, well, I want your pitiful offspring arrested for harassing my woman and damaging her shop."

Webb and Mendoza put their bodies between the adversaries. "Nobody is getting arrested today," the latter said.

At the same time, one of the other men replied, "They did no such thing, and you have no evidence to the contrary."

Brody snarled. "When I get my proof, I'll shove it down your throats. You're not the only one who can hire high-priced lawyers. I'll sue your fucking ass off. If I see those two little shits anywhere near that bakery again, you better hope I don't catch them."

"Are you going to stand there and let him threaten my sons? I want him arrested right now!"

Webb turned his head so they could all hear him. "Like we said, no one's getting arrested. Barker, get your clients out of here and keep them away from that bakery. Otherwise, I'll be filing harassment charges against them, and you can fight it out in court."

Barker was the taller of the two men and wisely ushered everyone from the room to the main lobby. Webb finally let go of Brody's arm. "That went well."

Running a hand through his hair in frustration, Brody tried to get his anger under control. He didn't want to take it out on the cops—their hands were tied in this mess. Without proof, they couldn't press charges, and with the lawyers involved, the teens wouldn't be allowed to answer any questions that might incriminate them. "They need to reinstate the draft—the future of our society is shit if we leave it to these punks."

"Ain't that the fucking truth?"

Mendoza nodded his head in agreement. "By the way, Egghead. I finally had a chance to track down the follow-up reports on Fancy's accident. The brake line had a jagged cut like it hit a rock or something. Her brother-in-law was interviewed back then and confirmed he and Patrick had gone four-wheeling the day before the accident at Holder Mine. Said they bottomed out a few times. The conclusion was that it had caused a small leak and was signed off as accidental."

Brody grimaced. In the past, he'd gone four-wheeling at the Holder Mine Campgrounds, north of Tampa, with some friends, but it had been a while. The place was a lot of fun, but the sport always had potential dangers. "Not the first time I've heard of that happening. A buddy of mine in the Navy lost a cousin that way."

"Hey, Webb!" They all turned to see a sergeant walking toward them, frowning. He handed the detective a slip of paper with an address on it. "A patrol car just called in. They've got a DB and think it's that missing girl. They said they hope you haven't had lunch yet."

"Fuck!" The detective went to his desk and grabbed what he needed while barking the info at his partner.

Brody stepped away from the officers and shot off a text to Ian.

> TPD has a reported dead body that might be the missing sub. Don't want to step on Webb's toes, but I think it's time to use a few connections and get the feds involved. Need a profiler.

The response was swift.

BOSS-MAN

> Fuck. Before I make the calls, confirm it's our girl. Send me the address if you have it.

"Evans!" Webb stood in the doorway, waving Brody closer. "Do you mind following us over there? We need your eyes and experience."

That was easier than he'd expected. "Sure. What's the address?"

After they confirmed Naomi's identity, Webb went with his partner to make the death notifications to the woman's mother. They then told Thomas Manfred out of courtesy so he didn't have to hear it on the news.

By the time the two detectives returned to their station, Ian and Brody had spoken to the captain in charge of the detectives, Vic Moody, and not so subtly convinced him to push aside his issues with the feds and call them for help. Trident Security had many connections, including Tampa's Chief of Police and others who could make the man's life miserable. Of course, they agreed to make it seem like it was his idea the whole time, ensuring he got the kudos when the case was, hopefully, solved. It was a safe assumption the first two missing women were long dead, but the killer was now seeking recognition for his work and placing the victims where they would ultimately be found.

At 5:00 p.m., the new task force was in place and met in a large conference room at police headquarters. If Brody hadn't been so disgusted with what he'd seen earlier, he would have greatly enjoyed the shocked look on Special Agent in Charge Frank Stonewall's face. The FBI supervisor and the Trident team had a mutual dislike for each other, having had quite a few run-ins before. What pissed the fed off even more was Ian had Stonewall's boss on speed dial. Larry Keon was the number two man in the FBI and the source of many of Trident's covert missions.

"What the fuck are they doing here?" Stonewall barked at no one in particular, but he was clearly referring to Ian and Brody.

"They're here on my dime," Moody responded. "Deal with it. Let's get started." Webb was right—Moody disliked Stonewall just as much as, if not more than, everyone else in the room.

Over a dozen members of the joint task force took seats as Moody and Webb began to fill them in. Brody glanced at the clock on the wall. Hopefully, it wouldn't run too late; he and Boomer had an early detail in the morning. He was bummed he wouldn't see Fancy later but glad the Trident women and friends had taken her under their wings. Harper, Kat, Shelby, Kayla, and Angie were taking her out to dinner and a movie—some chick flick the subs were dying to see. Kristen had been too exhausted with JD's sleeping schedule to join them but promised she would be there the next time they all went out.

With the discovery of Naomi's body, Ian had spoken to Mitch about reinforcing the rules of escorting the submissives home from the club. However, that hadn't helped the latest victim. From what they could tell, she'd gone back outside after Thomas had left, probably to get some things from her car. The crime scene techs had found groceries, including cat food, in the trunk of her Ford Focus and a famished cat inside the house. Naomi's phone was in her purse on a table in the foyer.

Brody wasn't taking any chances with Fancy, though, especially with those punks causing all sorts of trouble on top of the serial killer. After leaving the location where Naomi's mutilated body had been found, he swung by the Trident compound and grabbed the tracking bracelet he wanted her to wear until this creep was caught. The unassuming piece of jewelry had been used before when Angie and then Kat had been in trouble. The device had a GPS tracker and a one-way microphone that could be heard through a computer program if his laptop or tablet were close enough to the source. It had been a vital tool in rescuing the women after each had ended up being held hostage at different times.

At first, he'd used a medical alert bracelet for the device since they tended to be thicker, and most people wouldn't question it, but Angie and Kristen had convinced him to find something a little more stylish. Their point had been that if a bad guy knew enough about his victim, he might know they didn't need a medical alert tag. With the help of the jeweler who did many of the submissives' custom collars, Brody had come up with a design they liked yet still met his requirements. Tomorrow, after his morning detail, he would swing by Fancy's shop and put it on her—for now, it was in his pants pocket.

He had to get a few more tracking bracelets up and running. Angie and Kristen had nothing to worry about living in the secure Trident compound, but

Boomer and Marco wanted Kat and Harper to each have one, just in case. And he didn't blame them. Hopefully, this newly formed task force would find this sick bastard before another submissive went missing. And God help his next victim if they didn't.

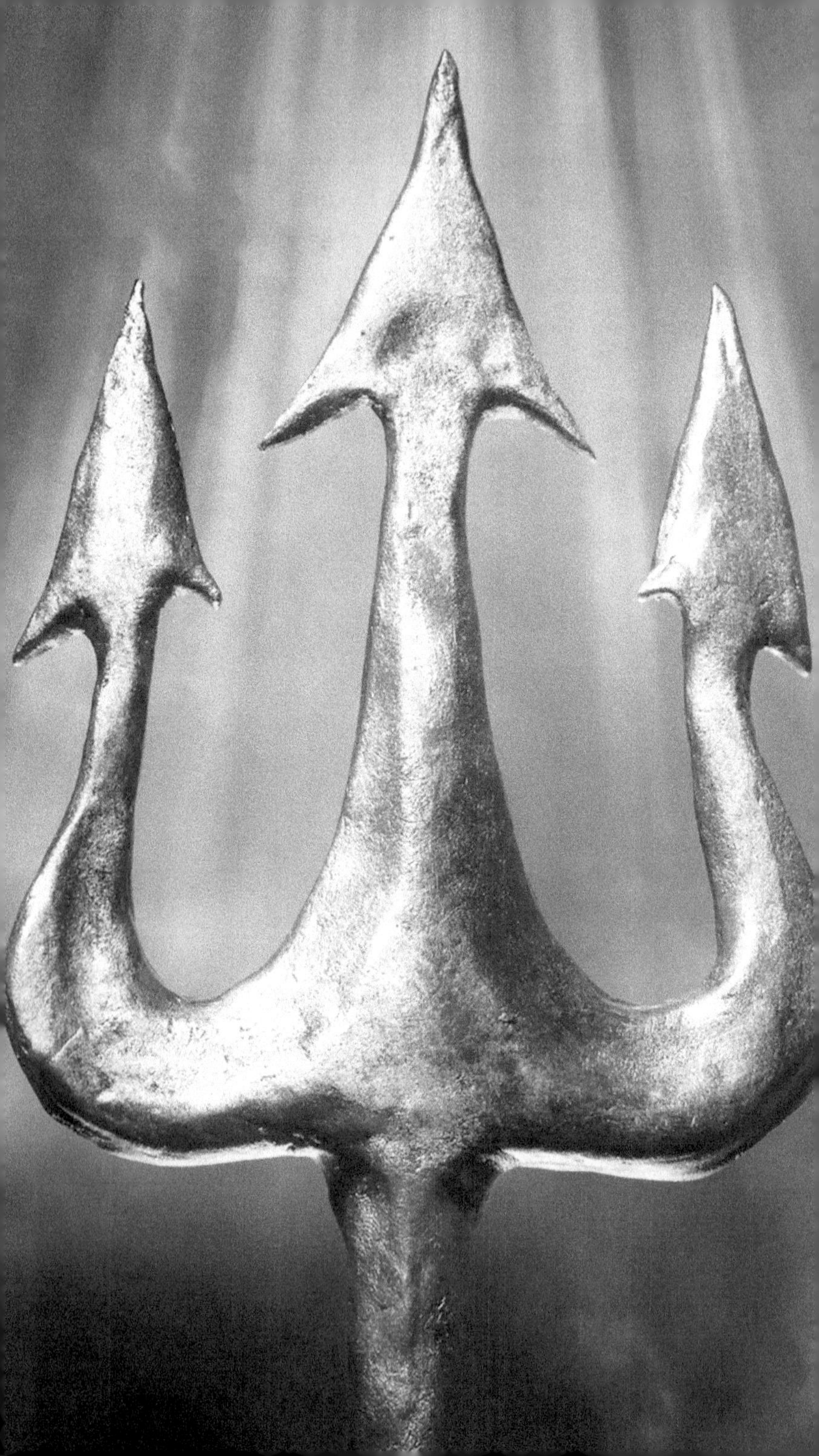

CHAPTER NINETEEN

Brody was glad the girls had invited Fancy out to dinner with them. It would give her a chance to get to know all of them better. If he had any say in the matter, which he did, she'd be a part of both of his families soon—here and in Texas. He knew they were headed in that direction, but he had to give her time to get used to their relationship before springing an engagement ring and permanent collar on her.

Was Christmas too soon? He sure as hell hoped not. He wanted everyone to know Fancy was his, and his alone for the rest of their lives. His father had always told him when he met the right woman, he'd feel as if he'd known her all his life. And that was exactly how he felt about his little baker. She was the second half of his heart and soul he'd been waiting for over the past thirty-six years.

It had been a long day with the two teenage shit bags, the crime scene, and the task force, and he was looking forward to vegging out in the hot tub for a while and just relaxing. The image of Naomi Nguyen's mutilated body was still fresh in his mind, and he continued to try, unsuccessfully, to shake it free. The sun had set about a half hour ago, but he enjoyed being in the spa in the dark; it soothed him. As much as he wanted Fancy in his bed tonight, he was due to get up far too early in the morning for the surveillance gig with Boomer. It would be best to let her get a good night's sleep since they were going to the club tomorrow night.

Speaking of tomorrow, he had to remember to drop his Navy dress whites at the dry cleaners after work so they would be ready for Ian and Angie's wedding. Fancy had taken that afternoon off from work and would meet him at the church after she made sure the cake got to the reception in one piece. He was also going to see if she would take the weekend of the hoedown off and accompany him to Texas. He couldn't wait to introduce her to his parents and siblings and was confident they would love her instantly.

As he made a right turn toward his neighborhood, his cell phone rang. Hitting the button on his steering wheel, he connected the call to his car's Bluetooth system, which automatically silenced the music from the radio. "Hello?"

A familiar male voice came over the speakers. "Hey, Brody, it's Corey. I'm at Fancy's shop. I saw someone run behind the building as I was driving past. He's gone, but... I think you better get over here. Is Fancy with you?"

His gut clenched. "No. She went out with a few girls for dinner. What's wrong?"

"I don't know. I don't even know what I'm looking at. I'm calling the cops as soon as I hang up with you. I think there's a dead body in the woods back here, but it's such a mess. I don't want to risk screwing up a crime scene."

Fuck! Was there a body like Heather's and the other girl dumped behind Fancy's shop? Maybe it was one of the missing submissives who had disappeared before Heather. Brody glanced in his side view mirrors and did a U-turn. "I'm less than five minutes away. Don't touch anything."

"I won't. Let me hang up and call the police. I'll see you in a few."

A few minutes later, Brody sped into the bakery's parking lot. It must be a busy night because he'd beaten the cops there. This part of town was mostly shops which had shut down hours ago and there was very little traffic. That was one of the reasons he was glad Fancy hadn't had insomnia lately, giving her the urge to bake in the middle of the night. Stopping near the back of the shop next to Corey's truck, he threw the gear in park and killed the engine. Grabbing his

Mag-lite from under the seat, he opened the door and jumped out. "Corey?"

"Yo, back here!" The man stuck his head around the corner of the brick building. "The cops are on their way, but apparently, the full moon is fucking with the call volume. Dispatch said they'll get someone here as soon as they can and not to disturb the scene. You can kind of see it without getting too close, but it's covered in a lot of brush."

"Let me take a look."

He rounded the corner and started walking toward where Fancy's brother-in-law was pointing. As he passed the man, pain shot through him, and his legs buckled when nearly 50,000 volts of electricity from a Taser being held on his exposed neck coursed through his body. His hand lost its grip on the flashlight, and he dropped hard and fast to the ground as his muscles spasmed out of control. When the device cut off after five seconds as it was supposed to, he barely felt the needle that was stabbed into his upper arm. As he tried to figure out what the hell had just happened he sank into a sea of darkness.

Russell Adams watched helplessly as the bastard who'd stabbed him in the chest earlier picked up an unconscious Senior Chief Evans. Using a fireman's carry, he loaded him into the bed of the retired SEAL's Ford F-150. The man pulled a tarp from his own truck and covered Evans with it before starting the Chevy and driving away in it.

Despite his wound slowly bleeding despite the dirty bandana he'd shoved in it, Russell tried to crawl through the wooded area to help the man who'd been nothing but kind to a fellow seaman. But the blood loss was making him weak, and he couldn't go more than a foot or two before stopping. He'd seen the man before in Fancy's shop, and according to the cute, blonde girl who worked with Fancy in the morning, the guy was the owner's brother-in-law and a city fireman.

Pain coursed through Russell's body, forcing an unwanted flashback into his mind. Russell's last tour in Iraq had been the worst. Assigned to Camp Bucca, one of the U.S. Naval bases in that part of the world, he'd been there through numerous attacks on American personnel, both on and off the base. They had been on constant alert for suicide bombers and Iraqis pretending to be allies when, in reality, they were trying to get on the base to kill as many Americans as possible. Russell had lost one of his best friends in one incident and missed being KIA himself by a mere five minutes. A suicide bomber had gotten close enough to one of the camp's manned gates to kill three naval guards who had relieved Russell and two others from duty minutes before. That was when his PTSD symptoms started taking over his life. Now medically discharged, he was wary of everyone—not a good way to be unless you lived on a deserted island.

Running footsteps caught his attention, bringing his mind back to the present. The assailant must have parked his Chevy nearby because he'd returned and was climbing into the driver's seat of Evans's Ford. Russell's heart plummeted when the vehicle backed out of the parking space and took off as if on a Sunday afternoon drive.

His head spun, and he stopped to rest again. Going after the truck was not an option. Neither was calling for help—the bastard had searched his pockets and found the cell phone Evans had given him and smashed it to pieces, and pay phones were hard to come by these days. There had to be a way to save himself and the senior chief—there had to be.

Russell collapsed at the edge of the parking lot, barely out of the bushes. No one was around, and even if there was, he didn't have the strength to yell or get their attention. Maybe, if he rested a bit, he could crawl across the lot and flag down someone driving by. *Rest... just for a minute or two.*

Glancing at his watch again, Boomer paced the parking lot in front of the Trident offices. Brody was fifteen minutes late, which was highly unusual—the geek was never late.

Boomer pulled out his phone and hit the speed dial for his friend. "Hey, Egghead. It's me again. Get out of Fancy's bed, if that's where you're at, and get your ass to work. If I don't hear from you in five minutes, I'll head out and let you know how to catch up with me. See you in a bit."

Hanging up, he climbed into his truck and started the engine. It was way too early to wake anyone else up. None of his teammates would appreciate a call at 0300. He could handle this detail alone as long as the guy they were supposed to follow didn't notice he was being shadowed. That was why the team liked to use two vehicles in this type of situation... they could hopscotch and alternate tailing the subject. The only problem was the guy they would be tailing usually left at 4:00 a.m. when there was almost no traffic on the roads.

After seven minutes, Boomer knew he couldn't wait any longer because it was a fifteen-minute ride to the target's house. Putting the truck in drive, he left the compound. Once he reached his destination, if he still hadn't heard from Brody, he'd send Ian a text. The last thing he wanted to do was wake the boss. It was like walking into a bear's den shouting, "Hi, honey, I'm home"—not a good, fucking thing to do.

Devon strode through the door to his brother's office, not even bothering to knock. "Any word?"

It was a rhetorical question. Brody had been missing for at least three hours, and Ian would have let him know if the status had changed. After getting the early morning call from Boomer, the eldest Sawyer had gotten into his car and gone looking for their AWOL teammate. In their business and experience, a missing man usually spelled trouble.

The geek and his truck were nowhere to be found. His boss had let himself into Brody's house to find it empty, then drove past Fancy's apartment. Ian didn't want to awaken the woman and worry her unnecessarily, but it was getting to the point where they would have to question her.

"No. The computer's not picking up any signal from his cell phone, and I drove all over the place trying to figure out where he might be. Cook will be here in about twenty minutes, but I can't think of anything he can do that I haven't already done." The new computer tech would need a starting point, and since they didn't have one yet, he'd be spinning his wheels just like everyone else. "I swear I'm ordering tracking devices and implanting them in everyone's ass around here. I'm fucking tired of people going off on their own and getting into trouble. Usually, it's the women around here, but the guys have done their fair share, too."

Dropping into a visitor's chair, Dev rubbed his tired eyes. You'd think after years of being a SEAL, he'd be used to functioning on little sleep. JD had been up half the night crying. Then after the baby was finally asleep, and his father had been just drifting off, Ian had called him at 4:45 a.m. "I'm worried."

"So am I, brother," Ian replied, the frustration in his voice was unmistakable. "But I have no idea where else to look for him. I've got Marco and the Omega team out searching the entire city for him. I called Chase Dixon, and he's sending one of his guys to relieve Boomer, so he'll be free in a bit. And I also just put a call into Isaac Webb to put an APB out on Egghead's truck. If you've got any other suggestions, I'm all ears." They both knew the police usually wouldn't take a missing person's report until twenty-four hours had passed, at the very least, but thankfully, they had plenty of connections and could bypass the waiting period.

"Do you think this has anything to do with the missing submissives? I mean, is it possible this guy is targeting anyone in the lifestyle?" Devon didn't know what to think. He didn't think a serial killer would stray that far from his routine MO and victim type, but then again, he'd never before seen or heard of what the bastard terrorizing the BDSM community in Tampa was doing.

Ian sighed and stood, picking up his empty coffee cup. "I don't know, but we have to consider every angle." He was about to round his desk when the landline phone rang. Reaching over, he stabbed the speaker key. "Sawyer."

"Ian, it's Webb—"

Devon flew to his feet. "Did you find Brody?"

"No. But I may have a lead. Just got a call from a patrol car. He found a half-unconscious guy in a parking lot with a stab wound. I pulled up at the same time as the medics. The guy was alert enough to hand the officer a business card. It's Evans' Trident card. Before we could question him further, the victim passed out. He's going to need surgery as soon as possible. I'm pulling up to the ER at Tampa General now."

Grabbing his keys and cell phone from the desk, Ian said, "I'm on my way. Wait a second... what parking lot?"

"It's for a few shops—a dry cleaner, a bakery, and two other stores."

As Devon's eyes grew wide, Ian's gut clenched. "Fancy Creations Bakery?"

"Yeah, how'd you know?"

"Fuck, I'll tell you when I get there. I'm on my way." Ian disconnected the call and hurried out of the office with Devon on his heels. "What the fuck is going on?"

"No clue, but I'm going with you."

Ian hopped into his car and sped out of the compound with Devon in the passenger seat, sending out texts to update everyone. Ian just prayed the victim, whoever he was, held on long enough to give them a lead to Brody if he had one.

Ian and Devon strode into the ER waiting room and made a beeline for Detective Webb when they spotted him standing with a uniformed officer. Webb turned their way, and Ian didn't bother with pleasantries. "Did you talk to him?"

The tall, black man shook his head. "No. The paramedics said he almost coded in the bus. The doctors are still working to stabilize him before they send him to surgery."

A "bus" was what many medics and cops called an ambulance, and "coding" was when a person stopped breathing and went into cardiac arrest. If this guy knew what happened to Brody and died before they could talk to him, they were screwed. "Fuck. What happened?"

The beat cop stepped forward. "I had the bakery on my list of properties to check during my shift.

Apparently, the shop's had a lot of vandalism lately." Ian knew all about that, so he nodded for the man to continue. "I was going to check behind the building, and suddenly, I saw this homeless guy on the ground at the back of the lot. Had just enough strength to flag me down, I guess. He was really out of it, and after calling for a bus, I got out the first aid bag and tried to stop the bleeding from a stab wound to his chest. I think the only reason he's still alive is he stuffed a bandana in the wound and laid on his stomach, which slowed the bleeding. He kept grabbing for my hand—I thought he was trying to stop me from treating him, but then I noticed this in his hand." The man held up a clear evidence bag with a dirty and bloody business card in it... *Trident Security, Inc., Brody Evans.* "Then he managed to speak, but all he said was 'help him.'"

"'Help him' as in 'help me?' Or 'help *him*?'" Ian asked for clarification.

The officer shook the evidence bag in his hand. "I understood it as 'help *him*.' As in help Brody Evans. That's all I got as the medics pulled up and took over."

"All right. Thanks, officer."

The man nodded and then went back to his paperwork. Ian turned to Webb and was about to ask something when a nurse opened the door to the treatment area. "Detective?"

Webb approached the woman. "Yes?"

"The doctor wants to send the patient up to

surgery, but he's awake and won't leave until he talks to a police officer. You have to hurry."

She held the door open for the man, but when Ian began to follow, she tried to stop him. "Sir, you can't—"

"Yes, he can," Webb told her over his shoulder. "He's with me."

Ian was glad the detective intervened because there was no way he wouldn't talk to the injured man, and he would've raised hell if he had to. When they entered the trauma room, the man was lying on a gurney with two nurses and a doctor doing everything they could to keep him alive. They attached the portable monitors and IV bags to the stretcher for transport. The victim's hips and legs were covered with a white sheet, and a pressure bandage was taped over his wound. IV tubes and monitor wires snaked from various parts of his body to whatever they were connected to. Beeps came from several devices, indicating the man was still alive.

When the detective stepped forward, a nurse said, "According to his Navy dog tags, his name is Russell Adams. You need to make it quick. We have to get him to surgery."

Upon hearing his name, Adams opened his eyes. Webb stood near the head of the gurney where he could be seen. "My name is Detective Webb, Russell. You wanted to talk to me?"

"Y-yes." The injured man's voice was raspy and filled with pain. "H-help him."

"Help who? Brody Evans?"

Adams weakly nodded and swallowed several times, trying to gather moisture in his mouth to speak. "Kid-kid... nap."

Webb's eyes went to Ian's in alarm and then back to Adams. "Kidnapped? He was kidnapped?"

"Y-yes."

Several monitors began blaring at once as Adams gasped for air. The doctor and nurses pushed the two men out of the way to get to their patient. Using his foot, the doctor unlocked the gurney and began rolling it toward the door. "We have to get him to surgery now, or we'll lose him."

Adams' hand shot out to weakly grab Ian's arm. "Fire... f-fire... m-man."

The staff raced the gurney to the elevator as Ian and Webb stared after them. "Fireman?" the detective asked. "What the hell did he mean by that?"

Ian shook his head and then led the way back to the waiting room. "I have no fucking clue, but you bet your ass I'm going to find out."

While they had been in the trauma room, Boomer and Marco had arrived and joined Devon. The three men stopped talking when Ian approached. "Do any of you know what this guy meant when he said a fireman kidnapped Brody?"

"Fuck!" Both Boomer and Marco spat out the

curse, but the latter scrambled to explain. "Fancy's brother-in-law, Corey Maguire, he's a fireman. It's got to be him. I knew something about that guy didn't sit right with me, but why the fuck would he kidnap Brody?"

"I don't know, but it's time to pay Fancy a visit, and she better not be involved in this... whatever *this* fucking is."

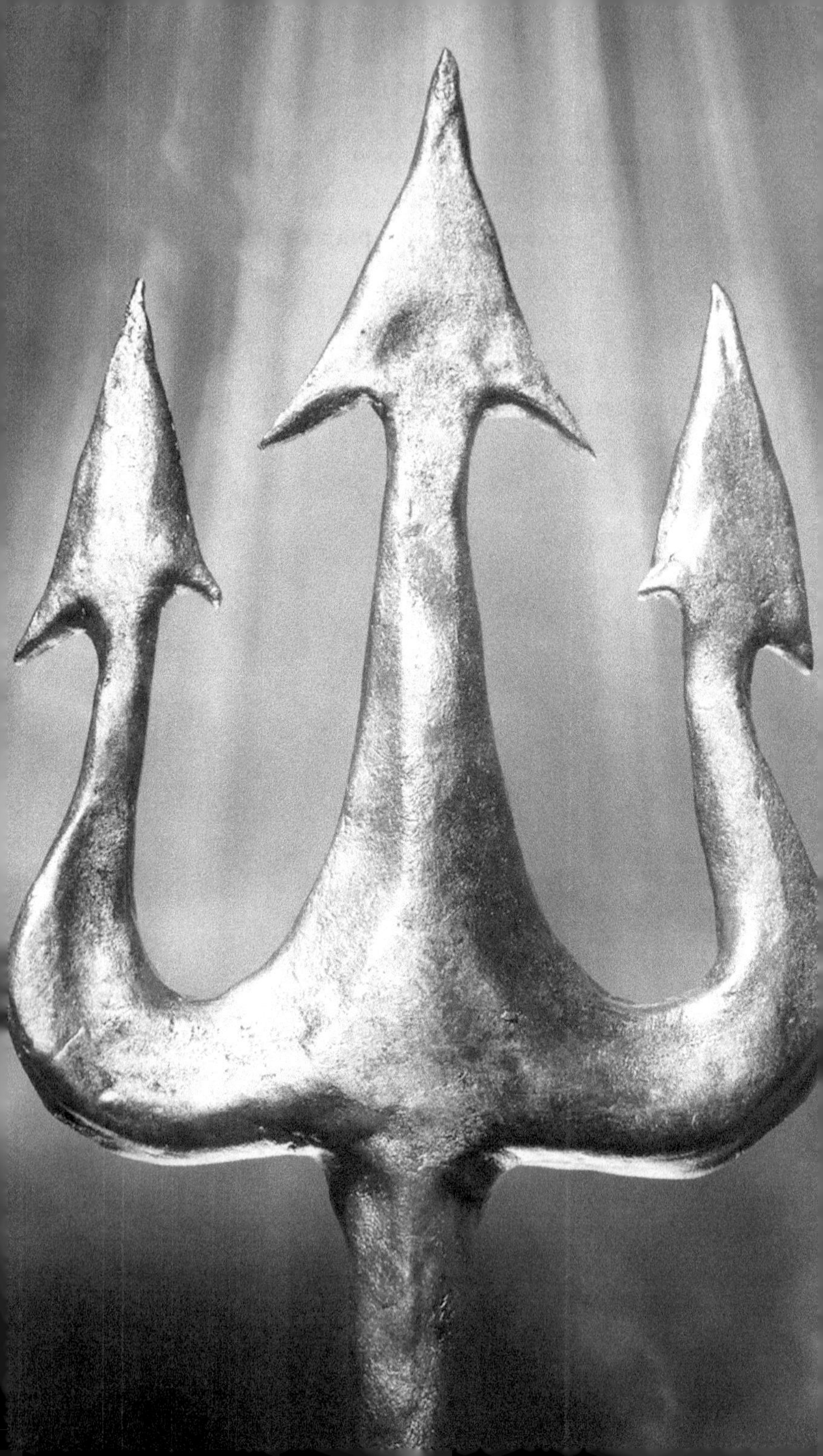

CHAPTER TWENTY

Fancy's jaw dropped as she pulled into the parking lot and saw two patrol cars and a crime scene unit. Sal was standing with one of the uniformed officers, and the relief she felt when she saw he was okay was brief. *What the hell had happened this time?* It couldn't be another vandalism, not with this much of a response.

Her gut clenched as she parked and hurried over to find out what happened. "Sal—"

He held up a hand, stopping her from asking the question on the tip of her tongue. "It's Russell, Fancy. The homeless veteran. He was assaulted sometime last night, back there."

She gasped. "Oh my God! Is he okay? What... who..."

The female officer hung up the cell phone she'd

been talking on and stepped toward her. "Are you Fancy Maguire?"

"Yes, I'm Fancy. What—"

"I need you to stay here, ma'am. A detective is on his way to speak with you."

Fancy was confused as she glanced around, trying to make sense of what was happening. "To me? But I wasn't even here. I don't even know what's going on. Is Russell okay?"

"I don't know, ma'am," the officer replied. "All I do know is they're taking him to surgery, and Detective Webb wants to speak to you specifically and told me to wait with you."

She didn't like the sound of that. It was almost as if they thought she was the person who had hurt the homeless veteran. She'd never hurt a fly. Pulling her phone out of her purse, she called the one person she needed right now—Brody. She groaned inwardly when the call went to voicemail. He was probably still on that detail, which had started in the wee morning hours. Not wanting to worry him until she could actually speak to him or had more information, she hung up without leaving a message.

Noticing the time on the screen of the phone, she turned to the cop again. "Officer, is it okay if Sal prepares the bakery for business? I can call in another employee to help him."

When the other woman nodded, Sal told Fancy,

"I'll call Jamie from inside. Don't worry, I'll get everything set up."

"Thanks. I'll be in as soon as I can."

Her employee took one last look at the back of the lot, where several crime scene techs were searching the area in a grid-like fashion, before shaking his head sadly and heading to the shop's front door. Fancy knew how he felt. While she didn't know Russell Adams well —he wasn't a very talkative man—he was very friendly and polite and didn't deserve to be assaulted by anyone. She prayed he was okay and realized she didn't know if he had any family who needed to be contacted. Maybe Brody would be able to help locate them.

When several vehicles pulled into the parking lot, led by a typical-looking, unmarked police car, Fancy was no closer to figuring out what was happening. The most likely scenario she could come up with was her vandal had come to do some more damage, and Russell had tried to stop him. After the vehicles had parked, she was surprised to see Ian, Devon, Marco, and Boomer climb out of them, along with a tall, black man with a shoulder holster on and a gold shield clipped to his belt.

Her gut clenched at their grim expressions, and she hurried to meet them. "Oh, my God. He's dead, isn't he?"

Ian's eyes narrowed as he snarled. "You tell us. Where did your brother-in-law take him, and why?"

Huh? "Corey?" Fancy shook her head in confusion. "What's he got to do with Russell? I thought Russell was at the hospital about to go into surgery."

"I'm not talking about Adams! Where's Brody?"

Now, she was baffled and getting more so by the second. "He's working, isn't he? He told me he was doing a detail very early this morning with Boo..." Her words trailed off as she realized Boomer was here and not with Brody. Fear began to flow through her body, causing her to pale and tremble. "W-what's going on? Someone, please tell me what's going on because I have no idea—"

Marco's glare softened as he held up his hand to cut her off. "Ian, I think she's telling the truth. She has no clue that Corey kidnapped Brody."

"What! What do you mean Corey kidnapped Brody? Th-that's crazy."

The detective stepped forward. "Let me start at the beginning, since we're just making you more confused at this point. My name is Detective Isaac Webb. On a routine check of your business for vandalism, a patrol officer found Russell Adams on the ground back there." He pointed to the far end of the lot where the techs were still working. "He'd been stabbed in the chest but was still alive. While the officer was trying to administer first aid, Adams handed him a business card—Brody Evans's—and said we had to help him. We didn't get any more from Adams until they were just about to take him up to surgery. He said that a fireman had kidnapped Evans. Now, do you have any idea why your brother-in-law would kidnap Evans and where he would take him?"

Fancy shook her head vehemently. She was frightened because Brody was missing, but there was no way Corey could be involved in it. "That's crazy! Corey kidnapping Brody? Why would Russell say something like that? I've known Corey for ten years, Detective, and there is no way he would kidnap Brody or anyone else. C-can't you track Brody's phone or something to find him?"

"We tried," Boomer explained. "There's no signal coming from it or Corey's. We need to take a look at your security camera video. There may be something on it to help us confirm or refute Corey's involvement."

"Yes... sure, of course. Come into the shop."

On trembling legs, she led the way into the bakery and back to her office. It was like being inside a gym locker with five large men in there with her. Boomer sat at her desk, and after her computer had booted up, his fingers flew across the keyboard. Four video feeds popped up on the monitor, but they weren't moving. The pictures showed the empty parking lot, the alley behind the shop, and the front entrance.

"Shit," Boomer said. "The feeds were turned off at just after seven last night. Nothing has been recorded since then." He glanced at Fancy before meeting Ian's glare. "Maguire has keys to the place and insisted we show him how the system worked in case Fancy had trouble. She okayed it." He turned back to Fancy. "Does anyone else here know how to get into the system to disable the cameras besides you and Corey?"

"No, no one." Of course, she'd given Corey the keys and passwords to the security system, never thinking he would do anything to harm her business—or Brody. She didn't want to believe he had done what they were saying he'd done, but the evidence was beginning to pile up, circumstantial as it all was at the moment. "I-I don't... I can't... why would Corey do this?"

Stepping out of the office, a grim-faced Detective Webb pulled his cell phone out. The only thing Fancy heard him say into it was "ABP" and her brother-in-law's name. Light-headed, she swayed on her feet, and Boomer jumped up, maneuvering the chair in front of him as Marco grabbed her arms to steady her. Settling her into the now-vacated chair, Brody's best friend squatted before her. "Sweetheart, where would Corey take him? We've already sent a patrol car to his apartment, and neither Corey nor Brody's trucks are there, and they aren't at Brody's house either. Does Corey own any other property or hang out somewhere secluded on a regular basis?"

"No. I can't think of any place, and he only owns his apartment, as far as I know. M-maybe some of the guys at his firehouse might have an idea." Her tear-filled gaze met Marco's worried one. "You don't think he'd..." She couldn't bring herself to say the words "hurt" or "kill"... she had to keep thinking this was all a mistake, and Brody and Corey would suddenly appear. They'd all laugh about the misunderstanding, and everything would be all right. But Fancy was coming to realize that was a dream and the reality was a nightmare. Why would Corey kidnap Brody, and what was his eventual goal?

A white mist floated through the darkness of Brody's mind. He was about to reach for it when the shock of cold water thrown in his face jerked him awake. As he sputtered and caught his breath, he found his arms were restrained behind him, and his ankles were shackled to the legs of the wooden chair he was sitting on. That comprehension was enough to shake the last of the cobwebs from his mind.

"Wake the fuck up, you fucking pervert!"

"Shout a little louder," Brody roared at Corey. "I don't think the fucking neighbors heard you that time."

The fireman punched him in the jaw, almost tipping him over. Pain shot through him, but he ignored it, trying to take in his surroundings and figure out how to get free. Tugging on his hands, he realized there was more than one pair of handcuffs on his wrists. *Shit.* He could have easily popped the chain links on one pair. They'd always practiced doing that in the SEALs, having competitions on who could get out the fastest. But the extra set made twisting them to the correct angle impossible. The bastard had done his homework.

"Don't worry about the neighbors. There aren't any for miles. No one to interrupt our fun."

The man walked behind Brody as the geek glared at him. Why had he never seen the craziness in Corey's eyes before? The guy was fucking certifiable. Glancing around, it was easy to see they were in a garden shed, but where was beyond him. There were no windows, so he had no idea what time it was or how long he'd been out. Around him, there were assorted tools, a lawn mower, and... *fuck him!* His chair was sitting inside a plastic kiddie pool, and from behind him, he heard the sound of a faucet being turned on. *This can't be fucking good!*

Turning his head, he saw Corey pulling a hose over and throwing the end into the pool. Water quickly covered the bottom and began to rise up the sides. To his left, he spotted something that made his blood chill—a car battery with jumper cables. As Jake would say, fuck a fucking duck!

Brody struggled to get free from his bonds. But between the extra care that had been taken to ensure he couldn't escape and the fact that he was still weak from the drugs he'd been given, his fight was useless. He doubted he could talk his way out of this, but he didn't have many alternatives at the moment. "Listen, my guess is this is because you don't want me dating Fancy, is that it?"

"She's too good for the likes of you. All you want to do is abuse her. Just like my perverted brother. Taking her to fucking sex clubs. How does it feel to be tied up? Huh? Is this what you do to her, you fucking pervert?" Spittle shot from Corey's mouth, hitting Brody in the face. "I saved her from Patrick, and now, I'll save her from you. Maybe then she'll realize what a real man is like."

Oh, fuck! Brody stared daggers at the man. "You cut the brake line on Patrick's truck, didn't you? And made it look like a rock had hit it. You caused the accident that killed your brother and put Fancy in a coma!"

Corey punched him in the face again, and Brody tasted blood on top of his fury. "She wasn't supposed to be with him! It was an accident! How was I to know her car wouldn't start that morning? But this time, she's safe. Nothing will happen to her. And after you're gone, I'll be there for her—just like before. But this time, I'll make sure she sees I'm the right man for her."

Yeah, certifiable was too mild a word for this guy, but right now is not the time to think of a better one. It's time to fuck that duck again!

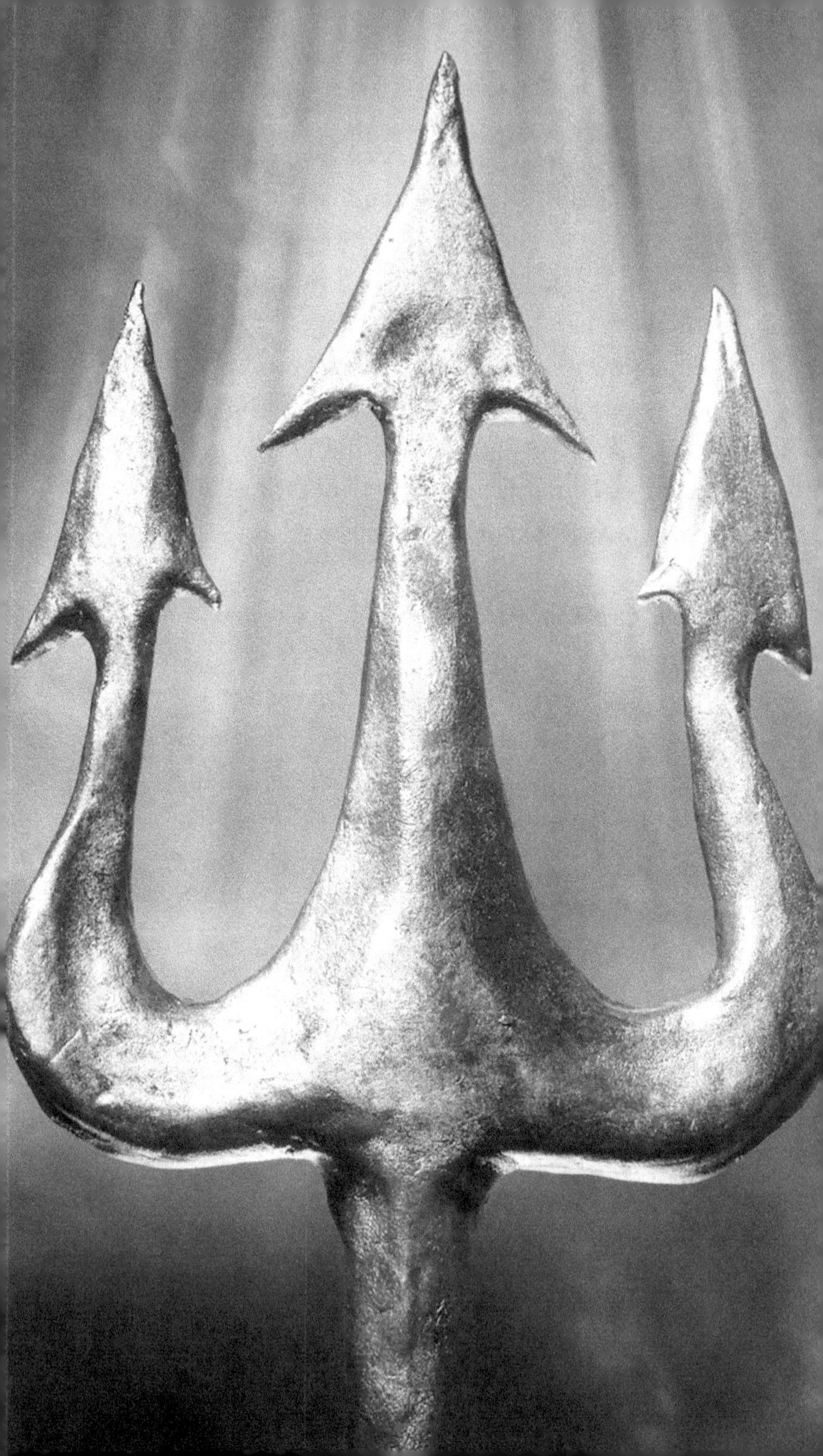

CHAPTER TWENTY-ONE

Ian paced back and forth in the war-room as Nathan banged away on his keyboard, attempting to find a connection between Fancy's brother-in-law and wherever he'd taken Brody. Dialing another number, Ian was trying to call in some favors to get an alert put out on the local news channels about the missing man and his truck. Hopefully, someone would call in that they'd spotted them. Boomer, Marco, and Webb had gone to interview Maguire's co-workers at the firehouse, but after the firemen had gotten over their initial shock at the current events, no one there had any idea where they might be.

While the Omega Team was also out scouring the area, Fancy was with Kat and Angie in the conference room, contacting the few friends she knew Corey hung out with on occasion who weren't in the fire department. Ian let her do it to keep her busy. In the meantime, Devon was going through the city's traffic camera feeds, trying to spot the geek's truck. Nathan had hacked into the system for him before starting his own search on Maguire's financial status, credit card purchase history, and anything that might give them a hint as to where to start looking.

As Ian hung up the phone, Webb and Boomer strode in, and the latter sat next to Devon. "We've got nada. Webb's got everyone out looking for them. Maguire's truck was found in a supermarket parking lot about two blocks from the bakery, so they must be in Egghead's truck."

Crossing his arms, the detective leaned against the wall. "I just called the hospital. Adams is out of surgery and in the ICU. It'll be touch and go for the next twenty-four hours, at least. They have him intubated and in a drug-induced coma, so we can't get any more info from him.

"DeAngelis went over to Maguire's condo with one of the uniformed guys and is knocking on doors again, trying to see if anyone we missed earlier is home now."

Boomer got Nathan's attention. "If you patch another computer into the traffic feeds for me, I'll help Devil Dog search them."

"Sure." The computer tech rolled his chair across the room to another section of Brody's vast console setup. Flicking the mouse on its pad, he brought it out of sleep mode. A satellite map appeared, and he paused, tilting his head to the side as he studied it.

The man's actions caught Ian's attention. "What is it?"

Nathan tapped the screen. "The blue dots are the trackers in the Omega team's phones spread out around Tampa, right? And all these red dots are everyone on the Alpha team. They're all here in the compound except DeAngelis, whose dot is over here." He pointed to the one a few inches away from the others on the map, which translated into miles. "The only one missing is Evans's dot, right?"

"Yeah, we know that. I checked this morning for Egghead's phone, and it wasn't registering." He stepped behind Nathan and stared at the screen. "Is it back up again?"

Webb leaned in, and Devon and Boomer stood to look over the computer geek's shoulder as Nathan shook his head. "No, but..." He grabbed the mouse and moved the pointer on the screen to an area north of the compound where a white dot was. "What's this one?" He clicked on the dot, and the info for a tracking device popped up. "Says 'Bracelet number one.' What the fuck is that?"

Ian slapped him on the shoulders in relief. "*That* is fucking Brody! He was going to give Fancy a tracking device to wear, just in case, because of all the crap going on with the vandalism and missing subs. He must still have it! Where the fuck is he?"

Rattling off the coordinates, Nathan zoomed in on the property and got the address on the north side of

Tampa. He quickly switched to another screen and entered the address into whatever database he was in. "Property is three acres in the snooty part of town, apparently. Three days ago, there was a fire in the main house, and it was pretty much a total loss. And looky here... Maguire's station house responded to it!"

Without being told, Boomer and Devon ran from the room to get their gear ready, but Webb stopped Ian in his tracks. "I gotta call in SWAT, Sawyer. You know I have to. Don't go all cowboy on me."

"If they beat us there, then it's all theirs. But I'm not waiting around for them."

Webb nodded as he dialed his phone. "Understood. I'll be right behind you."

As Ian hurried toward the conference room, Tiny and Kristen entered the front door. *Perfect timing.* "Big guy, I need you on guard duty here."

Inside the room, Fancy jumped to her feet. "What happened? Did you find them?"

"We think so—"

"I'm going with you!" She snatched her purse from the table.

Ian stepped in front of her and grabbed her shoulders. "Absolutely not." Before she could argue, he continued. "Listen, little one. I'm pulling Dom rank here for several reasons. One—Egghead would kill me if I let you within a mile of whatever's going on. Two —I have a feeling this has a lot to do with you, personally—you're the only connection between them. If

Corey sees you, it could set him off. I have to assume Brody's incapacitated somehow, which means we have to take every precaution. Stay here with the women and Tiny, and I swear I'll let you know what's going on as soon as I find out, okay?"

Tears filled her eyes, but she relented and nodded. "Please call me as soon as you can. I can't lose Brody, too."

Squeezing her shoulders, Ian placed a kiss on her forehead. He still felt like a heel from when he'd barked at her earlier outside her shop. "I will." Turning to Angie, he hugged her tight. "We'll get him back, I promise."

"You better," his fiancée replied. "He's walking me down the aisle in a few weeks."

"And he'll be there."

With a fist bump to Tiny on the way out, Ian ran to the parking lot and hopped into the passenger seat of the SUV his brother had running and waiting. Devon hit the gas before the door was even shut. Not seeing the detective's car, Ian assumed Webb was already on his way to the location.

Boomer was in the backseat, typing away on his phone. "Texting Polo and Omega. Where should they meet us?"

Hitting the speed dial on his own phone, Ian waited for Nathan to pick up the line in the war-room.

"Hello?"

Not bothering with announcing himself, the boss

said, "You better have a live satellite image up on your screen right now, or you just lost all the brownie points you earned five minutes ago!"

A snort came over the line. "I assume you want a staging area for everyone to meet up. There's a kiddie park one block over on Mercer Drive. The only structure they can be in is a shed of some sort about fifty yards behind what's left of the house on the west side of the property. My guess is Evans's truck is parked behind it under some trees because I can just make out the corner of a pickup, but I can't be certain it's his. Nothing else to report—it's all quiet from what I can see. I'll monitor it until you get there."

"Under no circumstances do you let any of the women watch the live feed," Ian warned. "If you do, I'll dump your body in an alligator pit, you hear me?"

"Loud and clear, Boss-man."

Hanging up the phone, Ian relayed the info to Boomer for the text before finding Webb's cell number in his own call log. He hoped like hell they weren't too late—aside from the obvious not wanting to lose a friend and teammate, Angie would fucking kill him.

Marco's vehicle flew down the street to where the target property was, and he slammed on his brakes. He'd been a lot further away than the rest of them, and

Boomer had sent him an updated text that they were now one house down from where Brody was being held—hopefully still alive. Not bothering to park the truck correctly, he jumped out of the driver's seat and raced over to where Webb was talking with Ian, Cal Watts, and the leader of the TPD SWAT. "I got here as fast as I could. How the hell did you get an entire SWAT team here so fast—make that two teams?"

Not only was TPD's team present, but so was the local FBI Hostage Rescue Team. Cal was head of the HRT and shook Marco's extended hand. "Believe it or not, we were around the corner at the old junior high school doing a joint active shooter drill." The large building built in the 1950s was scheduled to be demolished after a new school had been erected a mile away. The local law enforcement took advantage of it for training before it was destroyed. "Only took two minutes to load up and hightail it over here. We've surrounded the shed but haven't made contact yet—two positive heat signatures inside with no windows. One of my guys is trying to find a spot to snake a camera in before we let Maguire know we're here. We've evacuated the homes on all sides."

Wearing headphones, Boomer approached carrying a laptop. "Everything is muffled. I can't make out what's being said, but they're talking. The tag must still be in Egghead's pocket." It figured the first time they found a fault in the geek's microphone and GPS device was while they were trying to rescue him.

Cal listened to something coming over the comm set in his ear and responded, "Copy that." He then addressed the group gathered with him: "Shed is sealed tight. I can't get a camera in there without making noise. Ian, I know your team wants in on this, but you're too close to the situation. And we have more personnel than we probably need already."

Reluctantly, Trident's leader nodded. "Just because I don't like it doesn't mean I disagree with you. But God help you if we don't get Brody out of this alive."

Marco knew it had taken a lot for Ian to step aside, but the man was wise and experienced enough to know when it was necessary. However, that didn't stop Marco from wanting to go all Rambo and kick the shed door in to rescue his best friend. His boss gave him a look that said he understood, but it was best to calm the fuck down and allow HRT and SWAT to do their jobs. Nodding, Marco let the two teams do what they were trained to do and prayed it was the right decision.

The urge to panic was strong, but Brody shoved it to the back of his mind and tried to think of a way out of this dilemma—before his goose was cooked. "Listen, Maguire. She's all yours. Fancy was just a fling for me."

He almost choked on the lie, but if that was what he had to do to save Fancy and himself from this psycho, so be it.

"I knew you were just looking for another notch on your bedpost." Corey shut off the hose. The water in the pool was above Brody's ankles. "Should have thought about the consequences when I warned you off the first time."

He tried maneuvering the cuffs so he could snap one and then the other. Shackled to the heavy wooden chair, his options were few. "Well, consider me warned this time. You've made me see the light; you're the better man for her. Let's forget this ever happened. I'll walk away and leave her for you."

Sneering, the bastard attached the clamps of the jumper cables to the car battery. "Do I look stupid to you? The only person walking out of here when this is over is me. Then I'll comfort Fancy over the fact that you disappeared, and I won't have to do all that shit to her shop anymore."

What? Swallowing hard, Brody watched as Corey picked up the clamps at the other end of the cables. *Shit, this is going to fucking hurt!*

"You were vandalizing her shop? Why?"

"She was supposed to come to me for protection, not you!" He dropped one of the clamps into the water and slowly lowered the other to just above the surface. "You had to stick your nose and dick where they didn't belong!"

Brody realized this wasn't going to be a quick death. The bastard was going to shock him over and over again. He tried to pitch himself and the chair to the side and hopefully out of the pool, but he didn't have the leverage to do it in one shot before the electrical connection was made in the water.

"Corey, man, don't do—" His body seized as the current flowed through him. Pain was an understatement. It was a hundred times worse than the Taser. The air around him crackled, and his brain didn't register anything, but the agony every cell in his body was experiencing. This was it. He'd survived countless missions, idiotic childhood stunts, and a few extreme sports, and he was going to bite the dust at the hand of this deranged asshole.

Just when Brody thought he was going to pass out, the clamp was yanked out of the water, and his body sagged heavily. What had felt like an hour of being electrocuted had, in reality, been only a second or two. His throat was raw, and he concluded that the screaming he'd heard had been from his own mouth—involuntary though it was.

Thoughts of Fancy flashed through his mind, but he couldn't grasp one to hold on to. She was going to be devastated if he died. She'd come so close to not surviving the first time she'd lost a man she loved.

I'm sorry, sweetness. If I could turn back time and save you from another heartache, I would. I would've never pursued you if I'd known how this would end. I love you, Fancy-girl.

He'd barely recovered when another jolt hit him. His muscles went rigid, and his limbs felt like they would snap in half. Above his own screaming, he heard a crash, shouts, and then gunfire, but the electricity still coursed through his body. His heart pounded out of control. A white light filled his vision, then suddenly there was no searing pain, no sound, no anything, just darkness.

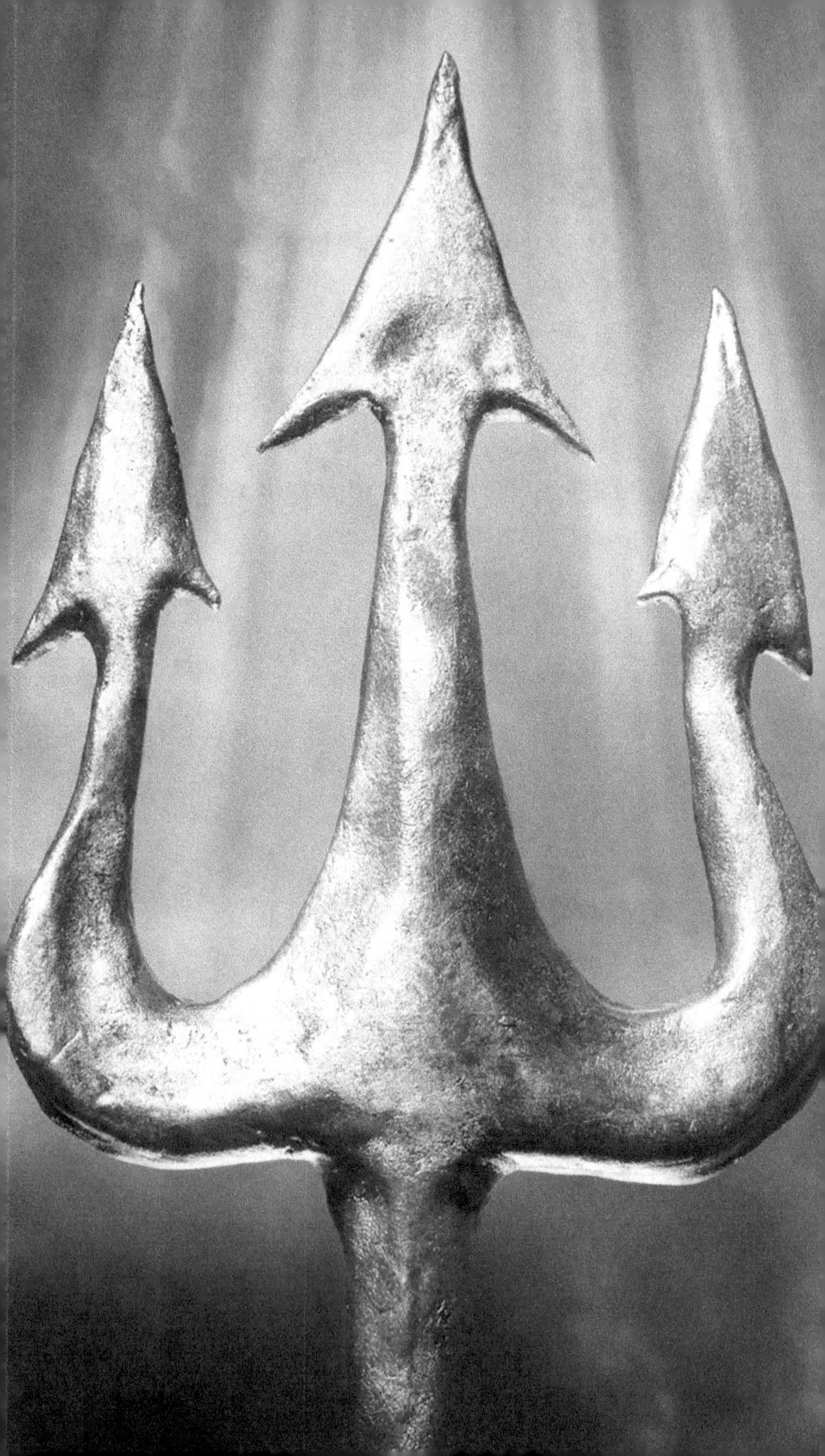

CHAPTER TWENTY-TWO

Ian waited with Marco and Devon as Cal grabbed a bullhorn and prepared to announce their presence to Maguire. Boomer was in the HRT's tactical communications van with one of the techs, trying to clean up the static from the device in Brody's pocket. The Omega team was gathered back by Marco's truck. They felt as helpless as everyone else and opted to stay out of the way. A paramedic unit and ambulance were parked up the street in case they were needed.

Devon was about to say something when Cal's hand flew to the comm device in his ear. "Shit! Take it!" he barked.

The Fed tossed the bullhorn onto the grass and took off at a dead run to the target property. Ian, Dev, and Marco threw protocol to the wind and hightailed it after him. Boomer came crashing out of the van to follow just as they all heard shouts and gunfire. As they neared the shed, with its now kicked-in door, Cal stopped short, and his fist shot up at shoulder height, silently ordering everyone behind him to freeze. They heard the "All clear" and "Get the medics" seconds later. Before anyone could get close to the door, two men in full tactical gear hurried out, carrying someone tied to a chair between them.

Shoving aside his shock, Ian pulled a switchblade out of his back pocket and lunged forward to help the others free an unconscious Brody. His hair was sticking straight up, and there were burn holes in his lower pants legs. Ian could smell seared hair and flesh as he cut through the Duct tape restraining Brody's wet ankles and legs.

"He's been electrocuted," said one of the men who had carried the big geek out.

After the others had gotten the handcuffs and tape off him, Dev and Marco picked Brody up by the armpits and legs, and someone kicked the chair out of their way so they could lower him to the ground.

As Marco opened Brody's airway, Dev felt for a carotid pulse. "Nothing! Start CPR."

Marco took a deep breath, tilted his best friend's head back, sealed their mouths together, and blew as hard as he could. In the meantime, Dev lined his hands up over their teammate's chest and began compressions as soon as Marco finished giving the breath. They worked in tandem until the paramedics and EMTs arrived to take over. One EMT pulled out an

Ambu-bag attached to a green tank, placed the mask over Brody's face, and forced the oxygen into his lungs.

Dev continued compressions as the other medic cut the shirt out from under his hands. As Marco scrambled to get out of the way of the rest of the arriving medical personnel, the medic slapped defibrillator pads and EKG leads on Brody's chest. "He's in V-fib! Need to shock him!"

The whine of the defibrillator charging increased in volume until a green light appeared on the device. The medic held his finger over the discharge button and yelled, "Clear!"

Everyone took their hands off of Brody's body, and when the medic hit the button, the unconscious man's entire torso jolted. Ian had a wry thought—it was weird that to counteract what the electricity had done to Brody's heart, they basically had to electrocute him again.

Devon checked for a pulse, and the EMT began squeezing the Ambu-bag again. After checking the monitor, the medic recharged the device and, once again, yelled, "Clear!"

Movement to his right caught Ian's attention, and he turned as Cal returned from inside the shed. The agent approached him. "Maguire's dead. My men heard Egghead scream, so I gave them the clear to take the door. The bastard had him tied to that chair in a fucking kiddie pool filled with water. He used jumper cables attached to a car battery. The gun he pulled on them, forcing them to shoot, was a Taser. Unfortunately, when they took out Maguire, both ends of the cables were in the water. Egghead was already unconscious when they cut the current off. I'm sorry, Ian."

His gaze returned to where the medics were still working on Brody and loading him for transport. He wished Maguire was still alive so he could kill the bastard himself. His voice was flat as he said, "Not your fault. You played it right. All we can do now is pray."

Fancy was numb. She'd been sitting in the ICU waiting room for the last few hours along with Brody's teammates, their significant others, and extended family. After Brody had been loaded into the ambulance, Ian and Marco returned to the compound to break the news. Corey had been shot and killed by the rescue teams, but not before he electrocuted his hostage. Ian hadn't gone into much detail, and Fancy didn't want to know everything that had happened just yet. All she wanted was for the doctors to come out and tell her she wasn't going to lose another man she loved.

The medics had been able to restart Brody's heart, but they'd intubated him to assist his breathing. He hadn't regained consciousness, and the doctors had told the stunned Trident group that the next forty-eight hours were critical. Fancy had gotten the impression they were surprised he'd made it to this point.

Marco approached, where she and Harper sat together, and handed them cups of coffee. Fancy thanked him even though she wouldn't be able to stomach the strong brew. They still had no clue what had led up to all of this—why Corey had kidnapped and tortured Brody in the first place. And if Brody died, they may never know.

Around her, everyone stood, and she looked toward the door leading out to the hallway as an older couple entered with Mitch Sawyer. They had to be Elise and Gerard Evans, Brody's parents. Ian had contacted them immediately about their son and arranged for a private jet to fly them to Tampa from Texas. Then Mitch had gone to the small local airport to pick them up when they'd landed.

The distraught-looking couple shook hands and exchanged hugs with nearly everyone present. Jenn broke down in tears again as she hugged Mrs. Evans, and once again, Fancy prayed Brody's two families wouldn't lose him because of her.

After Jenn had regained her composure, Mrs. Evans asked her a question, and the younger woman turned and pointed across the room to Fancy. She hadn't known what to expect, but Fancy fell apart when Brody's mother walked over to her with open arms. Tears poured down her cheeks, and she began to sob uncontrollably.

The older woman enveloped her in a warm embrace, which made Fancy cry even harder. "I'm s-so s-sorry, Mrs. Evans. It's all my f-fault."

The arms around her tightened, and a hand stroked her head. "Hush, now. First, my son is madly in love with you, so I think you can call me Elise. Secondly, Ian explained what he could, and I don't see why you believe this is your fault. You didn't know that man would do this. Neither did my son. Now we just have to pray that the Lord lets us keep Brody here on Earth for many more years."

Fancy didn't know where the other woman got her strength, but she drew some of it into her own body and mind, pulling herself together. Elise released her, gave her a genuine smile, and then turned to greet Kristen, who was holding little JD in her arms. Gerard Evans introduced himself to Fancy and insisted she call him by his first name. They were such a friendly couple, and she immediately liked them.

Another man, whom she hadn't noticed among the crowd, stepped forward and held his hand out to her. "Hello, ma'am. I'm Brody's older brother, Brett. It's nice to meet you, but I wish it were under better circumstances. Brody told me all about you when I spoke to him the other day. He's quite smitten."

Blushing, she shook his hand. "I'm sorry we're meeting like this, too. You're the Dallas police officer, right? He talks about his brothers and sisters often, but there are so many of you, I'm not sure if I'm mixing you all up."

"Yes, ma'am. I'm the police officer." His mouth turned up into a grin. "Just be glad the whole lot of us didn't come—you would need nametags for every-one." He gestured for her to take a seat. "Might as well get comfortable and get to know each other. I've got plenty of stories about Brody from when we were kids that you can use to blackmail him every once in a while. Did he tell you his other nickname is Frodo? He read *The Hobbit* and *The Lord of the Rings* trilogy long before they were turned into movies."

Forty-five minutes later, two family members at a time were allowed to go into the ICU and see Brody. They were given fifteen minutes every three hours, and as much as Fancy wanted to see him, she remained quiet as Elise and Gerard left everyone behind to see their son. Besides, she wasn't sure if she was allowed in the unit since she wasn't immediate family.

Friends, police officers, and even a reporter had been in and out of the waiting room. The latter had been escorted right back out by Tiny, who stood well over a foot taller than the nosy man. Detective Webb had told Fancy he would contact the local police in her Ohio hometown to have them inform Corey's parents of the incident and his death. She was grateful since she had no idea what to say to them. She'd spoken to her mother and aunt earlier, and as expected, Aunt

Denise had been more supportive. It wasn't that her mother hadn't tried, but the woman never knew what to say during times like these and usually ended up blurting out the wrong thing. Fancy was used to it, though, and she did her best not to let it bother her.

Boomer had gone down one flight to the surgical intensive care unit earlier and checked on Russell Adams's status. The veteran was stable, and the surgery had gone well. Ian had Nathan tracking down the man's family so they could be notified. During one of his few chattier moments in her shop, Fancy learned Russell was originally from Connecticut and still had family there, but she didn't know anything else. She'd overheard Devon and Ian discussing that they would cover all the man's medical bills, saying it was the least they could do since, without him, they may not have found Brody before it was too late.

When Elise and Gerard reentered the room, Fancy was surprised to see there was still time left for visitors. Brody's father waved her and Brett over. "Go on in, you two. Let him know you're here. I told them you were his fiancée, Fancy, so they would let you see him."

Grateful, she gave Gerard a peck on the cheek before following Brett into the restricted unit. Although the doctor had told them about the ventilator and all the tubes and wires attached to Brody, it was still a shock when they entered the room. Brett held her elbow in support as they approached the bed.

Brody was so pale, and his big body actually looked small with all the medical equipment around him. A sob threatened to escape her, and she swallowed it back down as she laid her hand on his and squeezed. There was no response.

The EKG monitor beeped with his steady heart rate, and the blood pressure cuff around his upper arm began to inflate. Brett placed his hand on his brother's blanket-covered knee. "Hey, Frodo. Got yourself in a bit of a pickle, didn't you? Well, I'm here with your girlfriend, and she's as pretty as you said she was. You better get your ass out of here because you know our sisters—once they find out you're in love, they'll want to meet Fancy at the hoedown. In the meantime, I'm telling her all the stories you probably don't want me to, but that's what big brothers are for." He squeezed Brody's knee. "We only have a few more minutes before we have to leave, so I'm going to step out and give you two a little time alone."

Fancy gave Brett a watery smile. "Thank you."

He nodded, clearly trying to keep his emotions under control for her sake. "I'll be right outside when you're done."

Once alone, Fancy pulled the only chair in the small room closer to the bed and sat. Her hand never left Brody's. "I'm so sorry, Brody. I still don't know what happened, but it's obvious it had something to do with me. Just... just don't leave me, please. I don't know what I would do if I lost you, too. I love you." Her voice cracked on those last few words, and she took a few calming breaths.

A soft bell dinged, signaling the end of visiting time. Five minutes had flown by, and it felt like only seconds. Standing, she leaned over and kissed his forehead. "I love you, Sir. Please come back to me."

The only response was the rhythmic beeping of the machines in the room and the ventilator inflating and deflating Brody's lungs. Giving his hand one more squeeze, Fancy reluctantly left the room.

CHAPTER TWENTY-THREE

Over the next forty-five hours, Fancy went from home to the hospital and back again. In the waiting room, she got to know Brody's parents and brother better. They told her all about the boy he'd been and the man he'd become before she met him. His teammates and friends rotated shifts in and out, bringing food, coffee, and whatever else was needed, even though they weren't allowed in the ICU unit to see him. They were keeping Jake and Nick in the loop by phone. Nick couldn't fly back again due to an upcoming mission with the SEALs, and Ian had convinced Jake to stay in San Diego with the new West Coast team until they knew more about Brody's condition. Back at the office, Colleen had reserved hotel rooms for Elise, Gerard, and Brett within walking distance of the hospital. The rest of the Evans clan stayed by their phones in Texas and took care of their parents' ranch. There wasn't anything they could do here but sit in the waiting room like everyone else, so they decided to stay at home where they could be of use. If Fancy hadn't already known Brody was a good man—protective, brave, loyal, and honorable—she would have known it just by his loving, extended family.

After Detective Webb had told Fancy that Corey's parents had been notified, she tried to call them, but her former father-in-law told her never to call them again and hung up on her. Apparently, they now blamed her for the deaths of both their sons despite knowing as little as the rest of them. From what her Aunt Denise had learned, the Maguires were arranging for Corey's body to be flown back to Ohio and buried next to Patrick in the plot that had been originally bought for Fancy. If this had happened six months ago, she would have been hurt, but now... she'd finally been able to let her husband go, and if it brought his grieving parents comfort, then that was fine with her.

At her bakery, her staff had taken over—God bless them. Jamie had suggested hiring her cousin to help out so Fancy could stay at the hospital. Fancy had met the other girl several times and had okayed her working at the shop. If she was a good fit, Fancy would consider keeping her on full-time, giving herself more free time to spend with Brody. If he... no, *when* he woke up, he would need her to help take care of him as he recovered.

Three o'clock rolled around, and Fancy would be going into the ICU to visit alone for the first time. Elise and Gerard had returned to the hotel for a bit to rest and would be back later, and Brett was on a phone call with his police department back home about a case he'd been working on. Harper, Marco, Angie, and Shelby would remain in the waiting room while Fancy went in for her fifteen-minute visit.

Several family members of other patients stood and walked into the unit behind her. Stepping into Brody's cubicle, Fancy closed the curtain to give herself a little privacy. Not much had changed in his appearance over the past two days. They'd cleaned and treated the burn marks on his lower legs and feet. From what the doctor had said, he would have only minor scarring from the second-degree burns, but he might lose the small toe on one foot where a third-degree burn had formed.

The monitors still beeped, but the good news that morning was when they'd briefly turned off the ventilator, the respiratory staff found Brody was breathing on his own. With the doctor's permission, they removed the intubation tube. Now, he had a nasal cannula sending oxygen into his nose. The doctor had been surprised, yet pleased with his EKG and stable vital signs this morning. The only problem was Brody hadn't woken up yet.

As Fancy pulled over the lone chair, the blood pressure cuff on his arm inflated again. On the bedside table was a silver package with moist applicators in it. They smelled like lemon, and she pulled one out and ran it over his lips to keep them hydrated as the nurses had instructed. Cupping his cheek, she stared at his pale but still handsome face. The stubble there tickled her palm. "H-hi. It's me. I'm here, Sir. Waiting for you to wake up and show me your beautiful brown eyes."

She only called him Sir when she was alone in the room with him. She didn't know if his family knew about his lifestyle, and it wasn't her place to tip them off. Some people didn't understand it, and Brody himself had told her his first impressions of the BDSM community had been one of abuse. It was as far from the truth as possible. She loved him, what he did to her, and how he cared for her. But this was a time she had to take care of him.

"Kristen was here earlier with JD. I just love holding him. I would love to have your babies some-day, and yes, I can still have them, as far as I know. Before I met you, I never thought I would get pregnant again. I didn't think I could go through another miscarriage and survive it. But you... you make me want to try, Sir. I would love to have a little boy with your dimples or a little girl with your eyes... maybe some of my freckles on her nose because I know how much you like them."

Swallowing hard, she continued. "Mara is trying to take her first steps, but Marco hopes she waits a few more days so her Uncle Brody can see her do it.

Your family, all of them, love you. Come back to us, please... I love you so much and need you. Please, Sir."

She still didn't receive any response from him and wondered if she ever would. *What if he never woke up?* Fancy couldn't stop the tears and sobs that spilled forth. She grabbed some tissues from the table and blew her nose. After wiping her eyes, she held his hand, stroked his hair, and told him all the positive things happening around them. She babbled about anything she could think of that might get through to him, but at the end of her fifteen minutes, she once again kissed his forehead and left without any response from him.

Walking into the private room, Fancy put on a big smile when she saw the patient sitting up in bed. "Good morning, Russell. I'm so glad to see you're awake. Boomer texted me last night to say they'd moved you out of the ICU. How are you feeling?"

Lowering the TV volume via the bed remote, Adams gingerly shifted in the bed. His voice was weak, and his skin was pale, but he grinned back at her. "Hi, Miss Fancy. I'm doing okay, sore, but okay. After giving me a few pints of blood and stitching me back together, the doctors think I'll be okay. Once they let me wake up yesterday morning, they took out the breathing tube. How's the senior chief?"

Placing one of the bags she'd grabbed from the bakery this morning on his bedside table, she sat in the chair next to him and swallowed the lump in her throat. "He still hasn't woken up, but the doctors will run some tests later today to see if he responds."

His eyes filled with regret. "I'm so sorry I couldn't save him—"

She grabbed his hand, cutting off the rest of whatever he was about to say. "There's nothing for you to be sorry about, Russell. If it weren't for you, it would have been too late, and he would never have had a chance. He's still alive and fighting, so we just have to think positively."

It was basically the same thing Brody's mother had said to her. What happened wasn't anyone's fault except for Corey's, and he'd paid for it with his life.

When Russell nodded in response, she said, "I brought you some goodies since I know how bad hospital food can be. I gave a box of cookies to the nurses from you, too, both here and in the SICU."

"Thanks. They're all really nice to me. I just hope I don't have any flashbacks while I'm here and hurt someone."

Fancy pointed toward the door. "Boomer made sure the nurses knew about your PTSD, so there's a sign on the wall next to your door that says to make noise and announce yourself when entering."

A knock on the open door had them both looking up, and Ian walked in. "Good morning, Fancy. Adams, how are you feeling today?"

"Good, sir."

Brody's friend and boss had obviously been in to see the Navy veteran before this morning. He stopped next to the hospital bed and inhaled deeply. "Damn, are those pecan rolls I smell?"

"Yes, sir, I think they are." Russell grinned. "Fancy brought them for me."

Chuckling, she pulled a smaller paper bag out of a larger plastic one and handed it to Ian. "You didn't think I would forget you loved them, too, did you?"

He took the bag from her. "Thanks, you're a doll. After this one, though, I'll have to start declining every once in a while if I want to get into my dress whites for the wedding." She doubted that because the man was in peak physical condition, just like the rest of his team. Turning back toward the injured man, he asked, "What are your plans when you're sprung from here?"

Adams shrugged. "I hadn't really thought about it, sir. Why?"

"I've got a proposition for you." Over his shoulder, Ian said in a raised voice, "Tori, come on in."

A brown-haired woman Fancy had never met before rounded the door jamb and strode into the room. She was close to Fancy's age and stood about five foot six. On a leash beside her was a beautiful Rottweiler. The large dog wore a yellow vest with the words "Service Dog in Training" on it. When the woman stopped a few feet from the bed, her canine companion immediately sat next to her, his stubby tail and butt wiggling with happiness.

Ian gestured to the man lying in the bed. "Russell Adams, this is Tori Freyja. Tori, this is Russell, and Brody's girlfriend, Fancy Maguire. Tori is a friend of a friend, and in addition to running a rescue for Bullmastiffs, she trains other rescues to be service and assistance dogs for veterans, specifically those with PTSD," he explained to Russell. "If you're willing, she has a ranch just north of Tampa when you get out of here. You can stay there while training your own dog. She'll teach you how, and it'll take a few months. After that, we'll sit down and discuss putting you to work and getting you a permanent place to stay. All the expenses for the dog are covered and then some. Tori's Healing Heroes is a non-profit, so all you have to do is learn how to train your dog to help you when you need it. You'll be expected to help around the ranch, which also has some therapy horses. The staff is experienced with veterans with PTSD, so don't worry about having any incidents there. Again, this is all up to you. You can decline if you want to."

Fancy's eyes welled up as she watched Russell's expression go from confusion to shock and then to awe that someone would do this for him. His gaze went back and forth between Ian, Fancy, and Tori several times in disbelief before it settled on the dog with its goofy face and tongue hanging out. "Is that... would he be my dog?"

Smiling and taking two steps forward, Tori patted the edge of the bed and said the word "place." Going up on his hind legs, the dog set his front paws on the mattress, and Fancy swore he was grinning. Tori stroked his big head. "This is Jagger, and he's about eighteen months old, from what we can tell. We pulled him out of a crowded shelter where he was scheduled to be euthanized. He's already started his basic training and will be ready to begin working with you when you're released from the hospital. Hold out your hand, palm down, and let him sniff you. He'll let you know when it's okay to pet him."

Russell did as he was told, and Jagger sniffed his hand enthusiastically. He then thrust his muzzle into the palm, demanding to be petted, and his new owner complied. "Hey, Jagger," he said while scratching the dog's ears. Everyone laughed when the dog groaned in delight. "He's awesome. I had a Rottie growing up."

"Sounds like it was meant to be then," Fancy told him as she stood, her voice thick with emotion at the lengths Brody's extended family took care of their own. And it was clear Russell Adams was now a part of that family. "Visiting starts in ten minutes in the ICU, so I'm heading up there. I'll stop in to see you before I go home later, Russell."

"Thanks, Fancy. I'll say a few more prayers for the senior chief. When he wakes up, please have someone let me know. And thanks, Lieutenant Sawyer, for everything. I honestly don't know what else to say."

Ian held out his hand for the other man to shake. "It's Ian. And you don't have to say anything more. It's the least I can do for your service and for helping us find Brody."

After Gerard and Elise had come out from their brief visit with their son, Fancy and Brett went in. On the way to Brody's cubicle, Fancy stopped at the nurses' station in the middle of the unit and handed a large bakery box to Sheila, the head nurse. "This is for everyone for taking such good care of Brody. Thank you for all you do."

The woman grinned. "Thanks for thinking of us. Whatever it is, it smells delicious." An alarm sounded, and she checked the monitor in front of her. Leaving the box on the desk, she led the way into Brody's cubicle, visibly not worried about anything. "One of his EKG leads came off. It happens after they've been on a few days. We rotate where they're placed so it doesn't irritate the skin too much."

"How's he doing today?" Brett asked.

Sheila checked the wires and patches on her patient's chest and found the loose one. The alarm shut off when she adjusted the patch. "His vitals are all stable, and he was moving around a bit in his sleep last night, according to the reports this morning. That's a good sign."

Fancy hoped so. She'd give anything for Brody to open his eyes and talk to her. Stepping forward, she grasped his hand and squeezed. "Hi. It's me. Brett's here, too."

To her surprise, his hand squeezed hers in response. She gasped, uncertain if she imagined it. "B-Brody? Squeeze my hand again."

Shelia and Brett's eyes widened as they realized what she'd said. All of them stared at where the two hands were joined. Slowly but surely, Brody's fingers closed around hers again. His mouth had opened seconds before his eyes did, and his tongue tried to moisten his dry lips. His sleep-filled gaze met Fancy's, and in a soft, raspy voice, he said, "You smell like pecan rolls, sweetness."

Bursting into tears of joy, she carefully leaned forward to kiss him. Neither noticed when Brett and Sheila left the room to tell the others Brody was awake and going to be okay.

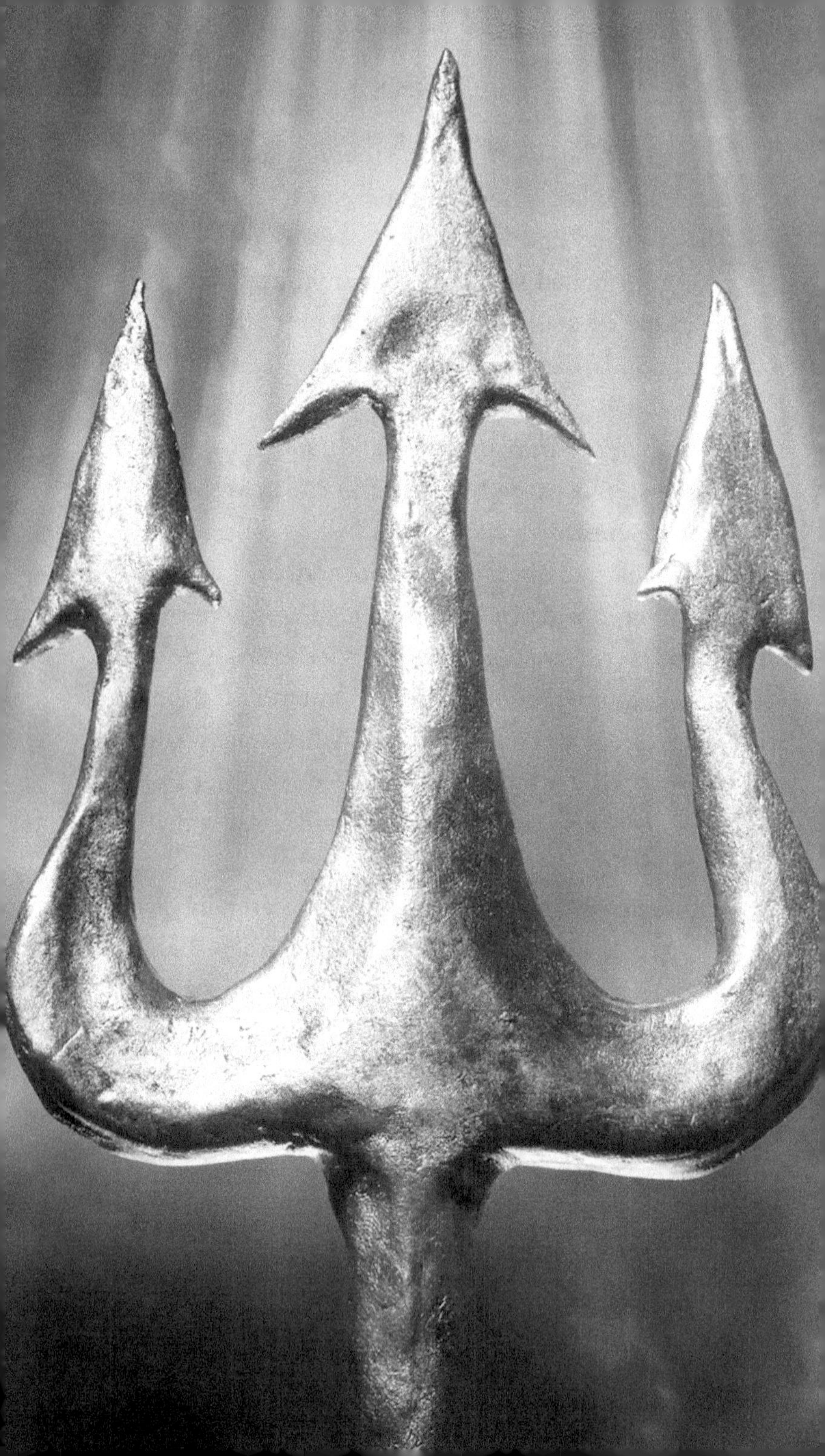

CHAPTER TWENTY-FOUR

"You look beautiful, Angie," Brody told the bride as her maid of honor, Kristen, gave a last-second adjustment to the veil. He was in his dress whites, trying to ignore the phantom pain from the amputated small toe of his right foot. If that were all he'd lost after being electrocuted to death before being brought back to life, he'd take it. The alternative would have been much worse.

After being released from his ten-day stay at the hospital, the first thing he'd done was have Fancy drive him to the Healing Heroes Ranch. He'd wanted to thank Russell for his part in the rescue and to see how he was doing. The man had recovered from his stab wound and had found a niche for himself at the ranch with two other veterans staying there. Brody couldn't get over the difference in the man. Russell's eyes were full of hope and happiness with Jagger by his side, and Brody was glad the man now had a positive future.

As Kristen left the room at the back of the church to join the other bridesmaids, Brody scratched an itch on his chest. The portable cardiac monitor had come off yesterday, but where the patches had been still irritated him like crazy. The doctors had made him wear the device for a few weeks to make sure there weren't any lasting issues from the trauma his heart had received. While everything seemed fine, he was banned from overly strenuous activities until he had a stress test next week. Thankfully, the doctors hadn't put sex on the not-allowed list as long as there were no acrobatics involved.

The worst part of the ordeal had been sitting down with Fancy after being interviewed by the police and telling her the details of why Corey had kidnapped and tried to kill him. As a Dom and her lover, he'd instinctively wanted to gloss things over and not reveal that Corey had been responsible for Patrick's death and was behind the vandalism at her shop. But she deserved to know, and he couldn't risk her finding out when someone from the press uncovered the truth. From what Detective Webb had told him, the Maguires were refusing to believe that their youngest son had killed his older brother. Grief would do that to people, and Brody wasn't sure he would be any different if he were in their shoes. When the police had executed a search warrant on Corey's apartment, they'd found evidence of the long-time obsession the man had with his sister-in-law. He'd been stalking her for years without her knowledge. His dating Nora had apparently been a ruse, and Brody felt sorry for the woman for having been used that way. He couldn't imagine the shock and horror she'd gone through when Webb had interviewed her after Brody's rescue. At least, the boyfriend she'd thought she had would never hurt anyone again.

Brody's folks had returned to Texas with Brett with the promise that both Fancy and Brody would be at the hoedown in two weeks. When his mom and he had had some alone time in the hospital, she'd asked him when he was putting a ring on Fancy's finger. Knowing that was her not-so-subtle way of telling him she approved of her future daughter-in-law, he'd laughed. After Fancy had finally returned to work on a daily basis, he'd run out and purchased her engagement ring along with a permanent collar. At Angie, Kat, and Kristen's insistence, the collaring ceremony had occurred three nights ago at The Covenant instead of waiting until after today's wedding. The ring he was holding onto for a little longer until he was certain she was ready for that next step.

As Brody escorted Angie to the vestibule at the back of the church where they would start their long walk down the aisle, a late arrival, dressed in a custom-made, gray suit, came rushing in the door. The man skidded to a halt when he saw them. Grinning broadly, US government spy T. Carter stepped toward the bride and brought her manicured hand to his lips for a kiss. "Don't want to get yelled at for messing up your makeup, little one. You look stunning. I'm almost tempted to whisk you away for myself, but I know better than to piss in Boss-man's cornflakes."

Angie grinned at him. "I'm so glad you made it."

"Wouldn't miss this for the world. The 'I'm never giving my heart to a woman' big guy is going down in a grand and spectacular way." He punched Brody lightly in the right shoulder. The spy had made a 3:00 a.m. covert visit to see him in the hospital before heading back to complete an assignment he'd been on. "Nice to see you up and walking on your remaining nine toes." When Brody opened his mouth to call him the usual "jackass" to which the response would be "asshole," Carter cut him off. "Ah, ah, ah... not in church, my friend. See you after the show."

He hurried to take a seat as the bridesmaids started down the aisle to their music. When Angie and Brody were in position, she squeezed his arm. "You know I would have killed you if you missed walking me down the aisle. I swear, I was starting to think I was cursed."

Hearing the nervousness in her tone, he smiled as he spotted Fancy sitting next to Kristen's cousin, Will, in one of the pews near the front of the church. "You wouldn't have had to kill me because that's the only way I would have missed this honor. Consider your curse broken, Angie. Now, let's get you down that aisle before Ian passes out or pops a blood vessel."

Two weeks later, Fancy sat in the passenger seat of the truck Brody had rented at the airport. As he turned off the main road, there was an overhead rustic sign announcing their arrival at Paradise Pastures, the horse ranch his family-owned. The two-hundred-acre spread was home to a decent-sized Quarter Horse breeding operation.

Fancy twisted her hands together as the butterflies in her stomach took flight. While looking forward to seeing Elise, Gerard, and Brett again, she was nervous about meeting the rest of the family. Her anxiousness increased as she took in the long line of trucks and cars parked along the three-quarter-mile-long drive-way. There had to be nearly fifty of them and more parked in a sizable lot the driveway opened into in front of the beautiful blue and white, two-story home.

She jumped when Brody reached over, took her hand in his, and squeezed. "Easy, sweetness. My sisters aren't going to attack you like a pack of wolves —at least not until they let you get used to them first."

"Oh, jeez. I'm just glad I've already met your folks."

Parking next to a big, white pickup with the logo for Paradise Pastures on the side, he turned off the engine. Leaning across the console, his hand went to the nape of her neck and pulled her close for a kiss—one she felt all the way to her toes. She could stay in the truck all day if he kissed her like that. But it ended all too soon. He looked her straight in the eyes. "Sweetness, my entire family will love you as much as my parents already do. And I'll be right by your side whenever you need me, just like you were there for me. I love you."

Giving him another peck on the lips, she replied, "I love you, too. All right. Let's get this over with so my stomach will settle."

He laughed as he exited the truck and walked around to open her door for her. She took his offered hand and let him help her down from the high seat. Leaving their luggage in the truck's bed, Fancy and Brody grabbed several boxes she'd packed at the bakery before they left. Cain Foster and Val Mancini had been scheduled to fly to Mexico in the Trident jet for a four-day fact-finding mission, so Ian had approved the pilot dropping Fancy and Brody in Texas on the way. She'd been grateful since she could bring lots of pastries for the big hoedown that they wouldn't have been able to get on a regular flight without paying extra for multiple bags. She and Sal had been busy yesterday making all sorts of pies, tarts, cookies, and cupcakes for everyone.

Fancy could hear the music and party guests in the yard behind the house, but Brody said it was easier to bring the baked goods in through the front door and leave them in the dining room for later. As they climbed the three stairs to the wrap-around porch, the front door swung open, and Elise and Brett were waiting for them. Standing with them was a woman who had to be one of Brody's sisters because she had the same eyes, nose, and hair color.

Brett held out both hands to Fancy. "Hey, there. Let me take all of those from you."

"Just make sure they don't disappear," his sister teased. "Save some of Fancy's goodies for the rest of us since all you did was rave about them when you got home."

When Fancy's hands were free, Elise pulled her into the foyer and hugged her warmly. "I'm so glad you're here." Releasing her, she indicated the woman standing next to them. "This is my eldest daughter, Doreen."

"Hi, Doreen. It's nice to meet you." Fancy held out her hand, but the woman embraced her instead.

"I'm so glad to meet you finally. Come on back and meet the gang." Before leading the way through the house, though, Doreen took the back off a sticker she was holding and put it on Fancy's shirt. It was then Fancy noticed everyone was wearing "Hello, My Name Is… " stickers over their hearts. While Fancy's was green like the one Brody was given and the ones Brett and Denise wore, Elise's was yellow.

Brody leaned down and whispered in her ear, "I told you we needed name tags. I'll explain the colors in a minute."

The group walked down the hall and through a huge kitchen before exiting the back door. Close to a hundred heads turned their way, and Fancy's eyes widened. "Oh my God. Are they all part of your family?" she murmured to him.

"Don't worry. We've done this many times before and have a system." Taking her hand, he led her to the top step and waved at the band that was playing. The fiddler saw him and, with a slash of his bow, stopped the music. Brody cleared his throat and raised his voice. "All right, everyone, you all know the drill. This is my incredible woman, Fancy Maguire. Fancy, this is the Evans family and friends. Those of you who are wearing yellow tags, raise your hands." When Elise, Gerard, and several others did, he continued. "Fancy, these are my grandparents, parents, their siblings, and spouses. You'll find their spouse's names under their name on the tags. Next up are the green tags. These are my brothers and sisters with their spouses or significant others. Red tags are the kids of said brothers and sisters. Who they belong to is on their tag. Blue tags are cousins, spouses, and kids. Purple tags are friends of the family. While not related by blood, they're related by heart."

Once she overcame her initial shock, Brody formally introduced her to his grandmothers, his paternal grandfather—his mother's father had passed a few years ago—and his siblings. Everyone else she slowly met throughout the day. The food was delicious, the yard games were fun, and the music was lively as Brody taught her how to two-step. Even when his sisters and sisters-in-law swept her up for a powwow about all things Brody, he was never far from her. If he weren't close enough to touch her, he'd wink and smile at her from a short distance away. But when he stood beside or behind her, he always found ways to make contact with her. Her favorite moments were when his hand would go to the nape of her neck and brush against her sensitive skin before giving her collar a subtle tug.

She now had two collars to wear. He had allowed her to keep the first one he'd given her for days like this when she was dressed casually because she loved it so much, and it was the first one he'd picked out for her. The one he'd presented her with during their collaring ceremony was gorgeous, though. It was white gold with diamonds and rubies spaced out along its length—he'd said the rubies reminded him of her fiery red hair. She wore it when she dressed up or if they were going to the club. But Brody liked it best on her when she wore nothing else and was on her knees waiting for him beside their bed.

She'd basically moved in with him after his release

from the hospital to help him recover completely, and neither one of them wanted her to return to her old condo. Fancy knew all about the engagement ring he had hidden in his dresser drawer. She'd overheard him on the phone asking her Aunt Denise's permission. Apparently, he'd already spoken to her mother and father, but knowing how close she was with her aunt, he'd also asked her. While Fancy had been tempted to sneak a peek at the ring, she fought the urge. She wanted to be surprised when he gave it to her. He'd mentioned to Aunt Denise he was waiting until Fancy seemed ready. It was a huge step for her to put Patrick to rest finally, and Brody was willing to wait. That, of course, made her love him even more. He wasn't pushing her deceased husband from her life, just accepting that Patrick had owned her heart first. Her love for Brody was different than that for Patrick. She couldn't exactly put it into words and couldn't say she loved one more than the other. But if it hadn't been for her marriage and love for Patrick, she may not have become the woman who was now madly in love with Brody. She couldn't play the "what if" game. She just knew he was the man she wanted to spend the rest of her life with.

It was quite late when the last hoedown guests had driven away. Everyone had chipped in to clean up, so all that was left to do tomorrow was take down the tents, tables, and chairs. As Fancy was helping Elise put away the last of the leftovers, Brody and his father strode into the kitchen. The elder Evans grabbed his wife around the waist and hugged her tight from behind. "As always, my love, it was a wonderful party."

Fancy smiled at Brody. It was clear his parents had experienced a long and passionate love affair, and they were still crazy in love after all these years.

Taking her hand, Brody led her to the back porch, telling his folks over his shoulder, "We're going for a moonlight walk. See you in the morning."

A round of good night wishes filled the air as Brody tucked her into his side. She wrapped her arm around his waist. "Where are we going?"

"A place where I can make you come and not worry about my parents overhearing us."

She gaped at his boyish grin and teased, "Oh, really? Is this a place you took your high school sweetheart when she was letting you do those three sexual positions with her?"

"Oh, you remember that, huh? Well, there's nothing to worry about. That was in my dad's old Cadillac, which went to the junkyard after my brother, Brian, blew up the engine during his senior year in high school. I've never taken any women up here, although I can't say the same for my brothers."

He was walking them toward one of the many barns on the property, but this one was an old, traditional, red building that she always thought all barns looked like. It was smaller than the other structures on the farm. However, it still had a large square footage. Fancy could smell the fresh hay as soon as they entered. Brody flipped a switch, and a dim light came on, just enough for them to see by. "This is where we bring the mares when they're about to foal so we can keep an eye on them. The rest of the year, it's mainly for hay, storage, and tack." Grabbing a blanket from a stack of them on a shelf, he stopped next to a wooden ladder leading up into the loft. "Go on up. I'll be right behind you, staring at your gorgeous ass, trying hard not to take a bite out of it."

Fancy shook her head at him and took hold of the ladder to start her ascent. "You're incorrigible."

"Yup. So my mother has told me many times over the years."

When she reached the loft, Fancy climbed over the last rung of the ladder, and sure enough, Brody was right behind her. There were quite a few hay bales, and he pushed several together, making a bed with a blanket hidden behind one stack. If someone came into the barn for some stupid reason this late at night, the couple would be completely concealed.

Pulling her close, Brody crushed his lips to hers. Her body was flush against his, and there was no missing how much he wanted her right now. Without ending the kiss, he lowered her to the makeshift bed and covered her body with his own. They went from zero to eighty in seconds. Her hands fumbled with the buttons of his cowboy shirt, then took care of his belt buckle and the snap and zipper of his jeans while he quickly got rid of her clothes. It wasn't long before they were both naked.

When Brody reached for his discarded jeans to find a condom, she stopped him. "We don't need that."

Stunned, he stared at her. "Are you sure, sweetness? You have to know by now I plan on putting a ring on that finger of yours and having as many babies as we can, but I don't want to rush you."

She wasn't sure if she would ever get used to him putting her before his wants and needs. Every woman deserved to have a man like him in their life, and she felt sorry for the ones who hadn't found theirs yet. "You're it for me, Brody... Master. I want to be your wife, your sub, and the mother of your children. And if it's okay with you, we can start trying right now. I've never been more certain of anything in my life."

His response was in his actions as he made slow, passionate love to her before rocking her world hard and fast. Fancy really hoped they were far enough from the main house and the ranch hands' bunkhouse because he'd made her scream several times before he found his own release.

As they lay nude in the afterglow of their lovemaking, Brody found his pants once again and reached into the front pocket. He pulled out a small velvet pouch. "I figured you would have noticed the bulge of a box in my jeans, so I've been carrying around this little sack, waiting for the right moment." The most gorgeous engagement ring she'd ever seen emerged from the pouch, and she gasped at the sight. The oval diamond was surrounded by ruby baguettes set in white gold to match her formal collar. Taking her left hand, Brody slipped the ring on her finger. It was a perfect fit. "You're all mine, Fancy-girl. Marry me."

EPILOGUE

Waiting in his office for Foster and McCabe, Ian studied the picture of the latest missing submissive. The serial killer had apparently struck again last night. While the Doms were trying to make it harder for the bastard to kidnap a sub, they couldn't be everywhere at once. Tara O'Brien had disappeared after driving home from an evening with her parents. She was a frequent visitor to one of the public clubs and had been in the lifestyle for a little over a year, from what her best friend had told Isaac Webb. And unless a miracle happened or the killer screwed up somehow, the task force was resigned to the fact they would find Tara's mutilated body within the next few days. Quantico assigned an FBI profiler to the case, and the agent would be at tomorrow's task force meeting. Ian hoped whoever it was would be able to narrow things down so they could come up with potential suspects. He was as fearful as everyone else around here that a woman from The Covenant could be the next victim.

Since Brody didn't have his medical clearance yet, he wasn't being assigned to any cases. Instead, his time was being split between intel gathering and helping the task force in case Ian needed to be out of town for any reason. Devon had also filled in while Ian and Angie had gone on a ten-day honeymoon to a small private island in the Caribbean. Aside from the staff, they'd had the place all to themselves.

No one had been surprised when Brody and Fancy returned from Texas engaged, and they'd thrown the happy couple a small party at Donovan's to celebrate. While Nick was out of the country with his team, Jake had been able to fly in after attending a meeting at the Pentagon with Ian. They were still chasing their tails over a white slavery operation that was being bounced around Central and South America, staying two steps ahead of the law. Several young American women had gone missing on tropical vacations, and at least two Canadians had disappeared after going ashore in Jamaica during a cruise.

A knock on the open door had Ian looking up. Foster and McCabe entered and took the guest seats in front of the desk. As Devon walked in moments later, Ian put aside the details on Tara O'Brien. Dev took what had become his usual spot, sitting on the arm of the small office couch. Leaning on his forearms, Ian regarded the two men from the Omega team. He and his brother had been watching them closely since they'd been hired almost a year ago. With multiple missions and a heavy caseload, it had taken that long to get the rest of the Omega team on board, settled, and training together. If a team was needed during that time, they'd combined Alpha team members with Omega. But now it was finally time to send the latter out on one final training mission to prove they could work together as a team. And every team needed a leader, which was why this meeting was taking place.

"While we have a little lull between cases, knock on wood..." Ian rapped his knuckles on the wooden desk, ". . . we're sending you out into the wilderness for the last training run—up in the Rockies. While she's technically part of the Alpha team, Lindsey will be joining you. We want her comfortable with both teams so we can move her around if need be. Your team will have less than what it needs for you to survive, so you'll have to work together to get to the extraction point, which is about a two-day trek from the drop-off. Dev and I have been trying to figure out who will lead this team, and I'm sure it's not a surprise that you both have been in the running."

The men nodded but didn't say a word. The Sawyer brothers hadn't made it obvious these two were being groomed for the top spot, but they hadn't been covert about it either.

Ian sat back in his leather executive desk chair.

"So, here's what we've decided. The two of you are going to be co-leaders." At their simultaneous raised eyebrows, he continued. "You both have extensive training and specialized experience the other doesn't possess. Foster, with your background in the Secret Service, you excel in urban scenarios and covert ops in social settings. McCabe, being Army Special Forces, your expertise is jungle warfare, so to speak. You work well together, bouncing ideas and strategies off of each other, and I honestly don't think either of you realizes it. We want you to continue working that way. When a mission calls for Foster's experience, he'll take the lead and vice versa with McCabe."

"If this co-leadership doesn't work out," Devon added, "we can always go back and reevaluate who should take the top spot, but after discussing it with Marco, Boomer, and Brody, we doubt that will be necessary. However, if either of you thinks this won't work, now's your chance to speak up."

The two men looked at each other for a long moment before Cain extended his hand. "Congratulations, partner."

Tristan grinned and shook the other man's hand. "Right back at ya, partner."

Before anyone could say anything more, Ian's cell chirped with an incoming text. A glance at the coded message told him his phone would receive a call in the next few seconds. When it rang, he held up his hand for everyone to stay in place as he answered it.

Knowing who was on the other end, he said, "Hey, Carter, what's up?"

"Ian," the black ops spy replied. "You know all those markers you guys owe me? I'm cashing them in. I need your help."

So much for knocking on wood.

Sign up for my newsletter and get a BONUS CHAPTER starring Brody, Fancy, Marco, and Harper!
BookHip.com/HACAKRX

Continue the Trident Security adventure with *Jack Be Nimble: A Trident Security-Related Novella* from the Heels, Rhymes & Nursery Crimes multi-author series. This is a standalone about T. Carter's future love, Jordyn Alvarez, and is best read after *Tickle His Fancy.*

Then read *No Way in Hell: A Steel Corp/Trident Security Crossover,* co-authored by J.B. Havens. This book takes place 4-5 years before *Leather & Lace: Trident Security Book 1* and provides more background on the Sexy Six-Pack and T. Carter. While reading both series is not necessary before reading *No Way in Hell*, it is recommended for optimum enjoyment.

Please note that *No Way in Hell* is NOT a romance story and does include graphic violence. If that's not for you, it's okay for you to skip it.

For the best reading order of the Trident Security series and its spinoffs, check out the printable list on my website - www.samanthacolebooks.-com/pages/best-reading-order.

Want to know what's coming next? Join my Facebook Group -
Samantha Cole's Sexy Six-Pack's Sirens.

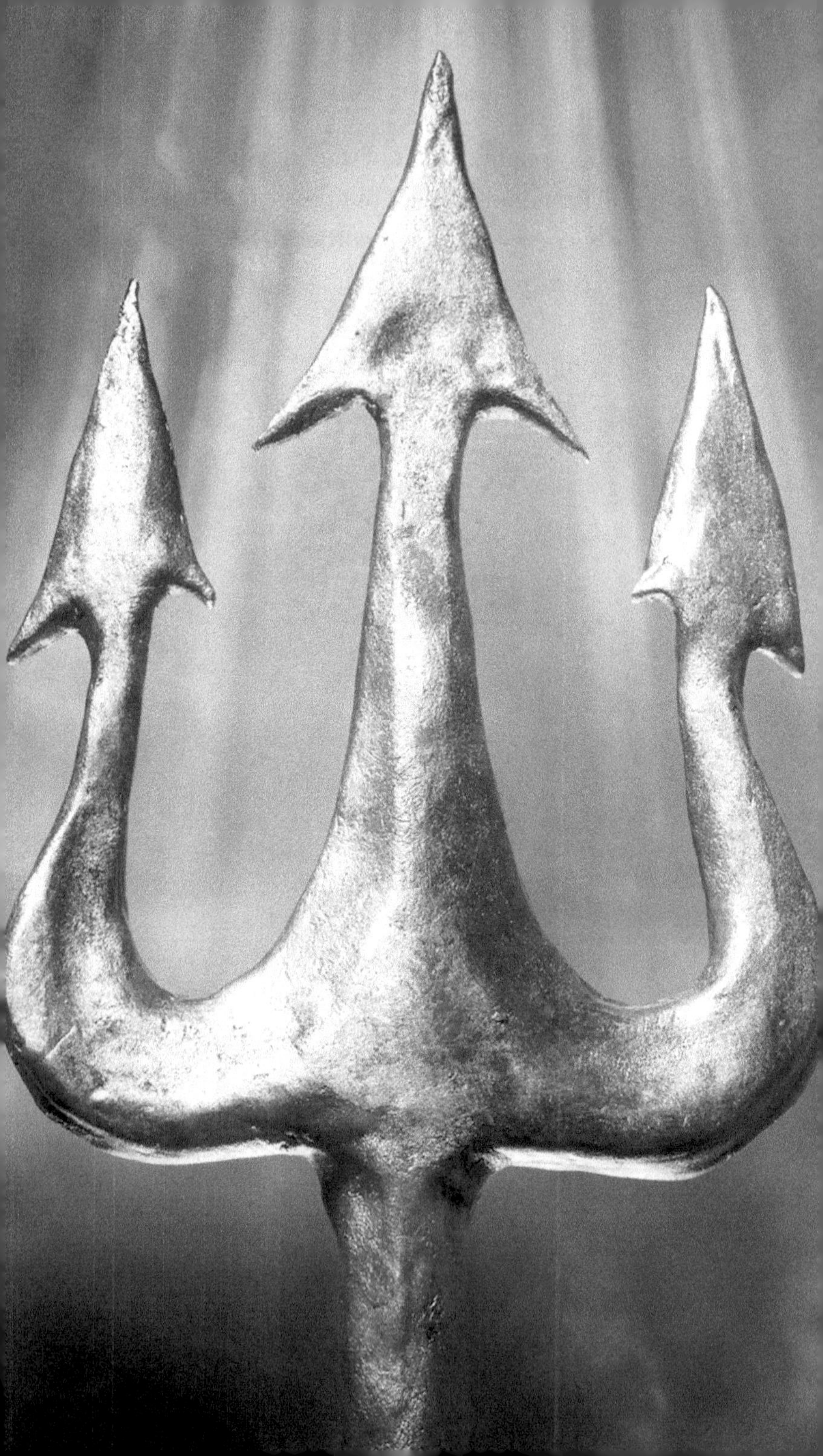

Jack Be Nimble

Laughter filled the outdoor recreation area, but Jordyn Cabrera Alvarez had no desire to play with any of the other children there. The Argentinian orphanage, near a small town a half hour north of Buenos Aires, was the last place she ever expected to call home, and she still couldn't bring herself to admit it was where she now lived.

For the first fourteen years of her life, she'd resided with her mother and father in their mansion in Recoleta, the most affluent neighborhood in Buenos Aires. She'd had everything a little girl could dream of—plenty of friends, a beautiful home with more amenities than most people could dream of, servants, and the latest styles of clothing, among other things coveted by the rich and famous. Everything she'd owned had been top-of-the-line, and no expense had been spared to make her happy. Her parents, along with the estate's staff, had doted on her, spoiling her rotten since she'd been an only child. She'd gone to private schools, taken lessons in horseback riding, and learned anything else she wanted to.

Her father, Santino Cabrera Perez, had been a wealthy businessman who'd been lucky enough to catch the eye of Regina Alvarez Huerta, a former Miss Argentina and a first runner-up in the Miss Universe pageant. Theirs had been a passionate love affair—maybe too passionate. While her father had never lifted a hand to Jordyn in anger, it'd been a different story with his wife. He'd been very jealous of the way other men would eye or flirt with his wife, and in his mind, no matter what, it'd been Regina's fault. The dutiful wife and mother had become an expert in hiding her bruises with clothing and makeup. It had taken years before a young Jordyn had learned that spousal abuse wasn't the norm in most families.

Her ideal life had come grinding to a halt three months ago when she'd arrived home from school one afternoon to find the house uncharacteristically quiet. The staff had been missing, and Jordyn later discovered that her father had told everyone to take the day off work. The teenager had been the one to find her parents' cold bodies in their bedroom. For reasons probably only known to him, Santino had shot Regina in the head before turning the gun on himself. The police had said the murder/suicide had taken place shortly after Jordyn had left for school that morning. In the blink of an eye, she'd become an orphan. To add insult to her tragedy, her father's greedy relatives had swindled his estate, leaving her penniless and alone. They'd wanted the money, just not another mouth to feed. Four days after the double funeral, her Aunt Ana Maria had dropped her off at the orphanage with barely the clothes on her back, since Jordyn's bitchy cousins had wanted all her beautiful things for themselves. Apparently, her father's family had bribed his lawyer, a judge, and a children's welfare agent in order to commandeer the estate and banish her to the orphanage.

It hadn't taken her long to realize that few children over the age of six or seven found new families through adoption. As it was, Jordyn was one of the oldest children there.

She'd attempted to run away when she'd first gotten there and managed to find her way back to her old neighborhood, only to find she'd been locked out of the home she'd grown up in. When she'd knocked on a friend's door, the girl's father had turned his nose up at her and told her she wasn't welcome there anymore. A few minutes later, a police officer had pulled up and taken her back to the orphanage. She'd been sure she would be punished when they'd finally gotten there, but Sisters Patrice, Rosemary, and Teresa had embraced her in their loving arms and did their best to let her know they weren't mad at her—just concerned.

Many a night, it was Sr. Patrice who'd sit on Jordyn's bed long after the other kids were asleep, when the teen's grief became too much for her to handle and she silently cried in the darkness. The nun, who'd been born and raised in Chicago in the United States, would pet Jordyn's hair and shoulders while singing soothing songs in both English and Spanish. Thanks to the woman's tender love and compassion, Jordyn eventually calmed enough to fall asleep.

Now, she sat in the afternoon shade with her back to the wall of the old, weathered building that housed the children's bunk rooms, the nuns' bedrooms, a kitchen, and a dining room. A similar building across the dirt yard housed the classrooms where the twenty-six orphans attended school. A few other structures dotted the landscape, including a cabin for Pedro Hernandez, the young handyman who did all the heavy work for the Catholic nuns who ran the orphan-age. The other building was a small chapel where they all gathered for an hour on Sundays. A local priest came every week to say mass, and several residents in the area also came to worship there rather than travel two towns over to the nearest Catholic Church.

Picking up pebbles, Jordyn tossed them into an old, chipped coffee cup sitting on the ground a foot or so away from her, as the other children played with each other. She hadn't made any attempts to befriend the others and had resisted any efforts they made to engage her in conversations or activities. The only time she interacted with any of them was while doing chores or if she had to be paired with someone for a school assignment. Otherwise, she wanted to be left alone to wallow in her own despair and resentment.

Preferring to be by herself also meant she was bored out of her mind most of the time when she wasn't in school. She didn't belong at the orphanage. She belonged with her friends, going to movies, shopping, laughing, and talking about boys. Most of the other children over the age of seven had lived at the orphanage for years, and their definition of fun was far different from hers. The nuns did their best to help all the children find loving parents to adopt them, even from other countries, but the older the children got, the less likely they'd find a new family. Jordyn didn't want a new family—she wanted her old one, or at least the one that included her mother. She'd never forgive her father for taking away her almost perfect life and everyone she loved. The image of her parents' bloodied bodies on the floor of their posh bedroom was one she'd never be able to erase from her mind.

"Jordyn," Sr. Patrice called to her from the doorway to the school where her office was located. "Come here, por favor." The nuns often spoke in both English and Spanish, wanting their charges to be bilingual, since many of the couples looking to adopt came from places where English was the primary language, like the United States.

Sighing, Jordyn stood and wiped the dirt from the non-designer clothes she was now forced to wear. As she trudged across the yard, she noticed a new white SUV parked next to the old, dirty pickup truck Pedro used. She hadn't seen it pull up to the orphanage and wondered who it belonged to. If it were someone interested in adopting a kid, it was highly doubtful they'd want Jordyn, and vice versa.

Sr. Patrice's smile lit up her face when she approached. As much as Jordyn hated her situation, it was difficult not to like the three nuns who ran the orphanage. Sr. Patrice was about forty years old and was an inch taller than Jordyn's five-feet-three-inch frame. Like the other two nuns, she always wore sedate clothing—twill pants or jeans, a short or long-sleeved, white or pastel-colored, button-down shirt, sneakers or loafers, and a navy-blue habit that covered most of her short brown hair. She had a kind face—one that, despite the circumstances, always made Jordyn feel safe.

"Sí, Sister Patrice?"

The woman tilted her head toward the open door. "Come inside, so we can talk."

Following the nun inside, her mind raced, trying to think if she'd done anything she'd be in trouble for. Although if she had, her punishment wouldn't be anything more than a look of disappointment from Sr. Patrice, along with a few extra chores. Since her one attempt at running away, Jordyn had quickly learned that disappointing the nuns was something she wanted to avoid, because whenever she did something right, the praise they lavished on her made her day a little brighter.

Sr. Patrice led Jordyn into her small office, and the young girl was surprised to see a man waiting for them. Although she didn't recognize him, something about him was familiar. He stood from the chair he'd been sitting in and gave her a tentative smile. "Hola, Jordyn."

Her eyes narrowed. How did he know her name?

Putting an arm around Jordyn's shoulder in support, Sr. Patrice said, "From what I understand, it's been a few years since you've seen Mr. Alvarez, but he's your uncle—your mother's brother."

The tall, dark-haired man squatted down so he wasn't towering over her. He spoke to her in Spanish, but his accent was definitely American. "Look at you, my little chinchilla. Do you remember me, your Uncle Iggy? I used to bring you saltwater taffy from California." He held up his hand, showing her a threaded band around his wrist. "You made this and gave it to me the last time I saw you."

Jordyn stared at the multicolored friendship bracelet as memories trickled in from the far reaches of her mind. She must have been six or seven the last time she'd seen Ignacio Alvarez, her mother's brother. He would come to visit several times a year, and always when her father had been traveling, since Santino had despised his brother-in-law, often referring to him as a piece of worthless trash. Despite her father's distaste for the man, Jordyn had fond memories of her Uncle Iggy—he'd always made her laugh and told her about the places he'd been, things he'd done, and people he'd met. She remembered making the bracelets with her friends, and Uncle Iggy asking if he could have one so he'd always have a part of her with him when he was between visits.

He was right—that'd been the last time she could recall seeing him. He'd stopped coming around, and Jordyn had almost forgotten all about him, since neither of her parents had ever spoken about him again. In fact, she'd thought he'd died or something. The memories of him now tore through her mind like a flash flood.

"You—you never came back. You said you would, but you never did." Tears began to fill her eyes. "Why? Was it something I did?"

His expression softened with regret and tenderness. "No, my little one. It wasn't because of you. Your parents and I had a disagreement, and it was best for everyone if I stayed away. I'm so sorry it took me this long to find out your parents were gone and Santino's family left you here. But I'm back now, and I'm going to take you to California. You'll love it there. You and I

—we'll be our own little family. I won't let anyone hurt you ever again, Jordyn—you have my word."

When he held out his hands to her, Jordyn couldn't hold back her sobs anymore. She flung herself into his arms and cried her heart out into his shoulder.

"Hush, my little chinchilla. I've got you. It'll be all right."

Ross, California
Two years later...

With a broad grin, Jordyn dumped the contents of her knapsack on the kitchen table—sixteen men's and women's wallets that she'd pilfered during her trip to Pier 39. The waterfront shopping center and popular tourist attraction was built on a pier in San Francisco and the perfect place on a sunny day to practice her pickpocketing moves. "How'd I do? Great, right? Not a single person realized I'd targeted them until I was long gone with the goods."

Uncle Iggy's eyes glistened with pride, despite his gruff voice. "Don't get too cocky, you. Cocky is—"

"Sloppy," she said at the same time he finished the sentence she'd heard millions of times since her dear uncle had started teaching her the tricks of his trade.

Not that he was a pickpocket—these days, his sights were set on valuable things which allowed him to afford a six-bedroom home in one of the most affluential neighborhoods in the suburbs of San Francisco. However, if young Jordyn was going to grow up to be a successful jewel and art thief like he was, she had to start with the basics.

It'd taken her months after moving with him to California before she'd started to question what he did for a living. According to what he let everyone else believe, he was an art appraiser and broker who travelled occasionally to procure requested items for the rich and famous. In fact, that was what he did on the side to look legit to the public and IRS. But his real income came from stealing some of the most amazing jewelry and art in the world and selling them to the highest bidder or whoever had contracted him to obtain them.

Jordyn had been begging him to teach her how to snatch wallets, without their owners knowing, and so many other fun things he knew how to do. She'd started calling him the Pink Panther, when no one else was around, after they'd watched some of the original movies starring Peter Sellers on Netflix. At first, her uncle had been resistant to teach her his illegal skills, but she'd finally worn him down, and Jordyn was on her way to becoming an exceptional student. Since learning how to disarm alarms, pick locks, and crack safes could be done in the basement of their home, where Uncle Iggy had a workshop set up, they'd started with that. Jordyn was able to practice on the numerous lock and alarm systems he'd collected, away from prying eyes. In fact, she'd cracked her first safe before she'd even got her driver's permit.

Uncle Iggy flipped through the stash. "I told you to do no more than five. You got greedy."

"You could've stopped me at any time." He'd been following her a close distance to make sure she didn't run into any trouble as she'd zeroed in on her targets. "Besides, I was on a roll."

He picked up a stack of empty post office mailers and handed them to her. "Send them back to the owners with everything in them."

Her brow furrowed. "Why? I thought—"

"You thought wrong, Jordyn. I'm teaching you things you'll need to excel at when we get into bigger and more dangerous jobs. These people were on vacation or enjoying their day off. The people you targeted weren't rich and will be relieved to get their money, identifications, credit cards, and personal items back. When I target someone, I know they have more than enough money to make up for what I take from them. They won't be worried about how they'll make their rent or pay their utility bills. If you don't have a moral conscience, then I won't be teaching you anymore."

She snorted and crossed her arms. "A thief with a moral conscience? Isn't that an oxymoron?" That was one of her favorite English words for some reason.

"Maybe. But it's the way I do things, and it's the way you'll do things too if you want me to continue to teach you."

Despite his big heart, Uncle Iggy had floundered in the beginning after bringing her to the States. He'd never been married, and raising a teenaged girl was definitely not what he'd been expecting to do at that point of his life. But they'd managed. He'd made sure she was healthy, educated in a local, private school, and knew she was loved. She'd made new friends, and when he had to go away on a "business trip," Mrs. Martinez, his widowed housekeeper and cook, would stay over. Although Jordyn insisted she didn't need a babysitter—she was sixteen after all—she was secretly glad the older woman was there in Uncle Iggy's absence. Mrs. M. was a cool lady and missed doting on her own children who were now adults with their own families scattered around the US. Whenever Jordyn had a question that she was too embarrassed to ask her uncle about, it was Mrs. M. who she turned to.

Uncle Iggy had eventually told Jordyn that, when he'd finally heard from a friend in Argentina what'd happened to her parents and then to her, he'd immediately gathered things he would need to get her out of the orphanage. He'd presented Sr. Patrice with a flawless, forged copy of Jordyn's birth certificate and letter from her mother, reportedly stating, that if anything happened to Regina and Santino, Iggy would be awarded full custody of his niece. A counterfeit passport in her name had eased their exit from Argentina instead of applying and waiting for a copy of her original one, which was probably in a dump somewhere. After getting copies of her parents' death certificates, Iggy had gotten full guardianship of Jordyn in California. At the same time, and at her request, he'd also petitioned the courts to let her legally drop Cabrera from her surname and allow her to go by Jordyn Alvarez. She wanted no part of her father's name after what he'd done.

When she'd asked Uncle Iggy why he hadn't hired a lawyer to try to recover her parents' estate for her, his reply had been that it would've taken a long time to go through legal means. He was rich enough to support both of them in the lifestyle she'd known before her parents' deaths, and he was leaving it all to her in his will. Instead of taking her father's family to court, with the help of several underground friends, he'd made sure the Cabreras lost everything they'd taken from her and more. To her satisfaction, the last she'd heard, they were penniless and in trouble with the law in Argentina. Fucking served them right.

Even though he was teaching her how to be a criminal, the last thing Jordyn wanted was to disappoint the man who'd rescued her from the orphanage. Sr. Patrice's smiling face popped into her mind. Maybe when she was making as much money has Uncle Iggy was in his profession, Jordyn would send some to Sr. Patrice. Despite the state's financial support, the orphanage relied heavily on donations. With some extra money, the kids could have nicer clothing and toys. Jordyn could be a Robin Hood and Santa Claus rolled into one kick-ass cat burglar. *Meow.*

"Fine, I'll return them. Maybe next time I'll tell them they dropped their wallet and hand it back to them after making sure they didn't know I took it." It would save her the trouble of mailing them. Taking the stack of mailers from him, she grabbed a pen and sat down. While he prepared their dinner—which entailed ordering a pizza to be delivered, since it was Sunday and Mrs. Martinez's day off—Jordyn addressed the tan envelopes with the information she found on the driver's license in each wallet. Hopefully, it was all up to date. She then wrote a small note for each, saying she'd found the wallet at Pier 39 and wanted to return it to the owner. Technically, that was true—she just left out the part where she'd found the wallet in their pocket or purse. When she was done, Uncle Iggy said he would drop the small packages off at the post office tomorrow while running some errands.

After the pizza arrived, the two grabbed their slices and drinks and took them into the living room to watch Argentina play against Bolivia in the Copa América, the South American Football Championship. Both of them were big fans, and it drove them nuts when Americans called it soccer. Jordyn had all but given up on correcting her new friends whenever the subject came up.

During the halftime break, Jordyn found herself blurting out, "Why did you stop coming to see us in Argentina?" It was something that'd been bothering her lately. Uncle Iggy had told her he'd had a falling out with her parents but had never gone into detail. "I mean, what was the fight about?"

Sighing, Uncle Iggy muted the volume of the TV and turned on the couch to face Jordyn. It took him a few moments to gather his thoughts. "I loved my sister. She was the light of my life, until she married your father. I'm sorry to say I never liked him. He was a possessive and jealous man. It's no secret that your father and I didn't get along. I wasn't educated enough for him—even though I graduated from a respected university. I didn't have enough prestige and was too crass for his liking. I, in turn, hated him for the way he treated Regina."

"He hit her a lot."

Her uncle nodded. "I wasn't aware of that for the longest time, since I wasn't around much. I only visited when Santino was out of town on business, and Regina was good at covering the bruises. When I found out, I lost it. I confronted your father when he returned home from a trip. Things got ugly. You weren't there, thank goodness. I think you were at a sleepover party somewhere. Anyway, I tried to convince your mother to take you and leave him. She wouldn't. She took his side, and when he forbade me from ever setting foot in their house again, she agreed with him. He threatened to tell the police I was behind several jewel and art thefts in the area—some of which were true, but others weren't. Up until that point, I had no idea he knew about my... extracurricular activities beyond being an appraiser and broker. Apparently, he'd kept it to himself out of respect for your mother—which is weird when you think about it. I guess he loved her in his own way, as cruel as it was."

Reaching over, he squeezed Jordyn's hand. "Believe me when I say it crushed me to stop coming to visit you and Regina. I tried to contact her a few times—I wanted to see you both and to try and get her away from Santino—but she refused to talk to me ever again."

Grief for her mother and hatred for her father threatened to explode from Jordyn's chest. She vowed then and there never to allow a man to raise his hand to her. She'd kill the bastard first.

Get *Jack Be Nimble: A Trident Security-Related Short Story* today!

OTHER BOOKS BY SAMANTHA COLE

***Denotes titles/series that are only available on select digital sites. Paperbacks and audiobooks are available on most book sites.

THE TRIDENT SECURITY SERIES

Leather & Lace

His Angel

Waiting For Him

Not Negotiable

Topping The Alpha (MM)

Watching From the Shadows

Whiskey Tribute

Tickle His Fancy

No Way in Hell: A Steel Corp/Trident Security Crossover (co-authored with J.B. Havens)

Absolving His Sins

Option Number Three (MMF)

Salvaging His Soul

Trident Security Field Manual

Torn In Half

Burning For Him

*****Heels, Rhymes, & Nursery Crimes Series**
(with 13 other authors)
Jack Be Nimble: A Trident Security-Related Short Story

*****The Deimos Series**
Handling Haven: Special Forces: Operation Alpha
Cheating the Devil: Special Forces: Operation Alpha

The Trident Security Omega Team Series
Mountain of Evil
A Dead Man's Pulse
Forty Days & One Knight

The Doms of The Covenant Series
Double Down & Dirty (MFM)
Entertaining Distraction
Knot a Chance
Finding His Forever (MM)
Reclaiming His Soulmate

The Blackhawk Security Series
Tuff Enough
Blood Bound

Master Key Series

Master Key Resort

Master Cordell

HAZARD FALLS SERIES

Don't Fight It (MMF)

Don't Shoot the Messenger (MFM)

Don't Burn Bridges

THE MALONE BROTHERS SERIES

Her Secret

Her Sleuth

Her Savior

LARGO RIDGE SERIES

Cold Feet

*****ANTELOPE ROCK SERIES**

(CO-AUTHORED WITH J.B. HAVENS)

Wannabe in Wyoming

Wistful in Wyoming (M/M)

COCK & BULL SERIES (M/M)

Scout

Rico

STANDALONES

Where the Broken Bloom

Scattered Moments in Time: A Collection of Short Stories & More

Sweet Revenge

The Sugarplum Fairy (M/M)

***THE BID ON LOVE SERIES

(WITH 7 OTHER AUTHORS!)

Going, Going, Gone: Book 2

***THE COLLECTIVE: SEASON TWO

(WITH 7 OTHER AUTHORS!)

Angst: Book 7 (M/M)

SPECIAL COLLECTIONS

Trident Security Series: Volume I

Trident Security Series: Volume II

Trident Security Series: Volume III

Trident Security Series: Volume IV

Trident Security Series: Volume V

Trident Security Series: Volume VI

ABOUT SAMANTHA COLE

USA Today Bestselling Author Samantha Cole is a retired police officer and paramedic who now writes heart-pounding romance in multiple forms—MF, MM, and ménage. From military heroes to rugged cowboys and small-town heat, her stories blend passion, loyalty, and danger in perfect balance.

Awards:

Wannabe in Wyoming (co-authored by J.B. Havens) won the bronze medal in the 2021 Readers' Favorite Awards in the General Romance category.

Scattered Moments in Time won the gold medal in the 2020 Readers' Favorite Awards in the Fiction Anthology category.

Where the Broken Bloom (formerly *The Road to Solace*) won the silver medal in the 2017 Readers' Favorite Awards in the Contemporary Romance category.

Sexy Six-Pack's Sirens Group on Facebook
Website: www.samanthacolebooks.com
Newsletter: samanthacolebooks.com/mailing-list

- facebook.com/SamanthaColeAuthor
- instagram.com/samanthacoleauthor
- bookbub.com/profile/samantha-a-cole
- goodreads.com/SamanthaCole
- amazon.com/Samantha-A-Cole/e/B00X53K3X8
- tiktok.com/@samanthacoleauthor
- youtube.com/@SamanthaACole-bp6yu

www.ingramcontent.com/pod-product-compliance
Lightning Source LLC
Chambersburg PA
CBHW072007190726
48293CB00001B/191